"*A fresh voice in urban fantasy reading this novel, you might alone …*"

—Laura Resnick, author of the
Esther Diamond series

"*If you're looking for a fun, fast-paced adventure, give Enter the Janitor a read.*"

—A Fantastical Librarian

"*[Enter the Janitor] was funny, exciting, and in some places, a near tear-jerker. In other words, an almost perfect start to a series.*"

—AudiobookBlast.com

"*Enter the Janitor is one of those books that makes you do a double-take when you see it. A book about magical janitors fighting the evil forces of Scum? How could this not be an instant classic?*"

—The Arched Doorway

"*Enter the Janitor is a unique and cleverly written book … bizarre, funny, exciting, and just a bit weird, all of which combine to make it a winner.*"

—Fanboy Comics

"*I loved The Maids of Wrath! This is a worthy successor to Enter the Janitor. The Cleaners universe keeps expanding in all the right ways. You'll never look at cleaning professionals the same away again.*"

—Jennifer Brozek, author of *Apocalypse Girl Dreaming*

THE MAIDS OF WRATH

THE MAIDS OF WRATH

THE CLEANERS BOOK 2

To Vicki—

Josh Vogt

*You wouldn't like maids
when they're angry...*

WordFire Press
Colorado Springs, Colorado

THE CLEANERS: THE MAIDS OF WRATH
Copyright © 2015 Josh Vogt
Originally published by WordFire Press 2015

All rights reserved. No part of this book may be reproduced or transmitted in any form or by any electronic or mechanical means, including photocopying, recording or by any information storage and retrieval system, without the express written permission of the copyright holder, except where permitted by law. This novel is a work of fiction. Names, characters, places and incidents are either the product of the author's imagination, or, if real, used fictitiously.

ISBN: 978-1-61475-373-5

Cover painting by Jeff Herndon

Cover design by Janet McDonald

Art Director Kevin J. Anderson

Book Design by RuneWright, LLC
www.RuneWright.com

Published by
WordFire Press, an imprint of
WordFire, Inc.
PO Box 1840
Monument CO 80132

Kevin J. Anderson & Rebecca Moesta, Publishers

WordFire Press Trade Paperback Edition April 2015
Printed in the USA
wordfirepress.com

DEDICATION

*To my sisters, who I love dearly and who
make me proud to be a big brother.*

CHAPTER ONE

Dani yelped and stumbled backward as the squeegee bounced off her forehead. A knee knocked the mop out of her hands, followed by a rubber boot which connected with her stomach. This racked up her butt's twentieth rendezvous with the floor of the supernatural sanitation company's training room.

The impact jolted her spine and forearms as she tried to catch herself. It also prompted a plastic crunch. She groaned and eyed a pants leg pocket, where a wet splotch started leaking through the material.

She undid the zipper and pulled out the cracked remains of a small bottle of sanitation gel. Barely a handful remained inside, and she dribbled this into her palm in the hopes of salvaging something from the mess.

Then she stilled as another squeegee whipped into the floor beside her—except this one sliced through the concrete like an axe splitting a particularly unlucky watermelon. She glowered at this as her attacker spoke.

"Your opponent is not about to pause and let you tidy up after every hit, Miss Hashelheim."

She grabbed the squeegee handle, thinking she could snap it back in a surprise attack. But her gel-slicked fingers didn't give her a solid grip on the embedded Cleaner weapon.

Between tugs and grunts, she tried to formulate a decent excuse. "I was … trying to … coat my hands … with a substance that'd keep … any Scum back."

Huffing and admitting defeat via squeegee, she lay back and tried to let her exasperation ebb away. Sweat trickled down her neck as she took inventory of her latest bruises.

While she admired the spotless ceiling of the Cleaners' training facility, a pair of boots—one of which had just planted its tread on her gut—stamped beside her. The bald head of her sparring instructor came into view as he frowned down at her.

"Miss Hashelheim," he said in a gravelly tone that would've made Sean Connery go weak at the knees, "I don't run a daycare and this isn't nap time. Get up and let's try again."

"No milk and graham crackers?" she asked. "How about a juice box?"

Her instructor, known to her only as Vern by the white stitching on his brown jumpsuit, retrieved both squeegees. He waved the one he'd hit her with before.

"If this had been properly chanted," he said, "it would've scalped you clear through."

Dani rubbed her brow as she stood. She'd be walking around with a lump for days. Body twitching in protest, she retrieved her practice mop and settled into a weary stance, one foot back for stability. For a moment, she considered rousing her power and seeing how Vern handled himself in an earthquake or gale. Her Catalyst abilities had been forbidden for this portion of training, though, which she found about as fair as not letting a person use their mouth in a pie-eating contest.

She tried to concentrate, to focus on where the next hit might come from. She could do this. She could—

Squeegees slapped first her right and then her left cheek. Growling, she jabbed the mop at Vern's impressive stomach.

He twisted like a beer-gut belly-dancer and pinned the mop along his side. Spinning, he yanked the mop out of her hands, jerking her forward so his kick planted in the middle of her back as she stumbled past.

Her left hip took the brunt of her twenty-first tumble. As her cheek cooled against the floor tiles, she debated which would be more humiliating: taking a nap right there or rising to face more defeat.

"C'mon, Dani," someone called from behind her. "Can'tcha at least pretend you're tryin'? It's embarrassin' to watch."

Pushing up, she glared back at Ben, who stood on the sidelines.

The janitor grinned and gave a thumbs-up with his left hand—the only one he had thanks to a supernatural disease which had infected his right arm, and a hungry demigod who'd used the Corrupted flesh as a snack. He kept the right sleeve of his blue jumpsuit pinned to where the limb ended just below the shoulder.

"You want a go with me, old man?" She regained her footing. "I'll thrash you so hard you'll end up back in diapers."

"Naw," he said. "I won't be any help in the ring, but I can do plenty good from here."

Dani faced Vern, who sized up her defense. "Yeah? And what good are you doing right now?"

"Why, I'm playin' the role of the inevitable distractification."

She rolled her eyes as she turned to keep Vern in front of her. "That's real helpful."

"Mebbe not helpful, but it's practical."

"Sure." She swatted a feint aside. "What's practical about distraction?"

"Let's say you're muckin' down in the Sewers, moppin' up a few clogs," Ben said, "when, oh goodness to gumdrops, a pack of Urmoch leap out all a-sudden, rarin' to see if you taste like bacon. Whatcha gonna do?"

Vern lunged and chopped a squeegee. Dani blocked the strike for once, but took a kick to the shin which had her hissing through her teeth. While Vern had more physically in common with a barrel than a ballerina, he maintained the surprising grace of the latter.

"Urmoch have pack mentalities, right?" she said. "I'd figure out which one was the alpha and—"

A glob of water smacked into her face and blurred her vision.

"One of them just threw a turd in your eyes," Ben said, choked with barely restrained laughter. "You're blind. Now what?"

She shook her head and swung wildly to block Vern's thrust. The mop flew from her hands, and she raised her fists. A hand grabbed hers and twisted it into a painful lock. She gasped as Vern spun her down to her knees. All at once, the water fell from her face, leaving the skin dry and her vision clear as she got within smooching distance of the wart on the instructor's cheek.

He gripped her red hair—what little had regrown so far—and pulled her head back to draw the edge of a squeegee along her throat. Ben hopped into her line of vision and chanted.

"Ding-dong, Dani's dead."

She scowled, ignoring Vern's proffered hand as she stood and grabbed her mop.

"So mature," she said.

"Hey, I ain't the one tastin' like bacon, princess."

She tossed the mop to Ben, who caught and tucked it under his armpit. He plucked a towel and water bottle out of a side pocket and handed them over.

Dani sniffed the bottle's contents, making sure the water didn't move of its own volition or smell of bleach before taking a swig. Wouldn't be the first time she'd accidentally sucked down an elemental spirit.

Speaking of which, where had Carl dribbled off to after being a poor excuse for a water balloon?

She scanned the training center for Ben's liquid sidekick. This section of HQ looked like a janitorial supply closet and Shaolin dojo had a drunken one-night stand, resulting in a room like neither but the byproduct of both. Weapon racks lined the walls, stacked with mops, brooms, dusters, vacuum cleaners and other cleaning implements. White tape outlined a dozen sparring rings on the concrete floor, while punching dummies stood in the corners, sporting decapitated heads, gashes and burn marks.

At last, she spotted a puddle rolling across the floor toward Ben. Sensing her attention, the sprite shifted its watery form through a series of geometric shapes. She struggled to decipher Carl's usual method of communication.

Apologies for wetting attractive human female, she thought he said.

"Just be careful where you splash me," she said. "I don't think elementals are immune to sexual harassment charges."

The elemental gurgled along, and Dani raised her eyes from him to the two women sparring a few rings over. She figured they were maids since the air stirred to life around them. From her observations, janitors exhibited more affinity with water, while maids worked better with the wind.

One maid fought with dual feather dusters while the other wielded a bucket and sponge combo. As the bucket-wielder swung high, the second maid darted under the swipe and rammed a shoulder into her opponent's sternum. The first maid reeled back until she slammed into a wall. She coughed and glared at her partner while rubbing her chest.

"For Purity's sake, Sherri, tone it down. I haven't even warmed up yet."

Sherri snorted and turned a hand to flip her opponent off without letting go of her dusters. However, the air shimmered and blurred the digit until she lowered it, scowling at her own hand.

Ben grumbled. "You gotta be kiddin' me. The Board expanded the foul-filter to block gestures too? Those muck-minded ⟋◆🅜&🅜☐✦." His voice fuzzed for a moment, negating whatever contraband insult might tarnish the Cleaners' shiny reputation.

The other maid returned to the ring, where they resumed trading blows with increasing vigor.

Putting her back to the maids, Dani looked at Vern.

"I think Ben needs a round or two while I get to be the distraction," she said.

Ben shook his head. "I got plenty of time bashin' bones in here, just like every other Cleaner. We had some good ol' fun, didn't we, Vern?"

The instructor grimaced. "You were a lousy student. Always rushing in with sloppy technique." He leveled a finger at Ben. "And don't assume losing an arm is going to keep you off the roster forever."

"I suppose I could always be addin' a few dirty tricks to my repeatatory," Ben said.

Dani frowned. "Ever consider one of those Word of the Day calendars?"

"Tried one once. I mebbe even remember a few of 'em. Gasconading. Circumlocution. Sesquipedalian." He grimaced as if tasting something sour. "Just way too much effort waggin' the tongue over so many syllaballistics." He winked at Vern as Dani rolled her eyes. "Anyhoo, until my turn comes, I'll keep on bein' the wind beneath Dani's wings."

Which means he's going to just keep trying to ruffle my feathers, she thought.

Vern started to retort, but a couple Cleaners entered the room and waved to get his attention.

"We'll resume in a few minutes," he told Dani. "Practice the moves I showed you until I return."

Dani wiped the sweat from her brow as she headed Ben's way. He now watched the dueling maids, their fight punctuated by shouts as they tried to jam feathers and soapy water down each other's throats. A pity the Cleaners didn't let their work become public knowledge. Dani could've made a decent side income by selling videos of their training bouts to MMA entertainment channels. Of course, that'd probably raise a whole new social debate: Could household chores make kids more prone to violence?

As she sidled up to Ben, Dani eyed the janitor, looking for any signs of discomfort. The cursed infection that had claimed his arm had also prematurely aged him; when they first met, she'd thought him in his seventies, rather than his true age of thirty-five. When the curse had been literally sucked out of him, the damage had also been reversed, restoring his middle-aged physique, including a healthy crop of black hair and a steely glint to his blue eyes.

But despite his assurances of feeling great, she occasionally glimpsed his former grandfatherly visage. A deeper wrinkle around the eyes when he smiled, a sag to his cheeks when he got lost in thought.

Catching her look, he grinned. "What's with the frowny face? Don't tell me I actually got to you with that little Carl-catapultin' stunt."

She took the mop back from him and placed it on the nearest rack. "Ben, why am I spending my summer vacation focusing on all this Cleaners kung fu? I should be working on getting better control of my powers instead all this wax-on, wax-off business."

"Actually, you won't learn how to operate the floor waxers until after you get a handle on joustin' with mops."

She sighed. "That's not the point I was trying to make. I don't need tools to summon my ability."

"Your body and gear are just as important as your powers," he said. "Just 'cause you can conjure localized natural disasters don't mean that's the only thing you oughta be ready to do. What if some Scum confronts you in a public area, where usin' your abilities would put innocent lives at risk?"

"I'd call in backup, I guess. Get a scrub-team on the scene."

"And if they didn't arrive in time?"

"All the better reason to work on fine-tuning my powers. That way I can make the manifestations more precise and reduce any collateral damage. I got a really tiny tornado worked up the other day. I mean, it could've spun in the palm of your—"

A cry rose from one of the maids, followed by the sound of a body hitting the floor. Dani and Ben spun to see the bucket-wielder sprawled on her back, blood streaming from a gash above one eye. Sherri stood over her, chest heaving, teeth bared as if to bite.

The prone maid started to rise. "Sherri, you—"

Sherri lashed out with a foot, and the other maid twisted just enough to take the kick in the ribs. She gasped and curled in on herself. Her head lolled as she fumbled for her bucket, which had fallen out of reach.

"What do you think you're doing?" Vern's shout echoed off the walls, enough command behind it that Dani nearly stammered a reflexive apology.

Sherri snapped her gaze at Vern, naked fury in her eyes, a primal fire that made Dani think of a rabid dog being teased with a slab of raw meat.

She gripped Ben's arm in alarm. "Ben, I don't think—"

The maid flung one of her feather dusters at Vern. As it flew through the air, the feathers snapped together into a black spearhead. Vern hollered as he ducked the missile, which plunged into the shoulder of one of the Cleaners behind him. The man went down with a scream.

Sherri swept her other duster around, and the air spun into a whirlwind with her at the center. She raised the duster above her head, where the feathers gleamed like razor blades, poised to plunge into the maid at her feet.

"No!" Dani and Ben echoed each other's cry as they rushed to intercept.

CHAPTER TWO

Ben moved a hair faster than Dani, long legs working in his favor. Grabbing a small plunger off a rack, he dashed toward the frenzied maid, who'd gotten at least one solid stab in. He threw the plunger with all his strength. It flew true and stuck to the side of Sherri's head.

Still got the good ol' aim, bucko, he thought.

With a shriek of rage, she reared and yanked the plunger away. Unfortunately, the tool wasn't chanted and he couldn't make it do anything fancy without his powers. Ben grabbed the dropped bucket and charged ahead, figuring he could at least stick it on her head and play the bongos until she got tired of dancing.

As he came close, however, the air swirled faster. It blasted into his chest and shoved him back onto his heels. Straining against the gusts, he checked on both sides. Vern and Dani leaned into the wind as well, unable to push closer either.

"Dani!" Her head jerked his way as he shouted. "Cut her off."

She braced herself while narrowing her eyes at Sherri, searching for the core of energy the maid used to sustain the gale. Then Dani made a chopping motion with one hand. The whirlwind died off. Ben sprinted in, bucket poised to wallop.

Sherri spun at him, snarling, eyes wide and glistening. She slashed for his throat; he blocked with the bucket. The feathers sliced through the bottom half, leaving him with … well …

There's a hole in my bucket, dear Liza, dear Liza …

Ben pouted as Sherri circled for another stab. "Hey now, missy. This was my favorite bucket of the last five seconds. We had good times."

He threw the bucket remnants, which merely clipped her shoulder. She thrust at his stomach and he lurched back. His reinforced jumpsuit turned the cut aside, but he had to keep back-pedaling as she rushed in to fillet him.

Then Vern performed his award-winning impression of a bulldozer and clobbered her from the side. Sherri fell, but rolled through and came up facing the fighting instructor. The feathers on her duster popped apart, and she flicked it at him as if in dismissal. A gust of wind lifted Vern and flipped him backward into a rack of training dummies. He bellowed and struggled to untangle himself from the unexpected orgy of rubber bodies.

Using the distraction, Ben grabbed Sherri's left wrist, which clutched the duster. He tried to yank her to the floor, where he could slam her hand down and force her to release the weapon. She pulled her other arm back for a punch and he raised his right arm to block.

Then he remembered—no right arm. Just dandy.

The roundhouse slammed into the side of his head. His jaw popped and all noise went distant, as if he'd plugged his ears with cotton swabs.

He managed to keep hold of her duster-wielding arm, and wrestled to keep it from coring out his heart while Sherri clawed at his face. Random blasts of air knocked him off-balance as he hopped around, dragging her into a merry-go-round of physical abuse.

Where was Dani?

Sherri grabbed the front of his jumpsuit, spun with a flurry of wind, and slammed him against the wall. The knock dizzied him for a second, time enough for her to stab at his face. He halted the cut an inch from the skin and stared into the maid's crazed eyes. Her face went purple as she strained to pin him like an oversized butterfly on a corkboard.

Her cheeks puffed as the duster edged closer. His vision narrowed until he saw nothing more than the gleaming feathers, chanted sharp enough to dice bone. The tip tickled his Adam's apple as he swallowed.

"Yo, Sherri!"

The maid looked to the side in time to take a faceful of wet mop. Screaming, she released Ben and reeled back as Dani whacked her across the face again. Dani held on to the mop handle as the cloth tendrils wrapped around Sherri's head like octopus tentacles, muffling the maid's cries. Sherri cut blindly with the duster, until one of the tendrils snagged her wrist and twisted it hard enough for her to drop the weapon.

Ben wheezed as Sherri tried to tear the mop off her face. Dani used the handle to keep the maid at a distance while forcing her into the middle of the room. Sherri dropped to her knees, and then her side as her struggles weakened.

At last, the maid fell flat, hands and feet twitching.

Dani jerked the mop, and it popped off Sherri's head with a sucking noise. The maid remained conscious but sluggish as she tried to rise. Dani dropped the mop and leaped on her, a knee to the back driving Sherri down while Dani clamped her wrists behind her.

"Get a bag and some ties," Ben shouted to Vern, who'd tossed the last dummy off. "We gotta neutralize her. You two," he pointed at the other Cleaners who'd watched the fight in shock. "Get the nearest handyman in here and then shoot a flare up the Chairman's nostrils so he knows there's been an emergency."

The Cleaners yelled into their handheld radios as they ran out. Vern limped over to a supply cabinet tucked into a corner of the facility. Ben joined Dani, taking one of the maid's arms so she could pin the woman's legs.

Once Vern returned with a black garbage bag and zip-ties, they drew the bag over Sherri's head, cinched it around the neck, and then hog-tied her. The garbage bag was a tool they normally used on Scum, chanted to allow the prisoner to breathe while dampening their powers. Staring down at the maid, Ben recalled when he and Dani had been similarly restrained. There were tricks to defeating such security measures—ones he'd used to spring them last time, in fact—but fortunately not too many Cleaners were privy to these.

At last, they all stood and exchanged worried looks. Dani's brow crinkled as she scanned him.

"You okay?" she asked.

He touched his throat where the duster had brushed the skin, and the fingers came away bloody. Ben grimaced and wiped them on his jumpsuit.

"Totally peachy, princess."

"You sure? She had you by the scruff there." Ben glared, and she raised her hands. "Just concerned, is all."

He sighed and stared down at the maid, who writhed at their feet. Not long ago, he'd have been able to handle this outburst alone without so much as a stubbed toe. Once one of the Cleaners' best employees, he'd wielded mop and spray bottle alike to wipe out Scum and Corrupt manifestations. But the Pure energies he'd once possessed had been stripped from him along with the condition that had almost claimed his life. A price he once thought he'd be okay paying.In the months since, though, he found himself increasingly bothered by the loss. For one thing, it kept his status as a Cleaner in limbo, since only empowered folks could technically be part of their ranks. Nobody seemed to know quite what to do with him beyond letting him train and educate the fresher recruits.

He noticed Dani still watching him, her normally bright emerald eyes shaded with worry, and made himself straighten and smile. No need to get her concerned. He might be powerless, but he didn't have to be helpless.

"Peachy," he repeated, forcing more conviction into his voice. "Thanks for savin' my ☺♦♦—er, yankin' my hide outta the fire there."

"Eh." She shrugged. "I lost track of who's saved who a while back. Don't make me start running a tally all over again."

He chuckled. "Sure thing. But thankya all the same." He eyed the mop she'd used on the maid, the same one she'd held to spar with Vern. "How'dja work the mop like that? I didn't think it was chanted."

She picked up the mop and shook it until the water soaking the cloth strings drained into her hand. She tossed Carl his way, and Ben cupped the bubbling elemental against his chest. They all looked at the maid and then at each other in concern.

"So what just happened?" Dani asked. "Some kind of Scum spell?"

"If it is, I ain't gonna be able to sniff it out," Ben said, feeling a pang of frustration at yet another lost skill. "Either of you sense anythin' mucky?"

Dani and Vern concentrated on the maid for a few moments, but shook their heads.

"Nothing," Vern muttered. "If she'd contracted anything in the field, it would've been detected and neutralized on re-entering HQ. No spells I can see or smell."

Dani's eyes widened. "Ben, wait. Something *is* off—"

Sherri bucked and flopped around, almost tripping Dani before she caught her balance and retreated a step. She raised the mop, ready to knock the maid senseless if she had any fight left in her.

Ben put his arm out to stop her. Sherri's movements had nothing to do with trying to get free. He could tell that much. They were mindless thrashings of panic and agony.

"You're right. Somethin's wrong," he said. "Get the bag off her head."

"What? But Ben, we just—"

"Do it!"

Vern knelt and reached to undo the bag. Before he could, however, Sherri gave one more jerk and went limp. Vern paused, and they waited for several heartbeats without the maid resuming her struggle.

Then he loosed the bag and tore it free. Dani gasped and even Ben, who'd seen his share of nastiness in this line of work, had to breathe out slowly to quell a surge of nausea.

Sherri's face had frozen in a twisted mask of rage as she stared up at them. Her bulging eyes had glazed over and bloody foam dribbled out from the corner of her mouth. Not so much as a twitch came from her cheeks or chest.

Dani pressed knuckles to her mouth. "Oh, ♑□♎ ... is she ...?"

Vern pressed fingers first to Sherri's neck and then her wrist. His expression darkened.

"Dead," he said.

CHAPTER THREE

Dani struggled to keep her composure as all-too-recent memories assailed her. She could only think of another maid who'd died ... thanks to her.

During what she now thought of as her "employee orientation," she and Ben had wound up in a desolate realm known as the Gutters; they'd been accompanied by several others, including a maid named Patty and a rather disturbing creature that called itself a *gnash*. Dani had convinced the gnash to guide them to a safe haven in exchange for its life. Along the way, though, she'd momentarily left the beast unsupervised, at which point it had turned Patty into a final meal.

Despite Ben's assurances that Patty's death hadn't been Dani's fault, the guilt still gnawed at her. This death tore the emotional scab wide again.

Shaking herself from the memory, she recalled that Sherri wasn't the only one hurt here. She ran to the other maid who lay motionless in a pool of blood.

Dani sighed in relief to find the maid still alive despite the mess. The maid rasped shallow breaths and had gone ashen. She whimpered as Dani probed the wounds, trying to recall what college studies she'd taken in preparation for med school.

Deep lacerations, possibly a punctured lung. No major arteries hit, it looked like, otherwise she probably would've already bled out. But internal bleeding would still be an issue.

She looked up to see Ben and Vern hurrying toward a newcomer—a thin, older gentleman who'd just entered the room.

She called out. "Ben, this woman's got to get to an emergency room. She could need surgery if she's going to make it."

He raised a finger, urging patience. "I'll do you one better."

The men exchanged a quick greeting, then Vern slipped out while Ben thumbed Dani's way. She moved aside as the newcomer hurried over and took her place by the injured maid.

While clothed in the same zippered jumpsuit nearly every Cleaner wore, the man moved with a professional and precise air that set him apart from most. The name on his uniform read: *Lopez*.

Lopez checked the maid over with measuring and probing techniques Dani recognized from medical texts she'd pored over. However, after the initial inspection, his procedure became anything but textbook.

He shifted around to kneel by the maid's head and clasped it between his hands. Then he began to sway from side to side while humming and chanting words just below Dani's threshold of comprehension. While his eyes remained closed, a green glow seeped out from between his eyelids, and a faint verdant aura lit the air around his hands and the maid's body.

Dani realized Ben had come up beside her, and she leaned over to whisper.

"What's he doing?"

"Lopez is a handyman," Ben said. "They're the finest you're ever gonna find at fixin' things—and people—if they ain't too far gone."

"A handyman? Isn't that what ... you know ..."

"What Sydney was before goin' Scumwise?"

She grimaced at his naming the entropy mage. Not only had Sydney been a flamboyant flirt and deceptive scoundrel with boundary issues, he'd also tried to hand her over to a cult. Not to mention she still owed him a date—a bargain she would've wholly regretted, except for the fact it had kept him from claiming an innocent life.

Ben nodded. "Yup. Handymen are almost as rare talents as you Catalysts, but there's more of 'em 'round 'cause they don't tend to blow themselves up before we get to 'em."

Dani sighed. "Lucky them."

"Even then," Ben said, "it's hard to find one as strong as Lopez here. He's got a real knack for the work. Been at it almost since he was a bouncin' babe."

Lopez smiled softly at hearing his name, but didn't pause in tending to the injured maid. Keeping one hand on her head, he tugged a small cloth out a pocket with the other and began patting it over her. Blood soaked into it without leaving a stain.

Not for the first time, Dani questioned the wisdom of the Cleaners keeping so much power contained within the company alone. What hospital couldn't benefit from magical rags to keep people and areas free from infection? How many more lives might be saved if handymen applied their abilities in disaster relief areas, rather than remaining hidden behind the scenes?

She closed her eyes and reached out with her power, trying to get a sense of what he was doing. The power snaked out of her, questing along to form an internal vision of the surrounding area, along with detecting any Pure or Corrupt magic at work. She sensed the earth beneath the floor, the recycled air, the electricity coursing through the lights and wires in the walls.

An emerald light suffused Lopez's form, making Dani think of a luminescent creature from the ocean depths. This light flowed along the maid's bones and veins until it bathed her entire body.

Suddenly, the light flared, and Dani grunted as her senses were shoved back into her body. She opened her eyes to find Lopez staring at her. Power dripped from his eyes like green tears and fell onto the maid's face, which looked a bit calmer, the skin a shade healthier.

Lopez shook his head slightly, as if Dani had intruded on an intimate moment. Then his eyes closed again, and he resumed his chanting.

Ben glanced at her. "Tried to take a peek, didja? Shoulda warned you. It's touchy work, and some handymen can get their knickers twisted pretty tight if you stick your nose in. Like bumpin' the elbow of a doc holdin' a scalpel while doin' brain surgery."

"Oh." Dani held hands out to the handyman to show she'd meant no harm. "Sorry. I didn't know."

Lopez's expression didn't change.

Ben cleared his throat. "Wouldn't recommend tryin' to chat 'em up while they're workin', either."

Embarrassed, she shuffled away and Ben followed.

"Handy*men*, huh?" she asked. "Don't any women get this kind of power? Seems a bit sexist if the Pantheon only imbues men with healing abilities."

"'Course ladyfolks can get the same powers," he said. "But you gotta admit, handy*person* just ain't got the same ring to it."

"Hmph. Glad to see we're still living in the twentieth century."

As Ben opened his mouth to reply, a voice echoed through the room.

"I've received reports of a disturbance."

Dani jumped as one of the walls shimmered and turned glassy, revealing a marble-tiled office with a steel desk at the center. The man behind the desk wore a white three-piece suit in sharp contrast to his ebony skin and dark eyes. A white fedora hung on a nearby hat rack.

Francis, the current Chairman of the Board, frowned at the scene, his gaze almost as cutting as his chin and cheekbones. He leaned forward, larger-than-life, and propped his head on a fist.

"Anyone wish to explain what I'm seeing?"

Ben stepped up. "If we had an explanation, mebbe so." He tilted his head toward the corpse. "This maid here—Sherri, I think—went full-on, bone-chewin' ballistic. Mebbe thought the color scheme here needed a little more red to liven up the joint."

Francis sighed. *"As always, Janitor Benjamin, your humor is ill-placed."*

"Naw, it ain't. I always know right where it is."

"It's really all we know," Dani said. "One minute, things are totally normal …" She thought for a second. "As normal as this place ever gets, that is. But the next second, we're fighting for our lives. Even after we subdued Sherri, it was like she went into some epileptic fit that pushed her over the edge. She died before we could do anything."

Francis' scowl deepened and he took notes with a golden pen as they related the details of the fight.

"Handyman Lopez? Do you have any insights?"

Dani hesitated, wondering if she should warn the Chairman against talking during the healing process. Then a voice spoke behind her.

"No, Chairman."

Dani jumped, not realizing Lopez had finished with the maid and now stood by her. He brushed silvery hair off his brow and gazed at Francis with gentle brown eyes as he spoke softly, his voice dusted by a slight Hispanic accent. "Chairman, this other maid will live, though I urge that she be transferred to Maintenance for at least a couple days. She has suffered intense trauma—not all of it physical—and needs ongoing care."

"Make sure to file the proper benefits paperwork. Do you have any idea as to what might've caused this violent outburst?"

Lopez raised his hands in a helpless gesture. "I've not had a chance for anything beyond a cursory examination, but detect no sign of physical or mental Corruption in the injured. I will have to perform a full plumbing before I can provide any real analysis of the dead."

Francis nodded. *"See to it."*

As Lopez left to deal with the patient and body, Dani stepped forward.

"I'd like to volunteer to help."

Francis fixed on her. *"Help with what, precisely, Janitor Danielle? I'm not sure how your particular skill set would aid the handyman, unless you've found a way to resurrect the dead via conjured lightning storms. While I understand you might wish to put your schooling to use, that isn't as applicable here."*

"Not that," she said. "I want to help figure out why this happened. Why Sherri went loco all of a sudden. You're planning on doing more than just a magical autopsy," she glanced over at the handyman, "or whatever plumbing is, right?"

Francis checked a paper on his desk. *"I believe you've been assigned to tools training for the next week. I have many others able to handle an internal employee investigation."*

"Sir, I feel strongly about this. I can do more if you let me."

She fought to not squirm under his gaze, always disliking how the Chairman could make it feel like she was trying to use the situation for personal gain at the company's expense. He considered her for a long moment before leaning back in his chair.

"This wouldn't have anything to do with the loss of Maid Patricia in the Gutters, would it?"

Dani looked aside, wishing he hadn't homed in on her motives so easily. Was she that transparent?

"Partly," she admitted. "I just want to feel like I'm contributing something. I can help, really."

"I'm sorry. There are others trained specifically for this situation. Perhaps in the future." His focus shifted. *"Janitor Benjamin."*

Ben's face lit up, and Dani fought down a rush of jealousy. Why should he get picked over her? He didn't even have his powers anymore. She kept herself from voicing the complaint, though, knowing it wasn't fair to the janitor and that it wouldn't do her any good. Once Francis set his mind, it took an act of God—or at least the Board—to change it.

"Yup?" Ben asked.

"Prepare a report of the confrontation and have it on my desk by this evening. I'd like your unique perspective on the events and it will give you something to do in your consultant role. In the meantime, I'll be assigning Ascendant Jackson a team to look into this further. That's all."

"Ah. Sure ..." At Francis' look, Ben chopped a salute. "Sir, yes, Chairman, sah!"

Francis faded from view and the wall returned to whitewashed cinder blocks. Dani and Ben sighed simultaneously and then looked at each other in mutual annoyance.

"Looks like we're both gettin' tossed the table scraps," he said.

"You'd think after what we did for him, he'd give us a little leeway." She turned toward the exit, but Ben caught her shoulder.

"Dani, Francis is just—"

"Doing his job," she said, more harshly than intended. "Just like everyone else around here is supposed to, including me." She faced him, fists planted on hips. "I'd really hoped when you announced me as a full-time employee that I'd actually be able to, you know, use my abilities out in the field versus puttering around here all day."

"Putterin'? It's the same old trainin' every Cleaner goes through when they're brought in."

"Well, maybe there should be some new training procedures," she said. "Plus some new gender neutral job titles."

"And at least you're gettin' paid for all this so-called putterin' now." His hand slipped off her shoulder. "I know you wanna be all go-go hero girl. Trust me, I get how that feels. But you still gotta be certified with the equipment before you can be assigned any major field work."

"Bull."

Ben blinked. Then he grinned. "Oh, look at you, princess. Slippin' past the foul-filter all sneaky like. I shoulda thought of that."

Dani waved the trick aside. "When I first got recruited, you were all about shoving me out into the field to get first-hand experience. Why are you so eager to keep me locked up, learning how to hold a stick properly?"

"Don't be blamin' me for that first bit. That was Destin's doin', remember? He figured stickin' you with me might getcha exposed to the Ravishing. Make your abilities more controllable-like with his Chairman powers."

"But that's not why you're taking this tack now, is it?" She leaned in, forcing him to meet her eyes. "Is it because you can't go out there with me?" Her anger flared as he shifted guiltily. "That's it, isn't it? You feel responsible for me, and you think if I go out without you by my side, I'm not going to be able to handle things."

He stiffened and glared at her. "It's nothin' like that. I'm worried for you, sure as shootin', but don't think I'd ever hold you back just 'cause I ain't able to do the work I want, either."

"Well that's what I am thinking," she said. "Honestly, Ben, despite what we've gone through, it's like you still think I'm a little girl and you have to be my grandfather, mostly minus the old man smell."

"Dani, I—" One eye twitched. "What do you mean, *mostly*?"

She started to chuckle, but jolted at a sudden thought. "♠︎♒︎♓︎♦︎! I totally forgot I promised Jared I'd drop by today. I have to go, otherwise I'll miss visiting hours. Want to join me?"

He looked ready to force the issue, but then pressed his lips tight. "I gotta write that report, and you know how much Francis loves his paperwork. The longer the better."

"Lucky you. Death by a thousand paper cuts."

"Say hiya to the kiddo for me."

She left the training room and headed for her quarters to clean up before going to the hospital. She strode along, joining the foot traffic of janitors, plumbers, maids, and the occasional white-suited Ascendant who deigned to mingle with the common sanitation workers.

After she'd been inducted into the Cleaner ranks, she'd asked for a map of HQ, having gotten lost more than a few times in the seemingly endless stretch of halls, storage rooms, and employee facilities. Ben had just laughed and told her about the team that had, a century before, set out to chart the whole of HQ—and hadn't been seen since. Rumors had it they still wandered the compound. A few of the more superstitious Cleaners occasionally held vigils with propane fueled torches, lighting rarely-traveled halls in hopes of bringing the waywards home.

And this was only the stateside operational center, not to mention the European and Asian headquarters. HQ, she'd learned early on, wasn't a terribly cohesive structure, as much as they tried to suggest this through company organizational charts—some of which would make an Escher painting the perfect semblance of sanity by comparison.

This branch was anchored in Denver, Colorado. Ben had tried to explain it once, saying the main portion existed "someplace a bit sideways to normal reality. I submitted a suggestion to officially call it wonkified space, but I'm pretty sure the Employee Suggestion box is just a disguised incinerator."

"You just get used to it," he'd said, waving vaguely. "Sooner or later. Hopefully. Or mebbe you'll find that lost survey team and bring 'em home, yeah? Focus on where you want to end up, and you'll get there like gravy goin' downhill."

As she walked, she reviewed the disturbing events in the training facility and tried to imagine what would turn someone so vicious. Had there been bad blood between the two maids? A quarrel over a man? Maybe a lovers' spat gone nasty? Those explanations seemed too simplistic for Sherri's savagery, plus her unexplained death.

Hopefully Lopez would be able to uncover an explanation while getting the other maid back on her feet. Maybe if Dani asked real nice, the handyman would let her watch over his shoulder when she had time off. She wouldn't use her abilities, of course. Totally mundane observation. Did handymen employ nurses or orderlies?

She let the thoughts fade into the background as another turn brought her into a familiar stretch of employee quarters. The doors all looked the same but she recognized hers by the pink smiley face sticker she'd placed on it.

She entered the sparsely furnished room she'd been assigned. Besides a bed and nightstand with a few tattered paperback novels, the main piece of decoration was the terrarium on the dresser, where an orange and red lizard lounged on a heat rock.

Tetris, her pet bearded dragon, cocked an eye her way in his usual inquisitive manner. Some girls wanted to own a pony. Some girls wanted to be a princess. Dani, however, had wanted to prove to her parents she could overcome her germophobic ways and deal with normal life enough to get through med school. Tetris had been her compromise, the one thing she'd learned to care about beyond her hygiene routines and gallons of sani-gel. Funny how a lizard could become a mental and emotional anchor—and funny how much she feared losing that anchor now that normal life involved maids going mad and buildings without blueprints.

A little voice rose in the back of her mind, listing various reptilian diseases that might claim Tetris' life: *Herpesvirus. Septicemia. Adenovirus* ...

Shutting down that old habit hard, she reminded herself that so long as she kept her pet within HQ, no infections could threaten him. Her work here protected him. The work helped her as well, giving her the ability to fight back against the filthy germs that once held her captive in terror. In turn, she could help others more directly with her Catalyst abilities. A circle of sanitized life.

The lizard scuttled off his rock to claw at the glass, stubby tongue licking the pane.

Ignoring his immediate pleas for attention—or food, more likely—Dani slipped into the bathroom. After showering, she shrugged back into her uniform, which always smelled fresh after she took it off for a few minutes. After putting on thick gloves, she dropped a handful of mealworms into Tetris' cage and watched as the lizard chased them down. She tickled him under the chin once he finished the last one.

"Need anything while I'm out?"

He gently bit the end of her thumb.

"You know I can't afford to get you a lady friend right now. Maybe once I get a raise; so figure somewhere between the next five and fifty years, 'kay?"

Once his water bowl was refilled, she stripped off the gloves, grabbed a fresh bottle of sani-gel, and slathered it on her hands for a full minute to satisfy the urge that'd been building ever since the maid incident. A knot of tension loosed in her gut as she breathed the fumes deep.

Sure. Rationally, she knew her new identity as a Cleaner combined with the suit shielded her from mundane contamination plus a range of Corrupt influence—but some things in life just refused to be rational. The gel remained a concession to this, a compulsion she might never leave behind her whole life.

With new gloves secured, she left the room and walked until she reached a hallway which dead-ended in a full-length mirror. She reached out and tapped the glass, letting a bit of Pure energy trickle from her to activate the portal. The glassways not only provided external access from various locations around the city, but also acted as portals between divisions such as Supplies, Maintenance, and the Recycling Center, where they kept imprisoned Scum and other nasties.

The glass shimmered and bulged, forming a translucent, feminine face. Glittering eyes focused on her.

"Destination?" the window-watcher asked.

"Saint Joseph Hospital," she said. "Containment ward."

"Employee authorization required."

Dani placed her palm on the glass. A chime sounded, and she shivered as a scan coursed through her. The chilly wave washed over her scalp, across her shoulder blades, and out the soles of her feet as the window-watcher inspected her down to bone and neuron for any sign of contamination. It left a tingling sensation in its wake, along with a metallic aftertaste which made Dani feel like she'd French-kissed a battery.

"Pass through." The face smoothed out, leaving the mirror featureless once more.

She took a deep breath to brace herself. She had yet to get used to traveling through the glassways. It wasn't just the brief discomfort. It was also the sensation of traveling much farther than the single step it took to go from one side to the other; a hop, a skip, and a jump over an empty space the size of the Grand Canyon, somehow landing on the far edge rather than tumbling into a bottomless pit. She'd woken a couple nights in a cold sweat, having relived the sensation in her dreams, but with messier results.

Stop being a wuss, she told herself. *Nobody else complains about this. Besides, it's better than driving across town. I hate having to file reimbursements for fuel.*

She plunged into the glassy surface. The frigid border swept over her, and for an instant she glimpsed an infinite corridor, with countless reflections of herself along the sides, each frozen in mid-step.

The other end of the corridor snapped her way. The space between contracted and the alternate versions of herself began to vanish. Dani braced to complete the step, as her momentum would propel her forward when she emerged.

As the opposing end of the glassway closed the gap, the nearest reflection on Dani's right reached out and grabbed her arm, which burst into flame.

Chapter Four

en frowned at Dani's back until the door slid shut behind her. He glanced around, made sure Lopez remained distracted with the wounded maid, and then plucked at his jumpsuit collar for a quick sniff.

Nothin'. She was just messin' with me. He took a deeper whiff. *Right? Right.*

He slipped over to the handyman and watched him work for a few minutes. Already a few gashes on the maid's stomach had sealed over and her breathing had evened. Nothing more Ben could do here.

"You got this?" he asked.

Lopez nodded without looking up.

Ben cast a worried look over at Sherri's body. He felt half-blinded without his ability to sense Corrupt energies anymore. There could've been charbeetles festering in her bowels, for all he knew, and the first hint he'd get would when they burned their way out to cover the room in flaming gunk.

He patted Lopez on the back. "Keep me in the loop, yeah?"

He headed for the exit and slammed face-first into the door, which had failed to open. Reeling, he slapped a hand to his nose. His grunt of pain echoed through the training room.

"Sonuva ..." He bit down on the curse before the foul-filter activated. After making sure his nose remained intact, he glared at the door and tried a variation. "Son of a bloody biscuit!"

The substitute swear didn't help alleviate the pain nearly as well, but it was better than nothing. Maybe Dani's tactic wasn't a bad idea. He needed to expand on his vehement vocabulary to get around the spell in more creative and satisfying ways.

Lopez looked over in concern, but Ben waved him away, trying not to flush with embarrassment. He eyed the uncooperative door as he eased his hand into a side pocket, and then groaned when he touched glassy shards.

"Aw, crap-on-a-stick."

After dumping the shards out onto the floor, he knelt and stirred a finger through them, seeing if there was any chance of restoring the access sigil. No such luck. It must've been shattered during the fight; not a glimmer of imbued energy remained.

"For Purity's sake ..." He grabbed his handheld radio and tuned it to the proper channel before clicking the button to speak. "Janitor Ben reportin' a little equipment malfunction. Monty, you readin' me?"

Static crackled for a few seconds before a voice cut through.

"What'd you break this time, Ben? We've had a bet running."

Ben glowered at the speaker. "It's my access sigil. Smashed to glitter."

"Yeah? What were you using it for? Hammering nails into your thick skull?"

"Har. If you're wantin' me to drop by and dole out the details, I'm gonna need a way to actually get to you. Whattaya say?"

"I'll requisition a new one. But it'll be a day or two."

"You're kiddin', right? I need a sigil to just walk around here. I'm not sittin' in one spot for two days until you can chant a new one."

"Hey, I've got a laundry list to work through that'd put a dry cleaners at a tar pit to shame. You should've taken better care of the one you were issued. And you know this new one will—"

"Come out of my pay. I figured." He leaned against the wall. "Fine. Dock me whatever's due, but can'tcha get it to me before I starve to death? Or gotta use the little boy's room?"

"I'll send someone to get you," Monty said. *"Keep your britches bleached."*

"Do you know how much that'd itch?" Ben asked, before hearing the click which signaled Monty had gone off-channel. He sighed and hooked the radio on his belt. Francis had provided the first access sigil after Ben lost his powers, since all of HQ's doors and glassways activated only when a Cleaner's Pure energies were sensed—a security measure to keep Scum from infiltrating the place, and also how management tracked everyone in the facility.

He pushed aside the temptation to call Lopez over to open the exit. Never a good idea to interrupt a handyman's healing. Sitting beside the door, he snagged Carl's spray bottle and held the water sprite at eye level.

"Learn any new jokes lately, buddy?"

An hour passed as Carl regaled him with humorous one-offs, which often involved birds for some reason, especially seagulls and pelicans. It was one aspect of elemental humor Ben had never quite comprehended.

Then footsteps sounded outside right before the door slid open.

"'Bout time."

Ben jumped up and nearly rammed into the heavyset woman who planted herself in his way. Putting a thick fist on a thicker hip, she slurped from a steaming coffee mug, which read *This is Not Your Day*. Dark brown eyes stared at him with hostile curiosity. Ben smoothed down his uniform as he recognized the other janitor, and Carl burbled through a series of shapes which roughly translated to: *Don't even think of trying to blame me for this one.*

They sized each other up while Ben tried to figure out the best way to break the ice—or iceberg in this case. He settled for a smile and wave as he secured the spray bottle on his hip.

"Heya, Lu. Good to see you. Alive that is. And not tryin' to kill me."

Lucy didn't twitch an eyelash. She'd been around since he and Karen first joined the Cleaners, and had worked with them on countless jobs over the years. They'd developed a comfortable camaraderie which had been lost after the job which left Ben infected and Karen deceased. Like everyone else, Lucy had kept her distance after he got out of quarantine.

The last time they'd been toe-to-toe, she'd headed up a team intent on keeping him and Dani locked down—albeit on Destin's orders before the former Chairman had been exposed as Corrupted. Ben had exchanged a few blows with her before pulling a downright dirty trick, even for an old dog like him. He'd kissed her. Of course, instead of slipping his tongue down her throat, Ben had given her a mouthful of Carl so the elemental could choke her unconscious.

Not the sort of thing anyone would hold a grudge about, right?

At last, Lucy took a heavy swallow of coffee and licked at the black grains between her teeth. She spoke with the lightest of Latino accents, which Ben knew only surfaced when she was holding down her emotions something fierce. "Why is it anytime an internal emergency is reported, I just know you're involved?"

"Y'know, I've been thinkin' the anti-Ben bias is kinda becomin' a thing 'round here ..."

She looked past him. "What's this I hear about a maid trying to bite people's giblets off?"

He turned and waved into the training room. "Why don'tcha take a look?"

Lucy craned her neck to see better. She sucked in a breath. "That bad?"

"One dead, another hangin' on, thanks to Lopez. No idea what triggered it yet, not that I have much to do with that kinda work anymore."

"Right. Well, I'm sure if it was important enough, they'd have sent a memo around to all the grunts by now."

"Right. 'Cause grunts always get them important memos." He hopped to one side and spoke to the space he'd just occupied. "So how've you been, Ben?" He hopped back. "Me? Why thankya, Lu, for carin' enough to ask. Things've been shook up a might bit since we last butted buckets." Ben lifted his arm to display himself. "Came out a little worse-for-wear, as you might see. But everythin' else is in the right place, doin' the right thing."

Lucy appeared unamused. "And the girl? Whatshername?"

"Dani. She's doin' just fine. You two should get reacquainted. Mebbe go get your toenails painted and have a slumber party."

Lucy pressed her plump lips together. "They won't release the official reports, but everyone says you got rid of Destin."

"Not so much got rid of. More like—"

"Rumor also has it the Board offered you the Chairmanship and you gave it over to Francis."

Ben tried to edge around her, but he would've had to leave his skeleton behind to squeeze through the gap between her and the door jamb. Her gaze and stance didn't budge. In another life, he could've pictured her as a drill sergeant. And not the shouty type either. One that could make the military minions want to demote themselves just by going still and fixing them with a particular look.

"Since when're you goin' 'round trustin' rumors? Look, I got an appointment—"

She took another slow chug of her drink. "Same rumors also say you're powerless now, since you're needing an access sigil and all that."

"I ..." Ben sagged. "Gossipin' just ain't good for company morale."

Frosty humor twinkled in her eyes. "I could have some real fun with this."

"Now that'd be downright immature of you, don'tcha think? Ain't you a big girl?"

She drained her mug and then peered at the contents at the bottom as if divining her next move from the settled patterns of the grinds.

"I've always been against cruelty toward helpless animals," she said.

"Should I be feelin' relieved or insulted?"

A shrug. "Eh. Room for both."

They stood side-by-side, Lucy lost in dark thoughts while Ben tried to figure out how he should feel toward her. Ben studied her out of the corner of one eye, and then realized she'd been doing the same to him.

She grimaced. "What?"

He stepped out into the hall, and the door slid shut behind him. "Just ain't seen you since our, uh, little encounter in the Recyclin' Center."

She tugged a few snarls out of her mess of black curls. "Yeah. Went on a rotation in Seattle. Bunkered down with a couple plumbers who'd run across a rotworm nest. Finally managed to flush the suckers out."

"Whatcha back here for?"

"At the moment? You."

His brows popped skyward. "Me? Look, Lucy, that pucker sucker-punch I laid on you? I know it kinda knocked you flat, but that was the point, and the only point, lemme tell you. 'Sides, technic'ly we weren't swappin' spit, since Carl—"

She whacked his arm hard enough he winced.

"Stow it. A bunch of us were in Supplies getting restocked when you put in your call. Monty ordered us onto volunteer duty and I pulled the short straw."

"Ah."

"Yeah. Ah. So don't think I won't leave you locked in the first broom closet we come to if you make this any more difficult than it has to be. Where do you need to go?"

He started walking and she moseyed after.

"Employee Records," he said. "I had an appointment to dig into some of the archives."

"A real appointment or one you've made up as an excuse to get a guide?"

"Real one, believe it or not."

"I don't believe it."

He paused and laid a hand over his heart. "Aww, I'm hurt."

Her finger thumped his chest. "Not yet."

"Listen, Lu, can'tcha just get me there and see? I promise, cross my heart and stick a cherry in my eye, that if I don't got a right and proper appointment, you can march me straight to the nearest broom closet."

She studied him for a moment and then tilted her head down the hall.

"So what're you looking for?" she asked as they resumed walking.

"I stashed some dirty mags in there before everythin' went britches over bonkers for me and wanted to see about gettin' 'em back."

She latched onto his arm and dragged him toward a side hall.

"Closet it is then," she said.

He managed to yank lose. "Sorry, Lu. I was just tryin' to get a chuckle outta you. Used to be that weren't so hard. But here's the truth." When he touched a breast pocket, the folded picture he'd slipped in there crinkled. "I'm lookin' for anythin' that might mebbe tell me what actually happened on my last job with Karen. Somethin' that'd finally help me find out what them Scum did to her."

She paused, and a look he couldn't identify flickered across her face. Pain? Anger? Did she think he chased a lost cause? Even Francis, with the authority he wielded, hadn't been able to provide Ben with much beyond what the public records already stated. He tried to meet her eyes, but she glanced aside.

"Lu? Somethin' wrong?"

She plodded ahead, and he hurried to match her.

"Let's just get this done before this coffee wears off and puts me in a really bad mood," she said.

"Yes'm."

CHAPTER FIVE

Dani yelled as she tried to simultaneously beat at her flaming arm and yank free of the hand gripping her. The glassway kept her frozen in mid-step, however. A growing strain tried to force her through to the other side, even as her reflection locked her in place.

Heat brushed her neck and cheeks. A rustling voice whispered in her ear.

"Don't think you can ignore us. You'll have to face us eventually."

The reflection released her to stumble out the other side. Her inertia spun her around and she reenacted one of Vern's takedowns, minus the instructor's assisting kick.

She sprang back to her feet, fists raised.

"Bad touch," she cried.

The mirror pane on this side, however, remained unbroken. Her reflection stared back at her with a mix of shock and promised violence. The flames along her sleeve had disappeared, not even leaving ashen streaks as evidence of the encounter.

Two other people stood reflected in the glass. A pair of Ascendants were stationed on either side of a double-doorway behind her. As she hurried to compose herself, they peered out from under the brims of their fedoras with worried looks.

"Something …" She tugged her uniform straight. "Something attacked me in the glassway."

The Ascendant closest to her, a thin woman with brown curls mostly hidden under her hat, cocked her head.

"Janitor, if there was anything aberrant in the glassway, the window-watcher for that route would've alerted us and HQ. You wouldn't have been allowed to come through."

Dani started to argue, but realized that from the Ascendants' perspective, anything outside of the normal operation of the glassways might also be outside of their ability to conceive. Plenty of rules governed how their world worked—even a magical one—and Ascendants were all about enforcing the rules. Plus, as Ben had warned her once, one of the costs of becoming an Ascendant was slowly shedding some of your more human characteristics, such as a sense of compassion or imagination.

So she tucked away the encounter until she could speak to someone else in authority about it.

"Here to see Jared," she said.

The same Ascendant raised a hand. "Sorry. Visiting hours just ended."

She plucked at an earlobe as she scowled. "Oh, don't do this to me. You don't know what kind of day it's been."

"Sorry, Janitor. Regulations state—"

Dan-ni? Hay air?

The voice bounced around inside of Dani's skull like a ping-pong ball, loud enough to make her cringe. By the Ascendants' looks of discomfort, she knew they heard it as well.

A moment later, the doors the Ascendants guarded snapped open hard that enough one of the top hinges tore out of the wall. The short hallway behind it looked more like an airlock than a passage, and it ended in a churning gray fog. The mist failed to billow out into the fore room, remaining unnaturally static.

C-c-c-comma pee lay, Dan-ni.

She traded looks with the suits.

"Has he been acting like this lately?" she asked.

The woman nodded. "We've had to re-secure the wards a dozen times this week, and he could still break out any time he wants, though I don't believe he knows it … or doesn't care. It's as if he is simply toying with us for his own amusement."

"At least he's entertained," she said. "I'd hate to see him bored, or maybe upset if he doesn't get a playmate."

The Ascendants hesitated as if they hadn't considered this. The other Ascendant coughed and stepped aside.

"Perhaps you could go in and say hello," he said. "Just for a few minutes."

Dani tried not to smirk as she strode between them. "Too kind."

Her pace faltered, though, when she came to the foggy boundary. She tried to wave it away, but the mist refused to budge from its unnatural border. At last, she took a fortifying breath and slipped inside the demigod's playroom. Fluorescent lights made hazy streaks overhead, but failed to penetrate the fog more than a few feet away. Dani lost sight of the walls after five steps, and prayed they hadn't reorganized the furniture too much. The bruises on her legs from her last visit had just faded.

As she stumbled along, she kicked aside rubber balls, Lego blocks, action figures, and one of those wooden ducks on wheels, which clacked as it rolled along. When she gauged herself to have reached the middle of the chamber, she spread her arms and slowly spun in a circle.

"Jared? Where are you?"

Dan-ni!

A dark figure leapt out of the depths of the fog and latched onto her with a full-body hug, arms around her shoulders, legs around her waist. Dani *whuffed* and staggered for balance as she caught the embrace. She leaned back so she could see the boy's black pupils, which were shot through with gold slivers.

Besides the eyes, Jared's half-human, half-Pantheon heritage only revealed itself in his grin, which stretched a bit wider than humanly possible, and showed off canines sharp enough to make any dentist get whiplash from a double-take.

Each time she noted this, she had a mini-flashback to seeing those same teeth sink into Ben's throat to feed off his energy. As always, she forced herself to shake off the revulsion the memory generated. Not the kid's fault his mother was a lesser member of the Corrupt Pantheon, and his father the insane former Chairman of the Cleaners. One couldn't pick their parents, but the hope remained that Jared might choose a better path than either of them had.

Jared released her and hopped out of sight with a single bound, trailing gray and white mist. Dani hurried to keep up with him—and then yelped as someone pinched the back of her arm. She swatted and grabbed a hand, turning to find Jared behind her all of a sudden. The fog made it difficult to discern, but she felt certain he couldn't have repositioned himself so quickly through any natural means.

Teleportation? Superspeed? The Board claimed Jared's powers would remain in flux until some unascertained threshold of maturity; until then, he continued to manifest and lose new abilities almost daily. At least this was a safer trick than the last time she'd visited, when he'd been belching poisonous gases and lighting them on fire with a snap of his fingers. Or when he'd started sneezing raw sewage everywhere. Or summoning giant cockroaches out of thin air ...

Hide-un-seekum, his disembodied voice crowed. *Hidded un seeked eww.*

She hugged him and laughed. "Yes, you did. Such a good game of hide and seek, too. I never saw you coming. Now stand still so I can get a good look at you."

Jared pouted, but went stiff-legged and straight-backed, shoulders pinched to show off his bony chest. Ever since being brought in for safekeeping, he'd refused to wear a shirt; anytime someone forced one on him, it disappeared within minutes, never to be found again. Dani couldn't tell if the jeans and tattered sneakers he wore were the same ones they'd found him in, but it sure looked it.

At least she figured out the source of the fog. Steam rolled off him as if he were a live coal tossed into a bucket of water. It swirled throughout the room and clung to every surface except her skin, which she felt oddly grateful for.

His inhuman eyes studied her in return.

"What?" she asked. "What do you see?"

Moo ore eww, tow dee.

Her mind slowly translated his faltering words. "More of me? What's that mean?"

Instead of answering, he leaped away into the fogbank, while his call echoed back from different directions.

Pee lay?
Pee lay?
Pee lay?

She spun in place, wary of another pinch. At last, he popped back into view, grinning and prancing about.

Pee lay, Dan-ni.

She reached out to keep him in place, but he vanished and reappeared on her left. She waved for him to stop long enough for her to focus on him.

"Jared, I can't stay long today, I'm sorry."

His dancing about came to a halt, and his face and shoulders fell. Disappointment emanated from him with such force that Dani felt like she stood in a surf, fighting the swell and tug of the tide. The pull of his emotions threatened to suck her down into darker currents of brooding jealousy that lurked beneath his childish behavior. The strength of his projections continued to shock her, and more than once she'd questioned the wisdom of exposing herself to it. Still, whenever she saw his smile and heard his guileless laughter, it reminded her of what they might salvage in him.

"Jared," she braced herself, both physically and mentally. "Jared, you need to draw your feelings back into yourself. Keep them contained. Remember what we talked about? No trying to force others to do whatever you want just because you're stronger than them."

He frowned in confusion.

Straw her?

"You are very strong," she said. "And people are vulnerable to you. If you aren't careful, you could overwhelm others, especially if they don't know how to shield themselves."

He pouted, but the waves of disappointment ebbed away until Dani breathed easier. Jared crouched and peered at her from under his black brows.

Ewe leaf?

She crouched to his level. "I'd stay longer, but I got out late from training today. Otherwise I would've gotten here earlier and could've played. Next time, I promise."

He reached out and tapped her forehead. Pulling back, he stared at the tip of his finger, as if seeing something there she could not. Hopefully this wasn't like the time he'd become fascinated with picking his nose and inspecting the results.

La dee dad tow-dee.

She frowned. "Yes. A lady dead today. A woman died while I was training. Jared, who told you about that?"

He shook his head. *New. Knotter.*

"Not her? Who?"

His face twisted. Faint auras glowed around his fists, the left hand glowing white, the right glowing purple-black.

Knotter. Knotter!

Dani clutched the sides of her head as his words turned to mental hammer-blows. The fog condensed into vague humanoid shapes which reached toward her with claws. Whispering voices scuttled through her thoughts, hungry, hunting—

Jared smacked the side of his head. The auras faded from his hands and the fog sank back into ashen curdles. Dani let out several slow breaths before straightening, while Jared looked at her as if expecting a spanking.

Sore me. Sore me, Dan-ni.

She grimaced as the pain retreated into a background headache.

"It's okay. I forgive you. You didn't mean to hurt me. Let's try again. I really want to understand what you're saying."

Jared screwed up his lips and projected the words with some effort.

Knot her. Knot her la dee.

She sighed. "Okay. You said that. Not her ... notter ... another? Are you saying another? Another lady?"

He nodded and bounced on his heels.

Goo hope towel. Tack me, Dan-ni.

"Hope towel? Oh, you mean the hospital. We need to work on your vocabulary lessons some more. Maybe you and Ben could study together." She glanced around, wondering when the Ascendants might cut off her visit. "Why do you want to visit the hospital?"

His gold-flecked eyes locked on hers. Low pulses of fear radiated from him and quivered along Dani's spine.

"Jared, what is it? You're worrying me. What's wrong?"

He licked his lips and shuffled closer. Taking her hand, he rubbed it against a smooth cheek.

40

Death, Dan-ni. Death in hope towel. It deer and comma hay air.

Trepidation rose as she translated his warped words. *Death in the hospital, coming here?*

To steal one of Ben's expressions … hoo boy.

CHAPTER SIX

Ben clipped Lucy's heels as she slowed. She thrust a shoulder back to make him retreat a step.

"Keep your distance, lover-boy."

He rubbed his forehead. "For Purity's sake, it didn't mean anythin'. Can'tcha understand I was a bit desperate right then? Y'know, to live?"

She raised an unplucked brow. "So you'd only kiss me out of desperation?"

He spluttered. "That's ain't—I mean, you …"

She shook her head in exasperation. "Muck and buckets, Ben. And you were complaining about not getting me to laugh."

"Yeah? Mebbe you could try a few knock-knock jokes. You know I've always been partial to 'em."

"I remember. Karen was always studying joke books to find ones you hadn't heard yet."

He grimaced. "Can we talk about somethin' else?"

"Sure. What's it like to buddy up to one of the most psychotic entropy mages we've ever dealt with?"

"Hey, you watch your words. Sydney and me ain't never were and ain't never gonna be bestest buds. Also, he might not take a shine to you callin' him a psycho."

"Would murderer work better?"

"A'ight. Howsabout we just cut the talkin' altogether."

"But I'm enjoying this too much."

"Can't have too much fun at once, don'tcha know? Ain't healthy." Ben patted the spray bottle on his hip. "'Sides, Carl's the only buddy I need."

Lucy nodded to the elemental, who swirled in hello. "How's he doing these days?" she asked.

"Couldn't ask for a better partner. Comin' on ten years together."

"You do you realize that makes you married by common law, right?"

Ben sighed. "You ain't gonna let up, are you?"

Her grin promised plenty more taunting. "You know the only way you'll ever recover your wit is to keep practicing. Don't worry. I'll be gentle. For now."

"Oh, yay, we're here. Can't talk. Gotta focus."

Lucy chuckled to herself as Ben strode past her. He headed for a door that looked carved from blue marble, with the words *Employee Records* chiseled into the stone.

She pressed a hand to the door which rumbled aside. A soft white light gleamed in the chamber beyond. Lucy waved for him to take the lead.

"After you, Mr. Bundle of Joy."

Ben stepped inside and closed his eyes as he crossed the threshold. He waited until he sensed Lucy enter and the door seal behind them. Then he gazed about, reminding himself to not try and absorb every detail at once.

They stood on a wide steel platform, worn to a dull burnish by the countless feet which had trod through here. It circled around to the far side of what appeared to be a bottomless pit, with further ringed platforms visible in the depths below. Pillared arches stood at regular intervals, and Ben knew if he headed down those other halls at random, he'd end up right back in this first chamber.

The ceiling was a dome of blue marble, etched with silver glyphs which appeared to shift and mingle with each blink. Curved glass panels covered every inch of the dome and reflected the source of light, which hung in the center of the space like a tiny azure sun.

The orb of Pure knowledge blazed in silent fury; occasional arcs of lightning shot into the dome and lit the panels briefly before fading. The whole chamber smelled of ozone and boot polish.

"This place always gives me the creeps," he said, trying to check out the orb without looking at it dead on. "It just ain't right. Makes me feel like I'm starin' at the back of my head."

Lucy shielded her eyes by his side. "Yeah. Trying to perceive seven interwoven dimensions can do that to you."

"Is that what they're up to these days? Golly jeepers. I'm gonna have to learn me some proper 'rithmatic if they go any higher."

With an electric spray, one of the glass panels detached from the dome and floated down to hover above their heads. The glass frosted over and a figure appeared at the center like a caveman frozen within a block of ice. Ben knew it was a man only because he'd met Rick in person years earlier, before he'd been elected by the Board as the newest in an ancient line of filing managers.

The Filing Clerk stared down at the janitors.

"Janitor Benjamin. You are late."

Ben tried to look contrite. "Rick, hey, sorry 'bout that. Bit of trouble in the trainin' center."

"Yes." Glowing lines of text whirled about Rick too fast for Ben to make any sense of them. "The maids. I already received a death certificate for Sherri Dabien and Chairman Francis has filed for the dispensing of health benefits for one Margaret Elmster. Your and the Catalyst's actions during the encounter have also been recorded."

"Must be nice bein' so connected to everything."

"My functions as Filing Clerk hold no consideration for my feelings about the position."

The panel dropped until the bottom edge clinked against the metal platform. Rick's image faded with a final warning. "You have half an hour. Use it wisely."

The panel shimmered and then melted into a translucent cube. Another shiver and it congealed into a glassy desk, complete with a chair, keyboard, and computer screen. The screen blinked on with a green flash.

Ben nudged the chair with a knee. It rolled smoothly on glass wheels, and he eased into the seat, trying to get over the feeling that it would shatter under his weight.

"Gotta love how user-friendly this place is gettin'."

"You know how to actually use a computer interface?" Lucy asked. "I thought you'd still be stuck on typewriters."

"I am a man of many talents."

"The first part of that statement is true, at least."

Ben reached inside his uniform and tugged out a manila envelope, thankful none of the items within were as fragile as the access sigil had been.

"What you got there?" Lucy asked.

He flapped the envelope. "This is all the info Francis scrounged up for me about Karen and our last job." Setting it on the desktop, he undid the flap and slid the contents out. The one item he'd removed, the photo of Karen, remained in his breast pocket; a talisman of sorts, as he thought of it.

Lucy frowned as she spread the papers out and shuffled through them. He ticked off what she would be seeing. A typed report which would've been sent for the Board's review, several notes in both Destin's and Francis' handwriting, and—

Lucy made a surprised noise and held the last item before Ben's eyes.

"What's this?"

He took the page. It presented a hand-sketched blueprint for a maze of tunnels which coiled in on themselves in a vaguely spiraling pattern. Certain spots were noted as major or minor junctions, others as nesting points for a variety of Scum critters.

"It's s'posed to be a map of the section of the Sewers where we went in," he said. "The official report says we was respondin' to an invadin' swarm of clogs. A simple burn-n-churn gig."

"So what's the problem?"

He laid the map over the keyboard and frowned at its familiar, yet confounding twists and turns.

"Problem is, I scanned this map into the system and asked for it to be ID'd and matched with any other junctions."

"And?"

He slumped back in the chair. "And it ain't nowhere to be found. Accordin' to all our big and fancy know-how and know-what, this part of the Sewers just don't exist."

"That's impossible."

The rasp in her voice made Ben look up. Lucy had gone still and fixed on the map with an intense stare. Curious as to her

46

reaction, he rolled the chair back a bit, giving her a clearer look.

"Best thing I can figure is mebbe this is a section of the Sewers we've somehow missed for hundreds of years, which makes us look downright shabby on the job, or …"

"Or it's not really the Sewers after all," she said, catching the line of his logic. "But still, that's impossible."

"Why?"

"Because …" Her gaze finally moved from the map to meet his. "You really don't remember, do you?"

"Tell me." He reached for her, but she shuffled a few steps away. Irritation bloomed, making Ben slap the chair arm and stand to glower down at her. "What's goin' on here, Lu?"

She scowled back. "What do you mean?"

"What's goin' on with you, huh? This has gotta be about more than our bump a couple months back or the fact that I ain't been sendin' you postcards sayin'*Wish You Was Here* since then. You got somethin' gnawin' at you, and it's dealin' with this."

He rustled the papers, watching as her gaze darted to them and then away in a guilty fashion.

"Didja know some of this already?" he asked.

She hesitated, breaths coming faster, and then nodded. "A little. I spent some time researching it myself."

"Why?"

"Why?" He pulled away from the fury which overtook her, turning Lucy from a plump janitor into someone he feared—if for a split-second—might try to rearrange his precious bodily bits in a way that would horrify Picasso. "Besides the fact that I knew Karen long before she ever became fond of you? Besides the fact that my best friend ended up dead for reasons no one's ever cared to explain to me? I don't know, Ben, why would I care about a silly little thing like that?"

She turned her back to him, but he could still hear the grief undermining her voice.

"All those months you spent in quarantine, I spent digging through as many records as I could get my hands on—anything even remotely related. Clogs. The Sewers. I looked at every job you two ever worked together, trying to find a connection, a link I could follow. Something about the situation didn't sit right with me, but

I could never pin down exactly what. And now you come back and all of a sudden are given access to information I never even knew existed."

As her tirade faltered, Ben lowered his hand, which he'd ineffectually used to try and shield himself from her wrath. He knew Lucy and Karen had been close before he came onto the scene all those years back—had it really been more than a decade since?—but the force of her resentment still blew away any response he tried to muster. What sort of apology could he offer? Another joke about a kiss would just get him walloped right then, that was for sure.

He just didn't remember enough, and those gaps in his mind remained as much an obstacle to him as Lucy's enforced ignorance did to her.

"How much did you get wrapped in it back then?" he asked.

She deflated, if slightly. When she looked at him with the glowing orb at her back, her face remained shaded.

"I was there, Ben. Not when it all went down," she clarified, catching his startled look, "but in the aftermath. I was part of the team Destin sent to pull you out after you radioed in an emergency status."

Ben leaned in. This was news.

"What'dja see? Please, Lu, I gotta know."

She held her hands out and rotated them as if manipulating an invisible Rubik's cube, reconstructing her memories of the experience. "I saw ... well, I saw the Sewers. We all did. We went in through a familiar junction and everything seemed normal. Until we found you, that is." Her hands dropped back to her sides. "The whole section of the Sewers had been purged. Scoured spotless. I doubt even the Board could've found a single bacteria in the place. Karen was gone. And you ..."

She shut her eyes. "You tried to kill me then, Ben. You were crazy. You took down Mickey and Julian and Sarah without even trying. None of us could get through to you until the Ascendants arrived. Can't you see why I might've been willing to believe it was happening again back in the Recycling Center?"

He sat and stared at his boots, elbow on a knee as he absorbed her words. At last, he lifted his head. Her expression remained wretched, and he wanted to kick himself with a steel-toed boot for having caused her so much pain, even unknowingly.

"Why ain't'cha ever come to me 'bout any of this?" he asked.

Her laugh went sour. "When? How? The moment we got you back, you were locked up tighter than a chastity belt. We thought you died in isolation. Then, when we found out you were still alive—and back on the job, no less—Destin and Francis kept everyone away. And even you shoved us back whenever we tried to approach, being so afraid of infecting us with the Ravishing. We had no way of knowing what was really going on while you kept aging and getting weaker, refusing any outside help. And all those years ... do you know how often I laid awake at night, wondering what had really happened to my friends? To two people I cared about more than anyone else?"

"You think I did it, don't'cha? You think I killed Karen."

Carl spouted in his bottle, a sharp rebuttal of that even being an option.

"Thanks, buddy." He swallowed as he faced Lucy again, but the fist in his throat refused to unclench. "A'ight. I get it. I ain't gonna blame you if you hate me for failin' her."

She shook her head and wiped at her eyes. "No. The Ben I knew would never have done anything to harm Karen. You loved her too much."

"The Ben you knew? So I ain't that guy no more?"

"Nobody stays the same forever. But what I mean is that even if you did something, it wouldn't have been of your own free will. You have to admit there's the possibility that something or someone got control of you down there. Made you hurt her at the very least. The Ravishing doesn't latch onto someone for no reason. There's always betrayal involved."

He stood again and walked over to the ledge, leaving her by the desk. A steel railing bordered the side, and he stared over this into the fathomless recesses of the chamber. Far below, white figures moved around on identical marble rings, while further down, other people sat at similar glassy desks which glittered in the orb's light.

Ben didn't pay much attention to the sights, his thoughts and feelings snarled into a distracting mess he couldn't begin to untangle. Soft footsteps alerted him when Lucy joined him. Despite her quieter tone when she spoke, emotions still wavered her words.

"Ben, I'm sorry. It wasn't right for me to dump all that on you at once. I should've … I could've …"

"Naw," he said. "You was right. I did push everyone away, and I'm payin' for that now. I figured everyone gave up on me so I gave up in return. For that, I gotta be the one to say sorry." He put his back to the ledge and offered her a tentative smile. "Lu, I'm a bullheaded, slack-jawed, knob-kneed fool who has a hard time zippin' his fly most mornin's, much less bein' quick on the draw when it comes to knowin' who really cares about the same things I do. I hope you can cut me some slack for that, at least."

She studied him for a minute, and then smiled back.

"Karen somehow managed to overlook all that, so I'll try to do the same." She blew out a whistling breath; most of her animosity went with it. "Whew. For a moment there, I really wanted to carve my initials on the inside of your skull."

"Well thankya for resistin' that particular temptafication. I'll ask Monty to get someone else to drag my hide around if it makes it any easier."

She coughed. "Truth be told, I didn't get the unlucky draw like I said earlier. I made Monty assign me to you."

"Why'dja go and do that?"

"Because I guessed you were up to something like this, and that you needed help but were too stubborn to ask. At least that's one thing that hasn't changed with you."

"You sure you wanna play tagalong? I ain't got no idea where this is gonna take me."

A firm nod. "I'll help you however I can, take you wherever you need to go, whenever. You don't just need a chauffeur, Ben. Without your powers, you need a combination seeing-eye and guard dog. Someone to help when things get messy."

"A'ight, just so we're clear, you're the one who just compared herself to a ♌♓♦♍♒, not me."

She snorted. "Finally. A bit of the old Ben. Maybe you aren't such a lost cause." She offered a hand. "So we're agreed? I help you and you keep me involved. You share everything you learn with me and vice versa."

He clasped her hand with his, reassured by her strong grip.

"Done and done," he said. "Now lessee what else we can dig up before Rick boots our butts outta here. That guy loves his schedules so much, I won't be surprised none when he marries one and settles down to have little schedule babies."

CHAPTER SEVEN

Jared leaned in close enough for Dani to smell an antiseptic odor clinging to him. He brushed the tip of his nose against hers.

Goo hope towel, Dan-ni. Stoop death.

He grabbed her wrist, and before she could pull away, the fog spun into a gray vortex with her at the center. The mist swept down onto her head and washed out her sight of the kid or anything else. Jared's hold vanished, leaving her stumbling in the void.

She held her breath to avoid breathing in the murk. Then the light plunged into darkness. Her feet tangled on a stretch of coiled rubber and she slammed against a wall. Rebounding a step only smacked her back into another hard surface. Clattering noises, like metal and plastic objects colliding, echoed about, revealing that she stood within a confined space.

A swipe of one hand hit a row of metal shelves. The other hand thumped against a wooden panel she hoped was a door. She finally forced herself still, tired of feeling stuck inside a life-sized pinball machine.

Where had Jared sent her?

She sniffed and caught a mix of citrus, pine, and soap. She tried another step, tripped over the rubber coils again, and caught herself against several hard wooden rods. Lovely. Had she racked up a high score yet?

She fumbled around until her hand landed on a doorknob. A twist and push let light into the tiny room, revealing … a janitor's closet. Of course.

A peek outside revealed a sterile-looking hallway, complete with beige wall tiles and linoleum floors. For a moment, Dani thought she might be back in some section of HQ. Then her eyes lighted on a sign on the wall: *X-Ray*. An arrow pointed to the left, alongside others which indicated the directions to restrooms, a lab, and the fire exit.

Dani recognized St. Joseph Hospital from a couple visits when she'd been interviewing for a possible internship. The medical center served much of the downtown Denver area, and must be the hospital Jared had been speaking of. Unfortunately, during one of her visits, she'd crossed paths with a patient who'd vomited what looked like chunky blood all over her shoes—but which turned out to be raspberry Jell-O. Dani had been left with a nurse until she got her hyperventilating under control. Not the best impression to make in front of people she wanted to work with someday.

Fortunately, no one stood nearby to see a young woman suddenly appear within a janitor's closet. After flipping the closet light on, Dani shut the door briefly and searched for the tools she could use.

She took a spray bottle filled with green all-purpose cleaning fluid and put it in one of the buckets, which she hefted along with a sponge-mop. A faded baseball cap hung off a corner of one of the shelves. She hesitated, thinking of all the scalp conditions the previous wearer could've suffered. However, after she slathered the inside of the cap with sani-gel, she jammed it onto her head to hide her red frizz of hair. A long shower would be needed once she got back to HQ, for sure, complete with delousing shampoo.

She already wore yellow plastic gloves and had more gel in a pocket. Hardly the chanted equipment the Cleaners provided, but it would all do in a pinch.

So armed, she slipped out into the hall.

Right as she did, a blast of noise made her jump to the side. Heart pounding, she leaned against the wall as if taking a break. The overhead intercom system squealed, and a voice babbled out codes and what sounded like a call for Doctor Snorkles to report to surgery. Footsteps pounded from the far end of the hall. Dani kept her head bowed as several orderlies ran past. Once they'd turned the corner, she let out a breath.

Jared's warnings about death had set her more on edge than she'd realized. Admittedly, death wasn't uncommon in a hospital, but Jared had seemed worried about a specific person—another maid, by the sound of it. How did he know these things? More to the point, what did he think she could do about it?

She tapped the radio on her hip and contemplated calling in before going any further. Then she reconsidered. If she found something valuable on her own, it might prove to Francis she didn't need to be babied any longer.

Where to, then?

Well, those orderlies had sure been going somewhere in a near panic. How far could she get before a hospital employee noticed her skulking about and had her escorted out by security?

Ben had once told her that no one pays attention to janitors. Time to put that to the test.

She tugged the zipper of her jumpsuit as high as it could go and pulled the brim of her stolen hat down a bit further. Holding the mop over one shoulder, she headed after the orderlies. She woke her power to its smallest degree and let tendrils of energy snake out of her and into the elements.

I'm just a janitor. She reinforced the thought over and over, trying to channel her belief into an insulating aura. *Nobody special. Nobody worth taking notice of. Just let me by so I can do my job.*

She took the same corner as the orderlies and found herself in a hall with a stretch of windows on one side. A glance outside showed a garden and walkways populated by nurses and wheelchair-bound patients basking in the fading sunlight. She eyed the lot of them as she hurried past, looking for anything amiss.

Unnoticed, she entered a waiting room where visitors slouched in padded seats, their expressions a mix of worry, exhaustion, and feeble hope. Just beyond this, she paused on seeing two men standing by a corner, their expressions strained, body language tense. The nearer one wore a black jacket with *Public Health* stitched in bright yellow on the back. The other had a lab coat over a button-down shirt and slacks.

As Dani eased closer, one of the orderlies who'd run by earlier appeared by the doctor's shoulder and offered him a clipboard and pen. After a quick signature, the doctor sent the orderly off and then returned to his conversation with Public Health Man. Dani set her bucket down and pretended to swab out a stubborn grain of dirt as she eavesdropped.

"This makes no sense," PH-guy said in a hoarse whisper. "Suicides don't occur in these numbers unless there's some environmental toxin or, I hate to say it, some religious nutjob convincing folks it's time to catch a comet to heaven. But so far as I can tell, none of these people have any link and nobody from my team has detected any triggers at the grocery store. There's no common denominator."

"What do you expect me to do?" the doctor asked. "I'm just trying to keep the rest alive. It's a miracle anyone made it here before bleeding out." He checked his wristwatch and sighed. "Got another surgery in ten. Think you can try interviewing some of the others? See if you missed something before?"

The officer frowned. "I'll give it another shot, but I haven't been able to get a single coherent statement out of anyone so far."

The men shook hands and headed in opposite directions. Bucket in hand, Dani trailed the Public Health officer. He opened a set of swinging doors by scanning an ID badge on a wall sensor. Above the doors, big block letters read EMERGENCY CARE, with a smaller band of red letters beneath stating: *Authorized Personnel Only*. She shadowed him inside.

Right within the unit, Dani stopped so suddenly the doors nearly slapped her butt as they shut.

Beds lined the U-shaped room, with a nurse's station against the near wall. Patients filled every bed, and each one looked like a mummy's stunt double from a horror flick.

Stained bandages swathed them all, especially around the arms, head, and neck. Red and black blotches seeped through the gauze. If Dani hadn't heard the men talking earlier, she might've thought these the victims of an explosion.

The faces she glimpsed looked like they'd been put through meat grinders, lips shredded, hands little more than stumps stuck in bloody mittens. A number of patients had been strapped in place, and most appeared unconscious or sedated.

The Public Health officer went to another doctor who stood near the nurse's station. They exchanged murmured words, and the doctor—almost skeletally thin in his coat—nodded to the bed on the far right. The officer went and began whispering to the patient there.

The doctor wrote on a notepad as he looked around the room, gazing at each patient in turn while scribbling furiously. Dani tensed as he slowly turned her way. He frowned for a second, as if sensing something amiss. His gaze swept past her, however, and she moved further into the unit.

As she shifted along, she caught snatches of conversations as nurses checked vitals and replaced empty saline bags.

"At least twice this many dead before the first ambulance got to the store …"

"Five in surgery right now. Dr. Lewis doesn't think many will survive the night …"

"This is insane. What makes so many people try and kill themselves all at once? Cashier said it was like some switch got flipped in their brains. One minute, all's normal. Next, everyone's grabbing any sharp object they can find …"

Dani moved to a structural column halfway down one side of the room and stood in its shadow.

Suicides? All of these and more at once? In the same place? This couldn't be natural. It must be what Jared sent her to discover.

She shut her eyes and extended her power throughout the room, seeking a clue to—

A palpable aura of decay suffused the Emergency Unit, making her gag and choke. The stink of rotted flesh clawed at her nose, and her eyes watered from the mix of urine, vomit, and antiseptic.

She nearly retracted her energies as the disruptive power assaulted her, but forced herself to push against the virulent energies. The longer she studied it, the less it felt like a focused attack on her and more a Corrupted presence brought in with the patients. Whatever the source, it didn't react to her probing. It must've caused such a negative reaction because of the natural opposition to her Pure energies.

Yet among it all, she sensed a faint glimmer of Pure energies outside of hers, like a candle guttering in a sleet storm. Letting this guide her, she slid out from her hiding place, alert for danger.

She started in one corner and tiptoed to each bed, giving each patient a once-over before moving on. The fifth stop held what she'd feared to find.

A woman had been laid out here, as shredded as the rest of them. Part of her outfit had been cut away to give doctors access to her slashed ribs and arms, but Dani recognized enough of the tattered remains to identify the make. A purple stain nearly obscured the stitched name on the left breast pocket.

Another Cleaner. A maid, if Jared had been right.

Dani chewed the inside of her upper lip. What was going on? First one taken by murderous rage, and now another having signed onto the suicide squad? Had something the maid done affected all these other people? Could it affect Dani, even now?

After checking the area to make sure she remained unnoticed, Dani leaned over the maid's bed. The woman looked pale and birdlike in her thinness.

Dani bent over and whispered. "Can you hear me? Hello?"

Whimpering, the maid tried to rise. Before the motion could draw attention, Dani set her mop against the side of the bed and gently pressed down on the maid's shoulders to restrain her.

"Hey, hey … no moving. Settle down." She smiled gently as the maid's eyes opened a sliver. "It's okay. I'm with the Cleaners too. Can you tell me what happened? Did something attack you? Blot-hounds, maybe? Dust devils?"

The maid murmured incoherently. Her eyes gleamed with tears and her shredded cheeks twitched.

Dani looked around. The nurses remained busy and the thin doctor continued his note taking without having moved an inch. Too public. She'd need a scrub-team brought out, otherwise there'd be no chance of trying to retrieve the maid without causing a commotion. She turned back to the woman.

"I need to report this to HQ. We'll get someone to take you back, maybe find a handyman …"

As her hand went to the radio on her belt, the maid's eyes snapped wide. Dani stepped back as she recognized the look on the woman's face—identical to Sherri's before she'd stabbed her training partner.

"Wait—"

With a cry of rage, the maid launched off the bed and grabbed Dani's throat.

CHAPTER EIGHT

ani lurched back and pulled free from the maid's clutches. She stumbled over the bucket she'd brought with her, caught herself on the end of the bed, and struggled to regain her footing.

At the cry and clatter, several of the patients woke with loud moans. The nurses shouted, but Dani paid them little heed even though she knew they noticed her quite clearly at this point.

Contain the maid, she told herself. *The scrub-team can wash away people's recollections of what goes on here afterwards.*

But that meant getting enough time to actually call in the scrub-team.

Dani ducked as the maid grabbed a bed pan and flipped it her way. It spun over her head; someone cried out as they became the unintended target.

Okay. First subdue crazy maid, then radio in.

The maid yanked her IV cord free from the bag. Saline solution sprayed across the bed and floor.

I really should mop that up before someone slips, was Dani's detached observation as she backpedaled, trying to figure out a defensible position. Her mop had fallen over from where she'd set it, well out of reach by now.

"Any of you nurses got some sedative?" she called out.

The maid stalked her way. Her features, already mangled, had twisted into demonic fury.

A young nurse appeared Dani's side, at first focused on the maid, and then staring at her.

"Who are you?" he asked. "Where'd you come from?"

"Sed-a-tive," she said. "Priorities, buddy."

With a yowl, the maid threw herself at Dani. One of her elbows caught the nurse in the face and he stumbled aside.

The maid whipped her IV tube around with the needle still taped to her forearm. She snapped the cord around Dani's neck. A twist and pull tightened it.

Straining for air, Dani grabbed the maid's wrists. With a twist of her hips, she heaved the maid over a shoulder as she pitched forward. The cord went slack and fell away. Dani sucked in a breath as the maid writhed onto her stomach.

While Dani had grabbed her arms, the maid had also clutched hers. With manic strength, she now used this hold to flip Dani onto her back.

The maid clutched Dani's uniform and bent in so all Dani could see were her hate-filled eyes.

"Kill ..." The maid shuddered and moaned the words. "Killll meee ..."

A pair of nurses leapt on the maid and struggled to pin her. Another nurse remained in the background, a syringe readied.

The first tickle of wind on her face warned Dani. As the air current accelerated, she tried to shift her sight into the elemental realm, to sever the channel of power the maid used to animate the air—but she moved too slowly.

A blast of air swept through the emergency room. It scattered stacks of paper, flipped trays and carts, blew blankets and bandages to all corners. Those nurses standing were slammed against the walls, the desk, the columns, to drop senseless once more.

The two holding onto the maid strained to anchor themselves. Both lost their grips and tumbled into the nearest beds, where patients screamed in terror and pain.

Dani let the wind skid her across the floor, past the maid, and against the foot of the bed where her mop lay. Gripping the handle, she rose to one knee and waited for the lull she knew to be coming.

Her power urged for her to employ it, to blow the lights in the room in an electric storm and fry the maid. To take control of the air and turn it into her own whirlwind.

Gritting her teeth, Dani subdued the volatile energies. She couldn't trigger her abilities in here. Too many potential victims.

The maid sagged, her bandages soaked red from reopened wounds. In that instant, the wind died.

Dani sprinted out and swung the mop with all her might. The spongy end caught the maid across the back of the head. It didn't lay her out, like Dani had hoped; rather the maid caught herself on her hands and spun in one motion, snarling. The wind picked up once more.

Dani raced by, crying, "Come on, then!"

She leaped over a prone nurse and bolted out the double-doors. A blood-chilling shriek resounded behind her, and feet slapped against the floor as the maid pursued. Bowing her head, Dani pushed herself faster, ignoring cries from the waiting room and squawks from the intercom.

At last, she reached a wider intersection and saw, in that instant, no one appeared near enough to get in the way of what she had planned. She spun and braced herself in the middle of the hall. No time to check the rooms she'd passed along the way. She just had to hope they stuck things like the nursery and cancer ward far from the emergency unit.

The maid raced her way, borne along like a banshee by her conjured wind.

"Sorry about this," Dani said.

She planted the mop and unleashed her power. The energies she'd fed into the earth triggered, and the floor bucked with a miniature earthquake. The fault line shot out from her feet in a tight zig-zag, building momentum. Tiles shattered and sprayed about as a wave of concrete and dirt barreled toward the maid.

Dani attempted to rein in the spell, but it felt like trying to hold back a stampeding elephant with a bungie cord.

The maid didn't hesitate in the face of the tumbling debris. She collided with it and clawed forward as if it was an opponent she could rake to pieces.

The gale she'd summoned blasted past and hit Dani with enough force to somersault her backward. She rolled against a wall, bruised but intact as the wind died off with a last howl.

Alarms sounded in the distance. People screamed and shouted at one another.

Dani shook her head, trying to focus. What had happened to the maid? Had anyone else been hurt?

She stood with a groan and staggered over to the mound where the maid had been. Dani edged around to the far side, where she spotted the other Cleaner.

The maid had been half-buried in shattered concrete and tile. As Dani approached, her head lolled and one eye opened, the other having swollen to the size and color of several red grapes. She had gaps where teeth once were, and one of her ears had been mashed into pulp.

"I'm so, so sorry," Dani said. "Just don't do anything. Let me call for help."

Blessedly, her radio had remained clipped to her belt. She grabbed it and thumbed the speaker button.

"This is Janitor Dani. I've got a ... a code red, or whatever is the highest level code we've got for emergencies. I'm at St. Joseph Hospital. Emergency Care Unit. There's been a ..." She swallowed hard. "Another maid gone berserk. Came in with a whole slew of attempted suicides and ..."

Dani paused as the maid lifted a hand with something gripped in it. The radio buzzed with a confused reply.

"Janitor, please repeat? Janitor Dani, can you respond? Can you confirm?"

At last, Dani recognized the object the maid held—a piece of rebar, snapped loose by the quake. The woman moaned two words she didn't catch.

Dani leaned in. "What'd you say?"

Several deep huffs shook the maid, and Dani recoiled on realizing the woman was trying to laugh.

"It's ... worthless," she croaked.

"What? What's worthless?"

The maid made a wet clicking noise in the back of her throat. "Ev—everything."

She raised the rebar and thrust it at Dani.

Dani reeled. "No, hey—wait!"

The rebar dropped from the maid's hand as she went into convulsions. Moments later, the woman's body went limp.

Dani dropped to her knees. The mop fell from her hand as she looked around, feeling battered in both body and spirit. Chatter continued over the radio, but she couldn't spare the attention to make sense of it. These deaths ... so senseless. What was happening?

She raised her eyes from the wreckage—and stiffened. A doctor stood at the end of the hall. The same doctor who'd been taking notes in the Emergency Unit, monitoring the patients.

He surveyed the scene, head tilted, showing no emotion beyond curiosity. She started to call out to him, to tell him to get back to the other patients and make sure his staff was all right.

Then he smiled. The distance didn't disguise the unnatural way his lips peeled back, so far it almost bared the entire top and bottom rows of his jagged, yellow teeth. Dani noted the black and blue discoloration of his gums and the way his eyes flickered black for half a heartbeat.

His face reverted back to normal, and his gaze shifted from the cooling body to Dani. He blinked as if he hadn't noticed her until right then.

She scrambled to her feet.

"Hey. Hey you! Got a moment?"

The doctor whirled with a flap of his lab coat and sprinted away.

CHAPTER NINE

Ben pointed at the screen, which displayed a scanned version of the puzzling Sewers map.

"See here? Lotsa these tunnels end without connectin' to another. No notes about dead-ends or that sorta thing."

Lucy's reflected the screen's glow. "Almost like they don't really end, they just—"

"Go somewhere else. Like another level. Up or down, mebbe, but who knows? If this is such an old part of the Sewers that we don't even got it on records, it might be 'cause it's buried or sealed or built over."

"Maybe." Lucy picked at one of her eyebrows. "But we got to you, remember? We went there to get you back, and we took the regular routes."

Ben chewed at the dead skin around his thumbnail. "When you found me, didja map out where we were? Spot any of the junction coordinatifiers?"

"No. We tracked you by the beacon spell your emergency call set off, plus your own energies once we got close enough. After we reached you, we were too busy trying to contain you and the Ravishing."

"So by the time you got to me, you coulda been fed into this area, led off the main routes and then back again on the way out."

"Without any of us noticing? I mean, sure, it was near chaos until we got back to HQ, but still, it's a stretch. When Carl started working with you again, did he know anything about the incident?"

The elemental sloshed about: *Wishing it so.*

"He weren't there," Ben said.

"Why not? You two went everywhere."

"Not always. Sometimes I made him skedaddle when Karen and I wanted a little ... er ... alone time on a job."

Her gaze went flat. "You're kidding."

At his flush and shrug, she scoffed. "Only you, Ben. Only you would try to be romantic in the Sewers."

"Hey, she didn't never complain none."

Lucy frowned. "So we're back to wild guesses."

"Seems like. I ain't got nothin' better at the moment. You?"

"Just what my intuition is telling me."

"And what's it sayin' with its tongue stuck in your ear?"

"That this was a trap." She tapped the screen over the center of the spiraling tunnels. "If this isn't truly part of the Sewers, then someone went to a lot of trouble to make sure it looks like it is. They lured you and Karen in with the promise of an easy job, and then clamped down once you got there."

Ben scratched his noggin as he considered the idea. He turned the real map this way and that to see if viewing it at other angles might trigger recognition.

"So we still gotta find out what this is a map of and how I get back down there."

"Get back?" Lucy echoed.

"Lu, this ain't just a strange little spot. It's where I lost my wife and mind. I'm bettin' any real info in our files has gotta be edited or removed. Guessin' if we got Destin back, we mebbe could find out how many piles he's swept under the rug, but that ain't likely happenin' anytime soon." He knuckled his chin. "I could try and summon Filth again, see if I could argue for her handin' Destin back over, but I doubt she's gonna cooperate. And gettin' Destin back ain't a big priority for the Board right now."

"Maybe not," Lucy said, "but—"

The radios on their belts sputtered to life.

"This is Janitor Dani. I've got a ... a code red, or whatever is the highest level code we've got for emergencies. I'm at St. Joseph Hospital. Emergency Care Unit. There's been a ..." A pause. *"Another maid gone berserk. Came in*

with a whole slew of attempted suicides and …"

Her voice cut off as an Ascendant called for confirmation.

Ben jerked upright. "For Purity's sake. What's she doin' there?" He scooted back from the desk and jumped out of the chair, shouting. "Rick? Rick!"

The desk flowed back into a flat pane which held the Filing Clerk's frosted image.

"You have two minutes remaining for system access," he said.

"Never mind 'bout that." Ben shoved the envelope at the glass. "Hold this for me, a'ight? Just store it with my personnel folder until I get back."

The orb of Pure knowledge crackled as the Clerk considered this. A pale hand slipped out of the pane and plucked the file from Ben. It vanished into the glass.

"Filed."

"Nice and tidy, like always. I owe you a beer."

Ben went to the door they'd come in through. Lucy opened the exit and trotted alongside him as he jogged for the nearest glassway.

"Ben, where are we going?"

"We gotta get to Dani."

"How? And do what? Ben, even if we could help, I haven't cleaned that hospital for years. I've no idea of the layout or where Dani might be by the time we get there."

He refused to slow. "Didja hear that call at all? I'm guessin' it's gonna be pretty easy to tell where she is. Just look for a buncha folks runnin' around, screamin' their knickers off and she'll be nearby."

"We aren't hearing any more chatter," Lucy said, waving her radio. "That means it's being dealt with. We're only going to get in the way."

"I ain't plannin' on trippin' up any field team." Ben stopped where the hall dead-ended in the usual full-length mirror. "But the kid's gonna need to see a familiar face after it all blows down—and someone's gotta run interference for her when the Ascendants start flingin' the rulebook at her and yellin' about whatever precious procedure of theirs she's trampled on." He raised his arm. "Who better?"

Lucy grimaced. "All right. We'll try, but I can't promise we'll get anywhere."

As she reached to activate the glassway, a face shimmered into view on the portal—though not that of a window-watcher. Ben scowled at the Chairman's projection.

"Francis, don'tcha dare block us. You gotta let me—"

"Yes, it seems I must," the Chairman said. *"The matter is more urgent than we guessed. Please see to Miss Hashelheim's retrieval. I'm sending in a scrub-team to deal with any fallout and tend to this reported berserk maid."*

Ben nodded in relief. "Thankya kindly."

Francis looked to his companion. *"Janitor Lucille?"*

She came beside Ben and bumped his shoulder. "I'm with him."

"Just as well. Please step through. I will see you transported as close as I can set you to Janitor Danielle's signal."

Ben pushed forward, Lucy on his heels as they popped through the glassy barrier. A flash of light blinded him for a moment, and then he found himself in a window-lined hall, with trees, shrubs, and empty sidewalks on the outside.

Footsteps pounded. Dani took the nearest corner and nearly ran straight into him. She stumbled back and swung a mop at his head, stopping just before she connected. Recognition and relief swam across her face.

"Ben … what … how …"

He pushed the mop away. "Francis sent us. What's happenin', princess?"

She looked between him and Lucy. "Doctor."

He cocked an eyebrow. "A doctor? In a hospital? That sounds downright suspicious."

Dani huffed. "Running away. He's got something to do with this. With the maids."

"How do you know?" Lucy asked.

Dani waved a hand in a circle. "His face changed. Went all nasty-like. Has to be Scum. And he was in the room with the maid and a bunch of other attempted suicides."

"You snuck in there?" Lucy asked.

"Felt major Corrupt energies in the place. Didn't recognize it as being him at first, but it had to be coming from him." She shook her mop, urging them into motion. "He's getting away!"

Ben popped his knuckles. "Scum playin' at doctor? Ain't the first time. All righty. We got this."

Lucy caught his arm. "Ben, the Chairman just sent us to get Dani back to HQ. We got her, so let's go. The scrub-team will take care of the rest."

He grinned at her, feeling the fierce joy of being back on the job. This was what he was meant to do, not dilly-dally around HQ, and he wasn't about to give up the opportunity so quickly.

"Naw. Francis just said to retrieve Dani." He patted Dani's shoulder. "He didn't say nothin' more than that. So long as we get her back to HQ safe and sound, we're technic'ly followin' orders."

"Ben, we're underequipped, underprepared, and potentially running into Scum territory."

"Ain't it great? Just like old times."

She shook her head, but returned a wry smile. "I can't believe I'm letting you talk me into this."

"Me, either. But I ain't complainin'. Can you get a whiff of where this guy's boltin' for?"

Lucy shut her eyes, and Dani mimicked her, both of them stretching out their magical senses to seek the man's Corrupt energies. Ben checked the length of the hall to make sure no hospital staff interrupted them. The area appeared deserted for the moment.

The women's heads cocked north.

"That way," Lucy said, and Dani nodded. "Moving fast. And down."

"Down?" Ben asked as they broke into a run. "Elevators?"

"Don't think so," Lucy said. "Look for stairs."

Dani took a slight lead, with Ben and Lucy a close tie for second. Ben's pulse thumped in anticipation of actually confronting Scum for the first time since his restoration. Maybe he didn't have his powers, but the people and creatures working for Corruption could still be put down by a good, old-fashioned knuckle sandwich to the softies. With Dani and Lucy along for the fun, they'd have no trouble turning this Scum into a bug smear on the windshield.

"There." Dani pointed at a stairwell door which stood slightly ajar. The three of them burst onto the landing and paused to listen.

Footsteps echoed below. Ben glanced over the railing and spotted a flick of white and a balding head two turns down.

"That's lookin' like him," he said. "Headin' for the basement. Mebbe he's got a getaway car stashed in the garage." He took the stairs down three at a time, praying he wouldn't twist an ankle.

A door slammed below. However, when Ben hit the landing the doctor must've exited on, it wasn't for the garage, but the B2 basement. Shouldering this open, he stumbled out into another wide hall. A side hall cut down into another subsection of the hospital. Ben ignored this as the far door—an enormous stainless steel block—swung inward, with just a few feet of space left before it closed. The ID sensor on the wall beside it flashed green, and then red.

"Got him cornered in the morgue!" he shouted.

He sprinted across and caught the door handle right before it shut. He strained to yank the metal slab open again, and then slipped inside. Rows of metal slabs and cabinets stacked from floor to ceiling all around him.

"Ben, hold up! Something's wrong with Dani."

Lucy's shout halted him, and he turned to see Dani stumbling to her hands and knees in the middle of the hallway. Her eyes were clenched shut, face scrunched in pain. Lucy had stopped to grab her arm in support.

Ben stepped their way.

"Dani?"

The door slapped shut. A clank reverberated as the lock dropped into place.

CHAPTER TEN

ani entered the hall right as Ben caught the door to the
morgue. She moved to help him, but after two steps, her
vision swirled. Black, icy agony lanced through her head,
and she felt herself drop like a puppet with cut strings.

Voices buzzed in the distance.

"Ben, hold up! Something's wrong with Dani."

Something grabbed her. She shook it off and fell sideways. The
hallway jittered and the walls wavered. Lights flickered all about as
the pain eased, leaving her gasping.

The walls solidified, but were no longer the dull concrete of the
hospital basement. Mirrors lined every surface and reflected her a
hundred times over in all directions.

Lucy had disappeared, as had the elevator doors behind and the
morgue entrance ahead, all replaced with the glassy panels.

"Jared?" Dani sat up, looking for the hybrid. "Jared, are you
doing this? You need to stop whatever it is. Bring the janitors
back."

Voices mingled, warbled and flowed around her as she stood.

Dani …

Dani, please …

Heed, Dani …

While most of her reflections appeared normal, she realized
several of them were off in little details. For instance, that one had

a mask of stone covering her features, while another had green hair instead of red. Dani started to study them closer, but then a light flared on her right as the nearest reflection pointed a hand of flame at the others.

"Back, mongrels! She's mine. You've no claim to her."

Fire sprayed out. Dani ducked as the flames shattered the opposing mirrors. The other voices cut off. When the heat died down, she risked a look at the fiery reflection.

As it stepped out of the mirror, its body burst into flames. Green eyes became miniature blue flames which flickered in the sockets, and liquid bands of scarlet and orange wreathed her.

Dani rose and glared at her fiery doppelganger. During her brief captivity with an extreme faction known as the Cleansers, she'd been shoved into a giant furnace during a ceremony to bring about the cult's dream of a fiery apocalypse. Within the flames, she'd faced down a burning replica of herself, which had taken control of her power for a time.

This had to be the same mimic. The one that had tried to convince her to give in to wanton destruction. Who had nearly made her kill Ben, among others.

She spat, and her spittle sizzled on the tiles at the doppelganger's feet.

"You."

"Me." Fire-Dani spoke with a black tongue, and ash puffed out with the rasping word.

"What are you doing here? I beat you already. Get lost."

A smile bared molten teeth. *"A single act of defiance doesn't mean you conquered me."*

"So this is what? Round two?" Dani bobbed and jabbed. "Give it your best shot, ♌♓♦♍♒."

The other's eyes narrowed. *"You're daring to call me a ♌♓♦♍♒?"* She went cross-eyed as even her own use of the word failed.

"Hah!" Dani punched the air. "Finally. I wondered if the foul-filter was ever going to kick in for you, too. Guess you're going to have to get creative like the rest of us."

Fire-Dani scowled. *"You joke around while I try to offer you a chance to save yourself from future agony."*

"Surprise, sister. This isn't the first time someone's claimed to want to save me. Fool me once, shame on me. Fool me four or five times …"

The mimic strode closer. As she moved, her blackened skin cracked around the joints, revealing lines of magma.

"The only reason the others haven't taken over is because I've kept them at bay. I'm the real source of your strength, Dani, whether you believe me or not. Without me, you'd be a whimpering mess, ready to piss yourself just like you did the first time that blot-hound tried to bite your face off."

Dani sidestepped, trying to give herself room to maneuver if the mimic attacked.

"Now you're just being—wait. Others? What others?"

Fire-Dani flicked sparks at the remnants of the other mirrors. *"Did you think I'm the only facet of your abilities? Fire isn't the only element you wield, silly girl."*

"Silly girl? That's the best you can come up with?"

The other Dani snorted. *"How could any single being, a human much less, command the power you do?"*

"Uh … maybe because I'm that awesome? My talent's pretty rare, they keep telling me." Dani paused. "And why'd you call me human? Aren't you just part of me? Something the Cleansers brought out?"

Her mimic cackled. *"And here we have another idiotic idea revealed. Why would you assume I came from you originally?"*

Dani licked her lips, which had dried in the heat emanating from … well, what was it, if not her reflection?

"If you didn't, why not explain where you really came from?"

"Isn't it obvious? We are of the elements. We embody the forces you wield so unthinkingly. You're a baby in diapers, thinking the world doesn't go beyond the edge of your crib."

"That's a little better than *silly girl*," Dani said. "But still kind of an infantile insult." She refocused on understanding what the creature said. "So you're like … like Carl. Ben's elemental partner."

The elemental's eyes flared, and the darkness behind the flames deepened.

"Nothing so ordinary. Drips like that bottled drudge can be scooped out of any lake or river. The ones you've snared—like me—come from a higher order, and are ashamed to be chained to such a feeble thing as you."

"Snared? Chained? What are you talking about?"

A fiery arm swept through the air, trailing sparks. *"When your powers first ignited, the energies you manifested drew our attention. We were not as ... awake before. Formless and free to move through our realms as we wished. Yet when we came to you, your power latched onto us. It imprinted aspects of you on us."* It stepped in, snarling. *"We're bound now. Slaves to your will, Dani. Are you getting it yet, or do I have to burn the words into tablets of stone and beat you over the head with them?"*

Dani backed away from the creature's searing fury, though instinctively she knew it couldn't hurt her here.

"I ... I didn't know ..."

"Obviously. Which is why I'm trying to enlighten you, seeing how you misconstrued my intent during our last meeting."

"Misconstrued?" Dani stepped back in, raising a finger. "You cursed me out, smacked me around, and then tried to possess me like I was nothing more than a mindless ... what was the word you used?" She thrust the finger out. *"Fleshbag.* That's it. Exactly how was I supposed to take it? Next time you want to enlighten me, give me a call and we can talk over coffee."

To her surprise, the elemental looked momentarily abashed. *"I suppose when you put it that way ..."* It ... she stared down at her fiery hands. *"We're slaves, yes, but even slaves can rattle their chains and look for a way to break free. I was still freshly awakened when we first met. I could claim I didn't fully know what I was doing, but that'd be a lie. I knew, deep down, but I was desperate."*

"Are other Catalysts the same way? Does anyone in the Cleaners know how this really works?"

A snort of ash. *"I wouldn't know. You're the first of either I've interacted with. But what's it matter?"*

Dani didn't answer as wild theories flew through her mind. Maybe this was why Catalysts were so rare, having to struggle not only with the volatility of their power, but also with these elemental creatures. Such a constant battle would be a distraction, if not a drain. How could she deal with it to avoid ending up dead or insane like other Catalysts she'd been warned about? And what if some of the upper management in the Cleaners did know? Why hadn't they prepared her for this sort of confrontation?

"Are you here to ask me to let you go?" she asked. "Or try to make me?"

The elemental's nose crinkled. *"The link is made, forged of our own foolishness, and can't be broken until the core energies leave your body forever."*

"You mean, when I'm dead."

"Oh, look. She's capable of learning after all."

"That's lovely."

"It's not an ideal solution, but if you're open-minded …" The elemental trailed off at Dani's look.

"So if letting you go is out of the question, what do you want?"

"To negotiate the terms of service. You need me, Dani. Otherwise the others will overwhelm you. They'll tear you apart from the inside."

"Why would they do that? It's not like I did this to you all on purpose."

"Some will try to gain control of your energies. To others, your death is the priority, since that's the easiest way for us to be freed. If you side with me, though, I can make sure they'll never trouble you. You've seen me deal with them here." The elemental gestured to the shattered glass around them. *"They'll stay quiet so long as you and I work together."*

Dani walked a slow circle around the mimic, while it watched her from the corner of its eyes. She tried to read the creature's body language, wondering if they had similar tics or tells. If aspects of herself had truly been imprinted on these creatures—a disturbing concept—then why couldn't she assume a few personality traits had been included? If that were the case, then Dani's instincts told her …

"You're lying."

Her doppelganger twitched. An ember popped out of one eye and melted into the floor.

"You dare accuse—"

Dani jabbed a finger at its midriff. Heat swept over her forearm, but she felt no pain as she forced the elemental back a step. The impulse to keep poking it rose, but she fought it down. *Got to be a little more mature.*

"I bet the only reason you have such a strong connection to me is because of the Cleansers, when they tried to turn me into a fire goddess. You're trying to make me strike a deal without really knowing the full situation." She waved at the broken mirrors. "Maybe you are stronger than the others—if they even exist—but I can tell you're afraid of something. I need you? Maybe. But you need me more, don't you?"

A growl trembled the elemental's fiery wreaths and flames licked out her nostrils. Dani imagined a dragon drawn out of its cave by foolhardy adventurers and, for a moment, doubted the wisdom of her aggressive approach.

"They'll come, just as I have. Eventually, they'll emerge and start struggling for dominance."

"If they do, I'll meet them head on, just like with you. I've been raring to have a real fight."

A sneer. *"Oh, you will. And when you do, you'll be sorry you refused me, and I won't be so willing to lend you my help then."*

"It's my power," Dani said. "You're just along for the ride. My coworkers are in trouble and I've got a job to do. You try to get in my way and I'll thrash you so hard you won't be able to light a match."

The elemental's body went white-hot, and the glass shards scattered about the floor began to melt and puddle.

"You think you can control me that easily?"

With a little growl, Dani reached out with her power, latched onto the creature's fiery being, and yanked it toward her with a mental command. When the elemental stumbled into range, she grabbed its throat and forced it to meet her eyes.

"Answer your question?"

The elemental writhed and blazed. The heat engulfed Dani, but didn't so much as singe her brows. She refused to let it, and it obeyed.

"You already burned off my hair once," she said. "Give it a chance to grow back a bit."

"Let me go!"

"Not my fault you guys got greedy, and I don't have time to argue about who sits where on the totem pole right now. So until you figure out a way to talk to me without verbal abuse, you're getting put into the naughty corner."

The elemental gaped, its mouth a miniature furnace. *"You'll regret this."*

"Doubt it."

She turned and flung the creature into the mirror from which it had emerged. It wailed as it plummeted into the darkness beyond; a falling star as it dwindled away.

The hall skittered sideways again, the mirrors faded into concrete, and Dani found herself in the hall before the morgue once more. The relief proved short-lived, however, for Lucy stood before the sealed door, cursing as she wrenched on the handle.

Dani ran to help, but the other janitor stepped away with a frustrated grunt.

"Where's Ben?" Dani asked.

Lucy kicked the door. "Idiot got himself locked in there with your fugitive doctor. Welcome back to reality. What happened?"

"Later. Ben first. Why doesn't he just open it from the other side?"

They exchanged worried looks, little effort needed to imagine the worst.

"We need to find another way in or—" Lucy began.

"I got this." Dani nudged the woman to the side, and then stepped back to prepare another mini-quake.

She feared the elemental's words might be true, that she'd find herself in a renewed struggle for control of her power, but her energies responded without hesitation. They funneled into the concrete walls and floor around the door. They agitated the earthen elements, loosening the bonds of stone and metal.

Right as she readied to crack the slab off its hinges, someone yelled on the other side. She hesitated, concerned about injuring Ben in the process of getting to him.

Then something slammed into the other side. A divot shot outward, the same size and shape a fist might leave had it been punching wet clay. Dani counted the knuckles in the imprint.

That settled it. Triggering the quake wouldn't be any worse than leaving him to deal with a creature that used stainless steel doors to play patty-cake.

CHAPTER ELEVEN

Ben grappled with the inner door handle, but it might as well have been flash-frozen in place. Muffled pounding came from the other side, but without an access key, the women wouldn't have any better luck than he did.

Someone chuckled behind him, dropping a slimy worm of unease down his back. While morgues were supposed to be sterile environments, the chilly air he sucked in held the thick flavor of rotting meat.

His hand dropped to Carl's spray bottle, but he didn't turn right away. The water sprite sloshed in trepidation. While Carl could animate himself independently, in the past Ben's Pure energies had bolstered the elemental's stronger and deadlier manifestations. If it came down to an extended brawl, he didn't know how long the elemental might keep up on his own.

"Carl," he whispered, scratching the bottle with a fingernail, "if things go nasty-like, you slip out under the door or whatever crack you can find and get back to the ladies. See 'em safe to HQ, hear?"

As the elemental gurgled grudging compliance, Ben made himself face the room, trying to appear confident in his nonexistent abilities.

Six open-air tables lay on either side, each occupied by a body draped with plastic sheeting. Several wall cubbies had been opened, pale feet visible within, tags dangling off the big toes. A side room held several autopsy tables, complete with hoses and drains to wash away unwanted bodily fluids.

Ben took this all in with a slow sweep. Fortunately, all but one of the occupants remained prone on their slabs.

The doctor stood at the end of the row, hands at his sides, long fingers drumming his thighs. A stethoscope dangled from his neck, the metal diaphragm at the end making Ben think of a third eye glinting in the man's sternum. An ID tag hung around his neck, but Ben couldn't read the name from this distance—though it wouldn't be of any help if the original doctor had been disposed of.

Ben curled his finger around the spray bottle trigger. "Heya, doc. Here for my checkup. Got this real awful case of 'too many folks dyin' today' and I'm kinda thinkin' you're involved."

The man glanced at the bottle, smiling mirthlessly.

"You are a Cleaner, I presume?" An inquisitive cock of the head. "Yes. Similar uniform. The insufferable arrogance is the same as I have encountered. The unfathomable sense of pride in your damnable work."

"Yowza. Talk about bad first impressions. Howsabout we start over and say hiya without slingin' spit at each other already?"

The man continued to rattle off observations. "Missing appendage. Amputated? Unconfirmed without closer observation. Impaired? Perhaps."

Ben cleared his throat. "So, doc, why'd you go Scumwise? What's your beef with us you want barbequed so bad?"

The doctor pushed his head forward and sniffed. "Yet there is something improper in your approach. No Cleaner I've faced has taken the time to attempt civilized discussion. Each sought to bring me low the moment they identified my loyalties. You are an aberration." The smile returned, but with more of a shark's hunger to it. "You have also not moved since entering. Do you fear a confrontation? Perhaps exertion would expose a weakness?"

Ben brandished Carl. "Don't be gettin' your hopes up, bucko. I just think we Cleaners and Scum never take the time to try and settle our differences in creative ways. Like ... spelling bees. Or dance-offs. Whaddya say? Mebbe a karaoke showdown? Arm wrastlin'?" He flexed his bicep. "Hope you're a southpaw."

Joints clicking, the doctor went to the nearest body and tore its sheet off, revealing a flabby man with wattles hanging from cheeks and neck. Like a striking viper, he snapped his mouth to the corpse's and breathed out, emitting a purple-blue mist. Ben clamped down on his rising nausea as the body's chest swelled, crackled and squelched as the miasmic breath filled it.

Just as fast, the doctor stepped back. For an instant, Ben saw the face Dani must've—eyes devoid of humanity, lips and cheeks pulled back to expose desiccated tonsils and a shriveled tongue caged behind pointed teeth.

He groaned as he recognized the nature of his foe. "Fleshmonger. Shoulda figured."

The doctor waved a hand at Ben as he turned to another table. "Take him."

The corpse sat up and oriented to the janitor. Its eyes glinted like obsidian chunks. Even as the corpse slid off the table, its nostrils and mouth melted into smooth, pale flesh, sealing the fleshmonger's breath within its lungs. Parts of the corpse jiggled disturbingly as it lumbered Ben's way on stiff legs.

Ben bent his knees as the corpse built momentum, and he leapt to the side at the last second. The corpse hit the door and bounced off, spun like a grotesque top and once more bulled Ben's way.

He darted around an empty table and kicked it in front of the charging undead. The corpse tripped and flopped onto its belly. Like a monstrous slug, it heaved toward him, flailing stubby arms.

"Blade, pretty please," Ben shouted.

He triggered the bottle. Carl sprayed out and congealed into a four-foot sword, while water flowed back over Ben's hand and sealed it to the grip.

As the corpse struggled to its feet, Ben chopped at its neck. The water-blade bit into flesh as hard as dried wood. No clean decapitation there.

He jerked the blade out and thrust for the corpse's lungs, hoping to release the Corrupt energies animating the body. The corpse grabbed the sword, however, and stopped it before the tip could tickle its chest hairs. Carl slithered out from the creature's grip before snapping straight again.

Ben ducked a clumsy haymaker and slashed at the creature's stomach. The flesh split enough to expose the pearly sheen of its innards.

When he cut in again, however, a fist clipped him under the chin. His teeth clacked shut, and black and white spots burst into his vision. He reeled and fell over the very table he'd kicked down. A hand clamped onto his boot. He lashed out. Fingers pattered the floor about him like maggots and his foot came free.

Ben rolled into a crouch as the corpse flung the table aside and charged.

At the last second, he dropped to his knees, pivoted and hacked across the man's thick legs. The blade bent as Carl struggled to hold firm, but he managed to cut down to the joints. Something popped. The corpse toppled, and the floor vibrated with the impact.

The creature rolled onto its back, and Ben yelled as he drove the blade into its chest. With only one arm to drive it in, the force of the blow almost tore his grip from the bottle; but Carl increased the pressure around his hand and kept it locked.

The corpse bucked and kicked. Ben yanked the blade free to ram it down again. However, when the blade came out, the fleshmonger's breath was expelled in a black cloud and struck him in the face.

Ben took a surprised breath and tasted putrescence. It felt like having his face shoved into an oil slick while someone pumped the contents of a porta-potty through his sinuses. His eyes burned, his lungs cramped, and his stomach threatened to jettison all escape pods and damn any sense of dignity.

Spluttering and gagging, he staggered free from the cloud. It dissipated seconds later, and the corpse lay inert at his feet. Ben stared at it, making sure it didn't so much as twitch. Once assured he'd dispatched it for good, he scrubbed the sweat from his brow and twirled the water-blade in a victorious salute at the fleshmonger who—

Who stood behind three more animated corpses.

"Now this just ain't playin' fair." Ben leaned against the nearest storage cubby, attempting to look cocky while giving his legs a chance to stop trembling.

The fleshmonger flashed his toothy grin. "Impressive. Yet futile, as you can observe. I'd hoped to use you as a further specimen, but I can see you would be troublesome to contain long enough for effective testing."

"Who's givin' you all this juice?" Ben asked as he fought to slow his breaths. "Filth? Pestilence? Pollution?"

The doctor's face did its quick-change act, letting him glimpse the monster behind the human guise.

"You think I would betray those who've gifted me? You do not comprehend the price paid. My parting gift is to provide you the end all Cleaners seem to strive for—as roach corpses ground beneath the heels of progress."

Ben struck a duelist's pose, something he'd copied from watching *The Three Musketeers* at least a hundred times. He flicked the water-blade.

"Bring it, bucko."

The doctor placed his hands on the shoulders of the nearest corpse. "There is more work to be done, and you've delayed me overmuch. Farewell."

He closed his eyes but didn't move, which confused Ben for a moment. Was he trying the "I can't see you, so you can't see me" trick?

A rumble in the floor drew his gaze to where the doctor stood—directly over one of the many drainage panels set in the concrete. Bands of black ichor shot out from the drain and cocooned the man in slime. When the bands retracted, the doctor's form shrank and flowed down with them. An instant later, he was gone, with nothing but a faint gurgle in the pipes and a ring of muck around the drain to evidence his departure.

The corpses remained standing and fixed on Ben, however.

Carl wavered, and Ben sensed the elemental's strength fading. He wouldn't be able to hold onto the sword form much longer.

"Splashdown," he said.

Carl quivered, trying to stay with him. Then the elemental rained to the floor. Rivulets drained away under one of the tables and the empty spray bottle fell from Ben's hand.

As if that had been their signal, the animated corpses lurched his way. They bumped into each other as they came; one even shoved a companion stumbling to the side in its haste to reach Ben.

"Sterility? Cleansing? Purity?" Ben tossed the half-hearted request to the Pantheon. "Any of you guys? If you were thinkin' of restorin' my powers, now would be a mighty fine time."

He waited a breath longer to see if a rush of energy would imbue him, renewing what he'd lost. But he remained impotent. Simply human.

"Figures."

He ducked as the first corpse came in range. A punch snapped past his head. Metal crunched, and he turned enough to see the morgue door buckle under the blow.

He dropped to the floor and tried to wriggle past their legs. A foot caught him in the ribs. A *snap*, and he screamed as jagged agony pierced him. He curled in to protect his vitals.

A hand grabbed his ankle. He shouted anew as one of the corpses yanked him up to dangle upside down, his hair and arm brushing the floor. The strain on his injured ribs sent a red wash of pain through him.

The room trembled, and for a moment Ben thought he'd been hit so hard he'd gone into shock.

From his inverted perspective, he saw cracks shoot along the walls surrounding the morgue door. With a rending of metal and stone, the door fell inward. One of the corpses leaped clear, but the slab crushed another flat. Bruise-colored gas spurted out from under one side, dissipated, and the creature stirred no more.

The crash left Ben's ears ringing, so Lucy and Dani's shouts were indistinct as they raced in.

"Mudmen," he cried in warning. The one holding him tossed him aside like so much litter.

His head smacked against a steel cubby door and he tasted blood before consciousness fled.

CHAPTER TWELVE

ani balked at the sight of living corpses, mouths and noses blank flesh, dark eyes brimming with malice. She cried out as Ben hit the cabinets along one side and fell out of sight behind a table. Before she could rush to him, two monsters lurched her way.

Lucy pushed Dani away from one corpse as it grabbed for her. Dani's survival instincts kicked in and she jumped out of the way of another fist. She cracked her mop across the nearest creature's head, but she might as well have been trying to bludgeon a bowling ball into submission.

The second corpse groped for Lucy, who darted past it. With surprising agility, the janitor vaulted two body slabs toward the side room within the morgue.

"Keep them distracted," she shouted as she raced out of sight.

"With what?" Dani cried. "A tap dance routine? Because I don't know how to dance!"

"Learn quick."

The second creature stared after Lucy for a moment and then refocused on Dani as if deciding she offered an easier target.

"What are they?" Dani jabbed the mop at the nearer creature's legs and face, trying to slow it. "Zombies?"

"No such thing as zombies," Lucy called back. "These're mudmen."

Dani eyed her attackers as she backed out of the morgue. "Mudmen? But one's a woman. Why is everything in this company so sexist?"

"It's just a name!"

Dani jumped to one side as one mudman charged and brought both fists down. They left twin craters in the floor, and the force of the blow vibrated through Dani's legs.

"Well, I don't like it."

"Tough, girlie."

Glass shattered in the other room, followed by the sound of running water.

"What're you doing in there?" Dani shouted, struggling to retain control of the mop. One of the mudman grabbed the other end. She yanked, and the sponge popped off in the corpse's hands.

"Washing my hands," came the calm reply.

Dani's voice discovered a previously unknown octave. "You're what?"

"Need the suds worked up well. Just hold on another second."

The corpse grabbed the mop shaft and began working its way toward her, hand over hand. Dani let go suddenly, making the creature stumble back into its companion. Using this distraction, she dove past them into the morgue, figuring she stood a better chance if she remained close to the other janitor. A fist and foot *whiffed* above her head, and she nearly tripped over the door she'd brought down. Stumbling down the main aisle, she banged shins and palms on the slabs to recover her balance, nearly skidding on some muck around one of the floor drains.

She turned to see the corpse with the mop snap it in two. It gave one of the jagged fragments to the second mudman.

Okay. Not exactly mindless brain-munchers. Maybe she would've stood a better chance against zombies. Weaponless and afraid to conjure her powers for fear of hurting Ben or trapping them within the morgue, she watched the corpses lumber toward her.

"This isn't funny. I'm going to get gutted."

"Were you this impatient as Ben's trainee? You need to learn to have some faith in your coworkers. Some of us know what we're doing."

Lucy stepped into view with both hands full. One gripped the handle of a high-pressure spray nozzle, like from a car wash, though this one had a black hose running back to one of the autopsy tables. The other held a fourteen-inch dissecting knife which dripped with soapy water.

She stuck her tongue to her teeth and whistled. The piercing noise ricocheted throughout the morgue and made Dani wince. The mudmen—mudpersons?—turned Lucy's way. The janitor triggered the spray nozzle.

Water jetted across the room with far more force and volume than the hose should've allowed. It struck one of the corpses in the chest and blasted it backward, pinning it to the wall where it wriggled like an insect on corkboard.

The second corpse started toward her, but Lucy remained focused on the one she'd trapped. A flick of her wrist plunged the knife into the creature's chest. A strand of suds trailed behind it like a pearlescent chain. Lucy yanked on the suds-chain, and the knife popped out and retracted into her palm.

A black cloud puffed out of the wound she'd made, and the corpse dropped limp to the floor.

All this happened so fast, Dani barely had time to catch it. She stared, slack-jawed, as Lucy aimed the nozzle at the second corpse, which had come within two paces of her. Another jet of water slammed it right where the first had hit. Another whip and yank of the knife, and the last corpse joined the first.

Silence swelled within the morgue, but for the drip of water and Dani's heavy breathing. Lucy stared at the two bodies and flourished the knife.

"And that is how you take down mudmen."

Dani could only nod, impressed by the woman's technique and confidence. Maybe there was something to learning how to handle the equipment.

"Thanks," she said as she eased back into the room.

"Don't mention it. How's Ben?"

Dani ran around to where Ben lay. She checked his pulse—strong—and noted his strained breaths and bruising along one side of the face. She patted his cheeks and gave him a gentle shake without success.

"He's not responding."

Lucy dropped the spray nozzle but kept the knife as she came over and checked out the unconscious janitor.

"He's just banged up a bit," she said. "Nothing a handyman won't see right in ten minutes. Let's get back to HQ."

"Dragging him the whole way?" Dani asked.

"Sure. You take his hands and feet and I'll provide moral support."

Ignoring the other woman's chortle, Dani slapped Ben's cheeks and shook his shoulders. After a minute of this, Ben groaned and his eyes flickered open. After a second, they focused on the women.

"Ladies." He glanced around. "I miss the party? Was lookin' forward to some cake."

Dani took his arm and started to pull him upright. He hissed.

"Watch it, princess. Mudman thought my ribs was a puppy that needed kickin'."

Lucy *tsked*. "What'd you do? Make fun of their shriveled peckers?"

"I think it had more to do with my bein' alive while they was dead. Jealousy's an awful thing." Ben groaned through clenched teeth as they helped him to his feet. "But yeah, formaldehyde sure does pickle things, don't it?"

Dani checked the area again and spotted the empty spray bottle.

"Ben, where's Carl? Did he—"

"He's fine. Just got a bit tuckered, so I sent him slippin' out when things got too down and dirty. He'll pop back up at HQ, if he ain't already beat us there."

With his arm over Lucy's shoulders and Dani supporting his other side, they made their way slowly back out of the morgue. Dani could tell Ben battled to not complain as they labored up the stairs, but by the time they got to the ground floor, he'd gone pale and sweat dripped from his forehead and chin. After a quick check of the hall, Lucy nodded them forward, and they reached the windowed stretch without opposition.

Then Dani noted the red light in one corner of the ceiling, and her mouth went dry. The glassy eye of a security camera aimed its unblinking gaze along the hall. It had recorded everything, including her prowling, Ben and Lucy's emerging from the glassway, and their chase of the doctor.

"Oh, no." Ben and Lucy looked at her in concern, and she pointed to the camera. "Someone's seen the whole thing."

"Don'tcha worry 'bout that," Ben said. "The scrub-team will deal with it. Fact is, I'm hopin' they'll have some records of what happened here. Maybe let us get a closer looksee at our Dr. Frankenstein."

Dani stared in disbelief. "The Cleaners have access to that kind of thing?"

"'Course," he said. "We're tapped into every security system anywhere we work. How'dja think we can mop up our tracks so well?"

"That's a little freaky."

"It gets better."

"What do you mean?"

"Save it for when we get back," Lucy said, bringing her radio out. "Janitors Lucy, Ben, and Dani calling for an extraction. Same glassway as last used by the Chairman to deposit us here."

"Activating," came the reply.

The nearest window pane flashed as if hit by a strobe light. Lucy took the majority of Ben's weight and helped him inside. As their backs disappeared into the glassway, Dani took one last glance at the camera, stuck her tongue out, and then followed them through.

CHAPTER THIRTEEN

She popped out the other side without encountering her elemental doppelgangers, which she silently thanked them for.

The team had been deposited in one of the many sterilization chambers used for bringing employees in from the field. While the blank walls hinted at nothing, Dani knew they were being scanned for contaminants by both technological and mystical measures. HQ must remain inviolable to preserve the integrity of their work. If any Cleaner set off an alarm, having been contaminated or Corrupted to the slightest degree, the room would be locked down until Ascendants arrived to deal with the situation.

Several benches and chairs provided spots for the Cleaners to rest until the scan completed, which usually didn't last more than a minute or two.

Lucy, having deposited Ben on one of the benches, now railed at him. As she shouted, her hands snapped all about his face, inches from hitting him. He didn't flinch, though he occasionally winced and pressed a hand to his injured side.

"What were you thinking, running ahead like that, letting yourself get trapped?" was the first thing Dani caught.

Ben wobbled his head. "Dunno. Mebbe I was thinkin': Oh lookee, gonna catch the bad guy and do my job. What shoulda I been thinkin', Lu?"

"Maybe about not getting yourself killed? Maybe that we could've bagged and tagged the guy if you hadn't mucked things up? Maybe that it wasn't your job in the first place."

"Hey, we're all back. We're safe. My face don't need no spit-polish."

"I'll stop spitting when you start showing some sense. I should've never listened to you. This is going on my record, I just know it."

"Lu, you're overreactinatin'." He shrugged Dani's way in a half-joking, half-pleading manner. "Gimme some backup here?"

Dani raised her hands in a *I'm not involved* gesture.

Ben's face fell. "Aw, princess, you too?"

"Don't try to guilt me into agreeing with you, Ben," she said. "You could've been killed."

"But I weren't. That's what matters, ain't it?" His forehead wrinkled. "And what made'ja go down like that, anyhoo?"

Uncertainty stalled her answer. What to tell them? Why did she feel so hesitant to reveal her encounter with the elemental? All Cleaners dealt with elementals at one point or another, she'd come to learn. Several others besides Ben had various elementals and sprites as ... well, coworkers remained the best word for it. Yet Dani wanted to delve more into the history of her specific line of talents and see if there was any truth to the fire elemental's claims before she revealed its presence to the others. What if they thought it a holdover from the Cleanser ceremony? A sign that she might not be stable and fit for work?

"Nothing," she said. "Just stumbled."

He eyed her. "You sure 'bout that? Looked mighty serious from where I stood. Like you was gut-punched by a ghost."

Dani looked at Lucy. "So there's no such thing as zombies, but ghosts are real?"

Lucy shook her head. "No such thing as ghosts either."

"At least, not in the traditionalistic sense," Ben said.

Lucy eyed him sidewise. "Was he like this when giving you employee orientation?" she asked Dani.

"Yeah," Dani said at the same time Ben gave a cheerful, "You betcha."

Two men entered the room. Lopez led the way, followed by the Chairman. The handyman went straight to Ben and began checking him over, while Francis took a stance at the head of the room.

Having donned his fedora, the Chairman cut a sharp figure wherever he went, his cleansing aura a constant radiance as if he'd swallowed a draught of sunlight. His power didn't just manifest in the visual spectrum, though. His position imbued him with several other talents, including the ability to extend his influence, for good or ill, over those around him.

Dani frowned, remembering the times she'd interacted with the former Chairman. Destin had made everyone around him feel worthless, little more than worms on a sidewalk.

In contrast, being near Francis lent a bit of steel to her spine and made her feel like the work she did, however menial, contributed to something meaningful and lasting. But his presence also woke a deeper twinge of worry. Tasked with managing the Cleaners' operations across the country, Francis rarely left his office except to deal directly with serious circumstances or threats.

"Heya, boss," Ben said. He exhaled in surprise as Lopez's healing energies tinged the air green about them both. Color flushed his cheeks and he straightened a bit. "We uncovered a bit bigger of a steamin' pile than we expected."

"I had a feeling you might," Francis said.

Lucy distanced herself from Ben slightly. "Sir, we ran into unexpected resistance at the hospital. A fleshmonger was present and animated several mudmen when we attempted to bag-n-tag him."

"Mudpersons," Dani said.

Everyone looked her way, and she flushed. Maybe not the time or place to propose the Cleaners update their vocabulary.

Francis fixed on Dani, and though she didn't sense any suspicion or hostility behind his gaze, she still felt under intense scrutiny.

"I'd like a direct account of your experience," he said. "While the memories are fresh."

Dani took a few moments to collect her thoughts, and then rattled off what she could of the events, from Jared sensing something wrong and sending her to the hospital to finding the maid along with the other attempted suicides, the ensuing fight, and spotting the Scum-doctor. As she spoke, Lopez's aura faded and he stepped to one side to silently listen while Ben stretched and prodded himself, testing the effectiveness of the healing. At last, she wound down to the showdown in the morgue and rescuing Ben.

Once she finished, Francis clasped his hands behind his back and sighed. When he finally looked down, it surprised her to find herself sweating as if she'd just finished a difficult exam. The others held silent until Francis raised his head.

"From what I've been able to discern," he said, "Maid Bethany—the one you fought, Dani—had been recently assigned to a deep clean of a local wholesale grocery store. We received an alert barely an hour before you discovered her that a mass suicide had taken place in that store. At least a dozen dead from self-inflicted wounds, with another score admitted to the hospital."

"How?" Lucy asked breathlessly.

Francis shook his head. "We don't know yet. I've a team on the scene at this instant, scouring for evidence. All we know is that one moment, everything appeared normal. The next, a good percentage of those within the store had taken to finding any means to harm themselves."

"That sudden switch is becoming a running theme with this whole scenario," Dani said.

"Maid Bethany," Francis continued, "was among the few who failed to inflict mortal damage before emergency services arrived and restrained the survivors, some of whom had also turned on each other. It may be that her Pure energies helped her resist whatever violent compulsion gripped everyone longer than the rest."

Dani shuddered, trying to not imagine the scenes Francis described.

Ben picked at the dark stubble on his chin and frowned. "I gotta argue with that theory."

"Of course you must," said Francis.

"Like we're all noticin', it's pretty samey-samey with the hoe-down in the trainin' room earlier. Two maids losin' their minds in two different locations? One of 'em inside HQ?" Ben shook his head. "I'd say the maids were the bulls-eyes and the rest of us got caught in the blast zone."

Francis considered this and gave the barest nod. "That would seem more likely."

"What's that mean?" Dani asked.

"It means we could be being targeted," the Chairman said. "It could be some new weapon being tested against us; if so, we must discover and stop it before it's used again."

Ben slapped his thigh. "Righto. Where do we start?"

Francis touched the wall he stood by. Golden energy pulsed out from his hand, and the wall turned into a screen which displayed a familiar hallway. A figure lurked along it, mop in hand, features mostly hidden by a baseball cap. Dani coughed and took off the one that had remained on her head. She tucked it behind her back.

"These are the video feeds we tapped," Francis said. "They've given us some potential leads."

"Just so we're clear," Dani said, "I'm not going to appear on the nine o'clock news as a terrorist, right?"

The Chairman chuckled. "Hardly. Any evidence of our presence is being wiped clean as we speak. Our scrub-teams are thorough."

"But what if something goes down in, say, a federally-owned building? A place with major security measures and—" She took in the slightly amused looks on all of their faces. "You mean you guys have access to government files and stuff?"

"And stuff," Francis said with a shade of a smile. "The extent and nature of our operations demands it."

"How is that possible?"

Ben grinned. "The FBI, CIA, and all them spook centers? They got office buildin's galore. And guess who's keepin' those buildin's tidy?" He spread his arm to indicate all of HQ. "Yo."

"Ben?" Lucy said.

"Yeah?"

"Never say *yo* again."

Dani kept staring at the video on the wall, considering the ramifications of the Cleaners' hidden power. "Geez."

Ben winked. "Fun, ain't it?"

"Scary is more like it. The White House …?"

"Has carpets vacuumed and toilets scrubbed like any other place. You wouldn't believe how filthy that place gets."

Francis cleared his throat, drawing them back to the screen he'd conjured. His fingers worked, and the images went into action, fast-forwarding so Dani vanished and shadows of normal traffic flickered past until a lab-coated figure raced into view. He paused it there. Another twitch of his fingers switched the screen to a front view, apparently from another camera Dani hadn't noticed. It zoomed in on the fleshmonger's face and then to the ID tag which flapped alongside his stethoscope. A white bar highlighted the photo and name.

"Dr. Thomas Malawer," Francis read.

"So he really is a doctor?" Lucy asked.

Francis shrugged. "Is. Was. Either way, we've confirmed his identity. Forty-eight years old, he's been published in numerous medical journals and has practiced at St. Joseph Hospital for the past decade. He's listed as a pathologist. A more complete dossier is processing."

Ben raised his hand. "Patholo-whatsit? Little words for the ig'nant folks, please?"

"A pathologist is a doctor dedicated to studying and dealing with diseases," Dani said. "Viruses, infections, and all that. I thought about going into that field when I first became a biology student." She focused back on the image. "Is that what we're dealing with? Some sort of super-rabies making these women go crazy?"

Lopez shifted his weight, entering the conversation with the subtle move. "No. There's no sign of disease affecting the first maid, magical or otherwise. Her body, mind, and energies are uncontaminated. Several of my associates have confirmed my initial diagnosis and I will, of course, analyze Maid Bethany when the body is brought in."

"Magical diseases?" Dani nodded to indicate Ben's missing arm. "Like the Ravishing?"

"The Ravishing is one of, if not the very worst of, them. Supernatural acceleration of virulent processes is a common weapon of Corruption," Francis said. "Diseases that feed off one's energies or resist even the most advanced medical cures. Others include bone rot, guttertongue, and legion spores."

"Sir, pardon the correction, *por favor*," Lopez said, "but legion spores are actually more of a parasitic invasion than a disease."

Dani grimaced. "Lovely. But we're sure what we're experiencing isn't caused by something this guy has whipped up in the lab?"

"So far as we can tell," the Chairman said. "It does not preclude the possibility that this doctor has developed a strain beyond our knowledge and ability to detect—though this is highly unlikely. My belief is he's been imbued by a member of the Corrupt Pantheon; why they would have chosen him as their servant eludes me. As you said, Ben, the maids appear to have been targeted, and the other wounded and dead would be innocent bystanders. Which leads me to the assignment I have for you."

He waved, and the video shifted into a satellite map which zoomed in on a tree-lined neighborhood. He pointed, and a red circle surrounded a house.

"This is the doctor's current known residence. It's likely he will have sensitive information secured in the privacy of his home. I need the place infiltrated and scoured from bottom to top for anything even slightly relevant."

Ben hopped off the table. He bounced on his toes and twisted from side to side to test his healed ribs. "Now that's what I've been waitin' to hear this whole time. When're we high-tailin' it in?"

"You won't be part of this operation, Janitor Ben."

Ben's joints all seemed to lock at once. "What?"

The Chairman turned to the two women. "Janitors Dani and Lucy?"

"Sir?" they echoed.

"Janitor Lucy is to be the team leader in this instance, with Janitor Dani as follow-up. I have two maids who have experience cleaning this residential community prepared to go onsite with you. You'll infiltrate the doctor's home and search out evidence of any Scum plot he might be—"

Ben strode forward. "Wait just one cotton-pickin' second. They both galumph back out into the field while I gotta sit here and suck my thumb?"

"While your knowledge and experience remains an asset within our training facilities," Francis said, "your lack of powers remains a liability in the field, as evidenced by this latest encounter."

"That was just a bit of dumb bad luck," Ben said. "Coulda happened to anyone."

"I'm sorry, Ben. I understand your restlessness. I've been lax in finding the best place for you within the ranks, and for that, I apologize. Once this situation is resolved, I swear your positioning will be my first priority."

"This is such ... such ... bull!" Ben grinned for a second. "Hey, it worked." Sobering, he turned to each of them, seeking support, for someone else to argue they needed him. Dani tried to meet his eyes, but had to look away.

With a snort, he stomped to the door but stalled when it refused to open. No one moved for a second. Dani could almost feel the heat waves of anger and embarrassment pulsing off him. She hurried over and pressed her hand to the door, letting her energies activate it.

He glanced at her with a clench of his jaw.

"Sorry," she mumbled.

"Can it, princess. Just go get the job done."

He exited and strode off. Dani watched his back, wondering if she should run after; having no words of encouragement or consolation, she let him jog out of sight and rejoined the others.

"Sir, is this really necessary?" she asked Francis. "I mean, sending Ben to his room? That's something you do to unruly kids, not employees."

The Chairman took his fedora off and fingered the brim. "Janitor Ben is undergoing a difficult transition time. While I understand his thirst for the job, the Cleaners need his expertise more than his action right now. He'll adapt to his new purpose, and in the meantime, it's our duty to see him safe where he cannot protect himself."

Dani frowned. The Chairman's decision made sense, but she couldn't help feeling traitorous to the man who'd risked his life for hers on more than one occasion. Yet she couldn't think of any way to debate further and had to let the argument drop for the time. Besides, the excitement of a true first field assignment proved too much to ignore.

"What's the plan?" she asked.

Francis nodded to her and Lucy. "Foremost, go get a few hours sleep. I'll not have my staff fatigued on the job. We'll monitor the doctor's residence until then for any signs of his return, though I suspect he'll avoid anyplace familiar now that he knows we've identified him. Meet in the garage, six AM sharp. In the meantime, I've alerted Supplies to be available for any equipment you need."

Lucy took Dani's arm. "We'll head there now."

The Chairman waved them to the door. "Dismissed."

CHAPTER FOURTEEN

ani trotted alongside Lucy until a couple turns had been put between them and the receiving chamber. As they went, Dani caught the other janitor glancing her way more than a few times.

"All right," she said after the fifth eye-bump. "What's up?"

Lucy didn't answer right away as she trudged ahead. She fixed on a distant point, and Dani could sense worried thoughts filling her mind. At last, Lucy sighed.

"Dani, I can understand your loyalty to Ben. It's not unusual for an apprentice to feel that way about their first trainer, especially one as ... unique as him. But nobody's perfect."

Dani laughed. "You think I see Ben as perfect? Hardly. He's my friend, though, and that counts for something in my world."

"He's my friend, too," Lucy said. "Or was, a while back. I'm not sure exactly where things stand right now. But one thing you've got to learn in this business is how friendship can make things tricky in the field. You can make bad judgments where friends are concerned. You can give them the benefit of the doubt where they don't deserve it."

She held a hand out to cut off Dani's response. "I'm not saying we have to be coldhearted robots. Emotions are going to be part of everything we do; there's no denying it. But you've got to try and keep some objectivity. Know where your priorities lie. In the bigger scheme, we're all just a handful of Cleaners among thousands, and our struggles can be chalked up to just skirmishes in the bigger battle. Even Ben knows better than to buck the system too much."

Or you at least hope he does, Dani thought, studying Lucy. *And why do you care so much?* She'd thought Lucy would've been more lenient, considering she seemed a flawed example of her own advice. If Lucy and her coworkers had succeeded in stopping Ben and Dani from their wrongful imprisonment, Destin might've remained in charge while Jared would've been destroyed. Still, she filed away Lucy's lecture for later consideration.

"Questions?" Lucy asked, catching her look.

"Just wondering if there's some orientation video I missed when I was brought in. What's the next bit cover? Why it's wrong to steal cash from the till? How to have a bubbly attitude while upholding our core values of customer service?"

Lucy's flat look cut through any further humor. "Keep that up and I'll start calling you princess, too."

"But do you really agree with Fr—with the Chairman's decision? I don't think sticking Ben on a shelf is the right thing. You have to admit, he isn't the type to handle forced inaction all that well."

"He'll deal. And it's not our decision. But that's not what we need to focus on right now."

Lucy stopped before a glassway portal and faced Dani. "If we're going to be working together, I need to know you can keep your head and follow my lead. No running off like Ben did, flaunting procedure to be a hero or because you think you know what's best. The Cleaners have existed for a very long time, and we have regulations for a reason. The people who ignore them end up being the people we bring back in dust pans and garbage bags. Ben's lucky to have survived as long as he has."

"Fine," Dani said. "I can't promise I'll be sweet little Miss Sunshine, but I'm as ready to get this job done as you are. And if it isn't all down to luck, want to tell me more about fleshmongers and mudmen? What're we going to need if we bump into the doctor again?"

Lucy pointed at the portal with her head. "Inside, first."

The portal deposited them into what at first appeared to be a hardware store. Dozens of rows of metal shelving stretched to a back wall, where a large door provided a glimpse into a warehouse structure, with pallets stacked into the distance. A forklift drove past the opening as they watched, yellow lights flashing. Dani drew her focus back to the smaller room and noted what kept it from being a true store: mainly the lack of checkout lanes and clerks, plus the fact that every item offered was some custodial tool of one sort or another. Vacuums, plungers, brooms, mops, floor scrubbers and waxers, pipe-snakes, buckets, and more, plus all manner of bottled chemicals that would eat through grime and skin just as much as Scum.

"How's your van stocked?" Lucy asked.

"The basics," Dani said. "Haven't had much chance to drive it yet with all the other training taking up my time."

"Sounds like a good enough excuse to give its tires a kick. Let's get what we need and stash it for the night." Lucy headed down the first aisle and checked out the equipment as she talked. "You'll want the regular setup to start. Buckets and sponges for containment. A few signs to set up wards around a job site—not to mention keeping people from getting in the way of your work. And the usual slice, dice, and stab array for when things get down and dirty."

Lucy took down a few squeegees from their hooks, tested their rubber-bladed edges on her thumb and smiled when they pricked a drop of blood free. She handed these to Dani, who kept half a pace behind.

"Will these work as well as the sword-on-a-soap-rope you used in the morgue?" Dani asked.

"So long you don't mind getting within groping distance." Lucy scanned the aisle. "Fleshmongers and mudmen aren't the worst sort of Scum you'll run across, but never doubt that they're a nasty bit of work."

"Think we'll run into any of them at the house?" Dani asked.

"Hopefully our doctor friend hasn't taken to storing bodies in his basement, but best to go in prepared." Lucy led her to a section filled with dust masks and other protective accessories. She stretched bands over Dani's head so a handful of masks dangled around her neck. "These can help your breathing if Scum try to stink-bomb you." Heavy-duty dishwashing gloves went over one forearm like a *maître d*'s napkin.

"Fleshmongers," the janitor continued, "often get their powers straight from Pestilence ... or even Corruption itself, for some of the stronger practitioners. Sometimes knowing which member of the Pantheon is fueling the Scum can help in knowing how to combat their energies. In this case though, we've no idea who Dr. Malawer represents, but we at least know what he can throw at us."

"Dead people. The not-really-zombie monsters. You do realize what any person with half a brain would call them if they were spotted in public, right?"

Lucy hefted a pair of mops with the fiberglass handles honed to spear-points. "Use these to give yourself more reach in a fight." She tucked the mops into the crook of Dani's right elbow, forcing her to pinch them to her side as they moved on. "We're not responsible for what silly things people choose to believe. But mudmen are one of the reasons we keep the bodies of any Cleaners stored in HQ."

Dani recalled her brief visit to Storage, the Cleaner version of a cemetery. "As ashes in tiny trash cans."

"Exactly. We'd prefer to not find ourselves dealing with Corrupted coworker corpses. Not good for morale."

Lucy snatched up an enormous plastic bucket and started dumping items into it: scrub brushes, hand brooms and dust pans, sponges, and gloves with the palms covered in steel wool. Then she hooked the bucket handle over Dani's left arm, making her sag a bit under the added weight.

"And these mudmen are different from zombies how?" she asked through clenched teeth.

"First off, mudmen aren't motivated by hunger or anything like that," Lucy said, strolling along.

"No brain munchies?"

That got the slightest smirk out of Lucy. "No munchies. They're more direct extensions of the fleshmonger's will. Think of them as flesh puppets, if that helps. Pretty dangerous if you let yourself get caught flat-footed."

"That's ..." Dani paused to adjust the growing collection of tools. "That's why they dropped after you popped their lungs open?

You were cutting their strings somehow."

A nod. "Good eye, girlie. Fleshmongers animate corpses by transferring parts of themselves into the bodies. Breath is a quick and easy method, and you can tell when that's the case by the sealed mouths and noses. But there are more permanent ways, like organ transplants and even blood infusions. Those are trickier and a lot messier to make the body lose its connection to the 'monger."

With both arms full, Dani couldn't resist as Lucy stuffed the many pockets of her jumpsuit full. In went a jug of industrial-strength cleaner, spray bottles of stain remover, liquid bleach, and a couple bundles of rags. Dani lugged these along, struggling now to walk straight as the janitor circled back toward the entrance.

"I think I get it," Dani said between huffs. "The pieces of the fleshmonger act as the core maintaining the spell."

Lucy flicked a silver trash can and it gonged. "Girlie wins the prize."

"For the record, I'm not so hot about 'girlie.' Dani works fine."

"Team leader prerogative. I get to pick the nicknames."

"Prerogative? More like an abuse of power." She called out as Lucy tapped the portal to activate it. "Hey!"

Lucy paused, turning with brows raised.

Dani did a full body shrug, making the equipment she carried rattle and bump. "What am I supposed to do with all this?"

"Get it to your van for morning. What else?"

"But—"

Lucy yawned. "See you then, girlie. Sleep tight. Don't let the bedbugs chew your eyes out."

The janitor vanished through the portal. Dani stared after, and then hurried to follow. One foot caught on a mop and she went down with a squawk. Equipment clattered as it rolled everywhere, and the bucket bounced once before coming to a stop in front of her face.

Bruised and breathless, Dani decided to remain on the floor for a bit and enjoy the view. *Maybe it's not that I'm bad at Cleaner combat. Maybe I just love gravity way too much.*

Footsteps sounded as someone emerged from the glassway and walked over. Black rubber boots planted themselves on either side of the bucket and a slim hand reached down. Flushing, Dani stared at it for a few seconds until she grudgingly grabbed the offer and hauled herself upright.

"Thanks," she said, "Would you mind—"

Her tongue became a rock which weighed her lower jaw down. She stared at the other person, caught between wanting to flee or fight.

The newcomer appeared to be her in every detail, except for the stone mask covering the face. Patches of green moss created the illusion of eyes, and Dani thought if she looked close enough, she could see little critters skittering between the cracks in the stone.

Finally, she rediscovered the art of speech.

"You must be my earth elemental."

The elemental mimic tilted its head, obviously hearing her. Instead of responding, however, it reached for her face.

Dani flinched, but kept from jumping away. Fingers brushed her cheek, not in a comforting or sensual way, but more testing the texture of her skin out of curiosity. Dani realized the hand had a slight translucence to it, and was formed from what appeared to be polished rose quartz.

The hand dropped away, but the elemental continued staring at her. Dani licked her lips. Would the creature attack? Try to possess her like Fire-Dani had? Yet the elemental remained unmoving. Another living reflection.

"Um … do you want something?" Dani asked.

The earth elemental crouched and began retrieving the scattered equipment. As Dani watched, it gathered everything and held it as she had just minutes before. Then it headed for the glassway. Dani caught one sleeve.

"Hey, I need to take that—"

The elemental jerked away from her. It stomped one foot, hard enough leave a crack in the floor. Dani stared at this.

"Oh-kay. No grabby hands. I get it. But I need that equipment. It has to go—"

It clutched the equipment closer to itself, then jerked its head at the glassway.

"You're … you're going to take it to the van for me?"

A slow nod. Grit drizzled from the stone face.

"I'm tired enough I won't argue, but … why?"

The elemental's blank gaze revealed nothing of its thoughts. With a snap, a line shot through the mask where a mouth might be. A voice ground out.

"We are not all unwilling. Know this."

It bowed without dropping anything, then disappeared through the portal.

Dani ran fingers through her hair and blew out a breath. Not all unwilling? So some of the elementals didn't mind being bonded to her? She found a teensy bit of comfort in the thought, but it also made her consider the flipside. Which ones might be raging against the bond? What would ... what could they do to her through it?

Hopefully, the earth elemental would honor its promise and she wouldn't be sent back to Supplies in the morning, unable to explain where all the equipment had gone to. Should she follow and make sure it did as it had indicated? Would doing so make it angry, since it would show she didn't trust it? Dani decided against trailing the creature, but determined to get to her van a little early the next morning, just in case.

She pointed to the glassway and spoke out loud to the other elementals connected to her, not knowing if they heard her or not.

"See that? That's how to influence people and win friends."

She exited Supplies and headed for bed, trying to ignore the feeling that hers weren't the only footsteps tromping along the empty hall.

CHAPTER FIFTEEN

Dani groused as she brushed her teeth and gargled with overly-minty mouthwash. She hated dreams. Hated them interrupting her otherwise blissful sleep, hated jolting out of them in a sweat, and—most of all—hated trying to remember the fuzzy details the next morning. Especially when she had the distinct impression the ones from last night hadn't been random neurons firing off into the void.

Something about a desert? An avalanche falling into a black pit?

Whatever. No dealing with weird dreams before coffee. Dani rapped the back of her head to dislodge the images.

Yet she remained distracted and oddly on edge. The hot water in the shower stung more than it soothed. Her uniform felt ill-fitting even though she knew it adjusted to any wearer's dimensions. When she went for her sani-gel to clear her thoughts and sinuses, she squeezed the bottle so hard the top popped off and goop splattered everywhere. Seriously? Two broken bottles in as many days?

She muttered as she went to Tetris' cage. Feeding him and tickling his belly usually sent her off for the day with a smile. Yet as she removed the terrarium lid he scrambled into the far corner and refused to budge. When she reached for him, he spread his spiky beard and hissed.

After a few attempts to scoop him out, Dani scowled at her pet. "You want to throw a tantrum? Fine. Be a brat." She tossed a few mealworms in and left, puzzling over his aggressive behavior.

Deciding her prickly mood would be improved with an abundance of caffeine, she dropped by HQ's twenty-four-hour cafeteria. She resisted ordering cheesecake for breakfast and instead filled the biggest thermos she could find with fresh coffee and wolfed down a sandwich made of toast, cottage cheese, and peach slices. She entered the garage while testing whether she'd gotten the ratio of cream-to-coffee right this time.

She found Lucy standing by her van. The other janitor jumped a bit when Dani stopped beside her.

"Dani? Weren't you just …?" She frowned at the driver's door.

"Sorry?" Dani asked.

Lucy shook her head. "Nothing. Just not quite awake yet. Thought you were already here for some reason."

Dani eyed the area for her earthen other, but saw no sign of it. A quick check inside the van revealed all the equipment stashed in the back, and she relaxed a bit. When she rejoined Lucy, she noticed the woman staring at the double pink stripes that stretched around the middle of the chassis and across the hood.

"Something wrong?"

Lucy traced the pink lines with her eyes. "It's just an interesting color scheme."

"Hey. My van, my choice on the paint job."

"Normally I'd agree but—"

Dani bristled and leveled her best glare at the woman. "There is *nothing* wrong with pink."

Giggles echoed throughout the garage, along with a few high-pitched squeals. Dani winced, wondering who let a cheerleading squad into the complex. Then she spotted the two maids heading their way.

Twins. Gorgeous twins, at that, wearing matching light green jumpsuits which accentuated their long brown hair and mocha-hued skin. They chatted as they approached, laughing and shoving each other with shoulders and hips.

Dani leaned in and whispered, "Lucy, please tell me the runway model twins aren't our teammates."

Lucy looked that way and groaned. "Cleanse me. Should've figured it'd be the Borrelia sisters."

"Hooray. They have a reputation."

Lucy gave her a warning look. "Chill, okay? You don't have to like who you're working with, but these two at least get their work done."

"Them? Scrubbing toilets and mopping floors? They look like they just walked out of a day-long spa treatment. I won't be surprised if they refuse to get in my van because it has a bit of rust on the bumper."

"Somebody sure woke up on the ♌♓♦♍♒⬒ side of the bed this morning," Lucy said.

Their conversation cut off as the twins neared, jostling each other. For a moment Dani imagined them wearing sleek crimson dresses and striding their leggy selves through a ballroom. Reality reasserted itself, and she noted the feather dusters on their hips and ... snakeskin-patterned cleaning boots. Of course.

Lucy stepped forward. "Janitor Dani, meet the Borrelia sisters, our maids for the day. Girls, this is Dani. She's still a little new, so be gentle."

The twins beamed at Dani, who squinted in the glare. Both girls hustled forward to envelop her in a hug, and she endured being squeezed between two firm bodies that smelled of flowers and strawberry lotion. The twins scooted back.

"So great to meet you," the one on the left said. "Love the short hair. Very daring look. I've thought about cutting mine a bit, but then we'd both have to, and my sister absolutely refuses to lose an inch. Maybe you could you convince her for me?"

Dani pinched the hair on the nape of her neck. "Actually, it's more a side-effect of being nearly burned alive by a Cleanser cult. I wouldn't recommend setting an appointment with their stylists."

The other twin gasped. "The Cleansers? I'm jealous. I've always wanted to have a go at them. Is it true what they say about them? That they dance naked around bonfires and get drunk on gasoline?"

"Close enough." Dani looked between them. "Okay. Rude question, but how am I supposed to tell you apart once we're on the job?"

Josh Vogt

"Simple," the twin on the left said, while both of them pushed their chests out, showing off the names stitched on the uniforms. "I'm Laurel, obviously, and this is Hardy. See?"

Dani's lips quirked. "Laurel and Hardy?"

"Well," Hardy drawled, "Hadara's my real name, but don't tell anyone else, okay? Just a secret between us girls. I'm thinking of getting it legally changed."

"You should." Dani coughed against the urge to burst out laughing. "You really should."

"Oh, I love your van," Laurel said. "Hardy, look at this pretty thing!"

Dani's mirth at the twins' names vanished as they circled her van, tracing the pink lines, patting the bumper, and leaving lipstick marks on the windows. They even cooed over the bumper sticker which read: *World's Sexiest Janitor.*

"It's so cute!" Laurel said on her second go-round.

Watching them fondle her van made Dani slightly ill. She hopped into the driver's seat, slammed the door, and fired up the engine.

"All aboard," she shouted. "Anyone not inside in three seconds gets left behind."

She started counting, praying they wouldn't take her seriously. But Lucy already occupied the passenger's seat, and when she glanced back, the twins had buckled in to the second row of seats. They smiled at her in the rear-view mirror.

"Yehaw," one cried, punching the ceiling. "Gun it, girlfriend."

With Lucy as her copilot and Laurel and Hardy in the back seat, Dani stomped on the gas pedal, certain something had gone very wrong with the universe.

▲   ▲   ▲

"Ladies," Lucy said, once they were halfway there, "you've been briefed on the situation?"

The twins nodded with—what else?—identical somber expressions.

Despite knowing she was being more tetchy than normal this morning, Dani couldn't resist a jibe. She just had the hardest time imagining these beauties breaking a sweat, much less dealing with actual dirty work. "You girls going to have trouble if we, you know, have to wipe up some dust or scratch out some mold with our fingernails?"

Lucy scowled at her, but the twins smiled back guilelessly.

"It's rough work, sure," Laurel said, "but we deal. We made some games up to take our minds off the tough stuff."

"Games?" Dani asked.

"Like pube bingo," Hardy said. "We invented it ourselves. You want in?" She rummaged in one of her pockets. "I think I've got an extra sheet somewhere."

With rising horror, Dani stammered, "Oh, that's … that's okay. It sounds … uh … different."

"It's pretty simple," Laurel said. "You just have to check off the boxes whenever you find pubic hairs in a new place around the house. Hardy won last week, but I'm only a box away this week." She perked up. "Oh! I call the master suite bathroom!"

"Hey." Hardy shoved her with a shoulder. "We agreed we couldn't claim any spaces until we get onsite."

Lucy raised her voice. "If we could focus?" She flipped to another page. "The doctor's house has a basic layout. Large dining room, kitchen, living room, and a den on the main floor. The basement was unfinished when he moved in, and we don't have any records showing what it might've been converted to in the meantime. Upstairs, we've got three bedrooms, including a master suite. Garage, of course. Huge backyard and pool. No pets, thank goodness."

One of the twins leaned forward to read over Lucy's shoulder.

"I recognize the place," she said. "It's one we've never cleaned, but we know the houses on either side for sure. The one on the left is the Goodwright's. They have the most adorable labradoodle, Skittles. She acts all vicious, but a few treats always brings her around. You'll love her." She pushed Dani in a joking manner, but the strength behind the shove almost made her steer off the road.

She got the van back under control as Lucy continued debriefing them. "Our approach is straightforward. Pull up, pile out. If the doctor is there, he'll be on high alert, so no sense trying to sneak in. We're splitting into two teams, one going for the front entrance, another through the back. We sweep the house clean, the back team taking the dining room and kitchen before heading into the basement. The front team takes the living room and den, and then heads upstairs. Understood?"

Everyone nodded right as the gate to the enclosed community came into view. As Dani braked beside it, a balding security guard stepped out and studied them from behind sunglasses. From his swagger, one might've figured him to be St. Peter checking the roster at the Pearly Gates.

Dani eyed the gun at his hip as she started to produce the paperwork Lucy had provided. Then Hardy nearly jumped into her lap to wave at the man.

"Johnny!" The shrieked name sliced into Dani's ears. "How you been, babe?"

"Laurel and Hardy, that you?" the guard asked, peering into the back of the van. A grin bunched his cheeks. "Where you been, sweet things?"

"We got a busy job, hon," Hardy said. "But we're back now. Missed us?"

"Like the desert misses the rain," Johnny said. He sucked in his gut a bit, and Dani had to swallow her gag reflex. "Making the usual rounds?"

"You know it," Laurel said, joining her sister in the increasingly crowded front. "Be good and let us in?"

"Anything for your pretty faces." Johnny retreated into his shack, and the gate slid open moments later. The twins blew kisses and waved as Dani pulled through.

As the twins laughed over Johnny's past and present attempts to flirt with them—which they described as *adorable*—Dani focused on counting off mailbox numbers. Every property they passed could've comfortably housed a family of twenty with room left over for the butler's cousins, twice removed. Whatever gardening company kept the lawns manicured probably got paid more than the four Cleaners' combined yearly salaries. With the early hour, the community appeared deserted, the houses quiet, blinds drawn, and no activity beyond a few sprinkler heads with spray flashing in the harsh morning sun.

Laurel and Hardy pointed out houses as they drove past.

"That's the Foley's," Hardy said. "Mrs. Foley always cleans her kitchen to a shine before we come in, but it still smells like a rat died in the garbage disposal."

"Better than the Hardmonts," Laurel said. "Remember when we found the video camera she tried to hide in the pillow, making sure we weren't stealing anything?"

"Or when Mr. Davids followed us around the whole time we were cleaning, just watching us and not saying anything?" Hardy shivered theatrically. "What a creep. He never lets us in to clean his office, either, and I'm glad. I really don't want to see what he hides there."

"Oh! And the Terristers? Their pool is practically a lake, but it's always full of beer cans and cigarettes. And I'm pretty sure Mrs. Terrister doesn't wear half the bikini thongs that clog the drains."

As the twins compared notes about the best of the worst houses to clean and the quirks of the owners, Dani navigated to the last house on this cul-de-sac.

"This is it," Lucy said.

Dani killed the engine and they all eyed the place. Ivy crawled over the stone walls, with black iron gilding the front door and windows. The dark panes reminded her of the dead eyes of the mudmen, and her chest clenched at the thought of what might wait inside.

"You forgot to mention every place in here is a freaking mansion," she said. "It's going to take forever to search each room."

"Then it's a good thing we get paid by the hour." Lucy hopped out and came around as Dani and the twins joined her. "Gear up. Dani, go with Laurel and take the front. Hardy, you're with me out back. First team inside the house radios the other. Stay on channel, and report anything out of the ordinary. Remember: hostile territory. Be on your guard."

They rooted through the back for their choice of gear. Laurel and Hardy went with feather dusters, dust pans and brooms, spray bottles and rags. Lucy took one of the steel wool gloves along with a mop and spray bottle which she filled with cleaning fluid. Dani tucked several sponges into one pocket, hung a squeegee on her belt, and picked out one of the spear-tipped mops and a silvery bucket.

The women looked between themselves and, with a silent signal, headed around to the sidewalk. They paused to inspect the windows, but not so much as a twitch disturbed the blue curtains.

"Let's get this over with," Lucy said, heading to cut across the yard.

Dani followed, but both women grunted as Hardy jumped up between them and snapped arms across their chests with bruising force. The twin ignored their confused glares as she stared at the lawn.

"Don't touch the grass," Hardy said.

"Something's wrong," Laurel added from over on the driveway.

Hardy looked over at the fence bordering the yard next door. "Skittles hasn't run out to bark at us. She always jumps the fence whenever we're around. Never misses a visit, no matter when we come."

Dani smoothed her uniform down. "You're worried because the neighborhood poodle isn't here to slobber all over us?"

"Labradoodle," Hardy corrected.

"Maybe it's just chained up," said Lucy.

The twins shook their heads.

"Wait there," Laurel said. "Don't step off the sidewalk."

Dani and Lucy watched as the twins headed toward the garage door at the end of the drive, where it butted against the fence of the next house over. Laurel peered over the fence, while Hardy hunched to check under the bushes lining the front of the doctor's house.

Her cry of dismay brought everyone running. Hardy pointed with her broom handle at a small mass half-hidden beneath a bush—right about where a dog might run across the yard after jumping the fence.

The canine skeleton lay under the shrub as if the dog had been sleeping peacefully when something slayed it. Not a scrap of flesh remained, though a stink of decay lingered in the area.

Laurel and Hardy emitted tiny wails while staring at the bones. Lucy reached across with her mop. A tap of the handle, and the bones collapsed into a heap, drawing another hiccup of grief from the twins. Dani tried, but failed to conjure sympathy for the dead dog. Maybe if it had been a lizard …

"He killed Skittles," said Hardy, with such hate in her voice she might've been speaking about a serial murderer.

The twins exchanged a look, their previously cheerful attitudes long gone, leaving a combination of ferocity and determination behind. Wind rustled around them, stirring the grass and leaves of nearby trees.

Valkyries, Dani thought. The transition in the twins' demeanor had her rethinking her behavior as they once more surveyed the grounds. Maybe she shouldn't have judged them so superficially right off. She tried to set her catty mood aside, realizing she'd been off balance since waking.

Lucy held her mop out like a divining rod and paced along the edge of the yard.

"The ground is chanted," she said at last. "Our good doctor placed a slopspell around the house."

"Translation?" Dani asked.

"Anyone crossing the property line uninvited gets a nasty curse called down on their head. Your flesh and organs liquefy and become so much fertilizer."

Dani eyed the lawn and gulped, thinking of how close she'd come to becoming a heap of bones herself. "How do we get past it?"

"The ground itself is acting like the core to the slopspell," Lucy said. "If you can disrupt that anchor, the curse should dissipate."

"Can do," Dani said. "Give me a minute."

She knelt and pressed a hand to the sidewalk to funnel her power into the earth. Now that Lucy had clued her in on what to look for, she quickly homed in on the slopspell. To her magically sensitive eyes, the curse looked like an enormous serpent coiled around the house, ready to strike anyone who stepped within range.

She triggered the earthquake and directed the disruption beneath the house rather than toward the surrounding properties. The earth rumbled. A second story windowpane shattered and cracks shot through the driveway. A trench ripped through the lawn and the Corrupt energies puffed away like so much smoke.

Dani rose and brushed her knees off. "Should be clear."

Lucy swept her mop-radar out again and appeared satisfied with what she sensed. "Disarmed. Okay, ladies, just like we planned."

Lucy and Hardy went around the side of the garage and disappeared toward the back, while Dani and Laurel headed to the front door.

"I'm guessing ringing the bell isn't the best option," Dani said once they found the door locked.

She stepped off the landing to check the windows along the side. Her footsteps crunched as she shuffled along, and she glanced down, expecting pine needles or wood chips. She froze, and it took great self-control to not hop back onto the front steps.

Bird, squirrel, and cat skeletons littered the area behind the bushes. Tiny bones ground beneath their boots as Laurel joined her in moving from window to window. Dani tried to ignore the noise, to not imagine little screams of pain as skulls popped under her feet. Laurel appeared undisturbed, intent on breaking in and making the doctor pay for the dead labradoodle.

To distract herself, Dani ventured a bit of small talk.

"So, Laurel, what do you and Hardy do for fun? Pube bingo sounds … um … fascinating, but it can't be all you do."

Laurel surprised her by blowing a raspberry. "Got that right, girlfriend. Our dad owns a ranch. Whenever we aren't making the rounds as maids, we're in the rodeo circuit."

"Like rodeo queens, doing the parade and that kind of thing?"

Laurel went onto tip-toes to peer inside another dark window. "No, silly. We were state champs last year for roping and barrel racing. Women's division, of course."

"Of course." Dani noted the woman's strong arms and long legs in a new light. First impressions were definitely not the wisest things to go off of, in this instance.

After rapping on the glass, Laurel plucked a feather from her duster. Eyes narrowed, she touched the edge to the glass and dragged it in a large circle. Dani winced at the nails-on-a-chalkboard squeal as the feather cut into the window. Once Laurel completed the circle, she pushed on the pane and the disc popped inside. No noise at its drop, which indicated a carpeted floor waited. Laurel reached through the hole and patted around until she found and flipped the latch.

With a triumphant smile, she withdrew her arm and shoved the window up. Before Dani could protest, Laurel hoisted herself inside and disappeared past the curtains.

Dani held her breath for an alarm, or shouts and screams. What other booby-traps might the doctor have rigged?

Laurel reappeared and offered an arm. "Upsy-daisy."

With a last look at the animal bones, Dani tried to reassure herself she wasn't go to become like them. She took the maid's hand and let herself be hauled into the shadowed confines of the fleshmonger's house.

CHAPTER SIXTEEN

Ben sat on the edge of his bed and stared at the wall of his quarters. He listened to the drip of the bathroom faucet, trying to slow his thoughts to match its monotonous pace.

A night of restless sleep and half-baked nightmares hadn't improved his mood. He wondered what they would've done if he'd shown up anyways and insisted he come along on the job. To save himself from further humiliation, he'd stayed in the room until he knew they'd be well and away. Better not tempt himself.

He scratched at the stub of his right arm. He'd heard of phantom pain, where people who'd lost limbs felt cramped, itchy, or burning sensations along the missing arm or leg. In contrast, ever since losing his arm, he'd experienced episodes of phantom power—instances where, just for a moment, he'd forget the loss of magic rather than flesh. He'd stretch out his arm and call on the Pure energies, ready to send Scum running for their mommas.

He squeezed his leg, using the pressure to reassert reality. *Better get used to it, bucko,* he told himself. *Not gonna be changin' anytime soon.*

Yet no matter how often he argued himself down that mental track, part of him refused to accept it. Refused to be shoved back down into an existence that lacked real power and purpose. How could he make the others see he could still contribute? Sure, he'd let the adrenaline get to his head with the fleshmonger, but it didn't give Lucy the right to verbally spank him like a raw recruit.

Ben stood and paced the small room. He tapped the new access sigil Monty had delivered to him the night before, saving him from having to get another chaperone through HQ. A metal one this time, harder to chant but less likely to shatter in a fight.

Funny how someone could take such a simple thing like opening doors for granted. Even the newest Cleaners could manage it without half a thought.

But for Ben, he might as well have taken one step forward and then sprinted a mile back. First, he lost Karen and fell from the height of his powers as an Ascendant. Then, after fighting to even remain a janitor, he lost his Pure energies altogether. Now he'd become so much dead weight.

He gripped the sigil through the suit and squeezed it hard enough for the disc to imprint on his palm. Ever since he was a kid, he always hated feeling like a target of pity. He refused to be a charity case. After Francis refused to kick him out on the streets like a stray dog, Ben had kept at the work partially out of a lifelong habit of stubbornness.

But what if nothing changed? Perhaps it would've been better if he'd let Francis scrub his memories and set him out on the street with a new identity. He was worse than worthless. Even Carl could contribute more.

Speaking of which … the faucet had stopped dripping.

Ben scooped up the bowl he'd used for a chili dinner and went into the bathroom. The water in the sink burbled at his entrance.

"You took your time, buddy."

Ben placed the bowl on the counter. Carl slopped back and forth, his equivalent of a shrug. The sprite flowed out of the sink, but retreated when his glistening edge encountered a few beans and sauce stains left behind.

Ben frowned. "Aw, don't get picky on me. Dribble in there and we'll go grab another bottle. C'mon. Waitin' for you got my stomach growlin' somethin' fierce."

The elemental spat water his way in displeasure, but slid into the bowl. Retrieving it, Ben left his quarters and headed for the cafeteria. On the way, he ducked into a supply closet and poured Carl from the bowl into a new spray bottle. After hitching this to his belt, he continued toward the promise of a solid breakfast. Maybe a hefty serving of bacon and eggs would do him a load of help. That was one good thing about his restored youth—it put off having to care about things like clogged arteries and heart attacks for another couple decades.

He entered the cafeteria, only to pause, startled. The place stood nearly empty. Normally the cafeteria served as a hub of activity, hosting teams in from the field who wanted someplace to recuperate, swap stories, and enjoy a bit of Cleaner camaraderie. Breakfast often involved a veritable river of coffee sweeping through, with Cleaners buoyed by donuts, bagels, and all the comfort food one could imagine. When one's job involved eliminating the darkest elements of reality, you learned to relish the small joys, such as an all-you-can-eat buffet line that never closed.

This morning, however, the platters of food remained untouched while a dozen Cleaners at most sat scattered about, a few in pairs, most alone. Everyone stared at their cups or empty plates. No noise beyond the occasional clink of silverware.

Ben eyed the empty tables and then checked the bulletin board by the door to see if he'd missed a memo. Wouldn't surprise him to have been left out of some company-wide meeting, but nothing appeared scheduled.

Carl made the bottle bump his hip.

Ben hummed. "Yeah, buddy. You feelin' it, too? Somethin ain't quite right."

Another bump and splash.

He scowled down at the elemental. "Whaddya mean? Chili ain't never given me indigestion."

He studied the room again as a rebellious thought rose within him: What did it matter if it felt right or not? Why should he care? He'd fought for this company almost his entire life, and both times when he needed it most in return, he'd been sidelined. If he hadn't learned his lesson yet, he'd better catch on quick. If they didn't want him on the job, might as well relax and let the company take care of itself.

He grabbed a tray and plate, shoveled enough food onto it to feed a pack of starving wolves, and headed for the exit, planning on eating and sulking in peace back in his quarters. His feet betrayed him, however, by taking him over to the largest group in the place—two maids and a janitor who sat in unified silence, mop and brooms propped beside them.

He slid in next to the janitor, who barely glanced his way.

"Where's everyone hopped off to this mornin'?" Ben asked.

"Who knows, who cares?" a maid replied.

"Well, I'm obviously carin', since I went and asked. If you ain't knowin', then don't be spoutin' off such a useless answer."

Their heads raised and the other maid checked out the name stitched on his uniform.

"You're Ben?" She leaned over the table. "*That* Janitor Ben?"

"Yeah. So?"

"So get lost."

He paused with a forkful of omelet halfway to his mouth. "'Scuse me, missy?"

"You lose your hearing along with your powers?" the other maid asked. "Everyone knows you've got some big curse hooked on you, and we don't want you passing it on to us."

The eggs plopped back onto the plate as Ben tightened his grip on the fork.

"We back in middle school or somethin'?" He glared at them. "The Ravishing's all gone for good, and I'm pretty sure cootie monsters still ain't real, unless you found one down in the Sewers."

"Funny guy," the janitor said. He leaned in close enough for Ben to smell the coffee on his breath. "Was it just a big joke when you betrayed Destin?"

"Betray—" Ben started to rise, but the janitor grabbed his belt and yanked him back down.

"You think people don't notice what you're up to?" the same maid said. "Getting your pal as the new Chairman and then blackmailing him into keeping you on? Fawning all over that Catalyst and making sure she gets special treatment?"

Her hand whipped out from under the table, and a dust pan caught him across the face and slammed his cheek to the table. His neck popped, and he groaned as he grabbed for her wrist. Disbelief roared through him, almost as loud as the blood in his ears. The maid kept his head pinned while the other janitor caught his arm and bent it behind his back, forcing him to drop the fork.

"You're a disgusting mockery of what it means to be a Cleaner," the janitor rasped in Ben's ear. "You don't even have the right to eat here with us." A slap sent Ben's plate flying over him, eggs and bacon scattering. Grease and syrup oozed down his neck and into his hair.

"What the ✗◆♍&ʒ is wrong with you?" Ben grunted the words out. The chanted dust pan might as well have been a clamp set around his skull. "Lemme go!"

His shout echoed through the cafeteria, but he might as well have yelled into an empty bucket for all the response it received. If anything, the janitor and maid increased the pressure. Ben could hardly hear them speaking beyond the creak of his bones and tendons. His shoulder strained half an inch from popping out and pain stormed inside his head.

The second maid sat within sight, but didn't even look up from the table as her companions manhandled him. Add a bit of drool to her expression and she might've been stoned.

"We're going to make an example of you," the janitor said. "Think it'll get the message across when a few of your fingers get pinned to the bulletin board?"

The top to Ben's spray bottle burst off, followed by a spout of water which whipped into the Cleaners' eyes. They cried out as they shielded themselves from the spray. One of Carl's diversionary tactics.

The pressure on Ben's head vanished, as did the grip on his arm. He rolled out of his seat. His shoulder slammed to the floor as he crawled away. No time to see where Carl went. He had to get away from these lunatics. Had to

He lurched to his feet and spun to face them. A growl burbled out of his throat.

Wait. Am I actually gonna let 'em kick me when I'm down? He'd show them what happened to people who called him a traitor. He'd gnaw their throats out. Tear guts out with his bare hand. Use the silverware to carve—

A blast of wind and water struck him and forced him back. The frigid attack soaked him and also dampened his rage enough for common sense to reassert itself.

No matter how furious he was, he couldn't face empowered Cleaners directly. They'd hose him down so hard and fast, he wouldn't leave so much as a muddy streak on the floor. And since when did he start planning to pummel them in return, no matter what sort of fuss they started?

The maid clambered onto the tabletop, pan and broom in hand, while the janitor had grabbed his mop.

Whirling, Ben sprinted away down the row. He started to call for help again, to bring the few other Cleaners in the cafeteria to his aid. Despite his earlier cries and the obvious conflict, no one else had even risen from their seats. A couple glanced his way, but with such dull eyes they might as well have been sleepwalking. Sleepsitting. Whatever.

Instead, he grabbed his radio and pinned it to his chest so he could manipulate the channel dial. Turning it to the Chairman's private channel, he shouted into the device.

"Francis, boot some Ascendants down to the cafeteria. Somethin's—"

A gust of wind hit him in the back. It blasted him down and shoved him across the floor until he knocked into a bench. The radio flew from his grasp and bounced back toward his pursuers.

"Janitor? Please conf—"

The other janitor stomped on the handheld. Plastic and metal shards flew everywhere.

Ben dove under the table as the mop slapped down where he'd been lying. The other janitor leaped on top of the table and stabbed the handle between the gap on the far side. Splinters fragmented off the tip as it narrowly thrust past Ben's chest.

He grabbed the handle and yanked as hard as he could, trying to snap the mop in half against the tabletop. For a moment, he and the other Cleaner played tug-of-war. Then Ben managed to get to his knees and shoved upward, his back on the underside of the table. The janitor yelled as he lost his grip on the mop and tumbled to the floor. Ben stood, flinging the table off his back, now in possession of the tool.

The maid paused long enough to help her partner to his feet, and the two faced him once more. The janitor sneered as Ben shoved the mop out to ward them off.

"What do you think you're going to do with one arm and no powers?"

"So glad you asked, boyo," Ben said. "Wouldja believe I've been practicin' somethin'?"

He stepped in and spun the mop, catching the business end under the armpit so the handle stuck out, braced between hand and chest. Before the janitor could duck, Ben whacked the handle across the side of his head. He carried through as the janitor stumbled into the maid, then whipped the mop in the opposite direction to crack it across the maid's head on the rebound.

As the two clutched each other for support, he twirled the mop free and stuck it out in front of him, parallel to the ground. He charged. The ends of the mop struck both Cleaners across the chest and threw them back as he bulled forward.

The three of them crashed onto a table. The janitor and maid struck their heads and lay dazed.

Ben hopped off them. He wiped his sweaty forehead on the mop before planting it like a king claiming victory on a battlefield.

"I owe Vern a beer, sure-as-shootin'." He scowled at the pair. "You ever wanna tussle again, kiddos, keep this in mind. Don't gloat, and don't never ask your enemy to prove what he can do. That's just beggin' for a whuppin'."

A glance showed none of the other Cleaners in the cafeteria had so much as looked their way. He considered approaching one or two of them, perhaps prod them into revealing what was going on. But the downed Cleaners stirred, and he decided now might be the best time to take off, before they recovered and regained the upper hand.

He called to the room in general. "Cail, you watch my back, a'ight? I got an itchin' feelin' we're gonna be steppin' in some steamin' piles soon enough."

Slapping noises sounded a few rows over and he glimpsed a puddle sliding under the tables. Ben jogged for the exit, both fuming over and befuddled by the Cleaners' abusive treatment. Even if people had been spreading rumors about him, their reaction to his presence was unnaturally fierce. Did it have anything to do with the maids who'd gone over the edge? He hoped not, but couldn't think of anything else that might explain what had happened.

Maybe Lopez had made progress in determining the cause. If anything, a full contaminant sweep needed to be run through HQ. If the cafeteria and its off-balance inhabitants were any indication, the Cleaners as whole might be in danger.

He hesitated at the exit and looked back.

The janitor and maid had risen and fixed on him like hunting dogs scenting their prey. The janitor brought out a squeegee from one of his large leg pockets while the maid brandished her dust pan and broom.

The fury in their eyes burned away any semblance of sanity. Their threats degenerated into howls and snarls as they advanced. They clutched their weapons with white-knuckled grips, the tools brimming with Pure energy even Ben could sense, like static plucking his hairs to attention. They weren't holding back in the slightest, and he didn't doubt they'd kill him if they caught up.

At first, he returned their murderous stares with one of his own. Hatred coursed through him, and all he could think of was their blood staining the floor, their hearts giving last feeble beats within his grasp, their chests caved in—

A jagged headache tore through his brain. He gasped and retreated into the hall. The pain shoved the rage aside for the time being and let him regain a semblance of control. What was going on? He'd never felt that level of viciousness toward anything or anyone but Scum. Them wanting to beat him to a pulp didn't mean he had to return the favor.

His footsteps pounding in synch with his headache, he raced off to find the handyman.

CHAPTER SEVENTEEN

ani and Laurel crouched right inside the window as their eyes adjusted to the interior lighting. Dani extended her energies into the walls and floorboards, trying to sense the composition of the place and what she had to work with if any fighting occurred.

No obvious Corrupt auras nearby, but she'd heard some more talented Scum could conceal their energies, keeping Cleaners from sensing them until it was too late.

She catalogued the nearby elements as quick as she could. Water in the pipes, electricity in the wires. Wood and brick framing, concrete foundation shot through with metal. Plenty to play with.

Withdrawing her powers, she took in the décor with her normal sight.

She didn't quite know what to expect in the house of a creepy, insane doctor. Skeletal chandeliers? Rusty butcher blades lying around with unidentifiable viscera strewn about the kitchen? Arms and legs sticking out from the freezer?

Whatever torture chambers her mind had conjured, it certainly hadn't considered finding a model house with furniture straight from a luxury lifestyle catalog. Neutral carpeting muffled their footsteps. Vibrant cubist paintings hung on most walls of the living room, and at first she mistook the black and gray rectangle on the main wall as yet another work of art. Then she realized it was a flat-screen television big enough to serve as a bed.

It all spoke of meticulously gathered and distributed wealth. Of a man who ironed the wrinkles out of thousand dollar bills before using them to buy the place in cash. Who organized the layout of each room with a compass and ruler, and planned out his meals for the year, alongside the return-on-investment spreadsheet which detailed how much he'd save on cooking said meals rather than eating out.

The absolute tidiness of it all made Dani want to knock over the nearest table lamp out of spite. How did a neat-freak doctor become corpse-loving Scum?

A whiff of cat pee made her nose scrunch.

"I don't think the litter pan's been changed in a while," Laurel said, mirroring her reaction.

"You think we lucked out and he's not home then?" Dani asked.

"Can't promise. Most Scum don't really give a flying fish about holding to a household chore schedule, so it's not any indicator of when he was here last."

Dani raised a brow. *Give a flying fish?* But what she said was, "Good point. Plus, when you can control dead people, who needs a cat for company?"

She set her bucket and mop down and got her radio out.

"Lucy, we're in," she whispered into it.

"GREAT." Both women jumped as Lucy's voice blasted off the walls. *"WE'RE ON THE BACK PATIO."*

"Volume," Laurel cried.

Dani fumbled until she twisted the right dial and reduced the speaker to a crackling whisper.

"Did I just hear my own voice from across the entire house?" Lucy asked.

"Umm ..." Dani looked at Laurel, who rolled her eyes. "Weird acoustics in here. Like you said, not likely that we were going to ambush the guy."

"No chance of it anymore," Lucy replied. *"Any signs of the occupant?"*

Laurel moved further into the living room, edging toward a side hall and a dimmer light switch. As she eased this on, the shadows retreated into the next rooms and halls over.

"Not so far," Dani said.

"Okay. We're in. Start scouting. Keep in touch. And stay quiet.*"*

"Will do."

Tucking the radio away, Dani joined Laurel, who remained a few paces back from the hall entrance. Darkness swathed it, though Dani thought she glimpsed a large number of doors lining the way. She nodded for Laurel to go to the dimmer switches again.

"You hit the lights for the hall and I'll be ready for anything that comes our way."

Laurel went to test which switch controlled the lights they wanted. Dani readied her mop, pointy end prepared to go into the other guy, and braced herself as the hall lights flared.

She frowned. "That's different."

Mirrors, not doors, hung every few feet down to the wooden door at the far end. The layout resembled the reality where Dani encountered her elemental others so much, she half-expected to see them standing in the panes. However, once she got close enough to the first two mirrors, she noticed a key difference.

Instead of reflecting the empty hall and themselves, the mirrors seemed to suck the light into them. Oily shadows roiled in their glassy depths, and Dani stopped herself from tapping the surface to see what would happen.

"What is all this?" she asked.

Laurel's feather duster snapped into its blade mode, and she held it against a cheek. "Can't say I know. It's weird. They're like dead glassways. But Scum don't use glassways."

"My guess is no touchie."

The maid hummed in agreement. "Good thinking. They've got an ugly look and feel. Maybe Miss Lucy will know what they are."

Dani stared at the far door. "I'm also guessing that's the den."

"Looks like."

"Great." She rolled her shoulders. "Ready to run the gauntlet of spooky mirrors?"

Laurel chuckled. "You're funny. I like you."

"That's me. The Catalyst comedian." Dani made sure her rubber yellow gloves were tugged on tight. She retrieved the bucket and tucked it under one arm, the open end pointed forward. The

Josh Vogt

mop went in the other hand. "I'll take the bucket run and you follow in case anything pops up behind me, all right?"

Laurel flourished her duster in one hand, a rag in the other. "Go for it, girlfriend."

Dani planted her boots and flexed her legs, building her nerve. She let a bit of power flow into the bucket to activate its defensive measures. Beside the mundane use of holding water and other cleaning fluids, the bucket had also been chanted to absorb a few Corrupt spells, diverting them from the Cleaner who'd come under attack. Dani hadn't done a run with one in the field yet, but no time like the present.

She sprinted for the den door, not taking even a second to look in any of the mirrors.

Halfway there, the bucket thumped as a hidden spell activated and hit it. With the slopspell on the front yard, Dani didn't want to guess what terrible fate she'd just avoided.

Mirrors whipped past, and she counted off the strides until stomping to a halt before the door. She grabbed the knob. Cords of purple smoke puffed out from the metal and wrapped around her gloved hand briefly before being sucked into the bucket as well.

A twist and shove, and Dani leaped into the room, mop raised, Laurel right behind her. As the twin kept watch on the hall, Dani glanced into the bucket. The Corrupt energies had been neutralized and transformed into a harmless sludge at the bottom of the container. When it filled, the protection would cease until it was emptied and re-chanted.

Hoping they wouldn't hit that threshold anytime soon, she turned her attention to the den.

Empty of the doctor, but full of filing cabinets. Rusted stacks of them reached to the ten-foot-high ceiling, some with papers jammed in so tight the drawers wouldn't close. Posters hung from these, much like the ones she'd seen in doctors' offices detailing how to properly open her mouth and go *Ahhh*. Except Malawer's collection was a bit dated.

Almost all of the posters were replicas of scrolls that belonged in a museum or a history professor's study. Egyptian hieroglyphics wrapped around scenes of people with animal heads pontificating over prone bodies. Enlarged pictures of Greek and Roman urns showed gods and mortals wrestling with snakes and skeletons. A number of the posters and hangings had been scribbled on. Black and red marker circled various figures, underlined stretches of ancient text and jotted notes in a jagged hand along the margins.

Dani squinted to make out a few of these.

Transformation?

Delay ... preservation? Mummified ...

Where did it come from? Does it matter?

She tapped the back of her teeth with her tongue as she thought. Weren't these a little old-school for a modern doctor to be studying? Seemed like a guy trying to learn how to drive by looking at depictions of the wheel being carved out by cavemen.

A desk sat in the middle of the room. Several stacks of books crowded the workspace, and Dani came close enough to read the titles.

The Cambridge Encyclopedia of Paleopathology, *The Archaeology of Disease*, and *Disease and Human Evolution* were the ones she made the most sense of. Not exactly pleasure reading.

Her eyes fell on a stack of papers weighed down by a fountain pen. Her pulse quickened as she recognized these were the same style the doctor had been writing on at the hospital when observing the suicide attempts. Could they hold some insight into his purposes?

She set the mop and bucket aside and snatched the papers. But her hopes dropped as she thumbed through them.

Besides the dates at the top of each paper—marked from several weeks back to just a few days prior—she could hardly read a thing. A few numbered lists of names which only turned out to denote people as Base Specimen #14 or Subject #3. A notation of EMW121 appeared in a handful of spots, but without context. Some of the subjects appeared to have statuses beside their numbers, including *Gestation*, *Progress*, and *Successful*.

The rest looked like so much chicken scratch. Figured. A doctor didn't need to write in code when their own awful handwriting obscured any meaning. This could just as well have been a self-prescription for Viagra, for all she could tell. Still, the dates were recent enough to warrant further investigation.

She folded and stuffed the notes into a large pants pocket and zipped it. Maybe someone at HQ could decipher them. In the meantime, they had to finish scoping the rest of the house. A scrub-team would need to come in and sort through these files. There had to be something valuable in here.

As she continued scanning the room, she brought her radio out.

"Lucy, we're in the study. The place is packed with books and files. It'll take a year to read it all, but maybe it'll shed some light on what Malawer is up to."

"Good to hear," Lucy replied. *"We just finished with the kitchen. The food in the fridge doesn't look like it's been touched in a month, but nothing else out of the ordinary. Moving to the basement."*

"Cool. We'll be upstairs. Holler if you—"

Laurel piped up. "Dani? There's something out here."

"Hang on, Lucy." Clipping the radio back in place, she joined the twin who stared down the hall. Everything looked normal as far as Dani could tell. "Something? Or someone?"

Laurel frowned. "Dunno. I thought I saw …"

"Yeah?"

"A woman. Walk between two of the mirrors about halfway along."

"Between? Like across the hall?"

"No. Between like she was in one mirror and then appeared in the one next to it without going through the hall."

Dani leaned out from the door far enough that she should've been able to see her head reflection in the nearest pair of mirrors. But the obsidian surfaces refused to cooperate, and she pulled back into the den.

"Did she look like Lucy or Hardy?"

Laurel shook her head. "No. She wore a dress, I think. Not a Cleaner."

"What'd she look like?"

Laurel's pretty face scrunched in concentration. "It happened so quick. Didn't get a good look at the face. Just the dress. Real deep blue, with sparkles on it. All glim-glam."

Dani studied the hall, bothered by the unexplained presence. A ghostly woman in sequined dress traipsing between black mirrors? How did that fit in with any of this? Or did Laurel really see anything in the first place?

The radio crackled. *"Dani? Report?"*

Dani raised it again. "Laurel and I are a bit weirded out by these mirrors. Nothing confirmed."

"*We've seen a few as well. They appear inert, but steer clear of them for now.*"

"Yeah. Figured. We're heading your way."

She tapped Laurel's shoulder, and the twin shook herself and smiled nervously.

"Ready?" Dani asked.

"You bet."

With the traps cleared by the initial run, they went back down the hall slower this time, shoulder to shoulder, though with their backs turned toward each other slightly so they could keep an eye on the mirrors they passed. Dani got the unnerving sensation that the panels weren't dysfunctional mirrors but windows to a realm of non-existence the hallway cut through. At any moment, she expected black claws to lash out and tear their faces off, or for freezing winds to howl between the voids and root them where they stood.

When nothing happened, they shared slightly embarrassed smiles before heading to where stairs led to the next story. The second flight cut along a wall, where four more mirrors hung.

They hurried up and found a main hall which split toward either end of the house. No mirrors here, though each path offered several doors. After a glance in each direction, Dani nudged Laurel.

"You pick."

Laurel headed to the right and Dani followed. The first two doors they checked turned out to be a linen closet and bathroom, with the latter decorated in a chintzy beach house style, seashell wallpaper, and glass bowls filled with white sand and shells. When Dani reached to open the next door, a slight noise made her hesitate.

"What's wrong?" Laurel whispered.

Dani pressed her ear to the door, trying to determine the source of the sound. It took her a second to identify it. Hissing? Chanting? No. Humming, and not from an air conditioner or a fan. Musical wavers, like a child who'd forgotten the words to a lullaby. Great. Little kids and lullabies were perfect for upping the creep factor in the doctor's house of horrors.

Her fingers tensed on the knob. "Someone's in there."

Laurel made a fist. Sticking a finger out, she spun it in a circle. Then two fingers, which she pointed up, then right. Her fist clenched again, and she shook it hard.

Dani stared and pulled back from the door slightly. "I have no clue what that meant."

The maid leaned in close so they could talk below their breaths. "Sorry. Basically, you rush in and clear any spells with the bucket as I follow. Then we cut right to dodge any physical attack. Hopefully that'll give us the element of surprise and let us take down any threat before it can react too violently."

Dani blinked. "Right. That's what I thought you were saying; just wanted to double-check. Good plan."

Counting to three under her breath, she opened the door and lunged, mop and bucket leading the way. She stopped so quickly Laurel bumped into her back and shoved her another step forward.

Both of them stared at the woman sitting in a rocking chair across the room, basking in a patch of sunlight that beamed through a dormer window. She wore a pink cashmere sweater, jeans, and had frizzy brown hair tousled around a fine-boned face.

At Dani's entrance, she rose, eyes and mouth wide in a comical expression of fright. The fear smoothed away a second later and a smile stretched her lips.

"Hello," she said. "Are you guests?"

CHAPTER EIGHTEEN

Ben peered out from behind a shelf stacked high with buckets and shoulder-strap vacuum cleaners, trying to remain unnoticed. After shaking the murderous janitor and maid, he'd since witnessed even more disturbing events as he made his way through HQ. Arguments devolving into fistfights in the halls. Cleaners sitting in the middle of the floor, gaze distant and hopeless. Janitors chasing Ascendants, waving mops and yelling something about pay scale injustice.

He'd just come from one of the supply depots, hoping to secure a new radio and get in touch with Francis. But Supplies had been locked down with no explanation posted. A mob of Cleaners had stood outside the main entrance, alternately shouting to be let in and threatening to bash in the face of the first Supplies staff who emerged.

Not daring to approach anyone for clarification, Ben had slunk off before anyone recognized him. Maybe one of the smaller supply closets would yield results. But moments after arriving at this one, he'd hidden behind a shelf as a plumber and janitor had stumbled in.

At the moment, he had front-bucket seats to two Cleaners bawling into each other's shoulders.

"It's just ... why care?" the plumber said between hiccups of grief. "Why bother? What does any of this matter?"

"I don't know," said the janitor. "I just don't know."

"Does anyone know how much we suffer? How much do we have to give before anyone even notices us? The Board doesn't care, do they? The Chairman doesn't care. Why don't we just give up?"

"I don't know. I just don't know."

The plumber hugged herself as sobs wracked her. The janitor threw an arm around her partner as they walked out of the room.

"I don't know. I just don't know ..."

Once the weeping faded from hearing, Ben eased out of hiding. He spat and ground the discharge under his boot. HQ should be the place he felt safest, but here he was, lurking around like a kid up past his bedtime.

What in blazes is goin' on 'round here? Has everyone gone loony?

It felt like HQ had been turned into a giant boiler with the heat and pressure skyrocketing. What would happen if it kept rising? It couldn't be natural, but he had no idea what might be causing it. Mass hysteria? People bingeing on way too many reality shows?

He threw his mop against the opposite stack of shelves. Even if he did figure it out, what could he do to stop it? He had a difficult enough time just trying to walk through the place without becoming a target. Someone, or something, was attacking the Cleaners, and they were succumbing to it almost without a fight, without even knowing the source.

This was his home. Everything that defined him existed here. If it all got flushed, where would that leave him? He had to hope—

A hand grabbed his belt. Hollering, he spun and swung. He checked the punch so it grazed Jared's forehead rather than slamming the hybrid to the floor. Jared leaped back and nearly toppled the shelf of buckets as he hunched and hid his eyes.

Ben forced his sphincter to unclench. Thank Purity he had his younger body back, otherwise this sort of surprise might've given him a heart attack. The ticker probably just aged ten years as it was. As his breathing slowed, he went over to the hybrid and urged him to straighten.

"Jared. Geez, kiddo, I almost ... well, I ain't thinkin' I'd have a chance at killin' you, would I? But I almost socked you a good one."

140

At last, Jared dropped his hands and pouted at him. His disembodied voice tapped inside Ben's ears.

Saw. Ree.

"S'okay." He scowled down at Carl, who had puddled beside his boots. "Thanks for the warnin'."

Carl swirled in a miniature whirlpool and then slid over to lap at Jared's tennis shoes. The hybrid laughed and tried to splash in the water until Carl drained back under the shelves.

Ben eyed the hybrid. "Why'd they let'cha … hang on. They didn't let'cha out, did they? You've gone and broke loose. Again."

Jared nodded miserably.

"For Purity's sake, Jared, you gotta stop doin' this. We're tryin' to protect you, but if you keep bangin' the boundaries, the more the Board's gonna figure you'll blow up in our faces one day. Can'tcha understand that?"

The hybrid drooped.

Lawn. Lee.

Ben closed his eyes for a moment, briefly awash with regret. "Aw, geez. I'm sorry, kiddo. I oughta visit more often. Good on Dani for makin' up for me bein' such a lollygaggin' loaf." He smiled softly. "Bein' locked up all day? I know just how much of a bum deal that is. Honest to goodness. But right now, I ain't lyin' when I say it's for your own good."

The hybrid looked around him to the door where the weeping Cleaners had exited.

Bay-en. Saw ick.

Ben rubbed the back of his neck. "Yeah, they're sick somethin' fierce. But I can't figure how they got that way. HQ's piled up so many wards, I bet we've got protection against some cruddy bugs that don't even exist yet. Should be downright impossible for anyone here to be dealin' with this. Mebbe a few folks bein' worked on by handymen, but not this sorta big, bad mess. Not everyone at once."

Jared hiccupped. And vanished.

Ben blinked at where the teen had stood. He turned in place, searching the confines of the supply closet.

"Jared? Kiddo? Hey, get yerself back here."

Another hiccup from a dark corner of the room, and Jared popped back in front of him. Ben put his hand on the boy's shoulder, though he doubted this would keep him in place.

"Nifty new trick, huh?"

Ta-ruck?

"That how you slipped out of containment?"

Jared waved his hands in denial. He tromped in place, exaggerating each footstep until Ben got the idea.

"You just walked right on out? They didn't notice none?"

Jared chortled and bounced in place.

"A'ight, we need to getcha back. HQ is too dangerous right now. If you stay here, Dani will be worried, and I ain't gonna be the one to tell her you got hurt on my watch, okay?"

Ho. Kee.

Jared pulled away and trotted out the exit. Ben grabbed his mop and ran after. He caught the teen as he turned down a fortunately empty stretch of hall.

"Hold on now. Where'd'ja think you're goin'?"

Jared pointed ahead. *Con. Tin. Mint.*

"How're you knowin' it's thataway?"

Jared shrugged. Ben watched his eyes, looking for any glint of duplicity.

"Jared, which way's the Recycling Center?"

Jared pointed left and up.

"And Supplies? Employee Records? The Board Room? The Chairman's office?"

As he listed off the sections of HQ, Jared pointed without fail, and while Ben couldn't confirm the accuracy, he didn't think the hybrid was lying. Nor did he think Jared knew the locations because he'd explored HQ enough on his own. The reaction was too automatic, too unthinking, as if he oriented himself by a mental map.

He made Jared face him while keeping watch for any Cleaners.

"It's 'cause of Destin, ain't it? Somethin' about being his kid and that sayin' about the nut not fallin' too far from the tree. Bits of what he knew are lodged in that big brain of yours."

Jared perked up. *Paw-paw?*

"Yeah. Paw-paw, for sure."

Ben scratched his stubble as he thought through the implications. Obviously the hybrid had inherited some of Filth's supernatural nature, and Destin hadn't been a weakling either when it came to throwing Pure energies around. The kid's constantly shifting powers were an assumed inheritance, but no one had guessed that he'd also gained specific knowledge from his folks.

If Destin had been involved in Ben and Karen's last job and the ensuing cover-up, perhaps Jared had inherited some knowledge about it as well, along with whatever else was locked in his brain.

Ben tensed as a shiver of hope traced his spine.

"Jared, before we getcha back, can you try somethin' for me?"

CHAPTER NINETEEN

Dani stared, nerves still tingling from the expected confrontation.

"Guests? Uh … sure, we're guests."

The woman clapped in glee. "Wonderful. It's been too long since we've had anyone visit. Would you like some tea?"

Oh, yes, Dani thought. *A perfectly normal reaction to people barging into your master bedroom unannounced. Why, I often have guests arrive in just such a manner, especially wielding cleaning equipment like overly hygienic ninjas.*

"If you don't mind my asking, who are you?" Dani asked. "Do you know Dr. Malawer?"

"Tommy?" The woman fiddled with a gold ring on her left hand. "Are you friends from the hospital? He should be home soon. He was here not long ago."

"Do you have some way of contacting him?"

The woman's lips dipped into a frown. "He was here not long ago."

"But when?" Laurel asked. "Don't you remember?"

The woman twitched a few times, and Dani couldn't help but think of a robot that had been presented with a logical paradox. A thought appeared to click into place, and her smile returned.

"Do you have any children? The kids might want to play. I could get some cookies."

She had yet to blink, Dani realized. Not so much as a twitch of an eyelash.

Dani glanced at the photos on the wall. Several of them depicted a father, mother, and two boys posed in various scenes. The mother and the woman here appeared identical, but it took Dani a few moments to recognize the doctor. The photos showed a chubby Thomas Malawer grinning through a full black beard while hugging his wife close. When she'd seen him in the hospital, he'd been at least a hundred pounds lighter and lacking the beard, but she didn't doubt it was the same man.

She swallowed, mouth having dried as she stared from the pictures to the woman who acted impossibly at ease with strangers infiltrating their house. Awful possibilities slithered into her mind, and she slowly backed toward the hall while Mrs. Malawer continued to smile as if her lips had been stapled into place.

"Please stay where you are, ma'am," Dani said.

The woman wrung her hands. "Would you like some tea? Coffee?"

Dani eased the door shut. Her last glimpse of the room was of Mrs. Malawer returning to her rocking chair, where she stared at her lap.

Laurel whispered harsh in her ear as she retreated a few paces down the hall.

"Dani, what's going on? Who is she? Where's the doctor? Why is she—"

Dani raised a finger as she got on the radio.

"Lucy?"

"Here. Was just about to call you. You should see this basement. It's something else."

"Lucy, did the Chairman's report specify if Dr. Malawer had a family?"

"Almost like a ... What?"

Dani glanced at the closed door. Had the knob turned slightly?

"A family! Did Malawer have a family?"

"Hang on."

She counted Laurel's heavy breaths until Lucy spoke again.

"Yes. A wife and two boys, a teenager and a one-year-old. They all died in an auto accident five years ago. Why?"

Laurel dark complexion turned a bit yellow as blood drained from her face. "Cleanse me. He didn't. Did he? I mean, he did, didn't he?"

Dani looked to the other end of the long hall, where two more bedrooms waited. Did a small shadow patter past one door?

"I'm betting some graves at the local cemetery are empty right now," she said.

Laurel's expression hardened as her shock turned to anger and disgust. "This guy's a straight up sicko."

Dani couldn't agree more, and was just about to say so when the house shuddered. Every light sputtered and dimmed. They went back-to-back, mop and broom raised. Dani could still make out the layout of the place, but all colors had gone dusky and a queasy purple glow coated every surface, as if the house had been painted to react with ultraviolet light.

The radio squealed to life.

"Dani, get down here. Something's—"

A deeper voice shoved Lucy's aside, and Dani and Laurel's units shook with the force of the words.

"Invaders. Defilers. You will be expunged."

A *pop*, and a wisp of smoke trickled out of the speaker. Dani thumbed the Talk button while twisting the channel and power dials.

"Lucy? Lucy! Hardy? Anyone?"

The house shook again, as if a giant had used it for a stepping stool. Dani went to check the staircase. Had the doctor returned? Did he prowl their way with an army of corpses?

No one appeared there, but when Dani turned back to Laurel, the master bedroom door had opened and Mrs. Malawer now stood behind the oblivious maid.

Mrs. Malawer's face had gone gray, eyes as dead as a shark's. Her lips twitched back, revealing twin rows of pointed teeth, identical to Malawer's monstrous visage.

"Laurel, look out!"

Mrs. Malawer pounced on Laurel's back. She bit down on her shoulder and the maid shrieked as she staggered. She dropped her broom as she grabbed for the claw snagged in her hair. Like a wolf dragging a rabbit back to its den, Mrs. Malawer yanked Laurel into the bedroom and kicked the door to close it.

Dani rammed the mop handle into the gap just before the door shut. The door resisted being opened, and she pried at it, yelling for Laurel to hang on. At last, the door flung wide, and Dani stumbled in.

Mrs. Malawer had Laurel on the floor, trying to rip her uniform to shreds as she bit at the maid's face. Laurel's suit turned aside the attacks as the maid grabbed for the feather duster on her belt. The air within the room shivered as she gripped the handle.

Dani swung the mop and struck Mrs. Malawer in the side. The woman rolled off Laurel with a howl. She gnashed her teeth at Dani, who raised the mop for another blow. Laurel sat up and snapped her duster at the mudwoman.

The feathers flared as a blast of wind flipped Mrs. Malawer back into her rocking chair hard enough to break the seat off the legs. A chunk of wood stuck out of Mrs. Malawer's thigh when she stood from the wreckage, but she gave it no notice. Growling, she gathered herself and sprang.

Laurel swung her duster like a tennis racket. Another fist of air hit Mrs. Malawer from the side. The woman struck the wall above the bed before dropping to the mattress. With an animalistic shriek, Mrs. Malawer scrambled off the far side and scuttled under the bed frame.

Dani hoisted Laurel to her feet by an elbow. "You okay?"

The maid had paled further, but nodded. "Stupid of me to get caught off-guard like that."

"Yeah. You should've totally seen the old housewife-turns-into-a-land-shark trick coming from a mile away."

Laurel scowled as she rubbed her head where her hair had been yanked. The two women turned to the bed. Mrs. Malawer continued to hiss and spit at them from underneath. Laurel's duster snapped into blade mode, and she eyed the cushions as if preparing to carve the bed to pieces to get to the undead wife.

The door slammed shut behind them, making them both jump. Another black panel had been hung on this side of it. In that instant of distraction, Mrs. Malawer raced out from hiding. Instead of attacking, though, she leaped past the flick of wind Laurel sent her way, ducked a swing of the mop, and dove for the mirror.

She passed into the black glass and vanished. Not a ripple marked her passage. Dani and Laurel hesitated, waiting for something to happen. When nothing did, Dani approached the mirror, watching for any sign of the wife's reemergence.

"Careful," Laurel whispered. "Could be another trap."

Standing as far as she could from the panel, Dani tapped the mirror with the mop handle. Wood thudded on glass. Daring a further test, she inched closer and placed a gloved hand on the surface. The boundary didn't give, no matter how hard she pushed.

Motion shifted within the blackness. She jumped back, ready for anything.

A lab-coated figure appeared, notebook in hand, scribbling even as he fixed her with a furious look.

"Dr. Malawer," Dani said, "I don't know if you can hear me."

"I can." His voice rang clear, as if he stood in the same room with them. "Ignorant. Foolish. You will be among the rest who succumb. It satisfies me to know this."

"Why are you doing this?" Laurel asked. "What are you doing? Lots of people have died."

Dr. Malawer licked his lips with a gray tongue. "And more will follow. My work nears completion."

"Want to gloat a bit more then?" Dani asked. "Since there's obviously no way I can stop a man of your brilliance, why not just tell me all the details of your master plan so I can marvel at how awesome you are."

Mrs. Malawer appeared and slunk over to lay her head on her husband's shoulder. Her face had returned to normal, but her eyes held a cold light as she stared at the Cleaners.

Dr. Malawer tucked his notebook away. He bent over and tugged the chunk of rocking chair out of his wife's leg. It left a puckered wound that didn't bleed, which he kissed before straightening to glare.

"Your actions confirm my analysis," he said. "No Purity in your actions. Only arrogance. She was right. Your kind deserves to be eradicated."

"She?" Laurel asked. "She who?"

"And what'd we ever do to you?" Dani asked.

A teenaged boy appeared in the black mirror, followed by a younger child who tottered up to take his mother's hand. Their faces held the same twitching unlife, like masks of skin pinned to their skulls and worked by invisible strings.

"It's a regular Addams Family reunion," Dani said. "Where's Lurch?"

Dr. Malawer sneered. "Failed humor. Similarly unsuccessful attempt to hide fear. Everything of the Cleaners is a façade. This is observed."

"You spend a lot of time observing." Dani flipped a hand at the notepad. "Taking all those notes. It must be nice feeling so superior. So distant, thinking the whole world is some big experiment for you to play with."

"The world?" A dry chuckle tore out of Malawer. "Perspective is necessary. This world is small. Insignificant. I've seen. What does one rat care for another?"

"I study medicine, Dr. Malawer, and it sickens me to see what you've let yourself become. You're supposed to uphold the Hippocratic Oath. Bring no harm. Preserve life. Not playing at God. Remember? Is there anything left of the man you once were?"

"She speaks of oaths. She doesn't know." He glanced to one side, then back at her. "I'm held to no oath but the one given to she who empowers me. The harm brought is to those deserving it. The lives worth preserving are here with me. None others. The price is paid. I fulfill my oath now and my family remains safe."

"Your family is dead, Malawer."

"No. My power brought them back. We are whole. Reunited."

Dani eyed Mrs. Malawer. "Uh huh. She seems quite the trophy wife, what with the fangs and all."

"Your fault. She defends her home. What mother wouldn't?"

"A mother who died five years ago. And your kids? I don't see them having great chances at a full and satisfying life."

The preschooler stopped sucking his thumb long enough to snarl at her. For a moment she thought the family might leap out of the mirror and attack. Her mind rebelled at the thought of having to put down a little boy, even if he was trying to bite her nose off.

"Mockery," Malawer said. "Futile."

"No." Dani jabbed the mop at him. "There's still a part of you that knows this is wrong. I can tell. You may be Scum, but you're not insane. At least, not fully. Why bother sitting around and arguing with a worthless Cleaner if I'm not getting through to you just a little bit?"

"Because I—"

Malawer's head snapped to the side. He stared at something beyond the border of the black glass and appeared to listen, but Dani heard nothing, no matter how much she strained. Finally, he nodded.

"Agreed."

The family vanished, and Dani sagged a bit. Laurel punched her shoulder, making her grunt.

"Girlfriend, you got some gumption."

"I don't think Malawer is impressed by gumption," Dani said. "Besides, what good has it done? What've we really learned?"

Laurel frowned and tapped her painted nails with each point. "Well, we learned Dr. Malawer took an oath with someone—a she—getting the power to reanimate his family in return for, you know, doing whatever it is he's doing to us. We learned whatever he's doing is almost done, so we need to figure things out quick. That he's using some sort of new Scum form of transportation, which maybe we could use to track him down when a scrub-team gets here. Oh, and that he'd do anything to protect his family—or whatever's left of them. It could be a bargaining point if we could get hold of one of them."

Dani stared at the maid. Then she shook herself. "Right. I mean, besides all that."

"I dunno. That's all I can think of."

Their eyes widened as the same thought struck both of them at the same time.

"Lucy!"

"Hardy!"

They grabbed their radios and frantically turned and jabbed the knobs and buttons, unsuccessfully trying to revive the equipment. Dani flung hers aside and went for the door, but balked on realizing the black glass covered the entire frame from this side. No doorknob. No hinges.

Letting her anger get the better of her, Dani started whacking the mirror with the mop. But no matter how hard she beat on it, the slightest crack refused to show. Only Laurel's nervous voice made her pause.

"Dani ..."

She turned, startled to see the wallpaper bubbling. The bubbles swelled, first into green buds, and then grape-sized pods that covered every inch of the ceiling and walls. A metallic hum filled the room. Several buds quivered.

"What's going on?" Dani asked. "What's Malawer doing?"

"I think I recognize these. Hang on ..."Laurel chewed a manicured nail until shock made her hand and jaw drop. "Cleanse me. Get your mask on. They're corpseflies."

"Like horseflies?"

Laurel snatched a dust filter mask out from a pocket. The buzzing increased, reminding Dani of cicadas.

"Corpseflies try to get into the body through any opening," Laurel said as she strapped her mask on. "Then they eat you alive from the inside out."

Dani rushed to get her mask on and tightened the strap. The mask sealed around her mouth and nose, purifying the air that filtered through it. Her eyes and ears remained vulnerable, however, and she made a mental note to stick a few gas masks and ear muffs in her van the next time she visited Supplies.

She set her mop against the wall. "Keep the bugs off me for as long as you can."

"What're you going to do?" Laurel asked.

Dani grabbed her squeegee and cut across the wall beside the door. A chunk of sheetrock tore away as the rubber blade sheared it loose.

"Make a new door," she said.

She carved out more sheetrock and insulation with each hack. She panted and sweat dripped off her nose by the time the first slash cut through to the hall outside, and she nearly lost her hold on the squeegee. Her muscles quivered at the thought of it tumbling out of reach. Yet her grip remained firm. Encouraged by the promise of freedom and spurred on by the buzzing of the rapidly maturing corpseflies, Dani dug faster even as her arms and hands began to burn from the effort.

With a sound like melons being squashed, the first crop of corpseflies burst out of their pods. Dani couldn't help but look over her shoulder as angry humming filled the air. Each the size of her thumb, the corpseflies had a metallic green sheen, obsidian wings, and wicked pincers that added clicking to the noise.

Laurel triggered a spray can she'd brought out, and Dani sensed the maid pouring Pure energy into the spray. It expanded into a cloud that smelled of lemon air freshener. A first wave of corpseflies dropped to the carpet, legs and wings twitching, while a few bobbed to the ceiling, out of range. Another handful of pods popped open and released more of the deadly creatures.

Laurel bumped her with a hip. "Don't stop. I got you covered."

Dani forced herself to focus on the wall and soon had a hole big enough to stick her head through. As she worked, she fed her power flow into the house wiring, latching onto the electrical energies waiting to be unleashed through every bulb and socket and appliance.

She chopped a stud into splinters and then carved down toward the floor. Just had to lengthen it a bit; widen it so they could squeeze through sideways.

Laurel continued spraying some bugs down and forcing others back with gusts summoned through her feather duster. Yet with each swarm she obliterated, more pods burst and added to the corpsefly numbers. Dani's hair fluttered about her head from both Laurel's attacks and the sheer number of insect wings stirring the air. Lemon scent mingled with manure, making her nose wrinkle behind the mask.

Tiny legs settled on her head, gripped her hair. She almost scalped herself with the squeegee when she swatted the corpseflies away. Back to digging. She whooped as a last few pieces fell away. Not exactly the Arc de Triomphe, but it'd have to be good enough.

She called to the maid. "Laurel, come on!"

A shove. "You first!"

Laurel backed her against the wall, guarding the retreat. Dani shoved her shoulders through, but her hips caught. A twist and lunge, and she spilled out into the hall.

Regaining her feet, she reached back through, grabbed Laurel's collar, and jerked her toward the hole. A mistake, for the motion caught the maid off-guard and made her latest attack falter. Unopposed, the corpseflies swarmed the hole, and Dani shrieked as several dozen smacked into her face. Pincers nipped her as she tugged Laurel through. She squinted, barely able to see as the insects skittered over her brow and eyelids. With one hand, she slapped her cheeks to dislodge the creatures, holding on to Laurel with the other.

Laurel choked and gagged as she tried to claw free of the bugs which swirled around her. Dani pulled her into the hole, determined to drag her out by force.

At last, Laurel shoved through. She fell the ground, thrashing and punching herself. Corpseflies surged out of the hole, but didn't immediately resume attacking the women as they flew down the hall. Dani dropped to her knees and tried to get Laurel under control before she did any more damage to herself.

The maid's mask had been torn to the side. Her lips were pressed tight, and tiny cuts covered her face and neck.

All at once, Laurel went stiff. She shook twice, and then clutched Dani close and opened her mouth as if to speak. A buzz emanated from deep within. Dani jerked back.

Looking sick with horror, Laurel clutched her throat.

"Dani … I swallowed one."

CHAPTER TWENTY

Ben paused outside of Employee Records to make sure no one tailed them. How Jared had stayed out of his room—*Admit it, Ben, it's a prison cell filled with toys*—this long without alerting the Board, he had no idea. At any second, he expected Francis and a team of Ascendants to swoop in at full aura and truck the kid off to the incinerator.

The door opened to his touch, a welcome response that made him feel, in a small way, like he still belonged. He and Jared entered the chilly archives. He couldn't tell if it was the same circular platform he and Lucy had been on the day before, but it looked identical. The orb of Pure knowledge hung beneath the glassy dome, which gleamed in the blue light.

Ben pulled Jared into the shadow of one of the steel pillars.

"A'ight, kiddo. Stay here and do whatever it is you do to keep folks from noticin' you. This'll just take a sec."

Jared put a finger to his lips and winked at Ben, who grinned.

"You got it."

He stepped out into the open and called to the dome.

"Rick, can I get that folder back? Betcha you're tired of holdin' on to it for me. I'll bring a beer by later."

The dome shimmered. Instead of Rick, however, a pale face appeared, wreathed in a white cowl. Fear jolted Ben and he fought to keep his composure. Had they tracked Jared after all? Would Ben be accused of underhanded dealings with the hybrid? Perhaps he should've returned the kid to his room straight away instead of dragging him along on a foolish hunch.

The Board member gazed down at him, face emotionless, stripped of its more human elements by the Board's proximity to the Pure Pantheon. A toneless voice cut through the chamber.

"Records are off-limits to all employees until the danger is deemed passed."

Ben stared at ... him? Her? Tough to tell.

"Danger? If you know what's goin' on, why don'tcha do somethin' about it?"

"The situation remains under analysis."

Striding to the railing, Ben leaned his mop against it and looked first at the orb of knowledge and then at the Board member.

"You ain't knowin', are you? You're just as ign'ant about what's happenin' as we are."

"All factors have not yet been calculated. The situation will be resolved as is determined most efficient."

"Well, while you're all up there punchin' the numbers, I'm still needin' my files back."

"Records are off-limits to all—"

He pounded the railing. "I handed that folder over for safe-keepin', not so you could lock it away!"

"Records are off-limits to all employees until the danger is deemed passed."

He rubbed one of his temples. "Great. They've put me on hold."

Shuffling alerted him to Jared coming out from behind the pillar. The hybrid glanced at the Board member's image and then tiptoed over.

"It's all right," Ben said. "I'm not thinkin' they're really here anymore." He leaned back against the rail and grimaced. "Waste of time. Without those files, I got nothin' to try and give your memory a little push. Mebbe you don't even know anythin' anyhoo."

Jared tapped his head, and an inquisitive look pinched his brows and lips.

"Yup. I thought mebbe your Paw-Paw mighta been involved in some shenanigans way back before you was born. Thought mebbe if you saw some of the stuff I've been studyin', you might make a connection. Bit of a long shot, but I don't got much else beyond those these days."

Jared made a clutching motion, as if trying to draw the words out of Ben.

Ben sighed. "The short of it? I lost my wife."

Wah. Eef?

"Wife. Karen. A gorgeous gal I loved very much, and ..." He frowned at Jared. "Do you even know what love is, kiddo? Has Dani told you about it at all, or is she still teachin' you the different sounds farm animals make?" A chuckle. "Not that we got love all figured out or anythin'. We weren't no perfect pair, no sir, no how, but at least we was a pair; I've ain't never been the same since she died."

His throat went scratchy, and the shadows in the chamber seemed to deepen as his mind once more approached the blank spaces in his memory.

"But I don't remember what happened to her. I don't know how she died down in the Sewers, or wherever we really went. And I gotta find out. It's ... just somethin' I gotta do."

He looked at his hand and envisioned Karen placing hers in his. The imagined sensation felt real for that instant, so much that he closed his hand, trying to capture her ghost. But the memory puffed away like dust tossed to the wind. He closed his eyes to clamp down on the tears threatening his composure. *C'mon. No cryin' in front of the kid.*

He forced himself to keep talking, though the words came out ragged.

"It hurts somethin' mighty big, Jared, losin' the person you cared for more than anythin'. Makes you almost not want to care anymore, 'cause you're just gonna get hurt again. You start thinkin' everythin's hopeless. Just this big, black drain inside you, suckin' all the good stuff down until you don't even know yourself anymore."

He paused to let his fluctuating emotions settle. Jared stared at the floor, not seeming to hear Ben talking anymore. Ben reached for him, but the hybrid shifted back, snuffling and wiping at his eyes.

"Kiddo, are you cryin'? Aww, c'mon. Now you're gonna get me started, and that ain't a pretty sight."

Jared scrubbed snot from his nose and shook his head hard. Before Ben could figure out what had triggered such a response, the hybrid ran around to one of the halls that led off from the main chamber. He waved for Ben to follow.

Ben sighed, snagged his mop, and jogged after. He knew they wouldn't get anywhere, not with the Board having locked the place down, but might as well humor the kid. The passage would be a return loop, depositing them back—

Into a completely new chamber.

Ben jerked to a stop. They'd entered a high-ceilinged vault with brushed steel cabinets forming the walls, numbered according to whatever system the Filing Clerk had enacted. In some ways the Records center reflected the current Clerk's mind, and the system changed whenever a new one was instated. It made the archives near-impossible to plunder, even if a thief was able to get around the intertwined dimensional loops imposed on the access points.

Ben glanced at Jared and marveled at how easily he'd circumvented the security. Maybe that wasn't such a paranoid precaution after all.

Propping his mop against a wall, he watched as Jared walked a circuit of the room, running a hand over various drawers as he went. On his second time around, he paused, opened a drawer and rummaged inside. Ben tried to keep his excitement in check. Maybe the kid was just messing with him. Maybe it didn't have anything to do with what he'd been talking about.

Jared drew out a slim book, bound in gray leather. He sniffed it, wrinkled his nose, and then trotted over to hand it to Ben, who wiped the sweat off his palm before taking it. His eagerness blunted a bit when he read the title, however.

A Comprehensive Treatise on Glasskin and Their Ways.

Ben turned the book to gauge the number of pages. *Comprehensive, huh? Must not be much to chew on.* He raised it for Jared to see.

"Whatcha pick this one for?"

Jared tapped his head again, and then tapped the book cover.

"Somethin' in here? Somethin' you … or Destin knew?"

The hybrid frowned at the book, then shrugged, as if uncertain why he'd given it to Ben in the first place.

"Guess while we're here, anythin' else you wanna show me?"

Jared scanned the vault, but shook his head.

Ben tucked the book under his right stub, and then took hybrid in a one-armed hug.

"You're a good kiddo, Jared. Just stay that way, a'ight?"

Jared cocked his head, confused. Ben placed the book in a pocket, retrieved his mop and then guided them out the way they'd come. The tunnel led out into the main chamber, which they exited, heading toward Jared's containment room. They walked in silence while Ben's thoughts ran down a dozen different avenues.

Glasskin? That was window-watcher business. Why would they have anything to do with janitors and the Sewers? Another mystery to tackle, if it wasn't an entirely false trail. He trusted Jared, but who knew how jumbled his knowledge was? Still, he appreciated the kid's effort. He shouldn't have slacked on visits. Needed to make that up to him.

They had to duck into closets and side rooms a couple times to let Cleaners pass by, but otherwise they faced no opposition in getting Jared back. When they reached a glassway, the hybrid shuffled in place, obviously not wanting to return to his room.

"You sure you can pop back in without bein' spotted?" Ben asked.

Jared grabbed Ben in another hug, his arms like wire bands strapped around him. Ben coughed a laugh as he pried free.

"No more stallin'. And thankya for this." He patted the book in its pocket. "Whatever it's for."

A shout whirled him around to see a handful of Cleaners racing their way.

"There he is! Get him!"

Jared moaned and tugged on Ben's arm, but Ben shook him off and pointed at the glassway.

"Get goin'. I can slog it faster without worryin' about you. Stay in your room until Dani or I fetch you."

With a final anguished look, Jared dove through the portal. Ben glanced down to where the hall split and then back at the Cleaners charging from the opposite direction. He fixed his destination in his mind.

"Carl, I'm sure hopin' you're still 'round somewhere."

Setting his jaw, he sprinted away, enraged coworkers on his heels.

CHAPTER
TWENTY-ONE

Dani supported Laurel's weight as they staggered down the stairs. Corpseflies buzzed about them, nipping and seeking entrance into their flesh, but the maid had re-secured her mask and the main swarm remained upstairs for the moment. The sound of even more pods bursting open followed them until the women nearly collapsed on the main floor.

Laurel breathed hard as Dani tried to formulate a plan. Her mind felt aflame as she considered and discarded half a dozen courses of action. Her power surged within her, wanting release, wanting to lash through the house in a wave of destruction. She clamped down and refused to let it take control.

The best thing would be to get Laurel out of the house and safe in the van, and then come back to retrieve Lucy and Hardy. The fact that the other Cleaners hadn't emerged from the basement made her dread what she'd find down there.

Turning the corner to the main hall, Dani stumbled to a halt. The front door had been replaced by a black pane of glass. The obsidian mirror blended with the walls the same as in the master bedroom. No getting out of the house the usual way.

They backtracked to the living room, swatting flies down by the dozens with each swipe. She halted on seeing the windows—

including the one they'd broken on entry—also having been sealed by the black glass. A dash through the kitchen revealed the sliding glass doors to the patio transformed as well, and she didn't doubt every other potential exit had been similarly blocked.

Trapped. And she'd dropped her squeegee in the panic upstairs. The sound of the growing corpsefly swarm made her balk at running to retrieve it. The upper level appeared engulfed by a green roiling cloud. The buzzing ground at her ears while the stink of manure clogged her sinuses.

Maybe Malawer had some secret escape tunnel in the basement. Dani could only hope. They couldn't leave without Lucy and Hardy anyways.

"We've got to get to the basement," she shouted over the noise of the flies.

Laurel nodded. She kept one hand pressed to her stomach, and Dani tried not to imagine what she might be feeling with the corpsefly crawling around in there.

When Dani headed for the basement stairs, however, hundreds of corpseflies swept into the kitchen and engulfed them. Their mandibles clicked and cut. Their legs scratched and both women dropped to their knees by the sink to try and get below the chaos.

Her and Laurel's screams were lost in the cacophony, and she needed no other encouragement to loose the storm she'd been building. The energies swept out of her, leaving her stunned and breathless.

Water spouted from the sink and hit the ceiling. Lights bulbs sizzled and popped, and jagged sparks shot out of every electrical socket. The water spread, mingled with the electrical arcs and, within moments, formed black clouds lit from within by lightning strikes.

Thunder rolled through the kitchen and dining room. Dani pushed Laurel to the floor as the storm broke.

Black storm clashed with green swarm. Lightning crackled, burning hundreds of the insects down with each flash and spark. Thunder buffeted like auditory fists, and the rain drowned any corpseflies that survived these first attacks.

After a few minutes of this, the thunderstorm died away into a drizzle. Insect corpses bobbed in the three inches of water on the floor, and a waterfall cascaded from the sink. A sweet smell of wet grass cleared away the manure stench as Dani splashed to her feet. Corpseflies crunched under her boots as she helped Laurel up.

"I've never seen a Catalyst's powers in person before," the maid said, wide-eyed as she surveyed the waterlogged house. "It's kinda …"

"Scary?"

"Cool."

Dani sniffed a laugh. "Yeah, well—"

Every wall on the main floor bubbled between one blink and the next. More green pods swelled into being.

Dani groaned. "You've got to be kidding me."

Laurel gasped and bent over, clutching her stomach. Dani clutched her arms to keep her from dropping to the floor.

"The fly?" she asked. "Bad?"

Laurel nodded, lips pressed tight. "Hurts." She bared her teeth. "I think … think it's …"

"Don't talk," Dani said. "We'll get you taken care of. Come on."

They splashed out of the kitchen. Pods burst all around them, but the remnants of Dani's storm kept the corpseflies from taking to the air immediately. They pounded down the steps to the basement, past a laundry room and toward the door into the main room.

Dani barged through, dragging Laurel along with her.

Lucy and Hardy spun from where they'd been inspecting a section of a brick wall. Lucy ran at them, shouting.

"Don't shut the—"

Dani turned and slammed the door shut right as a second wave of corpseflies flew toward her. Only then did she realize her mistake as the door sealed over from the inside.

Lucy stumbled to a halt. Her outstretched hand dropped. "— door," she finished. She slapped her thigh. "Great, girlie, now we're all trapped down here."

"Excuse us," Dani said as she navigated Laurel to a crate set in a corner of the basement. "Just trying to escape a swarm of corpseflies Malawer set loose on us. Sorry we didn't knock and give the secret password."

"Can it," Lucy said. "While I'm glad to see you're both fine—"

"Laurel's not so fine, actually. Swallowed a corpsefly before we could get down here. How do we get rid of it?"

Hardy rushed to her sister, while Lucy's expression turned bleak.

"Muck and buckets. This just keeps getting better."

"It was just one," Dani said.

"One is enough. What happened upstairs?"

As Dani related the events in the master bedroom, she checked out this section of the basement. No windows along the bricked-up walls. A mold-spotted concrete floor with crusty drains set in a row from one end to the other. Cardboard boxes and plastic tubs had been stacked in the corners, some of them marked *Trophies*, *Christmas Ornaments*, and *Photo Albums*. Other crates had arcane glyphs scorched into the wood, alongside hieroglyphics and Roman numerals.

A workbench crowded one side of the room, stacked with a wide variety of medical equipment. Microscopes, cryostats, blood tubing, clamps, scalpels, tissue processors, and more Dani didn't have any experience with yet. Racks of vials and tubes gleamed under the lights, and a mini-fridge had been stuck beneath the bench, where Malawer either kept chilled samples or maybe a favorite brew.

The construction at the far end of the basement held her attention for the longest, mostly because if its composition of human bones. Ribcages and skulls formed the base, large enough for someone—a sacrifice, maybe?—to lie on. Above this, femurs, humeri, and vertebrae had been wired together into twin arches that crisscrossed at the peak, where a skull leered down at the room. The four posts of the altar had been decorated with identical bone sculptures: a staff made of spines, with pairs of rib-wings flaring from the top. Finger bones formed the bodies of twin snakes which coiled around the staff to where shoulder blades had been set as their pointed heads at the top.

"Then they all went off for a family picnic and left us for the flies," she said, finishing her story along with the scan of the place. "This basement looks like a sacrificial pit."

"Kind of," Lucy said. "Hardy thinks it's more of a lab. But sacrifices were probably involved."

"I've interned at labs before. They don't use human remains to spruce up the joint."

"Those kinds of labs also aren't geared toward experimenting with Pure and Corrupt energies. Whatever Malawer is up to, my bet is it started here. We were trying to get a sense of the work he did before we got locked in."

Dani pointed to the larger bone decorations—the winged, serpent-twined staffs. "I'm confused. Aren't those symbols for medicine?"

"Actually, no," Hardy said from across the room. She had clasped her sister to her chest and rocked gently as she talked. "It's a caduceus. Lots of people think it's for medicine, but it's really a twisted thing when you know the truth. A wicked talisman in the wrong hands. The real symbol of medicine is called the Rod of Asclepius. It's just a single snake coiled around a stick."

Dani and Lucy stared at the maid, who held Laurel more tightly.

"I didn't take you for a mythology buff," Dani said. Of course, she hadn't taken them for rodeo champions either.

Hardy blushed. "Mr. Lopez has been teaching us some. He knows a lot. Real smart. And sweet."

Lucy took another look at the altar. "She's not talking mythology, either. Most of the aspects of Roman and Greek gods can be traced to earlier incarnations of the Pure and Corrupt Pantheons."

Dani moved near enough to the altar to sense the Corrupt energies infesting it. With the skull on top, it was hard to ignore the feeling that the altar watched them.

"Why's it so important that this is ... what'd you call it?"

"A caduceus," Hardy said.

"And the other thing?"

"The Rod of Asclepius."

"Yeah. Why the distinction?"

Hardy pursed her lips in recollection. "Mr. Lopez said a caduceus was a symbol of Hermes. Hermes was the patron of thieves and liars, and also the guy who took dead people down into the Underworld. Asclepius was all about healing and medicine, but today nobody realizes the difference. It got all confused after a while."

"So the caduceus is connected with bad mojo and death. Obviously someone remembers." Dani looked to Lucy. "Think this will help us?"

The janitor sucked through her teeth. "Maybe. But none of it'll do any good so long as we're stuck down here."

Laurel jerked in Hardy's arms and choked a cry. Dani and Lucy ran over to help Hardy hold her sister down as she bucked a few times, eyelids fluttering. Once she calmed, though with shuddering breaths, Dani noted the rapid pulse of the veins along her neck.

"What's it doing to her?"

"Eating or laying," Lucy said. "Corpseflies usually go for the heart first. Arteries are especially tasty. Either that or lay a bunch of eggs inside her that'll hatch and spread the swarm."

Dani gripped one of Laurel's hands and squeezed. "We can stop it, right? A handyman can get the bug out?"

Hardy looked to Lucy, who sighed. "Probably. But—"

"We still have to get out of here. Right." Dani scowled at the black mirror which blocked the exit. "I'm guessing you tried to radio HQ."

"Sure did. We're cut off. And these mirrors, even if they are some sort of new Scum passage, don't react to us."

"Dig out?"

Lucy shook her head. "These walls are reinforced, Scum-slicked with some defensive spells. No chanted blade makes a dent."

Dani paced the basement, staying clear of the altar and its corrosive aura. Finally she turned to the others and rolled her head to pop her neck.

"All right, ladies. That leaves the rough road out."

"What're you thinking?" Lucy asked, a disapproving squint already in place.

Dani lightly punched a wall. "I'm gonna crack this house open like an eggshell."

"And crush us in the process. Catalyst powers are hardly discriminatory toward friend or foe."

"Unless you want to watch Laurel get eaten alive or wait until Malawer triggers another trap, I don't see many other choices."

She and Lucy faced off until Hardy reached to the janitor.

"Please, Miss Lucy? Let her try?"

Lucy plucked at an eyebrow hard enough Dani thought she might tear it off.

"Fine," she said at last. "Do it. But for muck's sake, just don't let it get out of hand."

Dani grinned. "Yessir."

"How are you going to do this?"

"Just tear a simple crack through the basement and onto the lawn. We crawl free, get Laurel to the van, and zip out of here before any neighbors call the authorities."

Lucy snorted. "Simple. Sure." Another shake of her head. "Where do you want us?"

"Over in that corner is fine," Dani said, pointing to where Laurel and Hardy sat. Lucy joined them, while Dani went to one knee in the middle of the room and stuck her palms to the floor.

Taking a deep breath, she shut her eyes. Before she woke her power, she first worked on subduing the distractions. Concentration and willpower were essential to forming a spell. If she just threw raw energy into the elements, they would either collapse into a useless tangle of power or explode into an uncontrolled disaster that could wipe out the neighborhood. Kind of unproductive when her job put a high priority on saving lives.

She cleared her mind of the rising panic at Laurel's condition, and the sneaking guilt at being the cause of it. She ignored the rotten cheese smell permeating the basement and the cold waves flowing off the altar. She stopped listening to Lucy's heavy breathing and Laurel's whimpers. She pushed aside the sticky feeling of her jumpsuit, the damp plastic gloves, and squeak of her rubber boots. All of it went to the background as she honed her focus into a razor line.

Dani made herself the core of the spell, tying the cords of power to herself so she could cut them off at the proper instant. When the energies were anchored, she sent her senses out into the elements along with her power.

Glowing lines of energy bled out of her and into the ground. They dove into the earth, and she gave herself another few minutes to get a sense for how the dirt and rocks would shift. *We just need an escape route*, she told herself. *Let's avoid getting buried alive, shall we?*

At last, she felt ready. To her broadened senses, it felt like she clutched the house foundation in an enormous fist, ready to squeeze—but not to crush, so long as she maintained control.

Then, right as she prepared to activate the spell, the altar woke.

A cord of virulent purple energy lashed out from it and coiled around the lines of power she'd set through the earth. She gasped as her bones went frigid, and it felt like tiny ice bullets shot through her.

Lucy called out, sounding distant. "Dani?"

The magic within the altar pulsed and then retracted into a sucking void. She nearly fell flat as it sucked her Pure energies into itself. She shouted in denial as the altar leeched off the spell, draining it into a bottomless pit.

Her concentration wavered until she held onto the power by mental fingernails, refusing to let it be stripped from her. *This belongs to me!* she mentally cried. *You don't have the right to take it!* She'd fought to tame her volatile abilities, she wasn't about to let some pile of bones get the better of her!

All at once, the altar released its grip. The energy flooded free, snapping back into the spell she'd created. A magical backlash tore through her mind and soul, and the icy sensation burned away in the face of an internal heat wave.

For a moment, Dani thought of the furnace the Cleansers had placed her inside, attempting to transform her into a goddess of fire. She recalled the intense heat, the blaze which tried to sear her to the core.

The memory turned to ash as the fire built again, but inside her. It clawed along her spine and dug in to her shoulders, making her clench and shudder with unrestrained fury. The basement shook with her, and she dug her fingers into the floor, barely realizing her hands and knee had formed imprints in the concrete, as if her density had magnified.

"Dani, stop!"

Something shoved her away. As she briefly lost contact with the floor, so she did with the spell as well. The power she'd fed into it dropped deep into the earth, beyond her reach.

Fury soared as the heat stitched into the surface of her skin and tugged her into motion. Sulfuric fumes smothered her, and Dani found herself no more able to control her actions than if she'd been rolled up in a carpet and tossed into a lake of fire.

Her body rolled out of the hit. She stood, seeking her attacker. A stout woman stood nearby, yelling and waving her arms.

Lucy, her brain told her.

Threat, cried the flames. *Enemy. Hated one.*

The heel of her palm slammed into the janitor's face. Lucy stumbled back. Blood spurted from her nose and lips.

With that blow, Dani's rage puffed away. The threads of heat unraveled and left her in control and shocked at her violence. Lucy stared at her, a hand to her face. In the corner, Hardy cradled Laurel, eyes averted from the others.

Dani snatched for something, anything to explain, but the altar's attack and subsequent fit of rage had her thoughts jumbled.

"I ... I didn't mean ..."

"What've you done?" Lucy words came out garbled as she licked blood from her teeth and pinched her nostrils shut.

"It wasn't me! The altar ... it—"

Another rumble staggered them. Tools rattled on the workbench. Dani yanked Lucy clear as a crate fell from a pile to crunch on the floor where she'd been standing. As they stumbled back to the twin maids, the floor lurched. Grinding noises rose, and the ceiling shook as furniture crashed above.

A corner of the basement crumbled and fell away into a wedge of darkness. A loamy smell filled the basement, making Dani think of earthworms and mud. The Cleaners braced as the basement shifted, as if the house foundation had turned into a waterbed. The bricked walls bowed inward as the floor sagged, buckled, and rent.

The crack split the basement in half, cracked the outer wall, and widened into a V-shaped cleft in the earth with grass fringing the top. Dani rejoiced as sunlight streamed into the filthy place. She got behind the other Cleaners and pushed them into motion.

"Go, go! Quick!"

Lucy shoved Hardy, who shoved Laurel ahead of her up the incline.

As Dani moved to follow, another crack split off from the first and cut across her path. Both splits in the floor widened a few feet, and Dani found herself balancing like a surfer as the section she stood on raised and lowered.

When Lucy reached ground level, she turned back and saw Dani trapped on her side.

"Hold on, girlie. We'll get something to pull you out."

Dani reeled like a drunken surfer as the floor continued to lose solidity. The original hole expanded, crumbling more of the foundation, and the ceiling tilted, revealing more of the sky as the house fell in on itself.

She dodged as timber and tiles collapsed into the growing pit. With a clatter of bones, the altar slid and fell. The skull gave a final leer as if to say, *See you soon.* A bed plunged past. Wood and metal chips sprayed the side of her face as it struck the edge of her slab before it disappeared into the earth.

Dropping to hands and knees, she crawled backward as the floor continued to dissolve, leaving little room to maneuver. The walls of what had been the basement were now bare earth, curving around as if the ground had become a toilet bowl the house was being flushed down.

The speed of deterioration increased, and Dani sensed her lone support decaying beneath her. Panic threatened to seize her, but she pushed herself to stand. No time to wait for the others. If she didn't try to escape now, she'd be lost.

Across the increasing gap, a strip of broken concrete remained embedded in the earth. A potential ledge where Dani could cling until Lucy dropped a lifeline.

Terror gripped her lungs and squeezed as she gauged the unlikely landing pad and the nothingness below. But it was better than standing there until she hadn't a pebble left to jump off.

Heart slamming against her ribs, tongue choking the back of her throat, she gathered herself and leapt the crevasse. She bruised breasts, stomach, and thighs as she slammed into the ledge. The ragged stone scraped under her arms, and she cried out as one shoulder popped and almost made her lose her grip. Fingernails cracked as she dug in. Her feet kicked over emptiness.

"Hang on," someone cried from above.

"Hurry," she whispered.

The earth trembled. The ledge tore from the dirt. As she dropped, she snatched for something, anything to arrest her fall. Her hand came away with a dirt clod as she tumbled backward and into the abyss.

Something whipped around her waist and she jerked to a stop. Gravity reasserted itself as she swung and slammed her head and injured shoulder into the earthen walls. Warmth dribbled down her scalp. She tasted blood as she bit her tongue and cheeks to keep from screaming.

She hung there, trembling and staring down into darkness while one hand touched whatever had caught her. Turning her head revealed a stretch of green rubber leading back up and over the edge of the lawn.

A garden hose, tied in lasso fashion, had looped around her. She jerked as whoever held the other end dragged her upward. A grunt from Lucy.

"This girl is heavy. A little help, ladies?"

Air stirred around her, and a cushion of swirling wind lifted her. It wavered, however, and bumped her against the sides, so by the time she reached the top, mud smeared her suit and she spat pebbles and bits of roots.

The conjured wind tossed her over the edge and deposited her by two pairs of boots. Hardy threw her end of the hose aside and gave a wavering grin as Lucy helped Dani to her feet.

"I'd hug you," Dani said, holding her arm to her side, "but I'm kind of a mess."

Hardy bit her lower lip and grabbed Dani into a lung-popping squeeze. She clenched her teeth as her shoulder protested further, but she let the maid support her so her legs wouldn't give out in relief.

Once a scrap of strength returned, Dani got free and turned to survey the damage. She gaped.

The Cleaners had emerged onto what had once been the doctor's backyard, but none of the house remained. A massive sinkhole had opened and sucked down every last bit, including the garage and portions of neighboring fences. Dani limped over and peered into the depths, unable to see so much as a remnant board or brick. Her stomach flopped as she thought about how close she'd come to joining the rest of the rubble. Lucy stood beside her, arms crossed as she studied the hole.

"There goes any evidence we might've used to figure this thing out," she said.

Dani didn't look at the team leader, not wanting to see the blame in Lucy's eyes—or the bloody nose she'd given her. Then she remembered the stack of papers she'd stuffed into her pants pocket. A quick check revealed them rumpled, but intact.

"Maybe not," she said, zipping the pocket. "But first, we have to get Laurel to a handyman."

Returning to the twins, Lucy grabbed Laurel's feet and Hardy took her arms, and Dani trotted alongside as they hustled the maid around to the van and laid her in the back. Several house owners and family members had emerged from their homes to stare. Some pointed the Cleaners' way, but few seemed to notice their departure, with most of the attention focused on the sinkhole.

Dani threw herself into the driver's seat and didn't even give the others a chance to buckle in before pounding the gas pedal to the mat. Johnny the security guard was about to lose one of his precious gates.

CHAPTER
TWENTY-TWO

Ben peeked around the corner. Had he lost his pursuers?

A sponge whizzed past his face and struck the wall. Water burst from the sponge in balls, pelting hard enough to drive him to one knee. He caught himself with the mop, pushed back, and took off again as the furious cries of the other Cleaners followed.

Ain't the answer I was wantin', but at least it's one.

Panting from a marathon sprint through sections of HQ he never knew existed, Ben pumped his legs faster as his calves and hamstrings burned. How much further? Of all the times to be routed the long way to a destination, it had to be when maddened coworkers snapped at his tail.

A figure jumped out of a side room and into his path. Ben glimpsed wild eyes and a plunger readied to swing. He thrust the mop out like a spear and caught the plumber in the solar plexus. Another strike dropped the man. Ben paused to snatch the radio from his belt. Fingers grasped his uniform, but he pulled free and he ran on.

Struggling to keep hold of both mop and radio with one hand, Ben dashed along, trying to increase his lead. At last he came to a door that glowed with a soft green light, *Maintenance* stenciled on the center of it. He slapped a hand to the door and mentally ordered it to open.

Nothing happened. After another unsuccessful attempt, Ben hit the door with the mop and shouted.

"Lopez! Open up, *mi amigotomato*. Trouble brewin'."

The door remained shut, and Ben wondered if Maintenance had been locked down like Supplies. If so, where could he go?

As he turned to consider alternate paths, his chasers ran into sight. On seeing him, they slowed to a prowl, hyenas stalking a wounded gazelle. Ben checked around for Carl but saw no sign. Perhaps he'd outrun the watery sprite. Whatever the case, he stood alone.

Sighing, he clipped the radio to his belt and readied the mop.

"C'mon, fellas," he said. "Can't we chat about this? Beatin' up coworkers ain't no way to get a promotion, lemme tell you."

Their pace quickened, spurred by having him cornered.

He struck a pose, determined to go down swinging.

"A'ight then. To the pain."

He caught one in the face as they closed the gap, but then hunched to protect his sensitive spots as they fell on him, eschewing any magical attacks in exchange for a knuckle-to-bone beating. Ben choked as a knee rammed a nerve in his leg. He tried to fend off five strikes at once. A plunger whacked him across the shoulders. He tripped another, but took a kick to the face in exchange.

"Oy!"

Ben's attackers paused at the cry. He glanced between their legs to see another group stride into view. Dani led the way, her uniform muddy, her expression a mix of shock and outrage. She charged in unison with Lucy. The two women crashed into the other Cleaners, wielding mops like battle axes. The attackers resisted at first, but when Ben recovered and added his assault, they broke and fled.

A semblance of peace crept back into the area, disturbed only by soft weeping which drew Ben's attention to the two women who'd hung back. He recognized the Borrelia twins, a team of maids he'd heard plenty about but never had a chance to work with. The crying one clung to the other's arm, her face tight with pain, looking ready to collapse. What had happened out on the job?

Dani turned to Ben. "What'd I warn you about telling too many dirty jokes, huh?"

"Weren't my fault," Ben said. "Folks here in HQ have hopped on the same crazy-go-round those other maids were ridin'."

"It's spreading?" Lucy asked.

"Yeah it—son of a rabid rabbit, Lu, what happened?" Ben stared at the blood smeared across her nostrils, lips, and cheeks. "You try to head-butt your reflection again?"

Lucy scowled and scrubbed a sleeve across her messy face. "Your apprentice happened."

Dani returned the woman's glare with a stubborn clench to her jaw.

"She ain't my apprentice no more," Ben said, uncertain about the tension between the two women. He instinctively wanted to come to Dani's defense, but the guilt in the Catalyst's eyes made him wonder what had really gone on.

"Well, maybe she should be." Lucy's face reddened. "She's obviously not ready for field work."

Dani made fists. "I told you the whole way here, I wasn't in control. The altar did something to me; ratcheted up my anger to the nth degree and just made me lose it."

"Altar?" Ben echoed.

Lucy stepped in, bringing the women close enough to breathe each other's increasingly forceful huffs.

"Because of you, we no longer have a house to sweep. We could've figured out what Malawer was doing, but now anything useful is falling to the center of the earth and we barely escaped with our lives."

"Wait." Ben held his hand out. "What exactly happened to the house?"

"I know you're upset about this going on your record or whatever," Dani said, "but tossing all the blame onto my shoulders doesn't mean you were any less responsible, oh fearless team leader."

Lucy's haymaker caught Dani on the ear and made her drop her mop. After clutching her head, Dani shrieked and lunged, fingers outstretched as if to scratch her initials into Lucy's forehead. Lucy coiled for another punch.

Even as Ben moved to intercede, a yellow-green glow suffused both women, who froze. They appeared paralyzed except for the flickers of their eyes, where panic slipped in to replace the rage that had been flaring there.

Ben looked over his shoulder. Lopez stood before the now-open door to Maintenance. He'd raised a hand to each woman, who continued to twitch in the confines of the quarantine spell.

"Get them inside." Lopez nodded Ben to the Borrelia sisters. "I will handle these two."

Ben went to the twins and coaxed them into the chamber while Lopez manipulated the quarantine fields to march Lucy and Dani in after them.

Examination and recovery beds lined the walls, with several contained by privacy curtains. Another handyman emerged from one of these and hustled into the back, where more severe injuries were tended. A wash station sat in one corner alongside cabinets of medical supplies.

"Where's everyone gone off to?" Ben lowered his voice as it echoed. With the violence the Cleaners faced on a daily basis, it wasn't abnormal for every bed to be filled as handymen moved from patient to patient.

"My colleagues have been called to deal with injury reports throughout HQ," Lopez said. "People are not coming to be tended here as they should. Rather, the fighting spreads, and we have had to quell several suicide attempts. I only remained here on the Chairman's orders. It seemed he anticipated your and the team's troubles and set me to watch for you."

"Lucky he did." Ben set his mop aside. "Any of your folks actin' funny?"

"Not that I am aware. Tension is high, of course, but so far, my fellow handymen appear stable."

"Anybody figured out what's causin' all this ruckus?"

"If they have, they've elected to leave me in the dark."

Ben nodded at the frozen women. "How 'bout we pop the seal? I think they've cooled their heels enough."

Lopez studied Dani and Lucy for a long minute and then lowered his hands. The women animated, stumbling a bit until their captured momentum abated. Lucy turned her back to the others while Dani glared at the men.

"What the muck was that?" she demanded.

"Low level quarantine spell," Ben said. "Normally we use 'em to keep folks sittin' pretty until we can figure out how to keep 'em from spreadin' contagionisms."

Dani shook herself. "Felt like having a blood transfusion from a snowman."

"Ain't fun at all now, is it? Now you play nice, ladies, otherwise Lopez will stick you in time-out again." He caught Lucy's eye. "And since when has fist-fightin' been your way of dealin' with a job gone bad, anyhoo? If you both wanted to go at it, at least let me getcha a coupla pillows first."

Lucy and Dani exchanged shamed looks. The janitor broke the silence first.

"Sorry, girlie. It wasn't—"

"Wasn't you." Dani recovered some poise. "I know. So can we call a truce and promise no more bloody noses for either of us? We've still got to get Laurel looked at."

Lucy nodded, then went off to the wash station and wetted a rag to clean her face. While she mopped up, Dani related everything that had happened at the doctor's house to Ben and Lopez. The handyman had pulled back one sleeve to reveal a rosary on his wrist, which he thumbed through. He stopped at the wooden cross to rub it between his fingers.

His expression grew grave as Dani told of Laurel swallowing the corpsefly, and he stopped her before she went further with the story.

"This must be tended immediately," he said. "You should've told me that first."

Laurel had already been laid out on one of the beds. Hardy stood on one side and held her sister's hand. Dani took her other hand, while Ben and Lucy stood at the foot of the bed. The handyman ran his hands over the maid, palms an inch from touching, the rosary cross brushing her uniform. He stopped in the middle of her chest, and a green aura popped into existence around her. Laurel sucked in a breath and her face tightened.

"We're right here, sis," Hardy whispered. "Everything's going to be spiffy."

"The fly is in the chest cavity," Lopez said. "There is more foreign mass than should be accounted for a single creature, so I must assume it is laying eggs."

"You can get it all out, right?" Dani asked.

Lopez closed his eyes and flexed his shoulders. "May my gift be sufficient for this task."

The green aura his hands emitted narrowed to beams which shot from each finger into Laurel's body, like mystical scalpels and tweezers. He manipulated these with the practiced mastery of a concert pianist. Laurel shifted and moaned as he plucked one spot, prodded another.

As he worked, he spoke softly to himself. While Ben didn't know much Spanish, the rhythm of Lopez's words reminded him of a common prayer from the few times he'd been to church as a kid.

"Padre nuestro, que estás en el cielo, santificado sea tu nombre. Venga tu reino, hágase tu voluntad en la tierra como en el cielo."

"You're Catholic?" Dani asked, interrupting the prayer.

"Princess, what'd I tell you 'bout bumpin' around this kinda work?" Ben asked.

"Let him work, girlie," Lucy said.

Lopez shook his head. "It's all right." He smiled slightly while his hands never stopped moving. "So long as she doesn't intrude on the flow of energies, talking is not a disturbance."

"What?" Ben sputtered. "But way back when, you told me talkin' while you was workin' was gonna kill you and your patient both."

"That's because you kept trying to tell me rather awful knock-knock jokes while I was healing." Lopez made a face. "That's a whole new form of pain I simply can't bear, nor do I want the people I'm caring for exposed to it while they're already suffering."

Ben scowled. "Everyone's gotta be a critic."

The handyman's gaze flicked to Dani. "To answer your question, I was raised Catholic, yes."

Her brow furrowed. "So when you pray, are you actually trying to talk to God or the Pantheon?"

"The prayer is more of a meditative tool in the moment," he said. "It helps me focus. But no, I doubt the Pantheon heeds anything like prayers."

"Then why bother?"

"Because I believe my powers are a gift, and whenever one is given a gift, one should express thanks in return, or at least recognition."

"But you just said you weren't praying to the Pantheon."

Lopez's smile turned knowing. "Where does our power come from, Dani?"

"Hoo boy," Ben said. "Now you've gone and done it, princess. Just opened up a whole can of worms the size of pythons. We're talkin' mega-worms that could gulp you down without blinkin'. And you just done let 'em out of the can."

This time, Lucy elbowed him hard.

Dani squinted in concentration. "Our power comes from the Pantheon, of course. I've learned that much."

"Yes," said Lopez. "And what is the Pantheon?"

She looked to Ben, as if fearing being caught by a trick question. He splayed his hands in an *I warned you* gesture.

Dani strung the words out slowly, as if afraid she'd get docked points if she got it wrong. "They're the embodiment of the forces of Purity and Corruption in the world."

"Also correct. And who, or what, brought those forces into existence in the first place?"

"Uh ..." Dani's forehead wrinkled further. "Maybe the Force made the forces?"

"Sorry, girlie." Lucy crossed her arms. "The Force is up there with zombies, werewolves, and vampires. You won't find them anywhere in this reality."

Lopez twitched a finger and the intensity of the green aura around Laurel increased. "So what else would you consider as an option?"

"Never really thought about it," Dani said. "Of course, I didn't even know the whole Pantheon existed until recently, either. Still trying to wrap my head around them. Could they be aliens?"

Ben laughed. "Careful with the E.T. talk. You're gonna find most handymen are a bit more touchy-feely about their work than the rest of us common folk. Somethin' about fiddlin' with people's innards gets 'em all misty-eyed."

"Life is a sacred thing," Lopez murmured, "yet so fragile. I am honored to have been given the skill to tend those too weak or injured to help themselves."

Ben waggled his brows at Dani and mouthed, *See?*

She frowned back, and he had the sudden impression she'd been insulted by his cavalier attitude. She'd never mentioned any religious or spiritual leanings before.

"Wherever it all really comes from," she said, turning back to Lopez, "I kind of wish I'd been given your ability. It'd be a big help with med school."

"Not all physicians are handymen and not every handyman is a physician," he said. "Though the two have always been closely intertwined. Depending on the age and culture you consider, we have been called shamans, druids, medicine men, and many other things—some not as positive. We were among the Egyptians and Greeks and Romans as the earliest physicians. A portion of modern doctors have at least some small ability to induce healing through Pure energies, even if they aren't consciously aware of it."

Dani looked disturbed by this. "What's that mean for people who have the ability to cause natural disasters wherever they go? Are we what you protect the world from?"

Lopez's hands paused and he frowned. Ben came around and drew Dani away, though she moved grudgingly.

"Be right back, folks," he told the others.

Behind them, Lopez resumed praying. *"Padre nuestro, que estás en elcielo. Santificado sea tu nombre ..."*

"Wanna tell me what's eatin' atcha?" Ben asked once they got far enough away.

"Nothing's eating me, but a bug is eating her." She pointed an elbow at Laurel. "And it's my fault. Lucy's right. I'm not ready for this. Maybe I'm too destructive to ever be ready."

"It was your first official job, princess. No one's first job ever goes smoothly, I guarantify it. I gotta tell you about my first run-in with dust bunnies sometime."

She sighed. "Maybe. It just makes me doubt whether I'm cut out for this kind of work. The Cleaners are all about getting rid of messes, while I just end up making them and ..." She stared at her palms as if trying to read her fate there. "Ben, who am I here?"

His thoughts stuttered to a standstill. "Uh ... didn't I warn you 'bout lettin' them metafornicatin' mega-worms chew on your noggin'?"

"I really hope you mean *metaphorical.*"

"These are all questions I'm never thinkin' about until I've got at least three beers in my belly. So, unless you got a six pack handy ..."

She smirked, but the humor puffed away. She met his gaze, green eyes dulled by doubt. At least it wasn't the rage from before, but it still didn't seem like her usual self.

"Seriously, Ben. Who am I? Who do you see me as?"

He gripped her shoulder, trying to help her feel grounded, to know she didn't stand alone in her struggles.

"You're Dani," he said. "You're a Cleaner, a good kid, and the occasional pain in the rear."

Another brief smile before she bowed her head. "But am I Dani, the girl who's supposed to grow up and become a doctor? Dani the Catalyst? Dani the home wrecker?"

He chuckled and she grimaced, realizing what she'd said.

"I meant that last part literally."

"I wasn't suggestin' anythin' otherwise."

She scratched the back of her neck. "I guess I just wonder why I have these abilities. Am I meant to use them for something? Was I chosen to have them for a reason? What am I supposed to do?"

He waved between them as if warding off a stink. "What's this 's'posed to' and 'meant to' and 'chosen?' Talkin' 'bout things like purpose and destiny gets me thinkin' we're gonna gear up to go find some magical sword to defeat the dark lord in his gloomy old tower of nasty-wasty evil. It ain't like someone had you fill out a questionnaire while you was still in the womb and then stamped a job title on your soul. Your powers are just that. Your powers. Mebbe you wear the uniform and punch the time card, but it's still your choice to show up for work in the end."

"But this work is important to me," Dani said. "I care about this job and the people here. I want to do what I can to keep things safe and clean."

"And that's as good as puddin'. But if you start lettin' the Cleaners throw a shadow on your dreams, eventually they'll be eclipsed."

This time her smile stayed. "That was almost poetic, Ben."

He harrumphed. "Eclipsed was today's Word of the Day. Figured I oughta use it somewhere."

"I thought you chucked that calendar a long time ago."

"Mebbe I fibbed a bit about that part. But I mean this, princess. Never fix your whole life 'round your work."

"You have."

His brain recalled another Daily Word: *Touché*. "Sure, and see where it's got me? Look, a company's gonna fail you. A boss's gonna fail you. Your gear's gonna fail you. Sooner or later, everythin' and everyone is gonna get stripped away. Mebbe not forever, but you gotta know what'll be left standin' when it's just you versus the world."

She studied the floor, and Ben her spiky red hair as she considered what he'd said. Lopez's soft prayer floated over to them, a burble of words that teetered on the edge of music.

"Are you saying I should keep up with my doctor plans?" she asked at last. "Even though I'm more likely to break bones than set them?"

He squeezed her arm. "I'm sayin' you oughta remember it's not a choice the Cleaners should make for you. Or your folks for that matter."

Her eyes narrowed. "Have you been talking to them or something?"

He grinned. "Ooh. A nerve. I've heard about these. S'posed to be fun to hit."

"Bully."

"Whippersnapper."

"Old fart."

"Ballerina."

"Hey, you have been talking to my parents."

"Nope, but now I'm curious—"

"We need some help over here, guys," Lucy called.

They hurried back to find Lopez having repositioned himself by Laurel's head, his hands cupped like a bowl above her face. The maid's gaze flicked from each person as if seeking comfort from their presence.

"The eggs have been neutralized and the fly contained," Lopez said, "but I need you to restrain her. This next part will be ... uncomfortable."

Laurel pressed her lips into a thin line. Lopez brushed damp hair off her sweat-beaded forehead.

"Persevere, Miss Laurel. The pain will be temporary, I promise. The creature remains lodged within your chest cavity and I must draw it back out the way it came. Your flesh will knit itself together once it is removed."

Laurel swallowed hard, but nodded and clenched her eyes shut. Dani and Lucy each took a leg, while Ben and Hardy held the arms down. With a last look around, Lopez re-cupped his hands. The green aura poured out of them and into Laurel's mouth, forcing it wide as it entered her throat. Ben grimaced as her chest swelled and cartilage crackled.

Laurel shook all over, and everyone bent to the task of keeping her as still as possible.

Lopez clapped his hands together. A spasm tore through the maid, and Ben had to double his effort to keep her from ripping free. Tears poured down Hardy's face as she watched her sister struggle against the handyman's ministrations, but she didn't waver in keeping Laurel contained.

Laurel's jerking grew more violent, and twice she kicked hard enough that Lucy and Dani had to slam her legs back down. Ben's arm strained as he pressed almost his entire weight down along it. He glanced at Lopez. Fine lines of stress cracked the man's usual placid expression. Was something wrong? How much longer did he need?

At last, the line of green energy withdrew, and Laurel collapsed with a cry. The others fell back, though Dani and Hardy both rushed back in to hug Laurel. Lopez lifted his hands for everyone to see the emerald orb perched on his fingertips. The corpsefly hung within this like an insect in amber.

"Awful thing." He gestured to Ben. "Would you?"

Ben nodded, and Lopez lowered the corpsefly to the floor. Ben set his boot on the green bulb. When Lopez let his power vanish, the insect only got in a last flicker of wings before it was crushed beneath Ben's sole.

CHAPTER TWENTY-THREE

en scraped corpsefly guts off his boot while Dani and Hardy helped Laurel sit up. At Lopez's request, Lucy jogged over to get the maid a cup of water. Once she returned, Laurel took the cup in a shaky hand, swigged, swished, and then spat bloody water onto the remains of the corpsefly with vicious accuracy.

After draining the rest of the drink, she crushed the paper cup in one hand.

"When I see that doctor again," she said, "I'm going to hog-tie him before he can burp."

As everyone chuckled, Ben sensed hope sneaking back into the circle. It lifted his spirits to know not everyone had gone off the deep end. There were still some folks he could rely on, no matter how dark and confusing the situation became. Even the Borrelia sisters had a grit to them to see things through despite the hurt and tears. Perhaps they'd figure a way to cure whatever ailed the Cleaners after all.

While Lopez gave Laurel another look-over, Dani resumed her story, with Lucy interjecting at key parts.

"We get down to the basement," Dani said, "lock the corpseflies out, but realize one of those black mirrors sealed over the door behind us again."

"That's when she blew the house down while we three little pigs escaped by the hair of our chinny chin chins," Lucy said.

"That's not exactly how it happened." Dani rubbed her arms. "I worked a spell to crack the house foundation and give us an escape route. Before I triggered it, though, this altar did … something."

"That goin' in the official report?" Ben asked. "'Cause' Francis really don't take a shine to vulgariteness."

"*Vagueness.*" Dani looked to Lucy. "Does he do this on purpose?"

Lucy shrugged. "I've never been able to tell, honestly."

With a suspicious look Ben's way, Dani resumed her telling. "The altar tried to suck the spell away into itself, and I barely kept control. But when it let go, it was like it sent an emotional supercharge back down the line. This mindless rage just took over and had me ready to beat down the first person I saw."

"Like how the maids've been actin'," Ben said.

"Yeah, but it faded until we got back here." She and Lucy shared embarrassed looks.

"Did either of you ladies feel anythin' like that in the basement?" Ben asked the sisters.

The twins shook their heads.

"Nothing besides the usual heebies you get around Scum hideouts," Hardy said. "There were some massive Corrupt energies invested in the place, but nothing actively hostile as far as I could tell."

Lopez's eyes sparked with curiosity. "This altar. Describe it."

Even Ben got a cold knot in his stomach as Dani motioned about and traced the air, drawing an invisible outline of the bone altar, with its skull at the top and the strangely designed corner posts. How many innocents had Malawer sacrificed to build the thing? Patients from the hospital? Vagabonds off the streets? What was its purpose? He doubted it had anchored the core of whatever spell Malawer used to attack the Cleaners, as its destruction would've, or should've, undone the spell and negated the effects they still suffered under.

"So we figured these …" Dani looked at Hardy. "Cadu—sheesh?"

"Caduceus," Hardy said. "One stuck on each corner of the altar. Creeptastic. Dani thought it was a Rod of Asclepius but," she nodded to Lopez, "I told her what you taught us before. Was I right?"

Lopez pressed knuckles to his lips as he considered. "From what you've said, it seems to be the case." Hardy beamed while Lopez continued. "If so, it is intriguing. And disturbing."

"And important, I'm hopin'?" Ben asked.

"Likely. This Dr. Malawer does not strike me as the sort of man to build an entire altar imbued with Corrupt energies for nothing more than decoration."

"I dunno," Ben said. "I've seen stranger displays 'round here durin' Halloween. But we still ain't figured out who in the Corrupt Pantheon's got their claws in him. If it's a Petty, I've known a few who'll have their minions throw up false trails just to add to the clutter."

"I don't think that's what's going on here," Lucy said. "Everything in that basement looked connected, and that altar was the centerpiece."

"H'okay. So we figure out who the altar was built for and get the Chairman and Board to call down their biggest guns on 'em until they take back Malawer's toys and send him to bed cryin'."

"That presents a problem," Lopez said. "History muddles identity in this case. You can see both of the Pantheon's existence all the way back to the earliest civilizations. The Petty Hygiene? Both the Greeks and Romans worshiped a goddess known as Hygieia, and both civilizations took great strides in public health efforts, including building sewers, keeping water sources pure, and treating diseases in a more scientific manner. The Romans were even the first to consider things like microorganisms. Asclepius was the god of medicine and healing, and, I believe, the Primal Growth in earlier incarnations. The Pure Petties may have then been considered Meditrine, Hygeia, and Panacea.

"Miss Hardy was correct in linking the caduceus to Hermes." Lopez touched the maid's shoulder, and her eyes brightened. "While known as a herald of the gods, Hermes was also connected strongly to alchemy and transformative magics that could be used for good or ill."

Ben waved for Lopez to talk a little faster. The history lesson was fascinating, sure, but every minute spent discussing the

Cleaners' past was another minute HQ destabilized further. "And Hermes would be who now? Pollution? Pestilence? That don't sit right."

"That's the issue," Lopez said. "Hermes has never been directly linked to any one of them. If I were forced to single one out, I would say Hermes' actions mostly resembled those of the Primal Corruption, devoted to undermining and perverting that which is reliable and true."

Lucy jerked as if slapped. "You're saying we're going against Corruption itself?"

Lopez raised a hand. "You misunderstand. I only said that if I were forced to choose, but I believe the answer's more complicated. The Pantheon isn't a static thing, especially over millennia. Back then, their identities and actions could shift and merge. After years of study, I've concluded Hermes was a conglomerate. Facets of Primals and Petties we know today, perhaps from both Pantheons, combined into a single being by the people of the time."

"That's just dandy," Ben said. "If so, we got no idea who's stirrin' up the hornet's nest now."

Lopez drooped as he shed his scholarly air. "Without further evidence, no. We can't be certain."

"Hold on. Hold on. I salvaged these from the house." Dani flourished a bunch of papers, offering them to Ben. "Maybe someone else can make sense of them? Find a tie-in?"

He took them and frowned at the illegible handwriting. "This is so much scribble-scrabble to me." He passed them to Lopez, who read through them more slowly. "Why'd you snag these in particular?"

"When I first saw Malawer at the hospital," Dani said, "he was taking notes on the same kind of paper. I can read enough to see this has something to do with recent experiments, but no specifics."

Everyone held their breath as Lopez scanned the pages.

"His mind is in ruins, and his words are as crumbled and cracked to me as you." He caressed the papers as if trying to soothe them into revealing their secrets. "But I do sense echoes of the doctor's influence."

"Whatcha thinkin', Lopez?" Ben asked. "Try to snake the pipes a bit?"

The Maids of Wrath

"Do what?" Dani asked.

"Make a link between those pages and Malawer's shenanigans that fills in what we've been missin'."

"We can use these notes to figure out what Malawer's been doing?" she asked, looking concerned. "Isn't this trash magic divination? Like Stewart did? Please don't tell me we have to work with that rat again."

"It's kinda the same," Ben said, "but totally different."

Lucy whacked his shoulder. "Stop confusing the poor girl."

Dani perked up. "Actually, I get it. Stewart's trash magic wouldn't work here because Malawer never threw these pages away. They aren't garbage, just confiscated property."

Ben winked at Lucy. "Toldja she's smarter than I look." He refocused on Dani. "There's a buncha ways we can wade into the psychic muck that builds on items."

Dani's nose wrinkled. "Does it involve actual waders?"

He snaked his arm through the air. "Mebbe think of the doctor's mind as a lotta pipes. His thoughts flow through those pipes, makin' mental activity. These," he tapped the pages, "are an outlet. The good old doc poured out his thoughts and soaked those notes through. They ain't directly connected to him now, but they can still link back with the right handiwork."

"No good," Lucy said. "We don't have a plumber with us."

"Why do we need one?" Dani asked.

Lucy touched her own forehead. "Ben's talking about a variation of a technique the scrub-teams use to wipe us out from people's memories when we've attracted too much attention. Every team has a plumber who specializes in getting into people's mental pipes and extracting the memories we don't want flowing around in there." She waved around. "No plumber, no snaking the pipes."

Ben looked past Lopez to the deeper Maintenance wards. "There any plumbers bein' cared for in the back?"

Lopez shifted his stance like a knight readying to defend a castle gate. "Yes, but none are strong enough to manage such a thing without threatening their life."

Irritation crackled through Ben, and he struggled to keep it out of his voice. He'd forgotten how idealistic Lopez could be—usually at the most inconvenient ones.

"Lopez, this here's what you'd call an e—merge—ent—zee. Keepin' folks comfy can't be on top of the list."

The handyman's gaze remained steady. "They are my patients, Janitor Ben. I am bound to their recovery, and will not sacrifice their wellbeing for a possibly fatal divination attempt."

Ben waved his arm, barely hearing his blurted response. "They oughta be ready and willin' to give up their life for this company, like any of us."

"Ben!" Dani shouted. "You just told me—"

He chopped at her, and she wisely shut up. Ben stomped over to Lopez and stabbed at him with his eyes and hand.

"You really this much of a moron? For all your showin' off of those smarts for the pretty ladies, you can't even see how much trouble the Cleaners are in? That if this keeps gettin' worse, there may not be any Cleaners left to mop up the bodies?"

Lopez exhaled slowly through his nostrils. "I will not—"

Ben grabbed for the handyman's throat, ready to throw him to the floor and choke the infuriating stubbornness out of him.

Lopez shut his eyes resignedly, not even raising his aura. But a hand caught Ben's collar and yanked him back off his feet. He slammed to the floor, started to rise, but Lucy planted a boot in his stomach and scowled at him.

"Don't make me put effort into this, Ben. Just don't."

Ben jerked once more before falling back. The intensifying anger evaporated a second later, leaving him chilled to the core and aghast at his actions.

What'd he been doing? Attacking Lopez over a disagreement? What had made him so furious? For a moment, he'd seen the handyman as nothing more than an obstacle to be removed, an enemy to be defeated. A fight to be won at all costs, and burn the consequences.

He put his hand to his face, not wanting to see any of the others right then. "I'm … I'm fine. I'm fine. Sorry. Just got a little …"

"Out of control?" Dani asked. "Welcome to the club."

He sighed and forced himself to look around. Laurel and Hardy hugged each other tight, as if drawing strength from their closeness. Dani went through a quick routine of gel application while Lopez continued to watch Ben as if observing him from the other side of a window. At last he rolled to his side and pushed up.

"So it's happenin' to me, too. And here I was feelin' left out." He grimaced at Lopez. "Sorry."

"No need to apologize," Lopez said, relaxing slightly. "I can tell an imposed state from your normal self, well enough."

Ben nodded. "A'ight then. No plumber. How about tryin' a streaky mirror read? One of the maids could help if we got in touch with a window-watcher."

"Dangerous," Lopez said. "Performing that technique inside Headquarters risks exposing employees to contamination."

"Whatever's goin' on is already inside HQ and hittin' our people hard," Ben said. "A streaky mirror ain't gonna make us any more of a sittin' duck than we already are."

"We can't know that for sure," Lopez said, but Ben could see the uncertainty flickering in his eyes. "And if it doesn't work, we lose what little evidence we've gained."

"But we do know we're runnin' out of time,"Ben said. "The longer this goes, the worse it gets. I can't even guess why the bunch of us have lasted this long while most everyone else is goin' at it like rabid baboons."

Lopez opened his mouth—to raise a new objection, Ben didn't doubt—when a whisper interjected.

"Mr. Lopez? We'll help."

Everyone looked to Hardy, who smiled nervously in return. Lopez went to her and took her hand.

"Miss Hardy," he said, lilting her name with affection, "Don't feel compelled in this. There are other methods."

"Nobody's forcing her." Laurel stepped up beside her sister. "We're volunteering. Both of us."

"Are you—"

"We're sure," they said together.

A smile cracked his concern. Taking that as silent consent, Ben snatched his radio out and thumbed it on.

"Francis—"

"Already here."

Ben twitched at the near-instant response. "Cleanse me, it always grinds my gonads when you do that. Why didn't you holler our way before?"

"I had to finish corresponding with the Board and confirm the severity of the situation from my end."

"And what panic level are we sittin' at now?" Ben asked. "Should we all get a spare pair of underwear ready?"

"I've lost contact with both teams I sent out. The situation within HQ is deteriorating rapidly. Several divisions have been shut down, and the Board is trying to decide whether this warrants a full quarantine. Every Ascendant I've sent to subdue a violent outbreak has failed to report back."

"You ain't serious," Ben said. "Full quarantine? That's the only option the Board's smart enough to land on?"

"What's full quarantine mean?" Dani asked.

Lucy stared at Ben, who felt his face must mirror the disbelief on hers.

"If a full quarantine is enacted," Lucy said, "it's like a siege mode. Every Cleaner in HQ gets locked down like Lopez did to us earlier. Every glassway is closed, and no one can get in or out. Basically, we get packaged, sterilized, and stuck on ice."

"But if everyone's locked down," Dani said, "who's going to revive us?"

"The Board's responsible for endin' it if they think it's ever safe enough for their jelly-filled spines to handle." Ben swallowed against the sour taste filling his mouth.

Dani's laugh shredded around the edges. "Oh, wonderful! I've always wanted to leave my fate in the hands of a bunch of people who have less emotional capacity than a robot. And what about Jared? Does he get locked down, too? Do they have any idea how he'll react to them trying to quarantine him, or if it'll even work? They'll scare him so badly, we might lose any chance of keeping him from running wild."

"Let's not dump the whole bucket just yet." Ben lifted the radio again. "Francis?"

"Still here."

"There any window-watchers who could work with us on this? Can you link a glassway to this room?"

"I'm putting Window-Watcher Graham at your disposal. I'll be monitoring the situation from here, but I fear that's all I can do for the moment. The Board has denied me liberty to leave my office for fear of exposing myself."

"You could be exposed already," Ben said, "since we got no idea how this spell is spreadin'."

"Always one for cheery thoughts, Ben."

"Francis is grounded?" Dani asked, once Francis clicked off. "I thought he was top dawg around here. Got to call his own shots."

"Every dog's got a leash," he said.

"So what do we do now?" Lucy asked.

"Guess we gotta wait," Ben said. "Here's hopin' it ain't gonna take long—"

A rectangle of the wall shimmered beside the main door. Glassy blotches spread across it, like a puddle of water spreading without regards to gravity. The glass filled out to sharp edges which reflected the Maintenance room.

Ben went over and rapped on the pane. "Graham?"

The pane pushed out into a translucent face which sported a massive beard, made all the more impressive by its gleaming curls.

"Reporting for duty, per the Chairman's orders," Graham said. *"Looks like quite the party here. Any drinks?"*

"I'll send a growler your way once we've got things tidied." Ben sighed. "I'm startin' to owe beers to a lotta people." He waved for the others to gather round. "You all caught up on what's goin' down?"

"You mean besides half the staff acting like they took a puff from the crazy pipe? All of us on the skyline are getting pretty worried."

"Has any window-watcher been affected?" Lopez asked.

"Not that I've heard," Graham said. *"Though we don't tend to socialize much in the heights, know what I mean? So if someone did throw a mental loop-the-loop, I wouldn't have a clue."*

Ben stepped back so the reflection of his face overlaid Graham's projection. "We need to run a streaky mirror play with some Scum salvage. You know the drill?"

"Of course." Graham sounded insulted. *"But someone there must—"* His glassy eyes shifted toward the Borrelia sisters. *"Er ... them?"* His voice lowered to a tinny mumble. *"Janitor Ben, I don't know what you've heard, but they've a reputation."*

Dani stepped in and cocked a leg. "You make one crack about them and I'll find a way to kick through this pane and deposit your balls in your skull. Got it?"

Graham's glass face receded a few inches.

"I see. Very well. Can we get started then? I still have half an office building to clean before this evening and the sun's getting in my eyes."

"Ladies?" Ben swept an arm to the maids. "It's your show."

Lopez gave Hardy the doctor's notes, which she took as if holding a dead rat by its tail. She and Laurel approached the mirror and spoke with Graham in hushed tones.

Ben moved back to stand between Dani and Lucy. Lopez took up a station beside the twins as they worked, his hands twitching every so often as if wishing to help them. Yet he stayed out of their way.

"What's a streaky mirror?" Dani asked.

"Know how annoyin' it is when you spritz a mirror and wipe it down with a paper towel, only to find a buncha streaks left?"

"Sure." Dani frowned as the twins produced spray bottles and went to the wash station to fill them with soapy water. "I didn't think it was going to be so literal, though."

"It's a trick from an older book," he said. "Back in the days before radios and phones when paper was how folks stayed in touch."

"You mean back when you were a strapping young man?" Dani grinned. "There were dinosaurs then, right? Did you used to ride one to work?"

Lucy chuckled, earning her a scowl from him, which she duly ignored.

"Anyhoo," he continued, "Cleaners used to leave hidden messages for each other this way. Nowadays, mostly window-watchers use it, though some maids can pull it off. A bit back, someone figured they could use it to sneak info from Scum and, whaddya know, it worked."

He nodded at Laurel, who had wet down one of the pages with a few sprays. "This oughta do just fine. The notes are kinda like towels. The doc's thoughts should've left a sort of residue that, when they're wiped over the glass, should rub off, formin' the streaks. Then Graham projects a bit of a shiny show from his side, and the streaks act like a filter, makin' a pattern on this end we can interact with."

Lucy made a doubtful noise. "Assuming we can decipher whatever gets projected in the first place."

"Hey, I'm the office grump," Ben said. "Don't be shoe-hornin' in on my job description."

Laurel and Hardy both had damp pages, which they began to wipe across the glass, one twin starting at the top, the other at the bottom, and zigzagging until they met in the middle, where they drew a circle around Graham's transparent face. Gray streaks marked the path of the notes. The pages quickly turned soggy enough to tear and curl into fragments, which disintegrated with a few rubs of the fingers. They started in with two new pages, tracing designs in from opposite corners. Graham's face became the center of an increasingly complicated design, until the once-pristine mirror looked like a door carved out of birch wood, ornate enough to go on display at an art museum.

At last, the maids let the last flakes of paper fall to the floor. They kept flicking their fingers as if trying to shed a stubborn scrap of dead skin.

"Yuck," Laurel said. "Those notes had some major psychic grime sticking to them."

"Manicures all around?" Hardy suggested, looking to Dani.

"I'm down with that," Dani said after checking out her hand. "It'll be a get-the-corpseflesh-out-from-under-our-fingernails treat to ourselves. Ice cream after."

The twins whooped in unison.

Ben wished he could pinch his ears shut without being obvious. Good to see her finding a few friends in the business, though. Had she even seen her family since her recruitment? And what of her friends and classmates? He'd seen it happen too often, the new Cleaner—those who managed to survive their first few weeks, that is—so enamored by their abilities and overwhelmed by their new responsibility that they let their old lives and relationships slip away. Sure, the nature of the company didn't help, with its emphasis on dedication to the job. But there had to be a way to strike a balance between living in their muckraking reality and the one that remained mostly ignorant of the Cleaners' existence. Wasn't there?

He pulled his mind out of that whirlpool of worries when Graham spoke.

"Ready for the fun? Time for Graham to blow your minds with his light show."

"If you can help it, pretty please don't be blindin' us in the process," Ben said. "It ain't gonna help us none if we can't see what you're projectin'."

"Seriously?" Dani checked with the others. "Do I need to close my eyes?"

"No." Lopez's green aura flashed into being. "Any damage to the ocular nerves should be minor and almost immediately repaired so long as you do not move any further away."

Dani frowned and went with a compromising squint, one hand prepped to shield her eyes. The handyman's aura tingled on Ben's skin, and he kept himself from scratching as he prepared to observe whatever Graham revealed. They needed a few solid answers here; something to grab hold of and figure out how to throw right back into Malawer's shark-toothed face. What had set the first maid off? Why the suicides surrounding the second? Where did Malawer's power come from, and what formed the core of the oh-so-subtle spell infiltrating the Cleaner ranks?

And—he briefly checked the corners of the room—on a less pressing note, where had Carl dribbled off to?

That line of thought got snipped as Graham's glassway brightened like a window reflecting the midday sun. A square of harsh light struck the floor before their feet, and everyone took an instinctive step back as the Maintenance room heated ten degrees. The maids tugged the zippers of their jumpsuits down to fan their necks, exposing a tantalizing amount of cleavage. Ben briefly met Lopez's eyes as the handyman glanced that way.

Focus, Ben mouthed.

The handyman bobbed an eyebrow, but turned his gaze back to the light, where the gray streaks on the mirror started to flake off the glass. The flakes drifted into the square of light to twist and swirl in a growing column of dust, not unlike particles caught in a sunbeam. In this case, however, the particles kept a tight cohesion, forming first an ashen column, a wedge, and then several shapes so knotted and twisted they hurt to look at.

"This is it?" Dani asked, lowering her hand slightly. "I expected something a bit more … flashy."

"Don't encourage him," Ben said, nudging her hip. "Window-watchers will take any chance they get to show off for an audience and we need clarity here, not special effects."

"*Killjoy,*" Graham said. "*Every party has a pooper.*"

"Which is why we're all invited," Lucy muttered.

"Hush it." Ben edged closer. "Somethin's happenin'."

With a last flurry, the particles puffed out to the confines of the square of light and then snapped back into a central object that floated a few feet above the floor. Ben fought down his disappointment, for the formed object looked like nothing more than a deflated gray soccer ball, slumped toward the front, sagging along the sides.

Everyone stared at this for a minute, until Dani waved at the display in disgust.

"Are we supposed to make sense of this?" she asked. "Or am I the odd one out again?"

Lopez approached, hands spread as if trying to coax a frightened kitten back into his grasp.

Ben caught his arm right before he touched the ashen lump. "Lopez, you sure you know what you're doing?"

The handyman smiled. "Of course not. But while I will not risk those under my care, I've no such regards for myself."

"Not going to argue this one, seeing how our last one ended," Ben said, releasing him. "Just … be careful."

Lopez nodded in thanks, and reached to clasp the lump between both hands. Then he seemed to think better of this, and stretched out only one hand, his healing aura still gleaming about him.

The instant he touched the gray lump, he twitched as if hit by an electrical shock and a voice burst from his mouth, choppy and staggered on itself.

"Rooting Strain E—e—e—EMW121 in a n—nuh—ormal human being—labeled 'b-b-base specimen' for clarity—"

The handyman jerked back from contact and the voice cut off. He pinched his lips, but not before Ben noticed his trembling fingers.

"That was Malawer's voice," Dani said, checking around as if fearing the doctor had snuck in while they'd been distracted. "What gives?"

Ben watched Lopez closely, trying to make sure nothing affected the handyman other than surprise. The man appeared fine, if more leery of the object they'd summoned.

"I believe this is Malawer's mind." Lopez moved his hands around the sagging lump without touching it. "At least, a representation of it.

A shadow cast of his decayed thought processes."

"All thanks to yours truly," Graham said. At Dani's clearing of her throat, he hastily amended, *"And my lovely assistants, of course."* Another throat clearing. *"Invaluable, intelligent partners whose value is entirely undefined by their looks."*

At Dani's third cough, he groaned.

"Come on, lady. I don't have all day over here."

Dani winked at the Borrelia sisters, while Ben and Lopez returned to studying the shade of Malawer's mind.

"Guess it sorta looks like a brain," Ben said, "if one got microwaved and then given a massage with a hammer."

Lopez frowned. "Considering the man's current state, I wouldn't expect to find a healthy mind inside his skull."

"How much you thinkin' is locked up in there?" Ben asked.

"No way to know without letting it out," Lopez said. "And that appears to require someone willing to be an output channel."

"How'd first contact feel?"

Lopez grimaced. "Sullying. Malawer's thoughts leave a distinct flavor behind. Like choking on a bit of rotted cheese."

Ben placed a hand on his shoulder while the handyman glared at the phantasmal brain.

"You don't gotta do this."

The handyman sighed. "Yes. Yes, I do. Should exposure prove harmful, my abilities will help me recover faster than anyone here." He looked around at the others, gaze lingering on the twins. "Everyone please attend to whatever I utter. I may not have the best recall once this is finished."

The maids started to speak, but Lopez grabbed the projection and they were forced to be quiet as Malawer's voice once more burst out of him. The words seemed to cut through Lopez's throat, making it bump and flex with the effort. His muscles quivered and he tensed as if the projected mind attempted to throw off his touch. His fingertips dug in, worming deeper into the core of Malawer's mind. Statements switched mid-word as he tapped into new layers of the fleshmonger's thoughts.

"Esth—Esther, dearest. Beloved. L-l-l-onely. Promises broken. Forgive m—benefactor visited. Powers bestowed as promised. T-t-t-ogether soon—pah—Pure energ-gies-gies-gies rapidly escalate symp—symp—symptoms."

"There!" Ben jabbed a finger, and Lopez snapped to attention as he apparently heard what he said. He clutched tighter as the shadow-mind shifted in his grasp, as if trying to elude his searching.

"Initial challenge. Introducing trans-form-form-formed emotional contagion to c-c-c-Cleaners. Exhib-exhibit hyperactive ability to w-w-ward off disease and infection. Ffffirst t-two c-Cleaner tests only mild-ild-ildly successful."

Lopez's head cricked to one side. "Paradox. Paradox. Paradox. Once contagion established within clean-clean-Cleaner, acceleration of fffinal stages occurs. Fueled by pah-pah-Pure energies? Undetermined."

Lopez's arms began to tremble.

"Final stages reached too rapidly for condition to become infe-ec-ectious. Prevents spread. Must employ sec-secondary vvvector. B-b-base specimens may-ay-ay provide suitable hossst for incubation."

Lopez's eyes widened and rolled in their sockets. Ben kept his arm readied to catch the man in case the strain proved too much.

"B-b-base specimen found in the company of c-c-Cleaners! Infec-ected. Ongoing prox-ox-imity may be a positive ffffactor. Gestation appears indetec-eck-eck-table. Too soon to determine results."

Ben stepped back, feeling like a boulder had splashed down in his stomach. No. This couldn't be right. As he retreated past Lucy and Dani, they glanced at him and frowned, but refocused on Lopez.

As the handyman started to work his hands free, he loosed a last spurt of words. Malawer's voice almost sounded normal, weighed by sorrow and exhaustion.

"Esther. Beloved. Forgive me, but I cannot be alone any longer."

The handyman broke loose and staggered. Laurel and Hardy rushed to his sides and caught him before he buckled. Lopez wheezed, and when he spoke, his normal voice had been reduced to tatters.

"Highly unpleasant. Would not … wish it on … another. Will resume in a moment once I … catch my breath."

"Am I hearing this right?" Dani asked. "We're dealing with one of those magical diseases after all?"

Lopez took deep swallows. "An unheard of variation. Unimagined, even. I understand now why all our scans and wards have been ineffective. Malawer has not been attacking our bodies or minds or powers. Our thoughts and flesh remain uncorrupted, but he has subverted that which could overwhelm both. Our emotions."

He raised his head and tears gleamed on his cheeks. "He has created a virus that supplants our normal feelings with concentrated rage and depression. Once it advances far enough, every infected Cleaner will become like the first maids, unable to stop themselves as they launch into murderous rampages or fall to suicidal despair."

"And it's all my fault," Ben said.

They all turned to him. He stared back, feeling more distant from his coworkers than he ever thought possible.

Dani moved his way, but he thrust his palm out. "Stay away! Don'tcha get it? I'm the reason we're all in danger."

"What are you saying?" Lucy asked.

Ben held still, afraid to move lest he worsen the situation. Oily disgust slithered through him, twining around his chest and threatening to squeeze the breath out of him. Disgust at his foolishness, his ignorance. At how much he'd put at risk.

"The morgue. The mudmen. When we got separated, I was exposed but didn't think nothin' about it. Thought I was protected like I always used to be. Forgot I'm just another guy off the street when it comes to dealin' with Scum." He punched the inspection bed he stood beside. "Don'tcha see? Malawer wanted to infect regular folks—these base specimens he kept talkin' about. Usin' 'em as carriers to get close enough to Cleaners and pass it on to them."

He stared down at himself.

"I infected HQ. Malawer used me to slip his virus right inside. And the longer you're around me, the faster you're gonna get worse. Until we're all dead."

CHAPTER TWENTY-FOUR

ani's stomach churned and she smelled a rankness to the air she hadn't noticed before. She started to imagine cords of disease linking them all back to Ben, who stood as the center and cause of all their troubles.

Anger stirred its scaly head and hissed within her, and she felt herself rouse in response. How could Ben have done this? Any Cleaner who died was his fault.

Remove him! The desire to lance him like a pustular boil shrieked through her like a wind, and her breath huffed out almost hot enough to blister her tongue. Obliterate him. Scour his flesh from the bone and make him pay for the turmoil he'd caused. Such a stupid, arrogant person deserved to be ground down to dust and scattered on the wind.

With effort, she slapped these impulses down, recognizing their foreign nature now that she had a better idea of what to look for. It felt similar to controlling her own power. Except when she repulsed these alien emotions, they lingered much closer to the surface, coiling just beneath her skin, ready to lash out again the moment she relaxed at all. A look at the others revealed them to be struggling with similar violent desires. Even the twins gripped each other's hands hard enough she thought their fingers might snap in half. Only Lopez kept any sort of calm expression, though the steeliness of his gaze evidenced his internal conflict as he considered the situation.

Dani stepped forward, making herself a buffer between Ben and the others.

"Ben, you can't assume—"

"He's right," Lucy said behind her. "Even when you and I were pissed with each other, we didn't start swinging until we joined back up with him. And all the others chasing him ..."

"But the first incident happened inside HQ," Dani said. "Before any of us got near Malawer. He couldn't have infected you from outside the complex. It didn't start with you."

"Didn'tja listen?" Ben slumped beside the bed. "The first two tries didn't work. The maids died before they became infectious. Malawer needed someone to keep spreadin' it around, give it time to brew. Get strong enough to start takin' folks out in chunks."

He chuckled darkly. "I'm one ginormous idjit not to realize it before. I actually believed they was targetin' me for my reputation, for all the crummy rumors bein' spread. And all along, they were right. I shoulda never have been let back inside. I shoulda been let go a long time ago."

Dani crouched to meet his gaze, trying to establish a connection to draw him out of the malaise he was sinking into. "Ben, stop talking like that. That's Malawer's disease, not you."

He lifted his head, and the bleakness in his gray eyes made her think of the empty, dead landscape of the Gutters. "How're you knowin' that, princess? Where are my real emotions stoppin' and the fake ones startin'? I can't tell no difference." He motioned for Lopez. "You gotta put me into quarantine. For good, mebbe."

Lopez took up his firm stance from before. "I'm not convinced that will be of any help. If what you're postulating is true, though, then it may explain why those of us here are showing the fewest symptoms. They," he nodded at the four women, "went off on a job while you," he gestured to Ben, "only just arrived here to see me. We've been around you the least amount since your exposure."

Ben snorted. "While I've been runnin' all over HQ, gettin' everybody sick just by bein' here. This," he thumped his chest, "has been gettin' stronger in me. I'm a walkin' plague." He fixed pleading eyes on Lopez. "That's why you gotta put me away. Protect yourselves."

"I doubt locking you down will stop it from spreading at this point," said Lopez. "It's reached a critical mass, as Malawer hoped it would."

Ben made a fist, which he tucked behind his back. "Quit arguin' with me and just get 'er done. The longer you're exposed to whatever I'm carryin', the more damage it's gonna do."

"The damage has already been done," Lopez said. "But if we're the last to begin suffering the ravages, we may maintain clearer minds long enough determine a solution."

"We can figure this out," Dani said. "Don't give up."

Ben dropped his head back against the bed. "Dumb sods, all y'all."

She kicked him in the leg, drawing a curse as he rubbed his thigh.

"I'll inform my coworkers of what we've learned so far," Lopez said. "Perhaps with this new information, we can find a way to combat the disease."

He headed into the back chambers. Once he'd left, the others congregated around Dani and Ben, though Lucy and the twins still kept a healthy distance from the janitor.

"Tell us what happened in the morgue," Lucy said, glowering at Ben.

"How's that gonna help?" he asked.

"No idea. But we've got to start somewhere. So talk."

He sighed, but closed his eyes and narrated the events after the morgue door had cut him off from the others. Dani listened in rising disgust as he described Malawer forcing the breath of death into the bodies and how he'd taken out one of the mudmen before being overwhelmed. She licked her lips clean of imaginary grease and grime as he related the cloud of foul gas which had enveloped him in the process.

"That had to be it," Lucy said. "If I hadn't been so worried about saving your hide, I might've been able to contain one of them instead of popping their seals. That way we might've had a sample of the original contaminant."

"Let's hear it for Ben the Mighty and Powerful," he said, sagging even further. Dani resisted the urge to slap him, worried any aggressive action, even with good intentions, would unleash darker impulses. "Knowin' how I got exposed doesn't do no good."

"Then how do we stop it?" Hardy asked.

"This contagion is still some sort of spell, right?" Dani asked. "A constructed emotional virus, even. And every sustained spell or construct has to be grounded. Either the caster keeps it fueled straight from their energies or there's a core the energies have been anchored to. With something as nebulous and widespread as a disease, the core can't be contained within it like those in a blotdog or dust demon."

Ben raised a finger, then shook his head as if to say, *What's the use?* Dani cocked her head, not sure what the look had been for.

Laurel puckered her lips in concentration. "And it wasn't the altar in his house either, since that went kablooey."

"Kablooey," Ben said. "A word that's gonna be more and more fittin' here. You're all the powder keg, folks, and I'm the match."

"Then it's got to be Malawer himself," Lucy said, pointedly not even glancing the other janitor's way. "He's keeping the disease going with whatever powers the Corrupt Pantheon handed him. So long as he's alive—or at least whatever counts as alive in his case—the spell remains active. Neutralize him and it should unravel and take the constructed disease with it."

"Will that cure everyone who's already infected?" Dani asked.

A frown dimpled Lucy's face. "We have to hope so."

"Hope?" Graham asked from within the mirror. *"Foolish vestigial emotion."*

The vitriol in the window-watcher's voice had everyone turning slowly to face the glassway. All the gray streaks the maids had wiped across the pane had burned off in creating the thought construct, but now black cracks shot through the mirror, emanating from Graham's face.

"What'd you say?" Laurel asked.

"Why'd you say that?" Hardy asked.

Darkness bubbled into Graham's eyes and then dribbled into his cheeks and down into his beard, filling out the window-watcher's translucent visage as if someone poured ink into it from the other side. His grin was quite a bit toothier than before, and far less friendly.

"This connection will be severed. Initiating."

"I don't think that's Graham anymore," Lucy said, even as she ran for the mop she'd set aside earlier.

Ben finally roused, roared. "Lopez! Getcher ♋♦♦ back out here!"

"Analyzing," said Graham—or what had been him.

As Dani followed Lucy's lead to recover her equipment, a black cube shot out from the glass, looking formed out of night sky. When it struck the shadows of Malawer's thoughts, the construct evaporated.

"Analyzing situational threats."

The overhead lights flickered. A deep chuckle oozed through the room and dribbled down Dani's neck like a splatter of tar. She ground her teeth as she fumbled for her mop while the lights wavered. The twins were calling for everyone else, and Ben swore as something clattered and slammed to the floor, as if he'd knocked the bed over while trying to jump to his feet.

"Threats assessed. Neutralization initiated."

Dani stubbed her toes and banged her knees before her groping connected with her mop. As she turned, Lopez bolted back into the room and almost collided with her. His green aura bolstered the flickering lights, his presence alone fixing whatever technical issue threatened to plunge the room into darkness. The bulbs steadied and brightened so everyone clearly saw the creature which stepped through the glassway.

Towering twice as tall as any of them, the monster had eight multi-hinged appendages attached to a central, chunky body. Four of these acted as legs, while another four pointed up, twitching to where they ended in needle tips.

Its skin glinted with a crystal sheen and its segmented form alternated between being as wide as Dani's waist and as thin as the pane of glass it had just come through. In fact, it looked like the thing's body was composed of smoky prisms and panels which sucked the light into their depths. Graham's face had transferred from the glassway to the chunk which served as the creature's chest.

"Neutralizing," he said.

CHAPTER
TWENTY-FIVE

B lackshard," Ben shouted.

The creature skittered sideways, moving with shocking speed for its size and blocky structure. Its legs clicked over the tiled floor as it rushed at the maids.

The twins shot in opposite directions, their escape boosted by gusts of air. Two of the blackshard's arms slashed at them in tandem. Laurel got out of range as a smoky pane cut at her neck, but Hardy took a crystal block across the back, flipped once, and slammed into a Maintenance bed.

The blackshard scuttled her way, limbs poised to strike.

Dani instinctively woke her power and reached into the surrounding elements; but Lopez shouted at her.

"Do not! Too crowded."

Realizing he was right, that she'd likely injure the others in such close quarters, Dani clamped down on the spell she'd begun to fashion. She shuddered as her power writhed within her, not enjoying being cut off at the last second. It felt like getting a mental rope-burn as she yanked on the cords of energy and knotted them.

Laurel drew her hand-broom and dustpan and clapped them together. Sheets of wind sliced into the blackshard as she tried to distract it from Hardy, who sluggishly untangled from the bed and crawled away.

Lucy had dashed to the washbasin and turned the faucet on full bore. She cupped one hand under the stream and redirected it into a right-angled, high-pressure blast. With her other hand, she used the mop to soak up the spray and then flicked globs of water at the floor and blackshard. The creature stumbled as one missile splattered across Graham's glassy face—which gave Dani an idea.

On the drive back, she'd grabbed another chanted squeegee from the back of her van. She snatched this off her belt and ran in from behind.

"Dani, wait!" Ben shouted.

Dani side-stepped a kick from one of the beast's legs. She returned the kick and smashed a boot into one of the thin panes composing the limb. It cracked down the middle, and the black-shard sagged on that side. Its other three legs flexed. It bobbed and spun so Graham's face oriented on her. The two upper limbs which had been menacing Hardy now twitched above her.

Dani threw herself forward as the limbs plunged down. The impact almost knocked her off-balance, but she planted a foot and thrust the squeegee out.

The rubber blade slammed into the window-watcher's face. The chanted edge parted the crystalline skin like jelly.

Graham's face sank away—only to pop out on another black facet on the main body. The beady eyes oriented on her, and Dani dropped to her knees as an arm cut through where her head had just been. She rolled to the side as another limb chopped at her.

No chance to concentrate on conjuring another spell. She could only focus on dodging the glassy arms which looked sharp enough to sheer her in half if she moved too slow.

As she scrambled back out of range, the blackshard advanced, but skidded on the puddles Lucy had thrown down like watery land mines. When it fought to stay upright, the leg Dani had kicked shattered along the fracture. The blackshard staggered, reduced to three legs and a crystal stump.

Dani got to her feet and eyed its other legs for thinner spots. Lucy lashed out again with another blast of water. Laurel ran to her sister and helped pull her to safety while the blackshard focused on the Catalyst.

She dodged two more attempts by the blackshard to stab her face while trying to not let herself get backed into a corner. Water pelted the creature's back, but it ignored those attacks as they splashed off its glassy exterior. The smokiness within its facets seemed to roil as it moved, and Dani glimpsed her face reflected in the creature's body.

The closest reflection wavered and, for a moment, it didn't look like Dani at all. Another woman sneered out at her, face mostly hidden by long, dark hair.

Confused, Dani slowed her retreat as she tried to get a clearer look. One of her elemental duplicates?

When Ben shouted another warning, she realized the black-shard had hooked onto a Maintenance bed with one of its rear limbs and raised it to throw.

It flipped her way even as she tried to lunge to the side. The bed slammed into her. The metal bars cracked into her ribs, and only the minimal cushioning kept her skull from caving in. The bed drove her to the floor and pinned her there. Panic scattered her concentration and any chance of summoning her power as she flailed to get free.

The blackshard stomped her way. She screamed as one of its legs landed on her foot. Bone cracked. Blades of fire and ice stabbed through her ankle and knee as the weight of the creature crushed the ankle.

Tears of agony blurred her vision as two upper limbs cocked over the bed, poised to snap down at her face and chest.

They froze in mid-strike, swathed in a green glow. A glance to the side showed Lopez with hands outstretched, face gleaming with sweat. The quarantine spell couldn't contain the entire creature, however, and it struggled to break free, lashing out with its other limbs as it tried to reach the handyman.

As it fought, its leg remained on Dani's foot. Bone ground against bone. Tendons popped and tore, ripping further screams out of her. She gripped the bed and tried to shove it off, but collapsed again as the effort pulled on the trapped foot and shot excruciating pain along the leg.

The glow of the quarantine had faded some. The dagger-like limbs twitched again. Lopez shook with the effort of keeping the blackshard locked down.

Ben ran in and swatted the blackshard, aiming for the thinner segments of its limbs and forcing it to defend against him. Lucy joined him, and the cords of her mop coiled around an upper limb to yank it down. However, the blackshard used this connection to jerk Lucy closer in. An arm-limb slapped into her, and she skidded across the floor to lie in a heap.

Ben drove the butt-end of his mop into another leg-pane, and a crack shot through it.

The blackshard leaped straight up. Dani cried out as its weight came off her ruined foot. Its four arm-limbs punched into the ceiling and hooked into the tiles so it dangled, leg-limbs curled beneath it, ready to spear anything in range below.

Manipulating its upper limbs, it stab-walked across the ceiling, pivoting from one hanging joint to another, an obscene mix of spider and monkey as it followed Ben.

He danced beneath it, moving every which way as he tried to anticipate its strikes. The blackshard matched him easily, however. One hit sent the mop flying from his hand. Another strike spun him down. Blood splashed from a gash across his chest and forearm.

He tried to push up. Before he could, the blackshard dropped onto him, its legs caging him in. He curled into the fetal position, as if that might keep him from being squished.

Wind roared through the Maintenance room. It kicked aside curtains and shifted the bed which kept Dani pinned. The maids stood side by side, brooms aimed like machine guns as their gale sent the blackshard tumbling.

It rolled and clattered as it fought to regain its poise. Several limbs shot into the floor and braced as it levered upright.

Then it seemed to change its mind, and it shoved itself in the opposite direction, toward the double doors which led into the next chamber—where injured Cleaners lay waiting to be slaughtered.

Lopez ran in front of it, hands raised and blazing green.

"No puedes pasar!"

The aura of his quarantine spell flickered over the blackshard. It popped into existence around one leg, then winked away, only to envelop a second leg, and then switched to a third and back. The random, sudden containment of its limbs reduced the blackshard's advance to a crawl. Yet it forged onward, closing the gap with each stumble.

Dani bit back whimpers, too distracted by the pain in her leg to do anything. She scrunched her eyes shut and tried to focus, tried to force the energies to do her bidding; the spell kept collapsing and any strands of energy she threw out faded away.

"Help me." The words came out as a grunt, and she almost wept at the futility of them.

A spot of heat brushed her thoughts.

Why should we?

"You'd let us all die?" Dani gripped the nearest bed bar as if she could wring her flame-doppelganger's neck.

If you die, we'll be free.

"I don't think you really know that for sure," she said. "You weren't smart enough to keep from being linked to me. How do you really know what'll happen when that link snaps? Maybe it won't break after all, and you'll get dragged down into death with me."

The heat fluttered as a chill of doubt counteracted it. Whispers teased through her brain, and she imagined the elementals having a hurried council in the back of her head. Her pain and desperation kept her from being too disturbed at that moment by the thought of the elementals hitching a ride in her mind all this time. At last, the flame spoke again.

There will be a price. Favors owed.

"If we survive, I'll hear you out, I promise." Dani hissed as she moved too much and pulled on her ruined foot. "We'll find a way to make everyone happy. I just need enough focus to destroy the blackshard without hurting my coworkers."

Very well. We will hold you to your word.

The blackshard surged at Lopez. It struck out with two four-jointed arms. The handyman flew backward and hit the double doors he'd been guarding before dropping to the floor. His aura winked out.

"Lopez!" came the twins' cries. They started to rush in, no doubt about to be batted aside as well.

Dani filled her lungs and shouted as loud as she could.

"Get away from it! Now!"

The maids looked at her in surprise. They must've seen something in her eyes for they jumped back from the blackshard in swirls of air.

"Do it," Dani said through gritted teeth.

Our pleasure.

Dani poured her energy into a single magical punch and aimed it at the creature. She let fly.

The energies soared free, leaving her wearied enough that she could barely keep her eyes open to watch the results. For a moment, despair gnawed at her, as it looked like the effort would dissipate like her earlier ones. Then the energies snapped into a complicated knot of power that etched into the floor beneath the blackshard.

The tiles split into a wide pit under its legs. Two of its limbs caught the edges before it plummeted into whatever abyss the elementals had opened. As it strained to clamber out, upper limbs waving frantically, a heat wave swept through the room. The blackshard hesitated, as if confused.

Fire belched out of the rent in the floor. As the flames wreathed the beast, the facets of its body and limbs charred and cracked in the heat.

A keening noise cut through the room, making Dani and the maids clamp hands over their ears. Then the fire and the blackshard's wail cut off. At the same instant, every light bulb shattered and a curtain of darkness fell over the room.

What? No thank you? came the parting thought as Dani's awareness slip away.

CHAPTER
TWENTY-SIX

She woke to Ben's cursing.

"Son of a grout!"

"Sorry," said one of the twins.

"That was my hand you just stepped on. I kinda got a shortage of these, so I'd like to keep this one in workin' order."

"She said *sorry*," the other twin replied. "Stop being a baby."

"Dani?" he called.

"Over here." Her voice came out strangled and she coughed to clear it. "Still stuck under this bed."

"Hang on," he said. "We'll get that off you soon as we can, don'tcha doubt."

"Just be careful of my right foot," she said. "Pretty sure that thing broke it when it stepped on it."

"Aw, geez," Ben said. "Lopez? You with us?"

"*Sí.*" The handyman sounded groggy, but at least he'd survived. "*Uno momento.*"

"Lu?"

No answer from the other janitor. Ben sighed, and Dani heard the click of a radio being triggered.

"Francis, any chance we could get a bit of light in here? Hello?"

As he fussed with the handheld, boots crunched on glass, coming closer. Dani tensed for someone to accidentally hit her wounded foot, despite her warning. However, the twins came to her head first and felt along to the bed which sat on her chest and stomach. Going to either end, they hefted and shuffled it off to the side.

Dani sat up and breathed deep to fight nausea as movement woke the ragged pain again. She tried to ignore the parts of her body that screamed for attention and listened for the blackshard. Popping and sizzling sounded from across the room, but nothing to indicate whether the creature still posed a threat.

"Is it dead?" she asked.

"Can't tell until we get the lights blinkin' again," Ben said. "Let's guess that since we ain't dead in the dark, it's at least down for the count." More rustling. "Flashlight, anyone?"

Dani closed her eyes and shifted into the elemental spectrum of vision her power afforded. It took her a few moments to adjust to that perspective, seeing the floor and walls as sheets of earth and stone pierced by metal fixtures, wrapped in networks of water pipes and webs of electrical wiring. She sensed the others standing around nearby as the air rippled over their bodies, forming voids in her sense of the airflow. A prone figure—Lucy she assumed—lay near one wall, while Lopez squatted on the other side of the pit Dani's power had torn open.

At last, the handyman corralled his wits enough to activate his aura. The light revealed everything in gray and green, and the hues made Dani think of night-vision goggles from a spy movie.

Laurel and Hardy eased Dani up and returned her mop, which she leaned on as a makeshift staff to take the weight off her foot.

"Whoa, princess," Ben said. He pressed his arm across his chest to staunch the cut the blackshard had given him. "Sit down until Lopez can get a look atcha."

"Have to make sure it's dead first." She hobbled over to the pit, the twins at her sides. "Go check on Lucy."

Several of the blackshards limbs had fused to the sides of the pit, so the creature dangled over the drop. Its glassy body had bubbled in spots and turned to slag in others. A few limbs had been burnt straight off. Graham's face was nowhere to be seen. The entire thing appeared inert, though Dani had to keep from jumping whenever the skin pinged and cracked as the body cooled.

A moan drew her attention to where Ben helped Lucy. Lucy moved slowly, as if still stunned. A gash scored across her forehead and cheek, but otherwise she looked intact. The two joined the others as Lopez eased around the pit. Just being near him soothed the throbbing in Dani's foot. She refused to look down at it, dreading what she'd see. Getting the boot off without causing further damage would be a nightmare.

Ben whistled as he surveyed the inanimate blackshard. "Impressive piece of work. A clean shot." He looked around at the ruptured floor and charred ceiling. "In a manner of speakin'."

"What was it?" Dani asked. "Where'd it come from?"

"Blackshard," he said as he eyed the creature. "Corrupted glasskin. Leastways, that's what we figure. Some folks think they're behind urban legends like Bloody Mary and the Candy Man, or whenever you see a reflection in a mirror that ain't s'posed to be there."

He kicked a nearby limb, and a black shard chipped off. Lopez retrieved this and held it out for inspection.

"We could learn much from this," the handyman said.

Ben frowned at the remains. "Reality is no one's ever gotten a chance to confirm where they come from or what they want or who commands 'em. Whenever a blackshard's in the mix, they're either smashed to bits or wipe out anyone they come in contact with."

"Congratulations, everyone," Lucy said, as she leaned on Ben. "We just beat the odds."

In that moment, Dani felt the group drawing strength from one another in the aftermath. Swallowing took effort as fierce pride swept through her. This was what it meant to be a Cleaner— fighting back darkness and Corruption in whatever form it came, no matter the cost to themselves. Being here, being one of them … right then it meant more to her than any other purpose or glory she might achieve.

As if sensing her thoughts, Ben smiled at her from where he helped Lucy remain upright. All the doubt and hopelessness from earlier had vanished, revealing the janitor's old self, his grit and determination in wiping out a mess, no matter how big. This confirmed to her that the bleakness he'd momentarily staggered beneath had been symptoms of Malawer's emotional disease and not the true feelings of the man she admired.

Ben raised a brow at Lopez. "You up for this?"

The handyman nodded, though wearily. "I must be. It's my duty."

"Duty can—" Ben started.

"—be one of the few certainties we have right now," Lucy finished. "So let him have his."

Ben's lips pinched shut and Dani could see the effort it took for him to hold back some snippy response. He waved for Lopez to take the lead.

"A'ight, folks. The doctor's in the house. If we're good, we get lollipops after."

Lucy jabbed his stomach softly as he bustled her over to a bed and eased her onto the cushions. The maids helped Dani to another bed, but when Lopez came her way, she shook her head.

"Others first," she said. "I can hold for a few."

He frowned, but she pushed him off, trying to delay dealing with her foot for a few more minutes while building her courage. He shuffled over to Lucy and began to massage her cuts closed, letting his aura seep into them as he did. They sealed under his touch as she squirmed and winced. Then he moved to Ben and repeated the procedure.

The twins had escaped anything more serious than a bruise, and Lopez gave each a kiss on the hand, the relief evident on his face before moving to Dani. As he knelt to look at her foot, she caught Ben's attention.

"Talk to me," she said. "Distract me with lots of boring details."

He smiled in sympathy before turning thoughtful.

"I really don't wanna think about all this, 'cause it's gonna mean some mighty big stacks of paper to file a full report later."

Dani tensed as Lopez took her foot in both hands. The pain had become a background sensation, perhaps from shock, but she could still feel her flesh shift in his grip, as if he held a bag of mud and glass shards. Was this something even his magic could fix?

"What do you mean?" she asked.

He fingered the rips in his uniform. "We just learned Scum can Corrupt glassways now. That's fan-friggin'-tastic."

"They couldn't before?"

Lucy shook her head. "No. Glassways have always been immune to Corruption."

Dani glanced at the darkened glassway. "Why?"

Ben tapped a pocket thoughtfully, and Dani noted a square outline below the zipper. "Dunno for sure. Somethin' about the glasskin who originally made 'em. Somethin' in their nature." He opened the pocket, pulled out a slim book and studied the cover.

"What've you got there?" Lucy asked.

"*Glasskin and their Ways*," Ben read, talking half to himself. "Thought it was connected to somethin' else, but mebbe he meant it for this."

"He? He who?"

Ben shifted uncomfortably. "Jared got it for me, actually. I'd asked him about …" He glanced at Lucy. "About what we was studyin' earlier, but mebbe he got confused."

"When did you see Jared?" Dani asked.

"Why didn't you tell me about this?" Lucy asked at the same time.

Ben raised the book like a shield. "Later, okeydokey? It's complicated and if you ain't noticed, we got bigger problems right here. The main thing is, there might be somethin' in here that could help us." He tucked the book under the stub of his right arm.

A tingle started in the middle of Dani's foot, which grew into a distracting itch. She tried to not flex her toes, knowing it would only worsen the sensation. "You've never actually told me what glasskin are."

"They're really pretty," Laurel said.

"And made of glass," Hardy said.

Dani blinked at them. "That's a start."

"They're sorta …" Ben bobbed his head from side to side. "Artificial elementals."

"Artificial?"

"They ain't always been 'round," he said. "Folks think some of the earliest Cleaners made the glasskin, who then made us the glassways and taught us how to use them in return."

"Constructs teaching their creators how to use something they constructed?" Dani frowned. "That seems a little chicken-and-eggish."

"It's all hearsay, so choke it down with a salt shaker. But the glassways ain't never been Corrupted or breached like this in ... well ... ever."

"Oh." Dani looked between the glassway and the blackshard. "But if—"

She bit her tongue as Lopez squeezed her foot. Her vision flickered, and she must've blacked out for a second, for Laurel and Hardy suddenly held her arms to keep her upright.

Her foot shifted under Lopez's touch. She grabbed the maids' hands and gripped them as hard as she could. A miniature nova exploded in her ankle, and the room seemed to expand with it until Dani sat in the center of a sun which shot rays of pain rather than light.

This couldn't be healing. He wanted her to be in agony. He wanted her writhing while he gloated at the torment he caused. Fiend. Demon in disguise. Dani craved to bash his face in, to shatter his bones, to lop his hands off so he couldn't torture anyone ever again. However, the fit of pain kept her locked and unable to follow through with these violent visions.

Her ankle clicked into place. Her foot went rigid as the phalanges and metatarsal reformed, and blissful, tingling warmth replaced the anguish.

The room shifted back into proper lines, and she gradually regained her other senses—including the realization of how tightly she squeezed the twins' hands in her pain and momentary fury.

She peeled her hands from theirs, embarrassed by the sweat and nail imprints she left behind.

"Sorry."

"You got a strong grip, girlfriend." Laurel patted her back. "Ever think about steer wrestling?"

"All the time. It was either med school or rodeos for me." Dani flexed feeling back into her hands as Ben and the others eyed her in concern.

"You gonna live?" he asked.

"Yeah," she said, letting out a breath. "Holy schnitzel, that hurt."

"Healing often involves pain," Lopez said as he rose. "It is functional, but will remain sore for a few days. I'd recommend not letting anything else step on it, in the meantime."

"Sound advice." Dani dared to wiggle her toes. It felt like she'd hopped a marathon on that one foot, which was in desperate need of a soak and massage. Every bone felt in place, and her ankle actually rotated, versus sliding around.

Ben leaned in. "You were sayin'?"

Dani frowned in confusion, and then remembered she'd begun to ask a question before Lopez's bone-setting.

"Oh, right. If blackshards are Corrupted glasskin, wouldn't that mean glassways were susceptible all along?"

He shot off an imaginary gun with his hand. "Bang on the bullseye. Which gets me thinkin' blackshards ain't what we thought they were. And that throws another mess on the heap. How in the name of Hygiene did Malawer get a blackshard—even one of them—workin' for him?"

"Maybe it's not working just for him," Lucy said. "Maybe it's working for whoever gave him his power."

"That's what I'm fearin'." Ben shook his head. "So whoever we're goin' up against has blackshards as attack dogs."

"We beat this one, though," Dani pointed out.

"Barely survived, more like," he said. "And that was one blackshard goin' toe-to-toe with six of us—and you almost needin' a peg leg afterward. You really wantin' a rematch?"

Dani stood and tested the restored foot. She winced at a few twinges, but otherwise it took her weight, and she circled the bed a few times while the others continued talking.

"That book say anything about blackshards?" Lucy asked, jutting her chin at it.

"Dunno," Ben said. "Ain't had a chance for much pleasure readin' in between runnin' from coworkers and tryin' to keep my head from bein' cut off. And you know I always gotta look up the big words, so speed readin' is outta the question."

The other janitor snatched at it. "Give me that. Can't believe you didn't tell me."

Ben jumped back. "When was I gonna? In between you and Dani havin' a private roller derby match or when I was realizin' I helped cause all this? 'Sides, Jared gave it to me, and I'm thinkin' he wouldn't like it if I tossed it over to anyone else."

"What do I care what the twerp thinks? You promised to share whatever you discovered."

Lopez and the twins watched them argue while Dani racked her thoughts for something, anything that might give them a lead on Malawer. Her gaze settled on the Corrupted glassway and she thought of the rows of identical mirrors in Malawer's now-demolished house.

"Ben," she said, "Malawer's made a mistake. And we didn't even realize it."

His brows drew down. "Whatcha talkin' about?"

She pointed at the Corrupted glassway. "He left us a backdoor. A way to track down where he is. Maybe even follow it back to his hideout."

Ben stuck his tongue in his cheek while thinking, but Lucy was the first to shake her head.

"Good idea, girlie, but don't you remember? When we saw the same things in the house, they didn't react to us."

"Because we didn't know what they were," Dani said. "Now we do. Even if it's Corrupted, maybe we could still use it to get to Malawer. He used it to evacuate his family, so we know they at least follow some of the same principles."

Ben grunted. "Could be worth a shot. Any idea where to start?"

"Actually—"

Light flooded the room, leaving them all blinking in the sudden brightness. Lopez let his aura fade with a sigh, while Dani peered at the ceiling, which showed no sign of the blackshard having hung from it earlier.

"Uh, who put in new bulbs and tiles when I wasn't looking?"

"They grow back," Laurel said.

Hardy bounced on her toes. "Yeah! Whenever HQ gets damaged, it's got a built-in regeneration system. I think the Board makes it work."

"Self-healing construction? Nice." Dani refocused on the group. "But here's what I was thinking—"

Their radios squawked and they all reached for them in unison.

This is Chairman Francis. Can any survivors report in? I need a status update.

Lucy got on the button first. "We're all here, sir. The blackshard is down and we got scraped up a bit, but we're intact. We think we might have a way to get to Malawer."

"Can it be done within two hours?"

Everyone stared at each other.

"Two hours?" Ben asked. "Where'dja get that sorta timetable? Francis, what ain'tcha tellin' us?"

Static growled from the radios. Or was that the Chairman's own frustration seeping out?

"The Board has voted. They're going to invoke a full quarantine."

CHAPTER
TWENTY-SEVEN

Nobody moved for a count of ten. Dani watched the others, hoping she'd imagined the Chairman's announcement. Ben, Lucy, and the twins paled while Lopez went stiff and stared into the distance.

Ben twitched and spoke into his radio in a subdued voice.

"Can't be that bad already ... can it?"

"Bad enough. They analyzed what you found through the streaky mirror. Based on that and this blackshard incursion, nothing's going to convince them to rescind the order. Beyond the Maintenance sections, things are only getting worse, and we've had to shut down several glassways to keep rampaging Cleaners from escaping. Almost every interaction turns violent, and those who aren't trying to kill each other are nearly catatonic with despair."

"What about the handymen?" Lucy asked. "Lopez said they weren't being affected."

"True for the most part, and those Cleaners in their vicinity show less symptoms, but we've noticed several handymen behaving erratically. Their abilities may slow the disease, but it does not make them immune."

Laurel and Hardy moved to either side of Lopez, hands on his arms as if to protect him.

"But if we shut HQ down," Ben said, his tone heated, "there's gonna be nothin' left to stop Malawer."

"Right now, the Board believes the Cleaners are the greater threat to the public."

Everyone cried their version of, "What?" Some of the less polite versions were blocked by the foul-filter.

"Is it because of the suicides?" Dani asked once the clamor died down.

"Yes," Francis said. *"It seems that infected Cleaners project the negative emotions into anyone nearby to a greatly heightened degree. Any civilian within a certain radius will be drawn into the rage and depression our people are exhibiting. Plus, the disease progresses slower in someone who lacks Pure energies. The Board believes that shutting the Cleaners down will give them the time they need to develop an antidote, and that anyone outside the company will last longer without our interference."*

"Interference." Ben snorted. "Whatta lovely way to describe all the hard work we do."

"What about all the Cleaners out on jobs?" Dani asked. "The ones who haven't returned to HQ yet? Many of them are probably infected and don't know it yet."

"The Board would eventually be able to track down any Cleaners' location," Lucy said. "But with a full quarantine, any Cleaner stationed here, but currently outside of HQ is immediately snatched back when the lockdown is activated."

Dani whipped her hat off and flailed it in their faces. "This place has some seriously screwed up security measures. First a Recycling Center that implodes. Now we're all going to get imprisoned here forever?"

"At least we won't be dead, girlie. Just preserved."

"For who knows how long? We could wake up a hundred years from now."

"We have to be able to police ourselves," Lopez said. "If we get compromised—as we are now—it keeps us from turning on the very people we try to keep safe."

Dani slapped the hat back on and huffed. "Yeah but … but still. Why didn't I hear about this before?"

Lucy wavered between a smirk and frown. "It's in the Employee Manual. Your fault if you don't read the whole thing."

"There's an Employee Manual?"

Lucy stared at Ben, who wouldn't meet her eyes. "You never gave her a copy of the Employee Manual?"

He hemmed and hawed. "We really gonna waste time arguin' about who did or didn't do what? You know how much I hate all that philosiphocatin'."

Dani pointed at him and then thumbed at herself. "You. Me. Talking. Later."

He coughed. "I'm sure hopin' so, 'cause it'd mean there'll be a later to talk." He raised the radio. "Two hours, Francis?"

"That's the most I can give you. Can you do anything in that time?"

Ben looked around at the others, his posture battling between defeated and determined.

"Guess we're gonna find out." He stuck his radio onto his belt and tucked his arm behind his back. "A'ight, folks. We got our deadline. Now what're we gonna do with it? Dani? You had an idea?"

She jabbed her mop at him. "I'm still pissed about not getting a manual."

"Focus, princess. Deal with the Scummy doc first. Argue about me not saddlin' you with a few thousand pages of borin' homework second."

Dani sighed and closed off the part of her mind which had already begun inventing new curse words for Ben. She led them over to the Corrupted glassway and glared at the black glass.

"You said glasskin are elementals, right?"

"But not real ones," Ben said.

"Still," she said, "they're connected, and that means the glassways should have elemental aspects as well."

"S'pose so." He waved for her to go on. "What's that meanin'?"

"So," she ran a nail along the glass, "my powers let me sense nearby elements."

"Like we sense Corrupt energies?" Laurel asked.

"Sort of. It's more like seeing a different wavelength than normal, one tuned in to the elements my energies can affect. If glassways are connected to the elements, maybe I can use my other sight to figure out a way to access a Corrupted one too."

"And what're we doin' while you're lookin'?" Ben asked. "Thumb wrestlin'?"

"Give me a few minutes and a bit of space. And try to figure out another option." She nodded at the book still tucked beneath his stub. "Maybe see if there's something in there that can help after all."

Once the others had backed away, with Lucy trying to stab Ben in the chest with a finger while arguing over his mysterious book, Dani closed her eyes. But instead of seeking out her surroundings, she turned her focus inward and spoke to her mental stowaways.

Guys? Can we do a little huddle-up here? Things are getting—

The room shivered and slipped sideways.

—sticky.

Details blurred, the light dimmed, and Dani knew she'd entered the realm where her elemental others had confronted her the first time. Whether it existed in her head or some alternate dimension didn't matter right then; just that they'd responded.

"Thanks," she said as she turned around, confident her Cleaner companions wouldn't be able to see or hear the interaction. "I'm worried I might've used up all your good graces with the blacksha …"

Her tongue knotted. Instead of Fire-Dani or Earth-Dani, the figure before her looked like Ben, but if he'd been sculpted out of water. He smiled at her and inclined his head politely.

"Greetings, attractive human female."

"Wha … Ben?"

The smile broadened. "No, but I'm a good friend of his. And yours."

Ben's head spun into a brief shape, made of rods connected in a complex cube. Then the head reformed into the familiar features. Dani's heart rate slowed a bit as she recognized who this was.

"Carl? How?"

The water sprite bowed, an aptly fluid motion. "I'm tapping into your connection with the water elemental bonded to you."

"You mean the one I enslaved."

He grimaced. "Whatever the others think of their situation, it's not my choice of word. Either way, I can speak to you more directly here."

She walked around him, studying him from all angles. His head spun a full circle to track her.

"Where have you been?" she asked. "Ben could've used a little help earlier. Almost got smooshed."

"I trusted in everyone's ability to keep him intact. Not much I could've done against a blackshard." He spread his arms, the elbows bending a little too far the wrong way. "I've been pleading your case to the others. Trying to convince them to be more helpful when it comes to aiding you and Ben."

"Others?"

He tapped his head, and the finger plunged in and out of the watery boundary of his skull. "Your elementals. We've had a robust debate."

"Why?"

His eyebrows rose with a gurgling noise. "Why what?"

"Why have you been arguing for me?"

"Because Ben is my partner and friend, and I consider you a friend as well. Why wouldn't I look out for your wellbeing?"

"Are elementals supposed to be good at lying?" Dani asked. "Because none of you have a great track record so far."

His blink sprayed droplets from his eyelids. "Pardon? I wasn't lying."

"I'm sure that's true on a surface level." She put a fist to her chin, mimicking the famous Thinker statue. "But let's use a metaphor here. I'm sensing some deeper currents running through this conversation. Deep, dark, chilly currents, where who-knows-what might be lurking? You might go so far as to say your words are a deceptively calm river of logic that I fear being swept away when I wade out too far, only to be bashed against the rocks while struggling for the sweet air of truth."

His eyes rolled in their sockets. "Enough already. Subtlety has obviously never been a Catalyst characteristic."

"You going to tell me the real reason you're here? Otherwise I'll start describing the rocky rapids of white lies and the dizzying eddies of purposeful omission."

"Very well." He sighed, froth bubbling to his lips. "I want to help you remain empowered because I can only do so much to assist Ben these days."

"Help Ben? With what?"

"Staying alive." Carl raised rippling hands. "Ben is important. He needs to be preserved, but is more vulnerable than ever right now."

"Important?" Dani echoed. "As in what? He owes you money and you don't want him dead until he can pay you back?"

"Important as in the security code for a bank vault. Important as in a muzzle on a wild lion. As in a black monolith appearing on the moon."

She cocked her head. "Are you actually talking about Ben? That seems a little over-the-top. And how do you know this, anyway?"

"We water elementals are a bit more in touch with the fluidic nature of time than you humans." He smirked. "Shall I start describing time as a stream? Unlike earlier, it's actually a good metaphor. We can see a bit further in both directions, and there are so many different currents to decipher."

She raised a hand. "Spare me. So what're we talking about? Prophecy? Ben is some chosen one destined to save us all from an apocalyptic invasion of toilet snakes?" Dani thought of Ben's own talk about not getting locked down by thoughts of destiny or purpose. Could he actually be an altering factor in events yet-to-come?

"Hardly," Carl said. "What first drew us to him wasn't any vision of his future, but of his past. Something was locked away inside him at one point."

"What?"

Carl's shoulders swelled and shrank; his manner of a shrug, Dani assumed. "That is where our sight becomes blurry. We don't know exactly what. Yet. Our vision wasn't so precise, and any attempts we've made to see further have been blocked—which only worries us more. A memory, perhaps? An ability? A seed of something altogether alien? I was getting close to discovering it once. It was coming to the surface, but then"—his face pinched on one side—"the Ravishing. Losing Karen. Those events smothered it, and I haven't been able to uncover anything since."

"Were you there?" She stepped in as a terrible thought occurred. "Have you known what happened to his wife all this time? Kept it from him?"

"No. I wasn't with him when it happened, but it's part of the puzzle. Whatever he possessed before is still within him, waiting to be unlocked or unleashed."

"So you think."

"So we *know*."

Dani *humphed*. "Do you really? That whole incident obviously changed him in a lot of ways, not to mention his transformation back to his younger self and loss of his powers. How can you be sure whatever it was you sensed inside him before is gone now?"

Another thought jolted her. If Jared had drawn the Ravishing out of Ben, could he have also taken whatever it was Carl spoke of? She kept this thought sealed deep, though, not wanting the boy to come under elemental scrutiny, as well, in his vulnerable state.

Carl's whole body rippled. "Because if it had, there would be no doubt. The effects would've been seen and felt."

Dani's eyes narrowed. "For not knowing what it is, you sure seem pretty certain about a lot of it."

"If you see something fall into a lake out of the corner of your eye, Dani, you can detect the splash and waves and foam it causes, but not necessarily ever determine what the initial object was." Carl gave a bubbling sigh. "It's one of the reasons my kind placed me with him, to keep an eye on whatever developed and discern what needed to be done about it as early as possible—if anything could be done."

"You make it sound like he's going to turn into some kind of monster or nuclear bomb."

Carl looked aside. "We don't know what will happen. All we know is whatever Ben contains is powerful, likely dangerous. It will emerge sooner or later, and we need to be there when it does."

Dani wanted nothing more than to sucker punch the elemental right then, to see if she could slap his face straight off. This time, she recognized the mounting anger as entirely her own.

"You aren't really his friend or his partner," she said, keeping her fists by her sides. "You're a spy."

He winced. "That's unkind, Dani. I've saved his life a dozen times over."

"Because it's your job!"

The elemental's neck lengthened, thrusting the watery head inches from Dani's face. "Because I care for him!"

Dani wiped droplets off herself as Carl restored the semblance of a regular body. His scowl looked so much like Ben's it was disturbing.

"Maybe it was my duty at first, but his wellbeing has come to be a personal thing for me." His form shrank slightly. "Can we argue about my altruism later? You didn't come here to talk about this."

"Fine. Ben and I already have an appointment for me to ream him out. Shall I pencil you in for the slot after that?"

"Certainly. We'll have lunch. A few drinks. Perhaps go dancing after."

"Funny boy." Dani tucked her fists under crossed arms. "So you're helping me help you help Ben."

"Succinct enough. I've subdued the more riotous of your bonded elementals for the time being. It took some wrangling, but I've convinced them to play along until the immediate crisis has passed."

"Can they access the glassway then? Or tell me how to do it?"

"We believe so." He raised a finger. "But there's going to be a cost."

She scowled. "That's the part I've been waiting for this whole time. I already agreed to owe them favors for helping with the blackshard. What part of my soul do they want to try and cheat me out of now?"

"You don't trust them?"

"You bet your bubbling blue balls I don't trust them. Besides, I've made enough deals already. I made a deal with my parents about school. I made a deal with Sydney about a date. A deal with the Board about this job and Jared. I don't need another oath or contract hanging around my neck."

"Who said anything about making an oath or deal?" She started to protest, to say he'd just mentioned a cost, but he cut her off. "The Board's quarantine will trap the elementals along with you, and they don't want that to happen any more than you do. Helping them realize that clinched most of the debate for me."

Ah. Self-preservation. That, Dani could believe.

"What's this cost you're talking about then?"

He raised three fingers. Dropped one. "Pain. Opening the way will hurt."

"I can handle pain." Dani tapped her recently healed foot for emphasis. Enjoy it? No. But handle it? She refused to let anyone think her a wuss or coward.

"Not finished," Carl said. "The effort will also likely exhaust both you and the elementals for a time. You won't be able to pull off anything more than popping a soap bubble for a while."

Dani frowned, not liking the thought of being unable to help in whatever fight waited on the other side of the glassway. "I'll have to trust the others can handle Malawer and his cronies, then. But I'll still be able to swing a mop and squeegee. What's the third thing?"

"Beyond the initial pain, there's a high likelihood of magical feedback causing negative physical side effects."

"That's … vague."

"It's not like there's a lot of people running around doing this every day," he said. "Even your elementals are leery of the consequences. My guess? It'll be somewhere between intense headaches and going into a coma for a few days." He peered at her. "You're still sure you want to go through with this?"

Dani weighed the pros and cons. Carl presented an unpleasant range of options as to what she might experience, but were any of them worse than the quarantine? What if Malawer's disease proved incurable? She and the others could be preserved for years— decades or centuries, even. Her family and few friends she had outside of work and school would be left wondering what had happened to her. And what kind of world would they wake to, if ever?

She firmed her spine. "Yes. Tell me what to do."

He nodded, as if proud of her for making the right choice. Well, screw him, the double-dealing little sprite. Who was he to judge her either way?

"Up until now," he said, "you've been projecting your energies into the surrounding elements, making them an extension of yourself and using the elementals as a focus for your spells. In this case, you have to let the elementals project their energies through you." He toggled an invisible switch. "Kind of like flipping a vacuum cleaner's airflow into reverse."

Dani narrowed her eyes. "Project through me? Which ones?"

"All of them. At once. Those of fire, earth, air, water, and all the rest."

"All the *rest*? How many elementals did I get bonded to? Aren't there, like, only four big ones?"

Carl's gurgling chuckle had her wanted to stomp him into puddles.

"You think there's only one type of water?" he asked. "Only one type of wind? One type of flame or dirt or metal? My kin are a diverse species, and you've bonded to quite a thick chunk of the spectrum. It's what makes you so strong. Mostly, you've been manipulating the elements rather piecemeal. But here, every elemental at your command, no matter how great or small, must work in concert."

Dani shook her head. "Great. So I'm a weaponized periodic table."

Carl grinned. "An elementary deduction, my dear—"

"Finish that, and you're leaving here without limbs."

"I don't have them most of the time anyways," he said with a level gaze. "It's difficult to threaten my kind with physical violence, if you haven't noticed. At the worst, we get recycled into the atmosphere and, next thing you know, we're coming out of your spigots."

Dani glowered at him. "Doesn't mean I wouldn't get any satisfaction out of it. That was awful."

"Would you? And doesn't your power require a bit of emotional control? Something you're already on thin ice with, considering Malawer's disease."

She growled, but waved for him to continue. "Fine. Explain how this has to go down."

Carl moved around her, footsteps slopping on the tile, until he stood before the Corrupted glassway.

"Glassways are protected by an incredibly dense sheet of crystal; the glossy surface you see and touch before passing through. When you have the proper access, the glassway acts like ..." He made a circle with both hands. "Let's use the image of a vacuum cleaner again. It sucks you up and through the tube to the other end. But in this case, the tube is capped. You have to remove that cap, and the only way it's going to happen here is through brute force—which, fortunately, is your specialty."

"That's where the reversing the power flow comes into play?"

"Exactly."

"What then? The glassway opens and we step through to the other side?"

His watery form shivered. "It's not going to work exactly like it used to. The Corruption has made it unstable. Dangerous. Think of a regular glassway like a tree root. You flow through it from one end to the other. The Corrupted forces which have twisted this one … it's like they yanked the root out, leaving nothing but dead space, with plenty of bugs and moldy earth now filling it in. Sections can collapse at any time."

Dani massaged the back of her neck. "Rivers, vacuum cleaners, tree roots … we're really scraping the bottom of the comparison bucket today. Are we done here?"

"For now. But, Dani." His liquid features drooped. "Please don't tell Ben what I told you about him."

That had her snarling in his face. "Why shouldn't I?"

Carl held his hands together, pleading. "He has enough troubles already. He won't be able to do anything about what he contains, if he even accepts it exists at all. You have to believe that, whatever comes, I intend to protect him as best I can. Telling him won't help anything. It'll only distract."

She stepped in and shoved Carl's chest. While water splashed through her fingers, it forced him back with each push.

"If we survive this … if your buddies help like they promised … if I don't go brain dead or get stuck in quarantine"— she locked eyes with him—"maybe I'll think about keeping a secret like this from one of my closest friends. Now send me back. And next time we talk, don't you dare come looking like this."

CHAPTER
TWENTY-EIGHT

Ben looked up as Dani stirred from staring at the dark glassway. She wiped a hand on her uniform, leaving a damp spot before turning around.

He grinned and waved. "Welcome back, princess. Look who finally found us." He thumbed at the glob of water jiggling on his shoulder. "Almost worried I'd lost him for good."

Dani's expression turned guarded, almost hostile as she noticed Carl. The elemental had emerged from the wash station faucet and glided over to Ben not long after Dani had begun her inspection. Then she smiled—forced, Ben thought—and nodded to where Lucy and Lopez flipped through the book he'd finally handed over. Good thing, too, as Lopez proved quite the speed reader.

"How much time do we have left?" Dani asked.

He frowned. "It's only been a couple minutes. You lose track of time that much?"

"They find anything useful?"

Choosing to ignore her ignoring his question, he checked around for a spray bottle to deposit Carl into.

"Not yet," he said. "From what little of their mutterin' I've made sense of, it's mostly descriptions of the glasskin themselves, a few tips on summonin' 'em, and some notes about their music. Seems they're quite the singers."

"Can we summon one?" she asked. "Could one open the glassway?"

He scrubbed his chin. "I asked the same thing, but looks mighty doubtful. The summonin' instructions are a teensy bit complicatified. Needs things like stained glass windows or diamonds the size of your fist—I didn't pick up on everythin', but I'm pretty sure we don't have all the necessary whiz-bang to get their attention. Not even sure a Pure glasskin could work a Corrupted glassway, neither. It'd be like tryin' to drive a car when the steerin' wheel has been covered with rusty razor blades. Any luck on your end?"

She grimaced. "Can you call everyone over?"

As the others crowded around, Dani kept her gaze on their feet and passed her mop from hand to hand.

"I think I have a way in," she said. "Not going to take the time to explain it, seeing as we're short on that. If it works, I don't think the trip through is going to be a picnic stroll, so be ready for anything. The other issue is, the effort is going to wipe me out for a bit. I won't be much use on the other side."

That explains her actin' so fidgety, Ben thought. He could sympathize with not wanting to rush powerless into enemy territory.

"Think you oughta come along then?" he asked, already guessing her answer.

She flicked a flat look his way. "If you're going, I'm going. I won't be a helpless kitten, and besides, maybe I'll bounce back quicker than I expect."

Carl bubbled on Ben's shoulder, and she glared at the water sprite for a second before dropping her eyes again. Ben glanced between the two. What was with them?

"Let's do this before I lose my nerve," Dani said. "Everyone ready?"

There came a rush of folks darting around, collecting brooms, mops, sponges, and any other available tools. In the scurry, Ben snagged the book back from Lucy and zipped it away, though not without getting a look from her that promised interesting and intense conversations in their future. First Dani, now Lucy … he'd need an assistant to handle his Holler-at-Ben schedule soon enough.

Lopez scrounged a spray bottle from a cabinet; once Carl sat safe within and the bottle hooked on his belt, Ben joined the others by the glassway where Dani waited.

Her gaze swept across them. "Good to go?"

At their nods, she faced the glassway and placed a hand on the center of it. Everyone leaned in slightly.

Ben didn't know what to expect, but it certainly didn't include Dani's arm swelling to twice its normal size. She gasped and pressed the elephantine appendage harder against the pane, as if gravity tugged her that way. The black glass bowed inward. Fine white cracks shot out to the edges of the mirror. The cracks widened and splintered.

All at once, the darkness contracted, as if a giant fist snatched it from the other side and yanked it away. The outline of the glassway remained, but all it contained had vanished. The glassway looked … empty. More a hole where a glassway used to be than an actual passage.

Dani dropped her arm, which had reduced to its normal size. She remained stiff for a moment before the smallest groan escaped her.

"… *owie* …"

Ben caught her under one arm before she dropped to her knees. She leaned against him, breathing hard, and he helped her move aside as Lucy went to test the glassway. Her hand went through the boundary, and she stirred it before pulling it back out and checking to make sure all her fingers remained.

"How'dja do that?" Ben asked Dani.

Dani shook her head and blinked over and over. "Stupid periodic table … ow, ow, ow …"

He tried to meet her gaze. "You gonna be okay?"

"Fine," she said through gritted teeth. "Just tell whoever's stabbing the back of my head that they can stop now."

"Mebbe you oughta think twice about goin'."

That popped her eyes open. "I'm coming."

She got her legs under her and pushed up. One knee buckled, but she caught herself, straightened and turned slowly, each movement a minor triumph. As the others stared, she licked her lips while patting and pinching her cheeks.

"I can't feel my face," she whispered. "It's still there, right?"

"Yuppers. Sure you don't wanna tell me what's goin' on? Ain't never seen nobody pull that kinda stunt."

She sighed and gripped the mop to stop her hands from shaking. "Look, Ben. You've got your things going on and I've got mine. Right now, that's the best explanation I can give, unless you want to cough up the truth about that book you just so happened to get from Jared."

"I wasn't gonna keep it a secret, but there wasn't a chance, what with fightin' for our lives."

"Which we're still doing," she said.

"Right. Ain't forgettin'." He caught the others' attention with wave of his own mop. "Here's the deal, folks. I'll pop in and radio an all-clear—"

"Nothing doing," Lucy said. "Me first."

Without giving anyone chance to argue, she strode through the Corrupted glassway and vanished. Lopez headed in with the twins on his heels, leaving Ben and Dani to exchange rueful looks.

"Last one in has toilet duty when we get back," he said.

She bolted for the glassway, and Ben was happy enough to see her returning strength that he let her eke in right before him.

Yup. Definitely let her.

CHAPTER
TWENTY-NINE

ctually, he thought after he stepped through, *lettin' the others go first weren't too bad a choice.* The reeking wind howling down the tunnel they'd entered almost had him on his knees, dry-retching, and that was with five other bodies taking the brunt of it. It smelled like someone had condensed the essence of a garbage dump, mixed it with a septic tank, bottled it, let it age a few decades, and then forced him to chug the vintage through his nostrils.

"Masks," Lucy called from ahead.

Hooking his arm around the mop handle, Ben tugged the dust mask—which Lopez had had the foresight of supplying them with—over his nose and mouth, and pinched the metal band to activate the seal-spell. With a crinkle of cloth, the stench faded to a nose-wrinkling fart, though the wind continued to rake his hair back and sting his eyes if he looked too straight down the tunnel.

Half a minute later, the wind eased into a breeze, and he joined his companions in a huddle. One of the twins had her broom thrust out to summon a gust, streaming it ahead to counter the stink. Ben checked around their shoulders to see what waited ahead.

Sagging mud formed the tunnel, with soggy wood, rusty nails, glass shards, stone fragments, and other rotting detritus sticking out everywhere. They'd need to be careful as they marched ahead to avoid getting poked in the eye or through the foot. One of the perks of being a Cleaner meant not having to worry about contracting tetanus, but the pain would be inconvenient.

And don't you be forgettin', Ben internally groused, *that you ain't a proper Cleaner no more, bucko.*

"Where are we?" Hardy asked.

Lucy checked with Ben, who shrugged.

"No clue," he said. "This ain't the Sewers, that's for sure. Or the Gutters. When Malawer slipped away last time, he used the ol' Scum sludge express, but this ain't lookin' like any kind of pipe network. Fortunately," he looked over his shoulder to see the gleaming walls of HQ beyond the threshold they'd just crossed, "we don't have to worry about figurin' which way to go. Seems a straight shot from A to ..." He caught Dani's eye. "What comes after *A* again?"

Her face didn't so much as twitch. Hoo boy. Whatever she'd put herself through to break the way open must've been worse than he even imagined.

"Straight for now," Lucy said. "There were dozens of Corrupted glassways in Malawer's house. My guess is we'll bump into junctions soon enough."

"So we follow our noses," Ben said. "Always worked for me. The stronger the stink, the better chance we'll find Malawer at the source."

"Clock's ticking," Dani said. "Can we talk as we go, please?"

For half an hour they trudged ahead. Mud sucked at their boots and dribbled from the ceiling to plop on their heads, necks and shoulders. Ben felt odd being at the back of the line, relying on the others to handle the worst of it if a fight went down. But if they encountered resistance, he knew he needed to stay out of the way, though it grated his pride to a fine powder. He needed the action, the sense of accomplishment and contribution. For now he swallowed the bitter pill and didn't argue his positioning. Who knew? Maybe they'd be ambushed from the rear and he'd get a chance to show some Scum who was the boss after all.

Dani walked beside him, wincing occasionally when she put her right foot down and using her mop like a walking stick. Its pointy end plunged deep into the mud with each step.

"How're you holdin'?" he asked.

"Decent," she said. "I can still sense the elements around us, but couldn't push a pebble downhill if it meant stopping Malawer right here and now." A thoughtful glance at him. "Is this what it's like for you?"

"Sorta. 'Cept I can't even sense anythin' no more."

"I'm sorry. I didn't realize how awful it must feel."

He grimaced. "Yeah, it's suckin' straight from an exhaust pipe. But, you know, 'one day at a time,' and all that feel-better bull."

"Speaking of bull," her elbow poked his ribs, "what's the deal with Jared checking you a book out of the library?"

Ben looked ahead, but saw no variation in the tunnel. Seems they had the time.

He gave a condensed version of running into Jared in HQ and taking him to Employee Records on a hunch—one which had yet to pay off. Dani's expression grew increasingly glum as he told her of the hybrid's innate knowledge of HQ and its workings.

"I'll admit to bein' a teensy bit worried about him," he said, once finished. "He's been yankin' his chain an awful lot lately. And it's an awful short chain already. Don't want the Board slappin' a choke collar on him too."

"He doesn't mean anything bad by it," she said.

"Not now, mebbe." He sighed. "Makes me think of a kid explorin' the kitchen to see where mommy stashed the cookies. Seein' what he can get away with. Gotta admit, I think we've been lucky he hasn't wanted anythin' bad enough that he refuses to back down. But we say 'No' one time too many, and he might decide he's gonna get them cookies even if it requires a hostile takeover of the kitchen."

"Then what do we do? How do we do a better job of teaching him what's right and wrong? Should I make up moral dilemma flashcards? Multiple choice tests? It's not like there's a textbook on ethics aimed at half-human godlings."

"Eh, check the religious section of any bookstore. You'd prob'ly find one."

"Ben, I'm serious."

"So am I. I ain't sayin' you oughta read him bedtime stories from the Satanic Bible or anythin'. But a religious text or two might be a place to start, since that's where plenty of folks first learn about how it's bad to go 'round murderin' folks 'cause you like their shoes."

A frown scrunched her face. "I'm uncomfortable using religion to keep him in check. Had some bad experiences with it, myself."

He shrugged. "It's just a startin' point. I don't think it'd turn him into a nun or anythin'. Lotsa kids like hearin' those stories about miracles, what with people walking on water, healing the blind, and talking to animals. I bet Jared could even do some of that if he tried."

"But what if he decides he likes the stories about divine judgment and wrath more than the ones involving, you know, mercy, love, and other fluffier values?"

"We gotta give him the chance sooner or later," Ben said. "We gotta help him understand the world he lives in. Right now, I'm thinkin' he listens to us 'cause we're familiar. He might not even realize he could flip us the bird and walk. But if he ever gets there, I ain't sure what we could do to stop him."

"Trying to educate Jared on morality might only bring us to that point faster."

"It's a risk, sure 'nuff, but one that's been there ever since we started babysittin' him."

"You mean when I took responsibility for him."

He nudged her with his mop. "Ain't gonna let you shoulder everythin' by your lonesome, princess. You're gonna need a substitute teacher to step in from time to time, 'specially once you're own schoolin' starts again."

Her snort sounded clear through her mask. "You. A teacher. The same guy who doesn't even give me the textbook for my own job."

"Thing is, I kinda forgot that thing was even s'posed to be an Employee Manual after a while."

"What? How?"

"'Cause I kept usin' it as a pillow every time I read more'n a page or two."

She huffed a laugh. Dry and disbelieving, but at least it was a laugh.

They continued to exchange suggestions on ways to help the hybrid not grow up into a sociopath, psychopath, or any other career options that could end in high body counts. Ben knew they were distracting themselves from the eventual showdown with Malawer by worrying over an issue that assumed they'd survive what came next. His thoughts wandered to what would happen if they didn't finish the job within the allotted—and quickly dwindling—timeframe. Lopez's placing Dani and Lucy into a brief quarantine resurrected his memories of the months he'd spent locked up, slowly regaining the sanity the Ravishing had stripped him of.

The worst part? Quarantine didn't fully shut down the mind. One's body and powers were contained, but the mind chugged away, aware of time crawling past while the world went on without you. If they failed—if the disease wasn't cleaned up—would he survive another experience like that?

A *whump* interrupted his thoughts. Dani paused in describing her idea for making Jared a video series using hand puppets with names like Mr. Do-Good and the Sock Monkey of Doom.

A glance behind showed a large section of the ceiling a few yards back had slopped to the floor like an oversized cow patty. As they watched, a portion of the wall slumped into the tunnel, piling mud knee-high.

"Cleanse me," Dani said. "He warned this might happen."

"He?" Ben asked. "He who?"

The question got put on hold as he hurried to outpace another massive slough of mud which poured down from the ceiling. They caught up with their companions who'd turned to see the reason for their lagging.

"What's going on?" Lucy asked.

"When I forced the way open, it must've destabilized the passage," Dani said. "If we don't get out of here soon, we're going to be buried alive."

Even as she pointed back, chunks of mud, glass and rock caved into a pile which would've easily smothered any of them.

"Move it, people," Lucy shouted.

They ran at a hasty clip, boots crunching and slapping in the muck. The tunnel shook with their pounding footsteps, and Ben wondered how much their presence alone hastened the collapse. Mud clots continued to pelt them. Laurel slipped and clawed furrows in the floor as she scrambled back up with Lopez and Hardy's help.

A wall collapsed as Lucy ran by, and it took them a couple minutes to dig her pinned legs out. She swore through the whole process, which effectively meant they didn't hear a word she said. Sweat drenched them all by the time she got free. Then back into the race to escape becoming the world's smallest oil deposit.

"Opening ahead," Lucy cried at last.

This spurred them on faster. Ben had to squint as those ahead of him kicked muck into his face. Dani shielded her face with one arm and bent into the sprint as well.

They stumbled into the open. Everyone skidded to a halt, and Lopez nearly went down this time, but for bumping into Hardy, who flailed to keep them both upright.

Seconds later, the tunnel swirled in on itself and collapsed with a squelch. Ben stared at the closed-off passage with apprehension. No going back, even if they wanted to.

They'd entered what appeared to be a central hub. It was a circular cathedral of slime and mud a hundred feet across, lit by moldy orange luminescence. Black and green stalactites hung from a vaulted ceiling and dripped into vile puddles that reminded Ben of his brief time in Filth's realm. The fetid meat stink of the place slithered into his nose and squatted there.

Ten Corrupted glassways offered themselves, spaced evenly around the otherwise empty chamber. Deep tracks and ruts marked the ground, but nobody waited for them—so far as he could tell.

"Which way?" Dani asked, waving at the various passages.

"Can we even get through?" Laurel asked. "Won't Dani have to repeat her trick from before?"

Dani stammered, obviously not having thought of that, but Lopez jogged to the nearest one and shoved his hand into the pane. It passed in and out without resistant.

"They're accessible," he said. "Perhaps whoever constructed this didn't think anyone but Scum could reach this point, and so thought further precautions unnecessary."

"Or it means this network is so spankin' new, they ain't had a chance to secure it yet," Ben said.

"Lucky us," Dani said, breathy with relief. Ben eyed her, watching for more signs of exhaustion, but she held her ground.

"More than lucky," he said. "If Corrupted glassways are connected to Malawer somehow, and we can bag him, we might be able to keep the trick from spreadin' to other Scum. We don't need no more of their kind figurin' out another way to slip around."

"What do we do?" Hardy asked, eyeing the potential routes. "Split up?"

"No way," Lucy said. "Even if we each took one, we can't cover them all, and it'd leave us incredibly vulnerable."

"Yeah," Dani said. "Don't you girls ever watch horror movies?"

Hardy shook her head. "No way. Too scary. They give us nightmares."

Dani goggled at the twins, who flushed. "You're kidding. We've faced down walking corpses, flesh-eating bugs, and living crystal—and it's a few special effects that keep you up at night?"

Laurel flicked a breeze Dani's way. The ladies exchanged stuck-out tongues before Lucy's clap startled them back to attention. The janitor visibly worked to suppress her frustration and whatever stronger emotions the disease tried to draw out of her.

"What we need to do," Lucy said slowly, "is see if there's a way to figure out where these passages lead to. To discern which one Malawer might've traveled through most recently."

They headed to check out the glassways; then an idea shot through Ben and he shouted.

"Footprints! Nobody move!"

The others stared at him as if he'd blurted, *"Cthulhu fhtagn!"* At least they'd stopped walking.

"¿Cómo?" Lopez asked.

Ben swept his mop to direct their attention at the ground.

"There's plenty of tracks trompin' through here," he said. "But not near as much as there would be if it was a real Scum hub. Suggestin' again that it's all pretty new. Stuff's been dragged through, crawled, and slithered around. But how many footprints are you seein'?"

"Just a few," Dani said after studying the area. "Some claw marks, a bunch of things that look like someone got really pissed off and tried to stab the ground over and over."

"Blackshards," Lopez said.

Ben grimaced. "Prob'ly. I'm doubtin' the mud here ever really dries, so the more recent prints cover the old ones. Malawer musta come through here not long ago if he brought his family back this mornin'. Check for a buncha footprints all goin' the same way. That oughta make it easier for us to pick out which path they took."

"But, sir," Laurel said, "what if the doctor stashed his family somewhere else, then came back through to where he works?" Hardy bobbed her head, supporting her sister's idea.

"First thing, never call me sir. Makes me feel old." Ben flashed the maid a grin to show no hard feelings. "Second, not too shabby thinkin'. But with how close you all came to baggin"em earlier and everythin' he did to get 'em back, I ain't thinkin' he's gonna let 'em out of his sight again. They're with him right now; I'd bet my arm on it."

"All right, mister hotshot detective," Dani said. "Do we break out the magnifying glasses and deerstalker hats now?"

"Yuppers. Spread out, start markin' any human tracks— 'specially grouped up, in different sizes. Try not to make a mess of the paths any more than you gotta."

Bent low to stare at the churned mud, the Cleaners eased along, trying to step daintily in their heavy rubber boots. Ten minutes slogged past, broken only by someone's occasional curse as they tripped and splattered into the filth, followed by the others swearing and threatening the clumsy soul for potentially wiping out evidence. Followed by apologies as everyone cooled their tempers and returned to the search.

"Here!" Lucy called from one side of the chamber. They tromped over to see her pointing at a muddy patch where four sets of prints had dug in.

"That's gotta be 'em," Ben said. He sighted down his mop like a pool cue. The prints oriented toward two black mirrors clear enough. Unfortunately, a choppy patch obscured the last few yards, keeping it from being obvious which of the two the family had finally entered.

He stepped forward and used the mop handle to scratch Xs in the grime above the two Corrupted glassways. "Narrows it some." He glanced at Lucy. "How you feelin' 'bout two groups of three?"

Her expression remained deadpan. "No."

"Rock, paper, scissors you for it."

"No."

"Best two out of three. C'mon. Where's your fightin' spirit?"

"You don't want to see my fighting spirit right now, Ben."

"Easy way to solve this." Dani pointed at the Corrupted glassways in turn. "Eeny, meeny, miny—oh no."

Ben started to ask what was wrong, but the earth shuddered and answered that. Dani, with her elemental sensitivity, must have felt it coming before any of them. It didn't feel like the warnings of imminent collapse while running through the tunnel. This was the quiver and shake of something shaking loose.

Some*things*, he amended, as three mounds rose from the mud before them and blocked off the black mirrors.

The Cleaners retreated as mire slopped off the figures to reveal glistening obsidian forms in a riot of jagged shapes. Two looked like leafless black trees; their column-shaped bodies splintered into branches which ended in hundreds of needlelike appendages. The third was identical to the one they'd faced before, with eight jagged limbs split into awkward top-bottom arrangements.

"These guys again?" Dani cried. "Come on!"

"Scatter," Lucy shouted. "Draw them away from the portals, and then try to circle around to get through."

"But we still don't know which one," one of the twins said as they backed away. "How're we—Mr. Lopez, what're you doing?"

Ben stopped checking the chamber for any defensive positions and saw the handyman remained fixed before the blackshards, within easy reach of their deadly fractal limbs. He had his rosary out and thumbed the beads, but not a glimmer of his aura showed.

Ben hesitated, caught between the urge to hunker down or to run to the man's side. "Lopez, wanna let us in on your plan? 'Cause I'm hopin' that means you got one."

The man raised a hand without looking his way. "*Silencio, por favor.* I will handle this."

Ignoring Lucy and the twins' protests, Lopez stepped closer to the creatures and stared at their glinting forms. The blackshards were either taken off-guard by this nonviolent approach, or were calculating the numerous ways they could flay the handyman before moving on to the others.

Lopez spoke before either side could move, and while his tone remained soft, his words carried through the chamber.

"You are not mindless slaves," he said. "You once possessed great beauty and wove creations of Purity for a noble cause. We call you blackshards, a name invented in our ignorance of you. Others name you *grigori*, or fallen angels. But there is truth to the first, *sí?*"

His hand came out of the pocket, holding a dark chunk of glass. Ben recognized it as the piece of the destroyed blackshard he'd taken from the Maintenance Room.

The blackshards went still as if Lopez had hit them with a quarantine spell, but Ben saw no sign of magic at work. Could they possibly be bothered by the remains of their former kin? Did the creatures even have emotions?

"You are all connected, are you not?" Lopez said. "Shards chiseled from a whole. You see what the others see. Feel what the others feel. That is why you knew we would be here." He flicked the rosary Dani's way. "*Verla?* She is a Catalyst of untold power. She destroyed your kin as easily as one swats a fly, and she can do the same to you here and now."

Dani gaped at Lopez. Then she shook herself, planted her feet, and thrust the mop out as if readying for a joust.

"That's right," she cried. "You want fire? Oh, I can bring the fire. How about I drop a few tons of rock on your ... heads, or whatever body parts you have. I'll shatter you sorry excuses for overgrown mirrors so hard I'll have bad luck for the rest of my life. I'll—"

"*Eso es suficiente,*" whispered Lopez. Dani bit off her threats, but maintained her fierce glare at the blackshards. Ben tried to not look at her legs, which had begun to tremble.

"You knew coming here would mean your destruction," the handyman continued. "Yet here you are. With your reputation for being a cunning and elusive species, this speaks to me of an act against your free will. You have been herded here, forced to act as the doctor's bodyguards—a position far below your true stature. *No les pareces?*"

He reached out and laid a hand on the nearest black facet. Ben thought himself insane, but he would've sworn the blackshard flinched from Lopez's touch.

A segmented limb lashed out. The handyman stumbled back and blood trickled down his neck.

Everyone lurched to attack, but Lopez flung his arms wide and shouted, "No!"

He wiped at the bloody line across his Adam's apple, revealing a shallow cut and nothing more.

Lopez faced off with the blackshards again. "*Pido disculpas.* I will not touch you again without permission. But I give you this opportunity to leave without forcing us to destroy you."

A voice grated out from one of the creatures—though without mouths, Ben couldn't tell which one spoke.

"*Why would you spare us, human?*"

"All creatures can be redeemed," Lopez said. "Corruption is not a permanent state of being. Stand aside, and I will bend all my power to cleansing you."

"*We are bound to our nature as much as we are to one another,*" the blackshard said. "*We cannot be diverted by futile offers of purification.*"

"Then we would spare you in exchange for a favor." Lopez pointed to the two Corrupted glassways Ben had marked. "Tell us. Tell us which path to take, where the doctor lurks, and we will see to it he causes no further harm than he has already to you or the rest of your kind."

Ben imagined he could sense the blackshards' thoughts flowing between them as their facets flickered and glinted. He kept his knees bent, ready to bolt the instant the creatures showed any sign of attacking.

One of the tree-like blackshards flicked a branching limb toward the Corrupted glassways. It muddled the *X* on the right and drew a circle around the one on the left.

"*Here.*" The central blackshard scuttled forward and tapped Lopez on the chest with a crystalline tendril. "*Do not come this way again, or there will be death. If you do not rid us of the doctor's influence, we will pay much for our failure.*"

They scurried across the chamber and vanished into other portals as if fleeing a fire.

Everyone held their breaths for a minute after they'd left. Then Dani squatted right there in the mud, mop across her knees as she put her head in her hands.

"Untold power?" she muttered. "Nice way to put me on the spot. What if they'd decided they weren't too frightened to try for a bit of revenge?"

"Lopez," Ben squinted one eye at him, "did you just lie?"

"He bluffed," Laurel said as she and Hardy moved behind the handyman. "That's different. Right?"

"Sure. It means no more card games during coffee breaks," Lucy said as she used her mop to wipe her forehead.

"If the Lord exists," Lopez said, once more thumbing his rosary, "better to ask forgiveness for deception than for needless destruction of His creation, *no?*"

"I don't think those things were exactly part of God's original plan," Dani said. "If there was one."

"We all start out within it," he replied. "Even creatures of such evil deserve to know they are never fully lost to hope and forgiveness."

Dani frowned. "So when we face Malawer, are you going to give him a chance to fess up and take communion, too?"

"Malawer has caused much sorrow," said the handyman. "But at what point does one become unredeemable?"

"Uh, how about when he sells his soul for power, which he then uses to try and murder hundreds of people? How's that for a start?"

Lopez gazed around at everyone. "Would any of us have done differently, in his place?"

"What kinda question is that?" Ben asked. "Of course we would've." When Lopez didn't reply, he shrugged. "Well, way to preach the gospel of Purity to a buncha Scum. We should start carryin' tracts around. Mebbe switch the company uniform to fancy robes." He held up a hand. "Before we go, I gotta know ... where'dja learn that blackshards are connected like that?"

Lopez smiled. "In your book. It mentioned that glasskin often seemed to share information without overt communication. I guessed that blackshards might retain a similar trait. A lucky wager, *sí?*"

"Oui, oui, mi amigotomato," Ben said. He frowned at the others' winces. "What?"

They gathered at the glassway the blackshard had marked, but Dani hesitated at the threshold.

"Hang on. What happens if the blackshards are trying to trick us? What if this passage doesn't go where we want?"

"We gotta hope Lopez scared enough snot outta them that they didn't dare pull a fast one," Ben said. "We barely got more than an hour before quarantine hits. If this don't get us where we need to go, mebbe we'll have time to come back and try the other, but it's the best lead we got."

Lopez hustled in, followed by Lucy and the twins. Dani didn't even give him a chance to argue before ducking into the portal. Ben stepped through after, trying to not feel like the kid picked last for football team.

He had an instant to think, *This ain't right,* before he plunged into a river of freezing sludge.

CHAPTER THIRTY

Dani floundered and choked as frigid slime splashed into her face. She glimpsed her companions similarly stuck mid-stream as putrid floes and chunks of brown ice crammed around them. She'd lost her mop in the shock and wasn't about to dive under to find it, even if she had full-on scuba gear.

Ben's shout echoed as he dropped into the muck beside her, and his impact cascaded green-gray water over her head. Her dust mask kept it from getting in her mouth, but her eyes stung as droplets slipped in before she could clench her eyelids shut. It took all her self-control to not scrub her face with her dripping sleeves, as that'd only worsen the problem.

Blinking furiously, she got the smarting tears cleared enough to see Ben lodged armpit-deep in the sludge like the rest of them. He glared and writhed a bit.

"Ain't this lovely," he said. "I'll have to cancel my mud bath for tomorrow."

"Why didn't we come through the other end?" Dani asked.

"'Cause this ain't a regular glassway no more," he said. "Whatever they've done to Corrupt it has got it all bass-ackwards. Shoulda figured."

"Now what?"

He sighed and eyed the slop. "Now we try and swim."

"Swim?" Dani echoed. "I can barely move."

"I did say *try*."

"Guys?"

Dani twisted to see Hardy staring at the sides of the tunnel in worry.

"I think we're rising," she said.

Everyone stared at the walls until even Dani noticed a bump in the surface level. The arched ceiling came half a foot closer.

"Cleanse my colon," Ben said. "She's right."

"It was a trick," Lucy called. "The blackshards wanted us to drown."

"Hold on." He nodded at the dark panel they'd just entered. "We can go back out once the level rises enough."

He squirmed and kicked his way closer to where the panel hung a few feet above. As the surface continued rising steadily, he groped for the ledge. Once the bottom came into reach, however, his fingers bounced off the glassy barrier.

"No." He hammered the panel, but it didn't so much as flex. "Aw, c'mon!" He sagged back and looked her way. "Any chance you could—"

She shook her head. "Nuh-uh. I told you, it's not a repeat performance."

He slapped the muck, spraying her again. "Then what good is it?"

She stiffened, and then spat back. "Oh sure! Because you're a lot of help right now. Want to tally up who's actually contributed to our little escapade so far? Want to guess who's running laps around your score right now?"

His nostrils flared. "You do not wanna even start—"

"Would you two zip it?" Lucy cried. "I'm done listening to your pissing contest."

Ben rounded on her as much as the mire allowed, while Dani seethed at him from the side.

"Who put you in charge, anyhoo?" he asked. "Did any of us ask you along? No. You just barged in and figured you was the boss, like you always do. Always ready to tell folks when to bend over and take it, ain'tcha, Lu?"

Lucy bared her teeth. "Ben, don't—"

"Don't what?" he asked, mockingly. "Point out how useless you are right now?"

Lucy trembled with barely contained anger, but before she could retort, Lopez's voice thundered out.

"*Padre nuesrto, que estás en elcielo! Santificado sea tu nombre!*"

He had his eyes shut, shouting in an attempt to drown out their rising arguments.

"Oh, shut up with your stupid prayer," Lucy shouted. "I'm so sick of you acting like being a handyman is a high holy calling. It's not, hear me? You're just a muckraker, and you're going to die in the same stinking hole as the rest of us." When he didn't respond, her face purpled. "I'll be damned if I'm going to let your voice be the last thing I hear!"

She thrashed for Lopez, looking ready to throttle him.

"Leave him alone," the maids cried as one. Laurel caught Lucy's arm, but the janitor spun and snatched at the maid's hair. Hardy cracked a fist into Lucy's cheek, and the three of them clawed for control. Their shrieks and yelps bounced off the ceiling which had come close enough for Dani to touch if she tried.

Dani moved to help the twins, but Ben grabbed her collar.

"Let 'em duke it out," he said with a laugh. "Lu could use a thrashin'."

"Let go of me!"

She raked at his face, but he reared back. Another harsh laugh and sneer fanned her fury which swept through her in boiling waves. Her skin sizzled as she lunged at him, while he tried to shove her back. His malicious humor switched to rage a moment later, and he dragged her closer. When she fell against him, he slung his arm around her throat.

Dani jabbed an elbow back. He grunted and his grip loosened enough for her to wriggle out. Using his uniform for handholds, she yanked herself onto his back, where she wrapped her legs around his waist. She hooked an arm under his and then over the back of his neck into a half-nelson, straining to bend him double.

As he beat back at her, she saw the maids dragging Lucy under the surface while the janitor struggled for air. The twins' expressions were locked in vicious glee, not caring they were about to drown a fellow Cleaner along with themselves. Lopez floated an arm's length away. Tears streamed from his closed eyes, his expression one of utmost sorrow.

Filthy water made her shut her eyes again as the surface surged upward. Both her and Ben's heads bumped into the ceiling, knocking a last sane thought loose.

Is this it then? Is this how we go? Clawing each other's eyes out in some cesspit before drowning, quite literally, like rats?

She clamped her lips closed as she went under. For several heartbeats, she heard nothing but the thud of her heartbeat and felt nothing but Ben's lanky frame struggling in her grip. The shock of being submerged broke the spell of rage, for what little good that did. No chance to apologize now. Nothing to do but see if drowning was as horrible a way to die as she'd always imagined.

She tried to find Ben's hand, to give it a last squeeze in a pathetic reconciliation attempt. Her lungs burned while the frigid waters plastered her uniform to her skin.

A current sucked at her feet. The muck churned around her and tugged her down. She released Ben and kicked at whatever had grabbed hold, but felt nothing below.

The tug increased and tore her away from the janitor, who'd stopped struggling and hung limp. Then she tumbled down, lost in a swirl of brackish water.

She struck a hard surface, bounced off and spun. She tried to tuck into a tight ball, not just to protect herself, but to also hold in the remnants of air struggling to escape.

Another shift in direction. The back of her neck struck rough stone. The pain forced her breath out and she fought to not draw another. Red and purple light flashed behind her eyelids, and her body felt like an enormous bubble of pain, ready to pop.

Right as her lungs nearly overrode her survival instinct, the pressure built behind her and shot her out into an open space. She opened her eyes in time to see herself fly over Laurel and Hardy's prone forms. She hit and rolled across a metal platform that bruised her hips and arms as she came to a sprawled stop.

Her mask had torn off at some point. Where her body didn't feel numb, it twanged painfully whenever she tried to move. So she lay there, wheezing, and hoped nothing with slavering fangs or glowing red eyes tried to eat her for at least a few minutes.

At last, she summoned the strength to check on the others. Perhaps the fangs and eyes beastie hadn't gotten to her yet because it was still snacking on them. Might be good to find out.

Lucy was on her hands and knees a few feet away, and she glanced at Dani right before retching up another spew of muck. Lopez held her shoulders to steady her, his aura steady. The twins sat nearby, knees tucked to their chests, looking like kittens rescued from a washing machine. Dani figured she didn't look any better.

On the other side of them, a large rusted pipe jutted out from a wall of whitewashed corrugated steel. Murky water trickled to the floor as Dani eyed the opening. They'd come out of that? Hopefully after they dealt with Malawer, they could call a van to retrieve them, because she sure wasn't crawling back in there.

She took another look around, and panic jolted her to her feet. "Where's Ben?"

CHAPTER THIRTY-ONE

Ben opened his eyes to darkness. He tried to suck in a breath, but soggy cloth stuck over his lips. A spasm wrenched him, and he scrabbled at whatever blocked the air. The dust mask ripped away and he sucked a lungful, not caring who or what heard his gasps.

As his breathing settled, pinging noises caught his ear. It took him a few seconds to recognize the sound.

Footsteps on metal. A clip-clop of heels, as if he'd fallen into the path of a woman in executive attire stalking an office building. He licked his lips, tasted foulness, and tried to call out to them.

"Who …?"

"Shhhh."

The hushing whisper prickled his every last hair. He still couldn't see, but the footsteps had stopped and he sensed someone standing beside him. Had he struck his head? Might the blindness be permanent?

He jerked as a hand touched his thigh. "Don't …"

A finger—human, felt and smelled like—laid over his lips, while the other hand patted down his pants leg until it came to the pocket the glasskin book sat within. The person undid the zipper and slipped the book out. They flipped through the pages, and then the covers snapped together.

Ben tried to lift his head, to clear his vision, but both his strength and sight failed.

After another pat on his cheek, the touch withdrew and the footsteps receded.

"Wait …"

He flung his arm out to grab at the person's heels, but groaned as his wrist banged into a metal rod and sparks of pain crackled in his elbow. Kicking out in reflex slammed his boot into another metal surface, and the echo reverberated through and around him, giving him a sense of a cavernous space.

As if he'd rung a gong to summon his vision, dusky light filtered through what appeared to be a top floor of an industrial plant.

He huffed in relief and irritation.

Just a *myrk*, then. A spell of blinding and confusion Scum liked to slap on Cleaners to take them unawares. So why hadn't the caster killed Ben while he'd been helpless? Why take the book and stroll away? Had that been Malawer's wife, sent to intercept him? The use of a *myrk* niggled his thoughts, but he pushed it aside until after they dealt with the immediate emergency.

Groaning from soreness and growing exhaustion, he got to his feet and looked for the others. What had they been fighting about before the sludge had taken them? He couldn't remember. It had to be Malawer's disease growing stronger. Taking deeper root.

He checked himself over, mostly relieved to see Carl's spray bottle still strapped to his hip. He tapped the side.

"You okay in there, buddy?"

Carl spun into a tiny whirlpool. *What a ride.*

Ben checked over the railing, seeing a maze of pipes, platforms and chemical vats stretch into the distance.

"Any clue where the others are?"

Sloshing communicated, *None.*

"You get a look at whoever tried to fondle me, or did the *myrk* getcha, too?"

Carl whirled into a serpentine shape. *Sorry.*

"No worries. Can't win 'em all."

A further inventory check didn't cheer him much. No mop. His radio was still attached, but when he turned it on, the power light flickered and the talk button had no effect. Great. Someone needed to figure out a better way to waterproof and sludgeproof these things. He'd make sure to put that in his report.

He paused as his hand brushed the breast pocket containing Karen's photo and the access sigil. Tapping the chanted metal disc, he considered tossing it aside. Without it on his person, the quarantine would have no link to draw him back to HQ, unlike the others, whose Pure energies would allow the spell to home in on them.

Memories of being in quarantine battled with his belief in getting the job done, no matter the cost to himself. He recalled the long months of battling to regain his sanity and control of his abilities. Letting the horror of Karen's death and the Ravishing settle into a numb acceptance while the Board debated over what to do with him—all the while locked inside his body while people treated him like a lab rat. How would his mind react if he was forced into that state again? And would the emotional contagion continue to worsen within the confines of the spell? Would his control erode until there was nothing left of him but murderous and suicidal impulses?

He let his hand drop. All those fears aside, what good would he do if he remained free? If he even got out of this place, he'd only succeed in spreading the emotional contagion to anyone he encountered. If he wanted to ever consider himself a Cleaner again, whatever the dubious honor of the position, he couldn't willingly put innocents in harm's way.

Carl's spout of alarm turned him around in time to see Malawer stride into view from behind one of the larger nearby vats. His lab coat flapped around his skinny thighs, and he wore green surgical booties which had softened his footsteps. He halted on spotting Ben, and the two men stared at each other like gunmen poised for a high-noon showdown.

"An intruder." Malawer tilted his head. "Recognition. Infected specimen. Undetermined Cleaner variety."

Ben eased his hand to the spray bottle trigger. Plan A: Subdue Malawer until the others arrived. Plan B: Cut off the doctor's head and anything else that wouldn't stop wriggling.

"Heya, doc," he said. "Good to see you again. I've had this pain in my tender bits these past coupla days that I just can't get over.

Thought an amputation might help."

Two mudmen emerged from the shadows at Malawer's sides, noses and mouths sealed over. Glistening black eyes fixed on Ben.

Both wore ragged Cleaner uniforms.

Ben's gut twisted at the sight of the former coworkers' remains. Possibly part of the team Francis had sent out to investigate. No wonder they'd never reported in. He didn't recognize either of them, but seeing good people reduced to Scum droppings never came easy, no matter how many times it happened. Forcing himself to swallow stomach acid, he glared at Malawer.

"You run outta graves to rob, doc? It's a bit heartless turnin' friend to foe."

The doctor flashed his toothy grin. "Good then, that I no longer possess such an organ."

Malawer pointed at him, and the mudmen loped his way.

Ben considered whipping Carl out and making a last stand of it. In these close quarters, he might take one down before the other pummeled him senseless.

Plan C: Run like a bunny and salvage his pride later if he survived.

"Well, scrap it."

He turned and sprinted off with the undead Cleaners' steps echoing his own. A rusted stairway sat fifty feet down the way, leading to a lower level of catwalks.

He almost made it to the top step before another mudman dropped onto his shoulders from the upper landing and slammed him to the floor. His head struck steel, and he saw shark teeth and dead eyes descending before he blacked out.

CHAPTER THIRTY-TWO

Dani cocked her ear, thinking she'd heard a distant shout and clang. When it didn't repeat, she returned to studying where they'd arrived. They'd had a quick argument on Ben's absence, and determined the best chance they had of finding him was to move forward. A quick whisper on their radios produced no response, which disheartened her further.

Rusted piping and beams of all sizes, platforms, catwalks and stairs formed a metal jungle around them. A look through a hole in the landing revealed a concrete floor one flight down, and she counted at least five levels above. Light bulbs flickered in wire mesh strung along the occasional railing, and dusty fluorescent fixtures spotted the facility with curtains of chilly blue light. The only other illumination filtered through holes in the corrugated steel walls, and this was fading fast to twilight. Grime and rust invaded every surface, eating away at paint, tracking down the walls in old stain patterns and turning what must've once been a pristine building into a collage of green, brown, and gray.

The landing they'd tumbled out onto braced against one of the main walls. Three large vats had been built along this side, all of them two-stories high with labels like *Sulfate* and *Aluminum Hydrate* spray-painted on above warning signs that read *Toxic!* and *Danger!*

Dani wondered how people really needed such warning signs to avoid exposing themselves to industrial chemicals. Had there been a rash of deaths from folks munching on the stuff when they got bored?

An orgy of smells fought for dominance—fetid water, dust, and mold combined with acrid wafts which threatened to drain Dani's sinuses if she inhaled too deep. After all the muck they'd waded and swam through, she was going to give herself a full body immersion in a bathtub full of sanitizer gel once they got back to HQ. Maybe wearing a snorkel.

She extended her elemental senses and got a brief impression of the metal maze of the place, of a stony foundation and air circulating through countless gaps and chinks. Then her senses recoiled as if they'd touched acid. The whole facility felt poisonous down to the mortar and rebar. If elements could emanate hostility, then the entire facility was growling at the newcomers like an attack dog straining to break its chain and go for the throat.

Her companions regained their feet and joined her in surveying the environs.

"Anything survive the trip?" Lucy asked.

Their mops and brooms had vanished, but the maids produced dust rags and small spray cans of all-purpose cleaner. A few sponges got handed around. Dani still had a squeegee dangling from her belt. Lucy found her steel wool glove and tugged it on, while Lopez produced a bar of soap.

Lucy frowned, displeased by the final count. "Maybe this place has an old janitor's closet we can pillage."

"Do we really need those tools?" Dani asked.

"It's harder without them," Laurel said. "You just get used to channeling through them after a while."

"I don't," Dani said. "My power doesn't need an external channel."

"Technically, neither does ours," Lucy said. "But we're stronger for it. Being a Cleaner isn't just about what we do, but how we do it. Our tools are symbols of Purity, and symbols can imbue a level of power in themselves."

"Like Malawer using the snakes-on-a-pole motif?"

"Sort of. For Malawer, that altar and snake symbol were likely part of what transformed him into a fleshmonger. There must've been a ceremony, a trade of power for services rendered. Most Cleaners are born with their powers, even if they don't manifest them until later in life—or at all. Scum, at least the human sort, are a bit different because—look, it's in the manual, all right? Read it when we get back."

Dani snorted. "Right. This Employee Manual Ben forgot to toss my way. Anyone else actually read the thing?"

Laurel, Hardy, and Lopez raised their hands.

"Whatever." Dani shook her head. "We should move before it gets too dark."

Lucy checked her watch. "We've got half an hour to mop up. At the most."

"And much ground to cover," Lopez added.

"Well, haste won't make waste here." Dani headed for a flight of descending stairs she'd spotted.

They tromped out onto the ground floor, kicking up white powder which had them sniffling and choking back sneezes. Grouped together, they passed by rooms with doors broken open to show piles of rubber tubing, shattered windows, and half-collapsed desks. As they skulked through the bowels of the facility, Dani twitched at every ping and echo.

She resisted the impulse to feed her elemental senses into the surroundings again, put off by the negative vibe she'd experienced the first time. Did it indicate they had really found Malawer's base of operations, or was something else behind her heebie-jeebies? Lucy had said ghosts didn't exist, but did the Cleaners ever encounter anything of the phantasmal sort? Were there such things as haunted buildings, or did her nerves provide all the fuel her imagination needed to conjure leering faces in the shadows and make her certain they were being watched?

"I don't even want to guess what we're inhaling," she said as she waved off another cloud. "Probably going to die of lung cancer at thirty at this rate."

"We'll get a full scrub-down when we get back to HQ," Lucy said. "You could chain-smoke ten packs a day and still come out squeaky clean after Maintenance gets through with you. Perq of the job."

"Great. Remind me to snag a carton of cigarettes after this. I've been aching to get a new vice."

"Gross," Hardy said. "I could never kiss someone who smoked."

Dani grinned at the maid. "Don't worry. I'm not asking you to kiss me anytime soon. But I've heard the whole husky voice thing is sexy."

"Right," Laurel said. "About as sexy as having a rusty chainsaw whisper sweet nothings in your ear. Had a boyfriend like that once, and every romantic thing he tried to say sounded like a death threat."

Dani grimaced. "Okay. Maybe not smoking then. How about whiskey?"

"You like whiskey?" Lucy cocked a bushy brow. "Wouldn't have taken you for the hard stuff."

"After the girls and I have our manicure date," Dani said, "you and me are going to snag a bottle and see who's left standing."

Lucy gave a rare grin. "Deal."

The mudmen chose that moment for the ambush.

One raced out from between two stacked boilers and slammed into Laurel. They both stumbled to the side and into a side room and fell out of sight with a clatter.

Lucy and Hardy stepped to the front as two more mudmen raced at them from ahead.

Lucy flung a rag into the nearer mudman's face. The rag wrapped around the creature's head and then, when the janitor made a fist, sucked inward. The mudman's skull crunched into the size of a baseball and wrenched off at the neck. Purple-green gas spouted from the esophagus, and the body thudded to the floor.

As the second mudman closed the distance to Hardy, Dani searched for anything nearby she could use as a weapon. Hardy side-stepped its outstretched arms, grabbed one, and flipped the creature over her shoulder. Going to one knee, the maid whipped out a zip-tie and had the mudman's arms and legs hog-tied before Dani could blink.

Dani had her squeegee unhooked and moved to aid Laurel, but had to dodge the mudman which lurched out of the room with a metal table leg jutting from its stomach. She slashed its throat as it went past her, and it flopped backward, its movements slowing as the noxious fumes seeped out.

Laurel emerged holding a length of PVC pipe like a baseball bat. She lowered it on seeing the other two mudmen dealt with, and high-fived her twin.

"What was that?" Laurel asked. "A three-second twist?"

"More like two," Hardy said. "We're taking the trophy this year, for sure."

"For sure."

"A little help, *por favor?*"

They whirled to see a fourth corpse that had slipped up behind them, but which Lopez had locked in a quarantine spell. The mudman jerked in attempts to break loose, and the handyman flinched each time as the containing bubble thinned, coming closer to collapsing.

Lucy moved in, gloved hand raised. She paused, glanced at Dani, and stepped aside.

"All yours, girlie."

With a fierce grin, Dani thrust the squeegee into the creature's chest, which split like a rotten gourd. She jerked back as foul gas erupted out, and the animated corpse joined the rest on the floor when Lopez released the spell.

"*Gracias,*" he murmured.

Dani tried to eye him surreptitiously as he knuckled his temples. How much did that spell take out of the handyman? He didn't seem the complaining type; more one to push himself over the edge for the sake of his companions. But if he dropped from exhaustion in the middle of a fight, it would just divide their focus. She needed to monitor him and ensure they didn't lose the one person able to mend an otherwise mortal wound—and who might be able to heal Ben, should they find him before the worst happened.

Hardy kicked the mudman she'd bound. "At least we know we're in the right place."

Lucy pulled another rag out and sprayed it with pine-scented air freshener. "Unfortunately, it also means Malawer likely knows we're here as well. Since mudmen are extensions of the fleshmonger's will, he's probably detected the scuffle and gone into high alert. We're going to face more resistance as we go."

As if on cue, dozens of figures shifted into sight from around barrels and vats in all directions. A horde of mudmen surrounded them and moved their way, picking up speed as they came. The corpses wore everything from business suits to nursing uniforms to Hawaiian button-ups. Yet they all had the same mask of skin with two dark pits for eyes.

Dani stared in horror at the number of dead until Laurel grabbed her arm.

"Come on," the maid yelled.

She pulled Dani toward a lone stairway that hadn't been blocked off yet. Lopez waved for them to hurry, but Dani shoved him ahead and went last.

Discarding stealth for speed, they raced up three flights until the ceiling came into view, and then took a main walkway toward the far end of the plant. Mudmen thundered behind them, some taking the stairs, others crawling over the pipes and grilles in silence, their beady eyes fixed on their prey as they swarmed through the facility like ants hungry for a picnic morsel. Shadowy figures matched them below with loping strides.

Lopez's pace slowed, and Dani caught his arm to keep him with the others. His aura flared each time he faltered and renewed his sprint, only to waver soon after.

Breathing hard, they reached what she guessed to be the center of the facility. An enormous conical vat hung before them, half the width of the entire building. Its inverted tip fed into increasingly smaller containers below, and the walkway they'd chosen split around it.

The group paused briefly at the intersection while the mass of mudmen ran, crawled and climbed closer. In the breaths they took to gauge which way to go, their decision was nullified by the glut of mudmen which crowded either side.

The Cleaners bunched together for a last stand. Then Dani looked to one side and spotted a metal ladder welded between this level and the next higher. She waved everyone toward it, crying, "There! Up!"

She and Lucy took stances at the ladder base as the first mudmen ran in. Lucy threw sponges to either side, which shot out streams and wads of water on impact. The water-grenade knocked the nearest mudmen down like dominoes, while Dani prepped her squeegee in case any made it past the initial blast.

The maids made Lopez go first, and he scrambled up the rungs while they prodded his butt. They followed, taking the rungs three at a time and flipping over the railing at the top. Lucy hip-checked Dani toward the ladder.

"Right behind you."

As Lucy slung another rag into a mudman's face, Dani hooked the squeegee on her belt and started to climb. Once she neared the top, the twins grabbed her arms and hauled her clear. Feet planted, she leaned back over and yelled for the janitor below.

"Lucy, come on!"

Lucy threw a last sponge-bomb which sent more mudmen plummeting over the railing. Grabbing the ladder, she dragged herself up. Several mudmen crawled after her, clutching for her boots. She kicked one in the face and then lunged onto the upper level.

A mudman clambered after her, fingers torn to bloody shreds by the rusted metal. Dani chopped through the creature's forearms and a kick from Hardy sent it falling onto its companions. As the mudmen struggled to untangle themselves, Dani slashed the ladder rungs and bars until the top few feet creaked and fell away.

With their glittering eyes still fixed on the Cleaners, the mudmen filtered along different paths to find the nearest way to follow them. A few stuck fingers through gaps in the floor and clung to the underside of the walkway, only to fall away when the maids stomped on their hands and severed the digits.

The group hurried along the only direction they could go— forward, toward what they hoped wouldn't prove a dead end.

"What now?" Dani asked through her panting. "We keep climbing and eventually there'll be no place to go but down."

"There!" Lopez pointed ahead.

Dani squinted until she spotted what Lopez had.

One corner of the plant had been turned into a three-story office building, separate from the processing network that snaked through the rest of the place. The squat, brown and gray cube of offices had several lights on in the large plate-glass windows lining each level.

In a lung-cramping sprint, they made for the building, but balked once they emerged from the thick of the pipes and walkways. The ledge they had arrived on hung ten feet above and thirty feet away from the corrugated roof of the indoor offices.

Dani and the others looked all about for stairs, ladders or any way to get across, but this area offered no such escape. The nearest mudmen would be there within a minute, at the most. More boiled about on the ground floor, staring at the Cleaners as if daring them to jump down.

Lopez sagged against the railing and wiped at his slick face, while Lucy pounded fist to palm over and over. The twins eyed the way they'd come, on the lookout for any mudmen on their trail. Dark figures moved just out of sight, but rapidly nearing.

Dani grabbed the maids' arms.

"Can either of you do that flying trick?" she asked.

The maids shared an apprehensive glance.

"Sorta," Laurel said. "But not for long."

Dani waved at the gap. "All we need is to get over there."

"We could move ourselves," said Hardy, "But at that distance, tossing any of you across would hurt you bad."

"Could one of you hop over and then cushion us coming in one at a time?"

Another worried look, quickly covered by determination.

"We'll do our best," they said.

Laurel took a running jump, vaulted the railing, and soared out into the open. Dani held her breath, but the maid lighted on the opposite edge with just a tiny stumble. She turned and waved.

"Come on! I'm ready."

Dani and Lopez helped Lucy stand on the railing while Hardy got in position behind her. When Lucy glanced down, she gripped Dani's hands tight enough both went white-knuckled.

"I don't like heights," she whispered.

"And I don't like being dead," Dani said. She looked back at Hardy. "Ready?"

The maid nodded and tensed.

"Count of one," Dani said. "One!"

With a yell, Lucy vaulted off the railing. At the same instant, Hardy swept her arms out. Even without a broom, the blast of air slammed Dani painfully against the side.

Lucy floated for a second before plummeting toward the bare edge of the office roof. Another swirl of air from Laurel arrested her fall. Lucy dropped slower, passed over the edge, and rolled to a stop. Dani turned to urge Lopez on. However, the handyman waved her off with one hand.

His other hand pressed out toward a mudman that had appeared mere yards away. Lopez's arm trembled as he kept the creature caught in a quarantine spell.

"You next," he said through clenched teeth. "I will keep Miss Hardy safe."

"Hurry," Hardy told Dani. "More are coming."

Trying to avert her eyes from the expanse and the mudmen at the bottom of it, Dani braced herself on a nearby pipe and fixed her gaze on the opposite ledge.

"Count of three," she said. "One—"

The gust struck her back and she jumped in reflex. The delayed reaction didn't put the wind under her as much as necessary and she came in at the roof at a neck-breaking angle.

A few feet from impact, however, that worry vanished along with the wind. Gravity reasserted itself, and Dani dropped.

CHAPTER
THIRTY-THREE

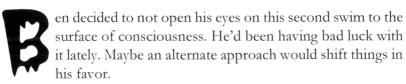

en decided to not open his eyes on this second swim to the surface of consciousness. He'd been having bad luck with it lately. Maybe an alternate approach would shift things in his favor.

"Breathing patterns have shifted. Subject is awake, but attempts to deceive."

Then again, mebbe not.

The slightest of movements made him aware of manacles clamped around his ankles, wrists, and elbows, the chains taut enough he could barely shift his weight. Numerous blunt and sharp objects pressed into his back, and his shoulders ached where the mudman had landed on him.

He cracked a lid and let the blurs swim into focus. Foam-tile ceiling. Drywall with peeling brown paint. Aged motivational posters hung askew in their frames, with words like *DEDICATION* and *INTEGRITY* paired with images of sunsets and eagles catching fish from a lake. Ben had no idea what a bird's diet had to do with *TEAMWORK.* Was the fish part of the team? Didn't seem like it got much out of the deal.

Finally he turned his attention to the clinking, jumbled platform he'd been shackled to.

He lay on a bone altar where a desk might've once stood. From the snake-and-wings sculpture on the one corner he could see, he guessed it to be identical to the one from Malawer's destroyed house. Even Scum were smart enough to back up their work these days, it seemed.

A stainless steel tray had been set beside the altar and Ben tried to not look too closely at the rows of bloodstained rods, saws, and scalpels.

Malawer shifted into view. He tucked a small digital voice recorder into a coat pocket and grimaced at the janitor. He looked almost normal, except for the gray of his lips and the circles under his eyes.

"Man of the hour," Ben said. "What's up, doc?"

Malawer gestured, and two mudmen wearing Cleaner jumpsuits took positions on either end of the altar.

"Why ain't I dead?" Ben asked. He had the feeling conversation was the best delay tactic here. If he could get Malawer talking, maybe it would give the others time to come to the rescue—if they'd arrived in the same place at all.

Malawer's unblinking gaze flicked his way. "You wish for death?"

"Nope. Just curious, since you ain't exactly been one to leave folks breathin' for long."

The doctor ran fingers down Ben's ribs, poked at his throat, and pressed on his bladder hard enough to make him wince.

"You are unique," he said. "Anomalous Cleaner. A base specimen? In part. But there is something more."

"That'd be my grizzled good looks." Ben arched his back to get a look behind him, but the mudman near his head pushed him flat. "What'dja do with Carl?"

"The elemental?" Malawer nodded at a miniature freezer tucked into a corner of the office. "Secured. Curiosity abounds. What effect will it have on injection into cardiovascular system?"

"Last I heard, shootin' water into your veins was a bit of a no-no." Ben moved his hips to keep a bone shard from piercing his kidneys. "So how's the family? Kids doin' well in school? Wife goin' to PTA meetin's, havin' tea and crumbly cookies with all the other dead moms?"

Malawer's brows crinkled. "Has humor always been so tiresome?"

Ben frowned. "Mebbe you just got a different sense of it. How 'bout this one: Knock-knock."

Malawer stood completely still, as if frozen in uncertainty.

The janitor sighed. "You're supposed to respond, 'Who's there?'"

After another moment, the doctor tilted his head. "Who is there?"

"A broken pencil."

When Malawer didn't respond, Ben prodded, "Now you say, 'A broken pencil who?'"

"A broken pencil … who?"

Ben let his head fall back. "Never mind. It's pointless."

Malawer waited a whole minute before pulling out his digital recorder and thumbing the record button. "Intriguing. Subject displays symptoms of some form of insanity."

"Aw, c'mon. I got another one. Hundreds of 'em, in fact. Knock-knock."

Malawer tucked the recorder away again. "Why do you persist in such banalities?"

Ben shrugged. "Dunno. I just crack 'em as I see 'em. Not my fault you've given up the ability to laugh to become a walkin', talkin' boogeyman. How's that workin' for you, anyways? Regrettin' becomin' a mass murderer yet?"

"Regret?" Malawer smacked his lips as if sampling the word. "No. Regret is wasted energy. Decisions are made and cannot be undone."

"Actually, they can. You just gotta realize you made a mistake. C'mon, doc. Admit it. There's at least an itty bitty part of you still in there, screamin' in horror at everythin' you've gone and done. That part of you knows your family ain't alive in any way that matters, and their bodies are just finger puppets you're wagglin' around."

Malawer slapped him. Ben knocked his head against the bones and tasted blood where his cheek had mashed against his teeth. Swirling and spitting to clear his throat, he grinned at the Scum.

"A full-blown emotional reaction, doc? And here I thought you weren't carin'."

"Emotion is wasted energy."

"Sure. Go all Vulcan on me. Die young and go broke."

Malawer frowned in confusion, and Ben sighed.

"Look, I ain't buyin' it. This heartless monster thing you've got goin'? You need a better actin' coach, 'cause you keep lettin' the mask slip. This thing you've created ... this emotional virus ... it's gonna destroy countless lives. Other families. Other guys with wives and kids like you once had. You think your family woulda wanted to be brought back like this? What would they think of what you've become?"

The doctor put his back to Ben. "They've thanked me."

"No," Ben said. "You thanked yourself. A mudman doesn't retain anythin' from the original person. They're just extensions of your power—a power you got only so long as you figured out how to sock it to the Cleaners, am I right?"

Malawer turned from the tray, now holding a scalpel with the tip broken off.

"Curious. Is it in the brain?"

Ben eyed the instrument. "I ... uh ... musta missed the conversation changin' tracks. What's my brain gotta do with your family?"

"When power was given to me," Malawer said, "I received new sight. Flesh and spirit divided. Energy, both of life and the Pantheons, became observable. All was revealed to me." He pointed the scalpel at the two mudmen guards. "Cleaner specimens provide insight into Pure energies. The skeins of power knotted within them. Yet you ..." He circled the altar, scalpel held by his side. "You lack these energies. Yet you contain something else."

"Yeah," Ben said. "The disease you got me all constipated with."

Malawer returned to his original position and gripped Ben's jaw, forcing their eyes to meet.

"No. This is deeper. It hides from my sight. I do not enjoy ignorance. I will discover the source." His face flickered from normal to the black-eyed visage. "And when answers are not observable on the surface, dissection may be required."

Ben pressed back against the bones. "Whoa. Hey now. How 'bout we get some anesthetic or somethin' before we begin, doc?

That's what you guys use, right? Or is that pesticides? Always forgettin' which is which."

"Unnecessary."

Malawer placed the tip of the scalpel on the base of Ben's throat. Ben started to shout, but one of the mudmen jammed its fist into his mouth. He gagged as his teeth sank into rotting flesh.

The first slice made him bite a finger off.

▲   ▲   ▲

A second blast of air punched up into Dani's stomach and knocked her eye level with the roof, but not quite high enough to clear it. Right as she fell a second time, Lucy's hand shot out and clamped onto her arm.

Dani's chest and stomach scraped over the rough edge as the janitor dragged her onto the metal sheeting. Dani vainly sucked for breath until Lucy slapped her on the back and her lungs decided to work again.

"Oh, no ..." came Laurel's horrified whisper.

Dani turned to see Lopez holding a trio of mudmen at bay. Hardy tugged on the handyman's uniform, trying to make him join her on the railing. Black eyes gleamed in the shadows just beyond their position.

Lucy shouted through cupped hands. "Come on! There's no time!"

Dropping his arms, Lopez spun and grabbed Hardy's hands for a second. Then he shoved her off the edge.

Laurel screamed. A blast of air buoyed Hardy, but Dani couldn't tell which maid had summoned it. Hardy flipped several times as she tumbled in, while Laurel flailed, raising gust after gust to keep her sister aloft.

Somehow, Hardy landed feet-first, but a leg twisted under her at the last second. She collapsed with a cry and fell backward.

Laurel and Dani dove in and grabbed the maid by each arm. As they caught her, Dani looked beyond to where Lopez raised a hand in farewell. A heartbeat later, mudmen swarmed in and drove him over the railing.

"Purity, no!" Lucy's cry deafened Dani for a moment.

The four of them could only stare as a waterfall of bodies swept the handyman away, tumbling down to the floor three stories below. Dani clamped her eyes shut at the last second, but couldn't block the faint crunches and thuds that echoed back up. The eerie lack of screams made it all even more surreal.

Laurel and Hardy held one another as they wept softly. Lucy kept shaking her head, as if refusing to believe what had just happened. The sudden loss rooted them all. Finally, Dani realized the distant clanks and tromping indicated more mudmen closing in throughout the facility.

"We ..."She looked around and licked her lips. "We can't stay here. We'll get trapped again. What do we do?"

Hardy rose on shaky legs. She opened a fist to reveal Lopez's rosary. When Dani raised her gaze from this, fury filled the twins' expressions, fueled by raw grief.

"We find Dr. Malawer," Laurel said hoarsely.

"And we make him pay," Hardy said, tucking the bead bracelet into a pocket.

Lucy shook herself and retreated from the edge. "Agreed. Let's see this done."

Arm slung over her sister's shoulders, Hardy limped along with them toward a corner of the roof where a hatch offered access to the top floor.

Dani used her squeegee to slice the lock off the hatch and pry it open, revealing a flight of stairs that fed into a dim hallway. After a quick check to make sure no mudmen waited below, they headed down.

The moment Dani hopped off the bottom step, she sent her elemental senses out and tried to sense any Corrupt energies in the area. If they searched each floor and room for Malawer, they'd run out of time long before they exhausted all the options.

Problem was, the entire chemical plant swarmed with Corruption, and the mass of mudmen made it impossible to pick out lone figures. Their footsteps reverberated through the air, and the air churned in their wake. Already dozens of them streamed into the first floor to seek the Cleaners who had eluded them. Other clumps of undead spotted the levels and rooms.

"There's too much going on," she said. "I can't figure out where he might be."

Lucy closed her eyes, as did the maids.

"There's a cluster of power on this floor." Lucy pointed to where the hall took a right turn. "That has to be where he is; or at least where he's secured the core of his spell. We destroy that and this all ends."

As they hurried toward the area she indicated, they took the corner and neared an internal stairwell. Still tuned in to the surrounding elements, Dani felt the floor vibrate and shouted a warning right before the stairwell door slammed open. Two mudmen lurched out, and footsteps echoed on lower landings.

Laurel flung a hand out and a blast of wind slapped one mudman to the floor, where Dani impaled it with the squeegee. Lucy caught the other one in the throat with a rag, which tore its esophagus out a second later as easily as razor wire.

Hardy rammed her shoulder into the door as another mudman tried to force it wide. She hollered as she braced with her wounded leg. Laurel joined her, both of them barely keeping the door closed. "Go," she shouted to Dani and Lucy. "We'll hold them here."

Lucy nodded in grim agreement. Dani hesitated, torn between getting to Ben and leaving her coworkers to face the mudmen by themselves.

"Are you sure?" she asked.

Laurel pushed her away. "Absolutely, girlfriend. We've got this. Go get that sucker and mangle him so bad we actually feel a little sorry for him."

"Not possible," Hardy said through clenched teeth.

With a last worried look, Dani joined Lucy in forging onward. Lucy seemed to know exactly which turns to take in hall junctions, and passed by numerous doors without bothering to check inside. Dani focused on keeping pace while ignoring the building mental resistance to their presence.

Her skin felt scraped raw by the Corrupt energies flowing around her, and her emotions fluctuated with each second. With one step, her hands shook with the urge to throttle the janitor. With the next, she stumbled and wiped at tears that threatened to flood out. Then she snapped back to a mix of fear and anxiety tightening her throat.

How could she trust anything she felt after this? How could she know if she was being manipulated or if she acted on her true emotions?

Finally, Lucy stopped in front of a closed office door. She sniffed and then snorted.

"In here." She glared at the door for a moment. "No wards." However the knob refused to turn when she grabbed it.

Dani raised her squeegee. "I could try—"

Lucy's kick broke the jamb and slapped the door against the inner wall. The two rushed in, and Dani noticed Malawer first as he straightened. Then the rest of scene came into focus.

Ben had been chained to a copy of the altar they'd found in Malawer's house. Blood streamed down his neck and a section of skin from his left chest and shoulder had been peeled away to reveal the muscle underneath. A mudman in a Cleaner jumpsuit had its fist rammed into Ben's mouth, who writhed as much as his bonds allowed, his eyes wide and furious.

"Cleanse me," Lucy said. "He's been using our people."

At her first step, the doctor pressed a scalpel to the janitor's neck.

"Don't move closer," he said. "His carotid artery is quite vulnerable."

Dani sensed Lucy tense to charge, and put a hand out to stop her. "Don't. He's right. Ben could bleed out in less than a minute."

The fleshmonger nodded. "Knowledgeable."

"Like I said, doctor-in-training here," Dani said. "What's your alma matter? Any chance you could write me a referral letter?"

"You will be subdued," Malawer said. "I will attend once finished with this specimen."

He waved with his free hand and the two mudmen moved to contain the Cleaners. When the fist popped free of his mouth, Ben licked his lips in disgust.

Then he jerked up and chomped Malawer's wrist.

Malawer hissed. He dropped the scalpel as he tried to yank free, but Ben hung on like a rabid Chihuahua gnawing on a pit bull.

Dani darted in and hacked one of the mudmen across the ribcage to release the fleshmonger's breath. Lucy grunted as the other creature took her into a bear hug. She stuck her steel wool-gloved hand into its face. When she ripped it away, the skin sealing the creature's mouth peeled off, and the creature toppled with a gust of the dark gas.

With his guards dispatched, Malawer tore loose from Ben and rushed for the door.

"You really think so?" Dani shouted.

She grabbed his lab coat as he brushed past and yanked with all her might. Malawer tried to slip his arms out, but one snagged and jerked him back. Lucy put a boot into his stomach, and he collapsed with a wheeze. The janitor leaped on him and pounded into his sides and face. Her gloved hand struck chunks of flesh free, and by the time Dani caught her wrist, much of Malawer's right side and face had been shredded to the bone. Yet he glared at them as if the shame of capture outweighed any physical pain.

"We still need him," Dani reminded Lucy.

The janitor tugged to free her arm and resume beating the man who'd caused them so much torment; but Dani kept her grip and Lucy's vengeful rage ebbed away.

"I remember," she said. "Let go, girlie. See to the old man."

As Lucy kept the doctor pinned, Dani went to the altar and chopped Ben's chains. She helped him roll off and to his feet, though he gasped when she accidentally brushed his exposed muscle.

"Careful, princess. I am a delicate flower, here, and he loved me not." He spat and then picked at his teeth. "Gah. Gonna be tastin' corpse for months. Could really use some mouthwash."

"Priorities," she said. "I'll get you as many gallons as you need from my personal stash, but only after we're done here."

"Right." They returned to Malawer, and Ben nudged the man's head with a foot. "You know what we need, doc. What core did you create to keep the spell goin'? Where's it contained?"

"It doesn't matter," Malawer said, words slurred by the ragged hole where his cheek had been. "My servants will overwhelm your companions in moments. Then they will finish you."

Ben grabbed Dani's squeegee and held it against the fleshmonger's throat.

"You ain't gettin' it, are you? Whatever you think about us bein' a bunch of do-good pansies, I won't hesitate to carve you like a turkey dinner until you tell us how to cure your virus."

"Desperation." Malawer gave a wet chuckle. "You attempt intimidation. Why? You have my body, but not my power. You have failed. Your time ends."

A flat voice slipped into Dani's mind.

All Cleaners, prepare for quarantine retrieval in ten, nine, eight ...

CHAPTER
THIRTY-FOUR

Ben froze at the announcement. From the others' stunned looks, they must've heard it as well.

"Not now," Dani cried. "Just a few more minutes!"

He groped at his breast pocket and yelled, "Hold him!" at the women.

Five.

Four.

Fingers snagged the metal disc of the sigil. Tugged it out.

Three.

He slipped the sigil into the doctor's breast pocket and jumped away.

Two.

O—

The voice died off, and Malawer jerked as if Ben had stuck him with a live brand. The fleshmonger writhed in the women's grips.

"What did you—" he started to say.

Their forms shimmered as white auras enveloped them. Malawer shrieked in pain and rage, but his cry cut off as the three vanished.

Ben stood alone in the office. He shuddered as the flayed patch of his chest burned with each breath, each brush of the air over bared muscle. He tried to avoid looking at the peeled skin as each glimpse made his stomach churn and knees wobble. The broken chains on his wrist and ankles jangled as he weaved where he stood.

Just a flesh wound, he told himself. Couldn't let the pain get to him. It was only his precious life blood leaking out, after all. Nothing serious.

He stared at where the others had been moments before. Had it worked? With Malawer trapped in quarantine, would the spell unravel? How could he tell?

Ben turned a weary circle. His thoughts drifted in and out of focus along with his vision. A large window looked out into the processing plant and he stumbled toward it. His hip bumped into the altar, and he paused to study it, to run a hand along one of the caduceus sculptures.

Was this the core? The thing could be a Scum equivalent of a nuclear bomb and he couldn't tell or do anything about it. Dismantle it, perhaps, but that wouldn't guarantee the dispersal of any energies invested in the bones.

You're useless here, old man, he thought. *Gotta admit it.*

He moved to the window, each footstep heavier than the last.

Fear. That was the real reason he'd slipped the sigil into Malawer's pocket, wasn't it? Nothing heroic. No idea what he would do once left behind. He just couldn't face going back into quarantine. He didn't have the strength. Didn't have the balls to accept the consequences of his mistakes.

Weakling. Coward.

He pressed his forehead to the pane and peered out. A look down confirmed his fears.

Mudmen. Dozens of them ringed the building on the bottom floor, shoulder-to-shoulder. The spell remained active, otherwise they would've all fallen over once the Corrupt energies animating them had been cut off. Malawer being quarantined hadn't disrupted the flow of power as he'd hoped.

He licked his lips again, tasted mud and the scraps of flesh stuck between his teeth. He ran a hand down his suit but came up empty of anything to get rid of the horrid flavors. *Not even a swish of water.*

That kicked his sluggish thoughts into gear enough for him to remember Carl. Not knowing why he bothered, he went to the mini-freezer and retrieved the spray bottle. Carl had turned to slush, and ice chips thumped the sides as the elemental tried to communicate.

Ben struggled to speak as well, his tongue a lead weight in his mouth. What was the point? They'd failed here. He'd bleed out soon enough, and the emotional contagion would continue to spread unchecked. The Cleaners—at least one of their bigger divisions—would be locked away, likely for good.

"Sorry, buddy," he managed to say. "Guess I just wanted to say seeya later."

Carl's swishing became more insistent, but Ben couldn't make sense of it.

"Been a good time, right? We did some good jobs. Had some fun. Say *hello* to your folks for me when you get back that way, a'ight?"

Icicles thrust through the plastic and pierced his hand. Ben roared and threw the bottle down.

"Son of a bloody biscuit! What was that for?"

He stomped, and the bottle split under his boot. Water splattered the floor. A few drops pelted his face and startled him back to awareness. The smothering feelings of hopelessness and defeat sloughed off him, and he realized how close he'd been to lying down and giving up.

And he'd just attacked Carl! He'd never thought it possible to be violent toward his partner, who'd gotten him through plenty of scrapes without complaint.

He knelt and tried to scoop the elemental's scattered puddles together. The ice fragments and droplets quivered and then rushed together. Carl's slushy form congealed into a hand with a lone finger thrust out.

Ben laughed and flicked the elemental.

"Thanks. I owe you. Almost lost it there." He chuckled. "Ain't no fair you bein' able to get past the foul-filter. Board's gotta realize the occasional ventin's good for the soul."

Carl flowed up and formed a chilly glove around his hand, which he squeezed slightly to indicate it was all good between them. Ben raised his hand and eyed his partner.

"Things sure ain't worked out the way I wanted," he said. "Gotta find where Malawer's playin' hide-n-seek with the spell core. Gotta end this before even a douse of ice water won't bring me 'round." He made a fist. "Can you gimme somethin' that'll make quick work of mudmen?"

Three six-inch blades jutted from his knuckles. A corner of Ben's mouth rose.

"*Snikt.* Heh. There's a reason we work together, buddy."

A closer inspection of the altar revealed the bones to be tied together by steel twine, and several well-placed slashes severed the main connections. The major sections tumbled apart, and he kicked and stomped the rest into worthless shards. By the end, sweat doused him while his chest and shoulder throbbed.

Another check out the window showed the undead mass below still standing, unaffected by the altar's destruction.

Ben leaned against the wall to catch his breath and let the room stop swimming. What else would Malawer have invested his power in? Something he would've kept protected ... something ...

Something worth protecting.

He pushed off the wall and headed for the exit, but paused with his hand on the knob. There had to be mudmen waiting for him just outside, and he had a worrisome track record with them lately. But what other way could he go?

A readying breath, and he yanked the door wide and cocked his bladed fist.

Mudmen crowded the hall outside, as he anticipated, each one oriented his way. Ben braced for the onrush, for them to pulp him with fists and feet.

None attacked. They just stared at him with dead eyes, arms limp, not the slightest shuffle.

After ensuring they weren't just waiting for him to make the first move, Ben stepped out. Easing by the unresponsive creatures, he began checking the doors to each room along the hall and found what he sought on the fifth try.

The door opened into a conference room that had been converted into a fancy dining parlor. A white lace runner lay across the twelve-person table, anchored by equally spaced silver candle holders and dinner settings. A half-drunk bottle of wine stood uncorked beside a pair of wine glasses and a stack of microwave dinners.

Ben's gaze tracked to the thin blonde woman who sat at the far end, hands in her lap as she stared at her empty plate. To her left, a husky teen slouched in his chair. On her right, a toddler had been strapped to a high chair. The baby might as well have been a doll, but for the occasional twitch of his pudgy arms and legs.

Ben shut the door behind him. The instant it clicked closed, the woman's head jerked up. Her black eyes shone with fear.

"Please," she said in a paper-thin whisper. "Do not." A purple, swollen tongue ran over her lips. "Do not take them from me again."

"Please." The teen echoed the sentiment without looking around.

The toddler bobbed his head. "I am nothing … without them."

Ben narrowed his eyes at the trio. "Malawer?"

A twitching nod from all three. Ben paced along the left side of the room as Malawer continued speaking through his wife.

"My body. Contained. My will. A distant echo. But my power—"

"Is in them, ain't it?" Ben waved at the boys and woman. "You shifted your energies, all the power needed to keep the virus churnin' along into them. They're the cores."

Their eyes shut briefly; all the confirmation he needed.

"I gotta admit. I get why you did it."

Three heads tilted. Black eyes blinked.

"Explain," said the toddler.

Ben pressed his arm to his side to keep it from trembling. "You loved 'em. You missed 'em. What father wouldn't? What husband wouldn't? They were your family, and they got taken from you. That kind of pain is plumb near impossible to imagine until you've gone through it yourself."

The family members emitted a low hiss.

"Don't preach to me, Cleaner," said the teen. "I'll not have your pity."

Ben clenched his fist. "No pity here, trust me. Mebbe the slightest bit of sympathy. I lost my wife years ago, doc, and it nearly wrecked me. I know how much it shreds you down to the bone. I woulda done near anythin' to get her back. I still would. *Nearly* anythin'. But this …" He pointed the blades at each in turn. "This is a line that never shoulda been crossed. And once you got 'em

Josh Vogt

back, were you happy? Was the love there? Were you an honest-to-goodness family?"

The three went limp again, and Ben imagined Malawer lurking just beyond sight, considering his words. He took a few steps closer to the family.

"No," he continued. "And y'know why? Because this ain't your family no more, and you know it. They died in that crash, and these bodies are just an extension of you, like any of the other meat puppets hangin' 'round this joint. Think of what you've done to 'em, doc. More than just defilin' their graves and stickin' a bit of your flesh inside 'em to keep 'em shamblin" round—you've turned 'em into nothin' more than part of your grand experiment. What kinda father, what kinda husband, would do that to the people he loved?"

The family writhed in place. Their faces twisted into pallid masks with gnashing rows of jagged teeth and pits of darkness for eyes. Ben halted a few feet away, ready to tackle the first to attack. Then they collapsed back into their seats.

"Lies," Malawer said in their intertwined voices. "The Cleaners are built upon lies; you seek to deceive me for no other reason than to cause me further pain."

Ben stepped over behind the teen. He placed his bladed fist across the boy's throat and looked at the wife, seeing the fleshmonger stare back at him.

"I'm givin' you an option—which is a whole heckuva lot more than anythin' you gave us. You tell me where you stuck the bits of yourself and I'll pluck 'em out, clean and simple. Keep mum, and I'll hafta turn 'em into giblets to dig them out. What's it gonna be?"

"Do not ..."

"Do not? You want a 'do not,' doc? Then *do not test me on this.* Choose. Tell me how to end the spell, or watch me rip 'em apart until I find what I need."

Ben's blood churned through him. Color seeped out of his vision until all was gray and flickering black spots. He held on, hoping Malawer couldn't sense how much he just wanted to collapse. A minute more of debate, and he'd be lucky to remain standing, much less string two words together.

Mrs. Malawer placed a hand across her chest, as if saluting a flag.

"Each piece is directly above their hearts."

Ben fought to keep his legs from buckling in relief. The success of his gamble invigorated him enough to last a bit longer. He sliced the teen's shirt open and saw the incision immediately. Carl retracted two of the blades so Ben could use the last to widen the cut. With the tip of the blade, he pried the flesh open and spotted the piece Malawer embedded there—a chunk of red muscle which pulsed disturbingly close to the rhythm of Ben's own pulse.

A stab, and he drew out the scrap of the fleshmonger's heart. It writhed on the water-blade until Ben wiped it off on the ground. A boot stomp; the teen spasmed and then fell still.

He tried to be more careful with the toddler, nicking the babe's skin and digging the scrap of Malawer out as delicately as he could. Once removed and destroyed, the child's eyes closed as if going to sleep.

When Ben went to the wife, her head lolled to look at him.

"You do not know," Malawer said. "So ignorant."

Ben paused with the blade poised over her breast. "Know what?"

The woman sneered. "What is coming. I am not the only one. Many more are devoted to seeking ways. Ways to end the Cleaners. You cannot begin to imagine."

"Howsabout you clue me in," Ben said. "Who's gettin' people to do this?"

A mad giggle slipped out of the corpse. "I am sorry to have failed. I wish I could have seen your destruction atthe end. You cannot fathom the coming devastation."

Her face went slack and her eyes dulled. Ben grabbed her shoulder and shook the body, shouting.

"What? Malawer, what'cha talkin' 'bout?"

Her head flopped back and forth. After a few more shakes, it became evident the fleshmonger had withdrawn his limited control.

Ben kicked the chair and pounded the table hard enough to rattle the dinnerware.

"No! Don't you say that and then hop off on me. We still gotcha, Malawer. I'll be seein' you soon, and you'll explain exactly what you meant."

Not bothering to be gentle this time, he carved out the last fleshmonger scrap and ground it beneath his heel. Thumps sounded out in the hall as mudmen dropped to the floor, released from Malawer's control. There'd be a massive cleanup operation for this job, he knew that much.

Exhaustion slammed into him, and Ben staggered over to collapse in the nearest empty chair. His wound felt ablaze and he fought for each gasp as he stared at the remains of Malawer's family.

A numbing chill spread across his left shoulder and chest. Why couldn't he stop shivering? Why did the lights dim no matter how much he blinked? Why couldn't he feel his right arm?

He chuckled as he realized the stupidity of that last thought. Purple flecks swirled across his vision even as he laughed at himself and laid his head on the table.

Ben, old boy, you can be one dumb sonuva—

He thought he heard a crackle, like a voice on an intercom. Before he could respond, however, the flecks whipped into a blizzard and dragged him down into the dark storm.

CHAPTER THIRTY-FIVE

Carl squeezed Ben's hand. The janitor grunted and kept his eyes closed. Sappy goodbyes took too much energy, and he had none to spare.

As the pressure on his hand remained, his senses flowed back into place one at a time. His cheek no longer rested on a table. The gripping chill had vanished, replaced by a soft warmth that wrapped his body.

And it wasn't Carl squeezing, he realized. Two smaller hands held his in a comforting manner.

At last, he surrendered and opened his eyes. Grit stuck a few lashes together, but he made out Dani smiling at him as she sat beside his bed. A glance down showed he'd been stripped to the waist, and bandages had been taped over where Malawer had sliced him open.

Beds ringed the room, each one filled with all manner of Cleaners, with handymen tending to various patients. A couple stood in the middle of the room, deep in conversation with the Chairman, whose back faced Ben.

Maintenance. So ... not dead. Hurrah.

Lucy moved into sight behind Dani, face rumpled by a worried frown. Ben slipped his hand out of Dani's and managed a little wave.

"Mornin', ladies. Good to seeya up and about. Guess that means the quarantine's been dropped."

"For a full day now," Lucy said. "You've been out for a bit."

Ben grimaced. "That bad?"

"Carl saved your life," Dani said, with an odd hitch to her voice. "He covered your wound and stopped the bleeding long enough for us to track down the chemical plant and retrieve you. It was close, though." She glanced at his chest. "They say it'll scar despite everything the handymen could do. Something about being operated on by a fleshmonger inhibited the healing, I guess."

Ben shrugged to sit higher on his pillow. "No tears here. Weren't exactly my best side, anyhoo. I'm sure Lopez did his best."

The women exchanged gloomy looks, which Ben only needed a second to decipher.

"Aww ... not Lopez ..."

Dani told him of the handyman's sacrifice, holding off the mudmen long enough for everyone else to leap to safety. Ben waded through the initial sorrow until he found the anger underneath, waiting to be aimed at the person responsible for a good man's death.

He pushed upright despite the tight pain that shot through his shoulder. "Malawer. Where's the ♌☾◆◆☾☐♎? He and I are gonna have a long, long chitchat."

Dani bit her lip, and Ben gripped the side of the bed.

"Tell me they got him contained," he said. "He couldn't'a slipped outta quarantine."

"He didn't. But ... Ben, he's dead, too."

Stunned, Ben slumped back against the cushions. "No. Can't be."

Lucy nodded. "When the Board released us, they kept Malawer contained, of course. They weren't too happy about the sigil switch you pulled."

"The day I start livin' like what makes the Board happy is the day after I get a lobotomy. What about Malawer?"

"Nobody noticed at first," Lucy said, "because he was preserved inside the quarantine spell. But when they tried to move him to a Recycling Center they released the spell to bag him and he dropped right there. His entire brain had been reduced to mush, as if someone stuck it in a blender."

Ben grabbed a fistful of sheets to try and contain his frustration. "That rotten … cheatin' … sonuva …" He glanced Francis' way. "… son of a motherless goat. He had a stop-gap installed."

"A what?" Dani asked.

"Basically the magical equivalent to a cyanide pill," Lucy said. "Concentrated knot of energy planted someplace vital, like in the brain or along the spinal cord. It's a measure Scum sometimes use on themselves in case they get captured and don't want to spill any secrets. It can be triggered consciously, or by some pre-set signal or code word."

"You think his being captured set it off?"

Ben frowned. "Mebbe partly."

"Just partly?" Dani asked. "What else could it be?"

Ben caught Lucy's penetrating gaze and quickly looked away. "Can't say for sure. They run a full scrub-down on his corpse?"

"No chance yet," Dani said. "Everyone's been too busy with the recovery effort. But they let us have a quick look at the body. Without his lab coat on, I noticed something strange about his skeletal structure." She handed him a folder. "Thought you might want to see this."

Ben opened the folder to find an x-ray sheet. He held it up to the light and frowned.

"This is the doc's?"

The women nodded. He turned the sheet this way and that, trying to make sense of what he saw.

Malawer's skeleton had been rearranged. The arms and legs looked normal, but every bone in his torso had shifted into the familiar shape of a giant caduceus. Twin serpents twined around his spine, and his shoulder blades flared out into feathery rib bone shards. Every movement must've felt like being shredded from within, a constant reminder of the powers he served.

Ben whistled. "That's takin' plastic surgery a bit too far in my book. I don't suppose we've made any headway figurin' out who his patron was?"

Lucy crossed her arms. "None. The virus is gone, so far as we can tell, but people are still having what the Chairman is calling 'emotional aftershocks.' Some are finding it difficult to reconcile what they did while under the spell's influence."

"Ain't surprised 'bout that," Ben said. "We didn't exactly end up in group hugs, now did we?"

Dani patted his arm and stood. "I've got to go feed Tetris. He's probably eaten his hot rock by now, the poor guy. You going to be okay?"

Ben forced a smile. "I'll be dancin' jigs by dinner."

She started to head out, but paused. "Oh. I'm going to visit Jared tomorrow. Join me?"

"You betcha."

Once she left, Ben tried to not squirm under Lucy's glare. How did she pull off the angry schoolmarm look so easily?

"What?" he asked.

She pointed at his leg. "Where's the book? The one the kid helped you steal. It was missing when we retrieved you."

Trying to recall the exact details himself, Ben related what had happened after they'd been flushed out of the Corrupted glassway. Lucy's frown went into a full-blown scowl the more he told.

"Could've been one of Malawer's mudmen," Ben said, once finished.

She huffed. "Uh huh. Since when do mudmen join book clubs?"

Ben noticed the Chairman had finished his discussion with the handymen. He waved at Francis, but the man simply nodded back and strode out of Maintenance. Ben pushed out of bed to follow, but Lucy blocked his efforts until a handyman hurried over.

"Janitor, you haven't been discharged."

"I need to talk to Francis," Ben said, still with one leg off the bed. "If I don't get to him now, he's gonna be buried in paperwork for a week after this muck-up."

"The Chairman said he wanted to speak with you as well," the handyman said. "But I told him a conversation should wait until you're fully recovered."

"I'm recovered. See? Awake. Breathin'. Refusin' to cooperate. Ain't that enough to show that I'm fine?"

The handyman cleared his throat. "Even if we let you go, your access sigil hasn't been returned, and no one has been assigned to escort you yet."

Ben looked to Lucy, but the other janitor retreated to the exit.

"I'll be back in a bit," she said. "Got to go check on something. Enjoy your chicken noodle soup."

"Couldja at least bring me somethin' to read?" he called after.

Grumbling, he let the handyman reposition him on the bed and check his bandages.

"No need to sulk, sir. This is for your own good."

Ben glared. "I ain't sulkin'."

"Of course not. If there's anything you need—besides further arguing—we'll be in attendance."

He left to attend another patient who'd begun moaning loudly, and Ben sank heavily back against the pillow.

Peachy.

CHAPTER
THIRTY-SIX

Dani napped for a few hours with Tetris lying on her stomach. She woke with the lizard clawing at her zipper. After scratching under his scaly chin, she secured him back in his cage along with a few crickets to keep him company. Then she returned to staring at the two letters that had been waiting on the dresser at her return.

She hadn't realized the Cleaners bothered with mail delivery; she hadn't even left a forwarding address at school after the semester ended. But at least these two pieces had been intercepted and funneled her way. The first sat thick and heavy, with the logo of a top-rated state medical school. The other had no return address and a light rosy scent wafted from it. She didn't know which she dreaded more.

Before she could give eitheroneanother thought, a knock came at the door. She jogged over and opened it with a quick press of her palm. The Borrelia sisters filled the entrance.

"We're heading out for a party," Hardy said with a toss of her hair. "You want to come?"

"A party?" Dani echoed.

"Funeral party," said Laurel. "For Mr. Lopez."

"Oh. Uh …" Dani plucked at a bit of hair that had flattened while she slept. "I didn't realize the Cleaners held funerals."

"They don't." Laurel waved the idea off. "It's just us doing it. And it's a funeral *party*, not a funeral. We promised Mr. Lopez we'd celebrate if he ever didn't make it back."

Dani blinked. "Celebrate?"

"Yeah," Hardy said. "He always hated how people focus on what they've lost. Said we should celebrate the memories we have and remind ourselves to make more while we can."

The twins smiled in unison, though not quite as brightly as usual.

"So, you want to make some new memories with us?" Laurel asked.

Dani returned a soft smile. "Sounds like a plan. Let me duck into the bathroom real quick, and we'll go."

She waved them into her quarters to wait while she freshened up. When she reemerged, Laurel stood gasping in delight over Tetris.

"Is this your lizard? He's so cute! Can we pet him?"

Of course they liked lizards. What Scum-busting, rodeo champion maids wouldn't? Dani nodded at the terrarium. Giggling, Laurel dug Tetris out with a firm but gentle grip and the maids proceeded to tickle the animal from tail to claw tip. Hardy squealed when Tetris nipped her nose, and Laurel kept running her fingers along his rows of spines. Watching the twins play with the lizard made Dani grin.

"I hate to admit it," she said, "but I really misjudged you two at first."

The twins shrugged without taking their attention off Tetris.

"Happens a lot," Laurel said. "You get used to it. Besides, what's it really matter what other people think? We're just us."

"Do you live in HQ full-time?" Dani asked. "I know Ben tends to sleep in his van, but that's not really an option for me, especially when this next year of school kicks in."

"No way," Hardy said. "We've got an apartment downtown. Got to have someplace to crash after a hard job." She grinned wickedly. "Or where you can bring a cute boy back to."

Dani flushed. With her conscription into the Cleaners and the ensuing training, it had been a while since she'd had a chance to think about anything remotely amorous. Not that her loathing of germs made any form of physical interaction all that attractive in the first place.

Laurel returned Tetris to his cage and clapped. "You should stay with us tonight!"

"You totally should," Hardy said. "We can get those manicures we talked about."

"Are manicures okay for a funeral party?" Dani asked.

"Totally," Laurel said. "And we can go dancing afterward. We know the best salsa clubs."

"I would've figured you more for line dancing and cowboy bars," Dani said.

"Yeah, we used to do that." Hardy grimaced at her sister. "But then Laurel broke the mechanical bull one night and they haven't let us back in since."

Laurel shoved her. "Would you stop bringing that up? It wasn't my fault."

"Was too."

"Not. Just faulty equipment."

"Oh, it was. Admit it."

Laurel and Hardy continued to argue as they headed out.

Dani grabbed the two letters and scanned them again. Which to open first? What would happen if she chucked both into the nearest incinerator? She didn't doubt one letter held pages for her to sign and dates for potential admissions interviews. Nor did she doubt the second had been written using words such as *dearest*, *darling*, and *date*.

Neither offered a path she felt ready to walk. At least, not right then and there. Strange how the dangers of bone-melting spells and Scum beasts trying to gnaw her face off seemed easier to handle than the unknowns of her continued education. Not to mention a romantic evening with a man who could turn objects and people to dust just by touching them.

"Dani?" one of the twins called after her. "You coming, girl-friend?"

She smiled at Tetris. "Some decisions can wait until after the weekend, can't they?"

He winked a golden eye, which she took as agreement. After tucking both letters into an inner pocket, she zipped her suit closed and chased after the maids.

"Wait up, you two!"

▲   ▲   ▲

Ben startled out of his ongoing sulk when a tan leather journal plopped into his lap. Francis and Lucy stood at the foot of his bed. Grabbing the journal Lucy had tossed on him, he tried to not look too grouchy.

"Chairman. Lu. What brings you two to check on this poor old invalid?"

Francis took his fedora off and rubbed the brim as he studied Ben. "The situation with Malawer, for starters."

"Funny. I wanted to talk to you about the same thing earlier. Thanks for the brush-off."

"Ben," Lucy said warningly, but the Chairman shook his head to indicate it was all right.

"I wanted you to rest," he said, "so you could provide a full report with a clearer mind. However, with what Janitor Lucy has brought to my attention, I figured the sooner we discussed things the better."

"This?" Ben tried to thumb the pages, but the journal slipped from his grip and tumbled to the floor. Lucy retrieved it, but didn't hand it over a second time. "What is it?"

"We'll get to that in a minute." The Chairman clasped his hands. "First, why not tell us what you were so eager to speak to Malawer about."

Ben explained the dialogue he'd had with the fleshmonger before convincing him to let his family go with a shred of dignity. "Right at the end, he let slip that there were others, other Scum linin' up like at a carnival shootin' gallery to see who can knock us down first and claim their giant teddy bear."

Francis' brow furrowed. "That brings us to another, possibly related concern. Have you made any progress with the packet I provided? The one with information about you and Karen?"

"A bit, with Lu's help. Why?" Feeling increasingly tangled in the bed sheet and hemmed in by his coworkers, Ben started to rise. "Didja find somethin' new?"

Lucy came by his side and put her hand on the uninjured side of his chest to gently press him back down.

"Easy," she said. "We did, but it hasn't cleared up anything." She raised the journal. "The book you had reminded me of something, but I couldn't figure out what until everything blew over. Then I remembered where I'd seen that title before. I recovered this from a few boxes I had in my personal storage. Take a look."

Holding the front toward him, she opened the cover. His eyes fell on the handwritten title on the first page.

A Comprehensive Treatise on Glasskin and Their Ways.

The same penmanship filled every page, with side notes scribbled in the margins. Ben stared at the cursive writing, unable to work his mouth for a long moment. At last, he took the journal from Lucy.

"This is Karen's handwritin'." He fixed a glare on her. "How'dja have this in your stuff?"

"Karen and I roomed together for a few years early on. Some of our belongings got mixed together. I always meant to get this back to her, but she never asked for it and it slipped my mind after a while."

Ben traced the writing and imagined Karen's voice dictating the words. "But this means …"

Lucy grimaced. "That the book you had before was the official copy she eventually got printed and filed. She was the author and these are her original notes. Before you came onto the scene, Karen had occasional obsessions she'd study for months at a time. The Gutters. Foreign Cleaner divisions." She nodded at the journal. "Glasskin and glassways. I never knew she'd entered it into Employee Records. Most of her pet projects ended like this journal—forgotten in some box or drawer."

"Janitor Lucy's reports and the witnessing of Corrupted glassways place these events in a new and disturbing light," Francis said. "And begs the question as to why someone went to the trouble of removing the first book from your person, and how they knew you had it in the first place."

Ben displayed the journal. "You think whoever took the book knows what happened to Karen and m'self?"

Francis shook his head. "Perhaps. Perhaps not. All we can know for sure right now is that someone is obviously tampering with glassways in an attempt to pervert yet another of our tools to Scum purposes. My main hope is Karen's old notes might hold some clue as to how this is being accomplished and help us anticipate and defend against any attacks on that front."

"Someone?" Ben echoed. "Malawer mentioned lots of others gunnin' for us."

The Chairman frowned. "There's no solid evidencethatany grand conspiracy is in play."

"But Malawer—"

"Was a fleshmonger responsible for the death of hundreds and the emotional compromising of our employees. Seeing what he did to his family, it is also likely he was wholly insane. We can't take his word at face value. Of course, there are always those who oppose us, but Scum remain a fractious lot. We've not seen any unified effort on their part in over a century."

Ben sat back, unconvinced, but it was his word against a dead man's.

Francis dug into a coat pocket and drew out a silver disc, which he handed to Ben.

"A new access sigil, for now. I'd like you to continue researching both matters. See if you can uncover any more substantive leads. Do be warned, however. The Board is considering a motion to place a permanent chant on you so you aren't able to evade another quarantine. They don't enjoy losing control of company assets."

"Heh. At least they still rank me as an asset," Ben said. "It's when I'm demoted to plain old ⌾♦ that I'll be worried."

Lucy smirked. "You're never too far from that."

He set the journal down and clasped her hand. "Thankya, Lu. This means a lot, just to have it."

She looked down and shrugged. "We'll deal with it later, all right? Just remember our agreement."

"You got it."

They talked a bit longer about the ongoing cleanup operation at the chemical plant, the failure to get anything helpful from Malawer's corpse, and how the news broadcasts were spinning the deaths at the grocery store and hospital. The scrub-teams would be busy for weeks.

After they left, Ben leafed through the journal until teardrops threatened to stain the pages and muddy the ink. Closing his eyes, he held his wife's journal to his chest and eventually fell into a restless sleep, one where he dreamt of Karen being dragged through an endless dark tunnel while he chased after, always too slow.

CHAPTER THIRTY-SEVEN

Still trying to shake off his night of disturbing dreams, Ben found Dani in the cafeteria. She nursed a thermos of coffee strong enough that his nose almost started bleeding after a whiff. He set down the stack of books he'd brought along and slipped onto the bench beside her.

She favored him with a bleary look and a grunt. Wearing a pair of jeans and yellow blouse, she looked worse for wear than after dealing with the blackshard. Her frizzy red hair was snarled all over and she kept scrubbing the dark circles under her eyes.

"What exactly happened to you?" he asked.

Her enormous yawn made Ben think of a lion opening wide for the tamer's head.

"The Borrelia sisters have a strange way of mourning."

"What?" He cocked his head. "This about Lopez?"

She nodded. "We started out by grabbing lunch, which somehow turned into a hunt for the best frozen yogurt—his favorite treat, apparently. Then they wanted to send some good vibes to wherever his soul ended up." She glugged several mouthfuls of coffee and smacked her lips. "That meant dancing. A lot of dancing. So we did a whirlwind tour of the clubs downtown. Ended up doing shots to toast his memory, which may have become a straight up drinking contest by the end. I'm pretty sure one of them carried me all the way back to the couch in their apartment. At least I woke up clothed. The girls were still out of it when I headed over here."

Dani grinned. "And for the record, whenever I head for the big trash can in the sky, I want people sending me off just like that."

"Dancin' and drinkin'? Sounds pretty torturifyin', but I'll do my bestest, princess."

She glanced at the books he'd brought. "What's this?"

"A few things I thought the kiddo might like readin'."

Her head went sideways so she could squint at the titles. "The Hardy Boys? The Adventures of Tom Swift? Choose Your Own Adventures? Ben, really?"

He leaned in to protect the books from her derision. "Hey, these here are classics. Once he finishes with 'em, I can introduce him to my favorite comic books. What'd you bring?"

She nudged a backpack by her foot. Ben drew it over and rifled through the contents.

"Aesop's Fables? The Brothers Grimm? Mother Goose? Uh, Dani, do y'have any idea how many of these stories are true?"

Her red eyes widened. "Seriously?"

Ben chuckled as he tossed the pack back to her. "Naw. Just ribbin' you. Good choices, though we're gonna have to make sure Jared won't try jumpin' over the moon for real. Oh. And this one's for you."

He hauled up the massive binder he'd kept hidden by his leg on the bench. When he dropped it on the table, the whole area shook. Dani stared at the block letters on the front: *Employee Manual.*

"Joy," she said, lowering her forehead onto the cover. "Homework. Not like I won't have plenty of that soon."

"You asked for it, and don'tcha ever forget it." He clapped her on the back, making her scowl. "C'mon. Let's go see how our favorite bundle of earth-shakin' power is doin'."

She stuck the manual in her pack and slung this over one shoulder. Her first effort at standing plopped her straight back down. She rose again with visible effort, pack sagging dangerously. Ben let her lead the way, mostly because it was a nuisance to activate any glassways without dropping the books.

The two Ascendants on duty admitted them without contest. As they entered Jared's containment room, Ben braced for whatever pranks the kid might be at today.

They both halted just inside the door and gaped at the place.

Jared lay on his stomach on the floor beside his bed. His tongue stuck out to one side as he focused on drawing within the lines of a Dr. Seuss coloring book. All his toys, which had once formed a plastic and wooden minefield, had been put away. The spotless floor looked freshly scrubbed, and Ben guessed running a white-gloved hand under the bed wouldn't result in so much as a speck of dust. Even Jared's dinosaur-themed sheets had been tucked in, tight enough that a quarter would bounce off the pterodactyl blanket.

"Jared?" Dani stared about in wonder. "Did you do all this?"

The hybrid looked up and beamed. His voice wove through the room.

Ah. Ben. God?

"Been good?" Ben chuckled. "You put the rest of us to shame, kiddo. What made you go for the deep clean?"

Jared pointed a blue crayon at them.

Mussy. Eww no lick.

Dani's shoulders dropped. "Oh, Jared. You think we've been staying away because your room was messy?" She went to kneel beside him and gave a quick hug. "We're your friends. Whether your place is neat or not doesn't change that."

"Does give us a little more sittin' room though," Ben said.

Dani frowned at him, but Ben winked.

"Aw, c'mon. Kid's got a sense of humor, don't he?" He waggled his brows at the hybrid. "Don't you?"

Jared cocked his head. *Hum. Her?*

"Hoo boy. Guess that's another thing we'll need to work on. 'Til then, we gotcha some presents to make up for not bein' around as much as we shoulda."

Jared let Dani draw him to his feet. *Prez. Dents?*

Dani sat on the bean bag chair and spilled her books onto the floor while Ben set his on the kid's bed.

"You betcha," he said. "Good stories from simpler times when you always knew the bad guy was gonna get flushed out by the end.

Not like all the modern twists and swivels where Jesus gives birth to himself, or the bad guy is the hero's time-travelin' granddaddy, or whatever else them loony writers dream up these days." He thumped a Hardy Boys novel. "This here's solid whodunit readin'. Good for the soul and easy on the brain. Whatcha say?"

Jared looked between the two book piles. He took Aesop's Fables and showed Ben the cover, where a horse conversed with a medieval bowman.

Hearse!

Ben chuckled. "Close, but big difference."

He waved the kid closer. Jared trotted over and plunked down beside him on the bed. He pushed the book into Ben's stomach.

Red. Tummy?

Ben cringed. "Read to you? Me? Sorry, but I ain't exactly the best storyteller. Mebbe Dani ..."

Dani's snores started right then. Ben and Jared looked over to see her slumped in the chair, her face buried in the crook of her arm. Sighing, Ben rummaged through his books and plucked out one of the smaller volumes.

"A'ight, kiddo. I'll read a bit. But that's one of Dani's, and I ain't gonna do it justice." He held up his selection. "How 'bout *Secret of the Ninja?*"

He hesitated as Jared snuggled beside him. Once they settled, Ben cleared his throat with a few coughs and a mighty hack. He turned to spit clear, but noted the spotless room once more and forced himself to swallow.

Then he read off the back cover.

"Somethin' mysterious and disturbin' is happenin' at your friend's dojo, and an ancient samurai sword's involved." He turned to the instruction page preceding the first chapter. "Warnin': You and you alone are in charge of what happens in this story...."

IF YOU LIKED ...

If you liked *The Maids of Wrath*, you might also enjoy:

Hellhound on My Trail
D.J. Butler

Mythology 101
Jody Lynn Nye

Working Stiff
Kevin J. Anderson

ABOUT THE AUTHOR

Josh Vogt has been published in dozens of genre markets with work ranging across fantasy, science fiction, horror, humor, pulp, and more. He also writes for a wide variety of RPG developers. His debut fantasy novel, *Forge of Ashes*, is a tie-in to the Pathfinder roleplaying game. WordFire Press launched his urban fantasy series, The Cleaners, with *Enter the Janitor*. He's a member of SFWA, the International Association of Media Tie-In Writers, and a Scribe Award nominee. Find him at JRVogt.com. He is made out of meat.

OTHER WORDFIRE PRESS TITLES BY JOSH VOGT

Enter the Janitor

Our list of other WordFire Press authors and titles is always growing.
To find out more and to see our selection of titles, visit us at:

wordfirepress.com

44557334R00194

Made in the USA
Middletown, DE
10 June 2017